Justin Scott was born in New York City in 1944 and grew up in Bayport, a small town on Long Island. He took a B.A. in history from Harpur College and an M.A. in American history from the State University of New York at Binghampton. Mr Scott has worked as a carpenter, a teacher, a dishwasher, a barman and a magazine editor, but for the last ten years or so has concentrated wholly on writing novels, among them the bestsellers *The Shipkiller*, *The Man Who Loved the Normandie* and, most recently, *A Pride of Kings*. Justin Scott is married to the actress Gloria Hoye and lives in Connecticut.

By the same author

A Pride of Kings
The Man Who Loved the Normandie
The Turning
The Shipkiller
Treasure for Treasure
Many Happy Returns

As J. S. Blazer

Lend a Hand
Deal Me Out

JUSTIN SCOTT

The Auction

GRAFTON BOOKS

A Division of the Collins Publishing Group

LONDON GLASGOW
TORONTO SYDNEY AUCKLAND

Grafton Books
A Division of the Collins Publishing Group
8 Grafton Street, London W1X 3LA

Published by Grafton Books 1986

First published in Great Britain by
Granada Publishing 1985

ISBN 0-586-05645-9

Printed and bound in Great Britain by
Collins, Glasgow

Set in Caledonia

For my wife, Gloria Hoye –
First book at Parmalee Hill –
And for our friends,
Mark and Marilyn Barty-King.

Prologue

In Munich they bracketed the limo with guard cars. When it stopped they hit the pavement fast – machine pistols in hand, eyes raking the traffic, pavements, doorways, rooftops.

Rome was worse. In Rome they put Mr Hammond in a plain Fiat, doubled the guard, shuffled routes and hotels daily, and prayed the Pope would declare martial law.

But this was London, and you didn't pile out of cars waving guns in London and Mr Hammond wouldn't ride a Fiat in London, so when his black Daimler limousine rolled magisterially past Harrods, Wheeler, Hammond's chief of security, followed at a distance in a quiet, grey Jaguar.

Wheeler was thinking that London was one of the last decent cities left where riding around in a classy limo wasn't an open invitation to get snatched. They'd had hits in London, for sure – IRA bombers, Arab fanatics, Balkan umbrella psychos – but they were the fringe element in political arguments and, besides, Charles Hammond wasn't a political target. He was a go-between, a deal-maker for big honchos, a fixer, not a fighter, a fixer who worked hard not to make enemies because enemies got in the way and Mr Hammond's job was to get things *out* of the way so people could do business.

The Daimler turned off busy Sloane Street and stopped, moments later, in front of a Dutch-façade terraced house on Herbert Crescent. Wheeler parked a hundred feet back on the quiet, narrow street and spoke by radio to the sidemen in Hammond's limousine.

Hammond, as usual, was already halfway out of the car. The sidemen jumped after him. They were good and before Hammond had reached the front steps, they had caught up and hidden the smaller man between them. Hammond was expected in the Dutch-front house. The door opened when they reached the landing and shut behind them a second later.

Wheeler glanced around the residential street, which was deserted but for the cars parked along the kerbs, and relaxed. He was tired. Mr Hammond was working something big and they'd gone non-stop since before Christmas. The last two weeks were a blur of airports and hotels. Now it was almost over. They'd be aboard the Jetstar in a couple of hours and in New York for New Year's Eve. No one knew they were coming, which meant no meetings, no escorts, just a last minute party at the CPS suite with some friendly rented ladies, and a late sleep New Year's Day.

There'd be UN appointments the next day, maybe a quick meeting at Comptel with Ms Thorp, then the long flight to Tana to celebrate the Malagasy elections, which-ever side won. Mr Hammond was friends with both. Wheeler lowered his window. It was warm for winter.

A London bobby rounded the corner of Herbert Cres-cent. Wheeler appraised him professionally. Big man, six-four at least, and looking even taller in his helmet. A man that size who could move fast, and this one walked like he could, was a dude to be reckoned with if he had a brain to go with his machinery.

Wheeler checked his rear view mirrors. The street and pavements were still deserted. He watched the door Mr Hammond had entered. The bobby drew abreast of it, bent down to look through the Daimler's smoked glass, and spotted the chauffeur.

Wheeler reached for his radio.

'Stay inside,' he told the men in the house.

'Righto,' came the reply. They were English, regulars with Hammond's London office. Wheeler travelled with Hammond, as did Rice, Hammond's exec, and Rice's secretary, an ex-FBI man who doubled conveniently as Rice's protection. The rest of the support staff was local. Hammond had offices in London, Tokyo, Washington, and Tananarive, to back him up in Europe, the East, the States, and Africa.

Wheeler switched channels and spoke to the chauffeur.

'Just give him your licence and registration.'

The chauffeur was Maltese, a new man, highly recommended, but still nervous and eager to please. 'Yes, sir.'

'If he gives you any trouble, send him back to me.'

'Thank you, sir.'

Wheeler watched the bobby walk round the Daimler and into the road. The chauffeur lowered his window and handed over his licence and registration. One of them fluttered to the ground. The bobby backed up and waited; the chauffeur got out of the car, stooped awkwardly, and picked up the paper.

Wheeler nodded his approval; the bobby was right not to expose himself, even in an obviously routine situation, just as he was right to check the Daimler's business outside the Overseas Club. Despite the fact that it was a legitimate private club for retired intelligence operatives – mostly British and American – its members' former calling might attract the wrong kind of attention. Idly, Wheeler wondered what business Hammond had there.

The bobby returned the chauffeur's papers and strode back to the pavement. Wheeler readied his own papers and murmured, 'All clear,' into the radio.

'Righto,' his man in the club said with relief. Hammond

was always in a hurry and no one liked telling him he had to wait.

The bobby spotted Wheeler in the grey Jaguar and again stepped into the road.

'Good morning, sir.' He touched his helmet.

'I'm waiting for a gentleman in the Overseas Club,' said Wheeler, handing over his international driver's licence.

The bobby held it between two thick fingers and angled it to read in the pale sunlight. He looked like a tough, young farm boy and very sure of himself. His hard eyes flickered quickly from the licence to Wheeler's face.

'Have you a permit for that firearm, sir?'

Tough son of a bitch, thought Wheeler, annoyed that the bobby had noticed the almost imperceptible bulge in his expertly tailored woollen blazer. He's got no gun and asking about mine as if I couldn't kill him in a second. 'In this pocket.'

'May I see it, please.'

'Sure.' He glanced at the Overseas Club door. What the hell would he do if Hammond came charging out and headed for the airport while his bodyguard's right to carry was being checked? He handed the cop his permit and picked up the radio mike to tell the sidemen to wait inside.

'The pistol, sir.'

'What for?'

'Serial number.'

'Right.'

He put down the radio, pulled the gun out of his jacket, snapped out the clip and handed it through the window, butt first. The bobby reached for it with one hand and returned his licence with the other. Wheeler took it and knew the instant both hands were full that he had made a lethal mistake.

The bobby's left hand filled with a gleaming sliver of metal. He was moving with a grace astonishing in such a

10

big man. He was thrusting like a dancer, lightning fast, and the stiletto extended like a snake's tongue from his enormous hand. It flashed in the sun, then disappeared in Wheeler's throat, just below the knot of his necktie.

The bobby slid the blade out of Wheeler's neck, shoved his face against the steering wheel, wiped the thin blade clean on Wheeler's sleeve, and resumed his measured steps towards Crescent Garden at the end of the street.

Charles Hammond came out first, the sidemen scrambling after him. Hammond was a short, stocky fifty-year-old man with ginger hair, bushy brows, and a full bristling moustache. He bounded down the steps like a tightly inflated ball.

The sidemen caught up with him at the bottom of the steps and hid him from view as they had on the way in. One of them was speaking into his radio, trying to raise Wheeler in the Jag, cursing the atmospherics that were blocking his signal; the other, who knew that Hammond's ruddy complexion stemmed from a dangerous heart condition, was worrying how to slow him down. Racing him wasn't the way. Hammond beat him to the Daimler's door handle – a basic tenet of Wheeler's security drill was that the chauffeur never left the wheel to open doors – he yanked it open and jumped in the back.

Leaning forward to rap the glass partition in his usual impatient *let's-go* signal, he called, 'Gatwick!'

The partition was already open; Hammond stabbed irritably at the button that closed it. 'I told you to keep this damned thing shut!'

The chauffeur turned around with an ingratiating smile and the lead sideman was halfway into the car before he saw the weapons in his hands. The chauffeur fired with his right and a cloud of white vapour spewed into Hammond's face.

11

The sideman thought it smelled like peaches. He arrested his forward movement and started to push himself back through the door. The chauffeur dropped the gas gun over the rising partition – freeing a hand to protect his face from the fumes which floated in the passenger compartment like a breath in cold air – and fired the silenced automatic in his left hand, twice.

The first shot went over the sideman's shoulder and cut down his partner; the sound of the bullet hitting him was as loud as the *pock* of the muffled report. The second shot slammed the sideman out of the car and sent him sprawling onto the pavement.

The Daimler lunged forward, smacking shut the open passenger door, whipped around the corner at the end of Herbert Crescent, and disappeared towards Sloane Street.

Wheeler held his face to the steering wheel and moved trembling fingers to the ignition key. There was blood in his mouth, but the steel must have missed his heart because he was still breathing. He clamped his fingers on the key.

His mind dulled by shock, he forced himself to wait. It seemed forever. If he was wrong, he'd waste his only chance to track Hammond. He heard a car start. Seconds later a white Viva pulled out several spaces behind him and raced away.

The watchdog turned the corner and only then did Wheeler start his own engine. Moving as little as possible to contain his bleeding, he steered the Jaguar out of the parking space. He caught up on Sloane Street. The Viva, all boxy and bright with glass, was chasing towards Knightsbridge, hustling to make the same traffic light as the Daimler which was turning right in stately procession through a jostling horde of black taxis.

Wheeler nudged his accelerator. The Jaguar shot forward, faster than he had intended. He careened through the turn as the light changed to red and dropped behind a newspaper van to hide from the Viva. He felt no pain, only a dull numbness that spread from his throat like a warning he had drunk too much booze. He knew he was handling the car badly, as if the steering wheel and the accelerator were operating in mirror image.

The newspaper van pulled off beside a news-stand, revealing the Daimler closely trailed by the Viva in heavy traffic. Wheeler tried to get the police on his radio. The controls were on the microphone, but when he got the right channel, he couldn't talk.

Carefully, he inclined his head and let the salty blood pour from his mouth. It splashed on his twill slacks and he thought, as he did every time he put them on, that a hundred-fifty bucks for a pair of pants was pretty good for a retired US Army MP. He'd worked for Hammond for years when one day Mr Hammond announced, as if seeing him for the first time, 'You look like hell,' and marched him into the best store in whatever city it was and bought him clothes while Rice was having kittens because they were late for a meeting with a bunch of bankers.

Emptying his mouth didn't help. He still couldn't speak. And he knew he couldn't drive well enough to force the Daimler off the road, not with the Viva protecting its flanks. He could do nothing but follow.

Hammond's form was partially visible through the dark back window: he was still sitting upright, but his square head lolled to the side as if he were sleeping. The Daimler changed lanes abruptly and Hammond's body fell out of sight onto the seat. A voiceless curse bubbled in Wheeler's throat. If they wanted to kill Hammond they wouldn't have bothered gassing him, but if they wanted him alive they wouldn't have used gas if they knew about his heart.

13

The Daimler veered to the left of the Wellington Arch underpass and swung round onto Park Lane, gaining speed in thinning traffic, then passed Marble Arch and took the Edgware Road. They were taking Mr Hammond north, out of the city. Wheeler followed doggedly, his hands and feet numbing, his vision alternately blurring and clearing, dread spreading like the numbness as he began to realize that he couldn't follow much further because he was dying.

BOOK I

1

Chamberlain thought for once he had made it home for the New Year. He had already missed Christmas, straightening out a plant security dispute that Comptel was having with the local cops in Rangoon. After seventeen years his folks were used to his erratic schedules, though his mother repeated wistfully that they had hoped he would have had more control over his holidays when he left the Navy. Unspoken was a plea to come home and settle down, and indeed minutes into his first pre-New Year's Eve Old-fashioned with his brother, Billy spoke for her.

'How much longer you going to play soldiers?'

'I'm out.'

'You know what I mean.'

When Chamberlain first left Connecticut, at seventeen, his folks would tell the neighbours, 'Pete can't say where he is,' though anyone who read the papers knew it had to be Laos or Cambodia, as the war finally winding down in Vietnam was no secret. But later, after an NYU College stint paid by Uncle, it got confusing. Where did US Navy SEALs operate in peacetime?

The Persian Gulf, for one place, training the Shah's forces before the revolution, then back to almost rescue the hostages, and losing more friends than he had in the South China Sea. The Mediterranean, for another, making a quiet point to Colonel Gaddafi. Even, surprise, the South Atlantic, delivering ammunition to hard-pressed British assault troops who had landed long on balls and short on ordnance.

Then he had let the CIA seduce him away from the SEALs. Out in force again, after the early seventies' débâcles, the spooks were working the waters of El Salvador and Nicaragua and had concluded that it was easier to teach underwater-behind-the-lines-demolition men to be spies than train spies to be SEALs. He had teamed up with his old Navy diving buddy Arnie Fast. Arnie, who had left the Navy years ahead of Chamberlain and was now a CIA hand with clout, brought him along to Europe, where Chamberlain – officially still in the Navy, though actually a civilian contract employee of the CIA – did some work at the bottom of the River Elbe, before hooking up with an anti-terrorist outfit the CIA was freelancing. Paths crossed and he had stumbled into the rescue of a kidnapped executive who ran the Munich office of Comptel Inc.

Comptel was an American-based international communications conglomerate, big in satellites and sat-com hardware, which had shot ahead of ITT in the early 1980s. At number thirteen on the Fortune 500 list it was used to buying what it wanted and it thanked Chamberlain with a job offer – international security troubleshooter. His business card read *Vice President for Security Analysis*.

'Amateur Asshole,' Arnie Fast had tagged it.

Chamberlain left the CIA, dropping his Navy cover story, and took the job anyway, because he saw a shot at finally parleying seventeen years of military and spook experience into a major win. Now, twelve months later, he was wondering whether a lot of business people enjoying first class air travel and a VP title were still penny ante. He confided as much to his older brother, the afternoon of New Year's Eve.

'So what do you want?' Billy had asked, paunchy at thirty-six, full of himself, and starting to make a buck building condos.

'A future.'

18

'You came to the right place.'

'Sand Bend? Since when?'

Billy gave Chamberlain's arm a playful punch and looked surprised at the resistance it offered. 'Still in shape?'

'That's one of the things they pay me for.'

'Let's take a ride.'

'I just got in. Mom wants to talk.'

'Mom wants you to take this ride.'

Billy's gleaming new Corvette, fire-engine red, was parked outside their parents' Cape Cod home, which was small and sheathed with asphalt shingles. He drove sedately into town, through the modest four corners business district – a post office, general store, package store, stationer's and rent-all – and down the river road. The sun was pale, its light thin, as high cloud moved in from the northeast. It had got a little warmer, guaranteeing the heavy snow forecast.

'You still breaking this in?'

'I take it easy. Too much to live for.'

'Then why buy a Corvette?'

'Because I can.'

Chamberlain remembered well that when you grew up on the shabbier side of the tracks in Northwestern Connecticut, a sleek Stingray seemed as satisfactory a possession as a teenage boy could wish for. Two miles along, Billy drove into the abandoned Sand Bend Fire Hose Factory. Once the employer for the entire town, it was a sturdy hundred-year-old brick structure. The river lay broad beside it, dammed for power. It had kept lawns, grand old trees, and soaring Palladian windows.

'Those windows gave me the idea. The light.'

'You're buying it?'

'Trying to.'

'To make firehoses?'

His brother shook his head in mock patience. 'Not firehoses. Condos. Apartments and offices.'

The windows arched the full height of each of the three floors. Chamberlain imagined the sun streaming on pale, polished wood floors. 'Nice.'

'And the river. It's like a park. It'll be beautiful.'

'What does the town say?' he asked, knowing that selectmen in this part of New England did not stampede to approve change.

'Town loves it. Goddamned Wetlands Commission is the big problem. They want a sewage plant.'

'Well, sure you're not going to dump in the river.'

'What are you, an expert?'

'I've spent a lot of time underwater, man. I don't like people messing it up.'

'I'm hoping to work something out, maybe build a plant with the town, maybe just engineer a septic. Pump it over the hill. It's workable. Everything's workable. So what do you think?'

'It would be a pretty place to live.'

'I'm glad you feel that way.'

'How come Mom wanted me to see it?'

'Want to be my partner?'

'Me?'

'Come on home. Have some fun. Make some bread.'

Chamberlain looked at the old mill. Behind the soaring windows he saw a prison where his father and grandfather had worked their days, saw the annual company picnics where the bosses told them how lucky they were, saw the invisible line right down the middle of the high school which divided those who were somebody from those who were mill hands, and remembered as vividly as if it were yesterday his seventeenth birthday when he joined the Navy and got the hell out.

'I already have a job. I got a good job. I make good bucks.'

'It's going nowhere. They're not going to move you up in the company.'

'I don't know that for sure. I'm in the company. I just have to find a better way to make it work for me.'

'I know corporations,' said Billy. 'I've worked for 'em. They're all the same. Comptel selects leadership from either sales or accounting, depending on whether they're making or losing money at the moment. Leaders rarely rise from production and never out of services like personnel and security.'

'They're paying me seventy-five grand a year.'

'Big hairy deal.'

'That's more than you do.'

'I'm just starting. Sky's my limit. You've topped out.'

'I want to come out of this job a winner.'

'You know how you win in a corporation?' Billy retorted with the zealousness of a recent convert. 'You sit holding your dick till you're forty-five. Then you start moving up, killing your friends. The guy with no friends when he's fifty-five is the new boss.'

Chamberlain stared at the red brick. Maybe it would be fun to ride around his home town in a Vet and rub in the old Brahmins' faces. 'Remember when you got married and I swiped the old man's car and the cops caught me with no licence? Remember how in the entire thirty pages of the newspaper the only place they could find to report my arrest was next to your wedding announcement?'

'Ancient history.'

Pete laughed. 'I still feel guilty about it.'

'Show the bastards. It's another good reason to come back.'

'I want to make a mark, first.'

'If you win any more medals you'll need a bigger chest.'

'Merit badges for hitting people.'

'At Comptel you're just a private slugger. You won't have to hit people working with me.'

Chamberlain had already concluded the truth in Billy's analysis. 'What do I know about plumbing and septic systems?'

'What did I know when I left Ma Bell? I'll tell you what I knew. I knew I wanted to be my own boss and do something that shows. Just like you.'

'Maybe I have to do it on my own.'

His brother looked away, getting frustrated. He said, 'Speaking of reasons to come back.'

Pete followed his gaze. He had already noticed the little Suburu station wagon pull into the rutted drive. A woman was getting out of a car with two little girls. All three were dressed up in their best coats and the little ones had black patent shoes. 'Is that Katherine Rodgers?'

'Katherine Grey. She married Buddy Grey.'

'Didn't he get killed?'

'Rolled his dump truck. Making Katie a widow.' He got out of the car. 'Katie.'

The girls came running. Billy knelt down and said hi to each as Katherine followed, shielding her eyes from the sun. She had been pretty in high school. Now she was beautiful, with the thick chestnut hair Chamberlain had admired from afar. But the little girls took his breath away, each so perfect looking and proud of the dress-up clothes.

'Katie. You remember Pete?'

'Sure. How are you?'

She took her hand from her eyes and extended it and Pete saw her eyes were greener than he remembered. She smiled and shook hands.

'Your children are so beautiful.'

She looked at them, proud. 'This is Rachel,' she said.

'And the little one is Jackie. Girls, say hello to Mr Chamberlain.'

Dazed, Chamberlain shook their little hands. They had tiny white gloves, and Jackie, the little one, offered him a candy, which he took with grave thanks.

'Tell Mr Chamberlain where you went.'

'We went to a puppet show.'

Chamberlain squatted down. 'What did you see?'

The five-year-old backed away, and for a second he saw himself as the child saw him – harder-looking than other adults, with small scars scattered randomly about his face, hands thick with muscle, a finger twisted from a bad break. The little one didn't notice or didn't care and blurted happily, 'Sleeping Beauty.'

'What happened?' He crinkled his grey-blue eyes to coax Rachel back; intrigued, she came, as carefully as a cat.

'A Prince woke her up.'

'They'll do it every time.'

They looked at him, eyes round and steady, expecting more, but he had run out of things to say, and they bolted suddenly to the river's edge.

Chamberlain stood up, favouring a knee that occasionally got sore. 'Great looking little girls.'

'Take after their mom,' said Billy.

'Are you home long, Pete?'

'Just for New Year.'

'You'll see him tonight,' said Billy. 'You're coming to the party?'

'Yes, I'm coming.' She looked at the factory. 'I heard you're going to buy this.'

'Trying to. Trying to get Pete to come home and help out.'

Katherine looked at him, quizzically. Chamberlain

23

shrugged. She called, 'Girls. Let's go. Mommy's gotta buy dinner. See you later, Billy. Pete.'

'You bet.'

'Great looking girl,' said Billy, when they had driven off. 'Sometimes I think of chucking it all for a weekend with Katie.'

'Careful,' said Chamberlain. 'Women with two little children *have* to get married.'

'So? Cute kids. She's even got money. Buddy's company had great insurance.'

'How long is it?'

'Long enough. She's paid her dues. Come on, let me show you around.'

Billy's New Year's Eve party started taking off around ten. Chamberlain had had a few drinks by then and was slipping more comfortably into his past. His distant past, he reminded himself. His childhood. Half his life had been away, yet some of the faces were as familiar as if he had never left.

Donny and Carol, who had gone together since they were twelve – married now with fifteen-year-old kids – still holding hands and still the best looking couple in the room. Kyle the wrestler and a young wife, his second, Jerry, Pete's buddy Phil's little sister. Tommy and Geeza, whose families owned the pizza joint and next door liquor store. Spark, Kevin, and Sherm. And Katherine, extraordinarily pretty, and very much alone. Her friends looked out for her, but it was hard for all of them, as Buddy had been the first of the group to die.

Others he didn't know, Billy's business associates, to whom Billy kept introducing him. The firehose factory dominated their conversation. It was going to be the hottest thing the town had seen in years, a boon to the economy, something the town could be proud of. The

24

septic was a bitch, all agreed. Billy's accountant took him aside and said, bluntly, 'Let's talk numbers.'

'But I'm not sure what Billy needs me for,' Chamberlain waffled, as the scheme began closing in on him. 'He's got people all over him.'

'Hey, this is just the first project and it's big enough for all of us. Danbury's expanding. This whole area's turning from farm to suburb. IBM's moving in. And ITT. We're the future.'

But when the talk shifted from business, they acted wary of him, sensing he had done and seen things they thought they never would, seeing in him history growing old. Most of them had been in college during the war or came of age after the draft was abolished, and today even *Rolling Stone* magazine had begun to publish romantic snippets about Vietnam and the colonial life in Saigon. The famous 'shelf', as they called Saigon's hotel terraces where spies and soldiers drank gin in the sun while the teenage hookers strolled by, sounded kind of pleasant twenty years later, and he wondered if the stories he had read about the British Empire would have seemed as silly to the soldiers who had been there.

'What's it like to look down a gun barrel?' Billy's partner Ron asked when he was drunk enough.

'Depends on the size.'

'Seriously.'

'You know you're not looking at a friend.'

The guy nodded, grave and a little sad, as if mourning a life which seemed short on experience.

The phone rang. Somebody answered, looked around the smoky living room.

'Pete! How'd they find you here?'

'Can I take it in the bedroom?'

'Make it fast. Don't want to miss the ball.' The television was turned to the celebration in New York where a lighted

25

red apple was to descend the Allied Chemical Tower at midnight. He lowered the sound and closed the door.

'Chamberlain.'

'It's Henry, Pete. I'm duty officer – '

'I know. What's up?' They were civilians, but the military expressions made them feel good.

'Mr Cowan wants you in the office.'

The bourbon he'd been drinking all night started trickling from his brain as if someone had pulled a plug. 'Mr Cowan' was Alfred Cowan, chief executive officer and chairman of the board of Comptel. Chamberlain could think of only one reason why, out of forty thousand employees world-wide, Alfred Cowan had chosen to call him on New Year's Eve, and that was a security disaster. Make that a *major* security disaster. With him in Connecticut, half looped in a snowstorm.

'We have a helicopter heading to Danbury airport.'

Chamberlain lifted the shade. Snow was still coming down a bitch. 'Tell the pilot to pick me up in the Rams Pasture at Newton. East of Danbury.' He imagined the town from the sky. 'Look for spotlights shining straight up a 140-foot flagpole. The Rams Pasture is a half-mile southeast of it. It's a dark space. I'll be on the road at the west end. Tell him to watch out for the trees and the telephone poles.'

'Hold on.' Henry relayed the instructions to the pilot.

'No, Pete. Pilot says he doesn't want to take the chance.'

'Tell that pilot that's what he's paid for.'

Henry went off and came back. 'He says it'll be breaking FAA rules.'

Chamberlain said, 'He's paid for that too,' and hung up.

'I'll drive you,' Billy offered, Corvette keys in one hand, Tequila in the other.

'It's snowing like crazy. I need a four-wheel drive. Where's your truck?'

'Getting a front end job.'

Katie got out of the chair where she had been quietly drinking a Tab. 'Where are you going?'

'You got a four-wheel drive?'

'Sure.'

'Can Billy run me to the Rams Pasture?'

Katherine looked at Billy's glass. 'I'll drive you.'

'Billy, tell Mom and Dad I'll get back as soon as I can.'

He made a fast general goodbye from the door. Katherine shrugged into her parka, picked up her long skirts and led the way through the snow to her car.

'This is really nice of you. I'm sorry to take you away from the party.'

'Where are you going?'

'My boss wants me in New York. He's sending a helicopter.'

'Wow.'

She started the car and headed for Newton. Chamberlain wiped the windscreen repeatedly with his coatsleeve. He wished he hadn't dragged her out. There'd be no one on the road but drunks, and soon even that seemed unlikely. As the road crossed Interstate 84, he saw all lanes were shut down. Katherine drove at a steady twenty and through the back of Newton to avoid the steepest hills.

'It must be great travelling around. Do you ever go to Europe?'

'About once a month.'

'Doing what?'

'Security.' She looked at him so he said, 'Let's say we have a plant manufacturing something a terrorist group wants. I help the plant design their security. Then I drop in one day and try to break it.'

'How?'

27

'Leave a note in the plant manager's safe. "Hi there. If I were a terrorist, you'd be in trouble." Like that.'

'They must love you.'

Chamberlain laughed.

She made it through the town and parked across from the Rams Pasture in a dark Mobil station. The police were next door, lights barely visible in the snow. Chamberlain opened his window a crack to listen for the helicopter.

'Why do they need you tonight?'

'They probably lost something.'

'And they want you to find it?'

'I wouldn't be surprised.'

'How do you do that?'

'Buy it back.'

'Is that what you did in the Navy?'

'There's my ride.'

It came down like a brightly lit stone, plummeting out of the sky, blowing snow, and flashing red and white lights.

'Thanks again,' he yelled over the rotor roar.

'Happy New Year.'

He bolted for the machine, which was hovering warily a foot above the snow-covered field, drove through the prop blast, found the door, hauled himself aboard, and slammed it shut. It was a super-luxury ship, about as quiet inside as you could make a helicopter.

'Go!'

'There's cops coming,' the pilot yelled, pointing at the patrol car flashers approaching the edge of the field.

'Well, what the hell are you waiting for? A parking ticket?'

'He was waiting for you, Mr Chamberlain,' a woman's voice answered behind him. 'I hope it was worth it.'

Chamberlain turned to the passenger seats. The cabin was dark so the pilot could see. In the dim lights of the instruments he saw a woman – dark-haired and wrapped to her chin in a fur coat. She indicated the seat next to her as the helicopter soared into the night. Chamberlain buckled in.

'I'm sorry. I didn't know he had a passenger, I wouldn't have told him to land here.'

'I presume the roads are a mess. They were further north.'

'You know my name, but I'm afraid I don't know yours.'

'Helen Thorp.'

Uh oh.

Helen Thorp. Number two in the company. Girl genius, Alfred Cowan's right hand, first-class ball buster, and very likely heir apparent to the thirteenth largest corporation in the world. 'Any idea what's happening?'

'None. But I'd be happier if an accountant had come aboard instead of a security man.'

'I don't know about that,' Chamberlain smiled. 'If you have to send a helicopter for an accountant, you're probably in pretty deep trouble.'

He felt the last fumes of bourbon burn out as she replied, 'I'm used to good news from accountants. Would you close that curtain, please?'

He shielded the cockpit and she turned on a reading light, opened a typed draft of the annual report, and began to mark it with a gold pencil. Her coat turned out to be sable. It spilled open at her throat, revealing a silk scarf, grey, a perfect colour bridge between her rather pale skin and thick jet hair. She was only in her early thirties, but fine lines beneath her dark eyes, and a full, sensual mouth, made her look wiser than her age, more mature, more knowing. All in all, Chamberlain concluded, an astonishing-looking woman mysterious with achievement.

She caught herself chewing her lip, removed her glove and smoothed her lipstick with the tip of an exquisitely manicured finger. She glanced at the window, noticed Chamberlain watching her in the reflection, looked through him, and returned to her reading. He got up, stepped through the curtain and took the empty co-pilot seat.

'Do you know what the fuck is going on?'

'Aside from the fact that some hick police force has my registration numbers,' the pilot replied icily, 'no.'

Chamberlain tried the radio. But Henry said, 'Mr Cowan said nothing on the radio.'

He signed off, surprised. Comptel manufactured some pretty classy, very private radios, and he knew for a fact, having chosen the equipment himself, that this was uncrackable by anything less than the gear used by the NSA.

The storm began thinning over the Connecticut coast. Ground lights appeared in patches and by the time they landed on a Hudson River pier, the sky was half-clear. A limousine took them to the Comptel Building on Sixth Avenue. Helen breezed past lobby security and into the private elevators. Chamberlain followed, making a mental note to test security one night soon with a dark-haired woman in a fur coat. As the elevator expressed to the executive floor at the top of the fifty-storey tower he looked at his watch.

'Happy New Year.'

To which Helen Thorp replied, 'Let's see what's going on first.'

2

Alfred Cowan, the balding chairman of the board and chief executive officer of Comptel Inc., was a heavy, broad-cheeked man in his early sixties. His powerful Ed Asner forearms were planted on his desk in an impatient let's-get-down-to-it posture. An unknotted black bow tie dangled from the open collar of his pearl-studded dress shirt. And his dinner jacket, evidently hurled off as he stormed in, had landed at the far end of his enormous office, splayed over an armchair like the urgent shadow of a diving hawk.

'Good party?' Helen called from the door.

'My wife thought so.'

She crossed forty feet of carpet briskly, and stopped in front of Cowan's desk. Chamberlain, following, stopped too, beside and slightly behind her as she shrugged out of her coat. Underneath she had an expensive-looking sweater and long, pretty legs in ski pants.

'What's up?'

Cowan grinned, unpleasantly. He had the hard blue eyes that Chamberlain recalled from their previous and only meeting. 'Guess who got himself kidnapped.'

'Who?' Helen asked warily, and Chamberlain sensed multiple layers of testing and competing between mentor and protégée. His own thoughts skipped to a half-dozen Third World capitals, and the Comptel executives in each worth ransoming. He had guessed right. The conglomerate had lost something and he was going to have to buy it back.

'Your boy.'

'*Hammond?*'

Her whole body stiffened, and she reeled, or flinched, as if she had been hit. The sable slid to the floor and piled around her legs in deep, shimmering folds. Chamberlain picked it up and draped it reverently over one of the leather armchairs that circled Cowan's desk. What, he wondered, was he doing here? He had guessed wrong, after all. Hammond, Charles Hammond, was a freelance, not a Comptel employee.

'When?' Helen asked. 'Is he all right?'

Cowan looked like he wanted to kill something. 'I got a call from London. Crocker. He's third VP for – '

'I know who Crocker is,' she interrupted, recovering quickly, Chamberlain thought, very quickly, a nice quality when the shrapnel was flying. 'What did Crocker say?'

Cowan had yet to acknowledge Chamberlain's presence, but now a severe glance in his direction announced that the chairman of Comptel was addressing him too. 'Crocker's holding down the London office. The rest took off for the south of France, *en masse*; goddamn holidays. Crocker heard it on the news. He tried to get Rice to confirm. But that snake-eyed bastard wouldn't talk to him.'

'Who is Rice?' Chamberlain interrupted.

'René Rice,' Helen replied. 'Hammond's chief of staff. In other words we know nothing.'

'Have you tried the police?' Chamberlain asked.

'Crocker said Scotland Yard is investigating. All the radio knew was two of Hammond's bodyguards were shot dead and a third is missing, along with Hammond.'

'Dead?' Helen asked.

'Two dead. One missing. No Hammond.'

Helen sank into the chair nearest Cowan's desk. Her hand rose tentatively to her scarf, but in an instant she bounded to her feet and dialled London on Cowan's telephone. Waiting for the connection, she drummed her pearl-grey nails on his desk. 'Hammond can't be kidnapped.'

'You got any proof he isn't?'

'Of course not – Alfred, do you realize what this means?'

'That's why we're here, isn't it?'

He glanced mournfully at his dinner jacket, pulled the tie from his neck and dropped it on his desk like a soiled napkin. 'Well, Pete, how you doing?'

'The lines are jammed up,' Helen snapped, dialling again.

'Hogmanay,' Cowan said. 'Every Scot in the world is calling home drunk.'

'They had to pick tonight?' She tried dialling again and Cowan repeated, 'How you doing, Pete?'

Chamberlain said, 'Pretty good, Mr Cowan. Considering.'

'You were up in Connecticut.'

'My parents.'

'Apologize for me. Where are they, Greenwich? Darien?'

'Sand Bend.'

Cowan shrugged. 'Sorry to screw up your holiday.'

'That's okay. This looks like Munich all over again.' Didn't hurt to remind the boss why he had been hired.

'Not quite. The guy you rescued was my employee. This Hammond . . .' He shot an angry look at Helen, busy dialling a third time. 'This guy's a problem.'

'Hello. Hello. All Seas? It's Helen Thorp calling René Rice.' She brushed silky hair from the phone. 'When will he be back? . . . Would you please tell Monsieur Rice to call me at Comptel in New York.' Then, with a mirthless wink at Cowan, she said, 'Since I'm on the line, let me speak to Mr Hammond.' Cowan nodded, acknowledging the ploy, but clearly, she was out of luck on that score too. She said thanks and hung up.

'Stonewalling?'

'With boulders. She said that Hammond's in Tananarive.'

Chamberlain started to ask, why not phone Tananarive, but she thought he was asking where and cut him off, irritably. 'Malagasy. Madagascar? Big island off the east coast of Africa? Indian Ocean? Weren't you in the Navy?'

'Only under water.'

'Listen, Alfred, it's six, London time. If they answered at six in the morning, they're obviously waiting for a ransom call. I better go to London. Talk my way into Rice's office.'

'No,' said Cowan. 'Pete goes to London.'

'Why?'

'He's done this kind of thing before.'

'Wait a minute, Alfred. This is no ordinary kidnapping.'

'Pete's qualified. Don't forget he got our Munich guy back from those German freaks.'

'Goddamnit, Alfred, we're talking about Charles Hammond. Pete kicked doors down to get that man back. It was sheer luck he wasn't killed. We can't take that sort of chance with Hammond.'

Chamberlain wanted very much to explain that kicking down the door in question was a last resort, when every instinct screamed at him that the ransom was a trick, when Arnie Fast had also agreed they were going to kill the man anyhow, that there came a moment when taking action was less risky than sitting around hoping things would work out. He wanted very much to explain this, but Helen Thorp had the settled eyes of a ship's captain, and he had learned long ago that explaining things to captains did not pay. And if the truth be told, he *had* spent a month of nights replaying the split second when if one person had moved an inch differently, Comptel would have needed a new man in Munich anyway.

Cowan defended him, undoubtedly for reasons of his

34

own. 'Pete is more than a door-kicker, Helen. He's a troubleshooter, if you know what I mean. He keeps up. He's on top of stuff like this.'

'In the Washington office,' Helen replied coolly. 'Troubleshooter means ex-military, retired FBI or has-been CIA.' She studied Chamberlain a moment. He stood his ground, held her gaze, wondering what the hell she had against him. 'You look too young to be retired FBI and too smart for the Navy. Where'd you go from there? CIA?'

Chamberlain grinned a grin he hoped looked sheepish. What he really wanted to do was give them both the finger and walk out. But an invitation to join the Chairman of Comptel in his office, after hours, was a once-in-a-lifetime opportunity. 'Guilty on two counts. I don't know how smart I am, but I was a Navy SEAL before I joined the spooks.'

Helen kept boring in. 'Did you leave the spooks on friendly terms?'

Again Cowan answered for him. They were like a long-married couple conducting a fight through a guest. 'After Pete got back our Munich guy, I made him an offer he couldn't refuse. I know a few people, so I was able to smooth things over for him.'

Chamberlain said, 'I can still go back for favours, if that's what you're asking, Ms Thorp.'

'*Intelligence* favours. Information. Not guns. Not blowing up ships. That must be understood.'

'It's understood.' So she knew about the SEALs. She knew everything. Why the games?

She turned back to Cowan, as if Chamberlain had left the room. 'The question is, Alfred, how much ransom do they want and how much should Comptel contribute.'

'Wait a minute,' said Cowan, 'Hammond's not an employee,' and Chamberlain realized, *that's* what they were fighting about.

'Also,' Helen sailed through his objection, 'what can we do to help René Rice deal with the kidnappers when they make contact?'

'He's not an employee,' Cowan repeated. 'He works for a bunch of different companies.'

'Alfred – '

Chamberlain interrupted her. 'If I can suggest. Since Mr Hammond works independently for several corporations, maybe you and Ms Thorp could poll the others and put together a fund. Share the burden.'

'Wonderful idea,' said Helen, and Chamberlain felt great.

'Maybe,' said Cowan.

One of the twin teletype machines behind his desk buzzed to life, startlingly loud in the muffled quiet. Cowan swivelled around to read the printout.

Chamberlain glanced at the console. 'That's the private link.'

'Probably Crocker in London. I gave him tonight's code.'

Comptel Inc.'s original conglomerate base being in telecommunications, the company possessed an especially exotic internal information network, including two distinct telex systems. The first served regular business and communication with the rest of the world. The private link was reserved for plant heads, district managers, and the top company officers. Six people in the New York City corporate headquarters, Chamberlain knew, and he was certainly not among them, had access to the second system.

The machine ceased. Cowan, who had watched it fill the paper, broke the long silence that followed by ripping the paper from the platen. He turned around slowly and placed the sheet on his desk. He looked bewildered.

'Crocker?' asked Helen.

'No.'

'Who?' She sensed Chamberlain tightening beside her.

36

'I don't know.' Cowan twisted the paper sideways so she could read it.

YOUR BID IS EXPECTED AT THE PENDRAGON AUCTION. LANCELOT.

3

Lady Janet Isling awakened in darkness, her hair prickling against the linen pillow-case. Silently, she edged her hand under the pillow. She was inches from the gun when powerful hands seized her wrists and jerked her upright.

An electric torch blazed in her eyes, blinding her. She struggled, but when they turned the room lights on she realized that there were two of them and the one holding her was too strong. She went limp to save her strength and put them off guard.

Burglars was her first thought, house breakers surprised to find her sleeping in the seemingly empty villa. Many of the big houses were closed at this time of year when the permanent residents abandoned the South of France for Paris or Christmas skiing in the Alps.

That they would try to rape her, having found her naked and alone, she had no doubt. Nor did she doubt that she would shoot them both as soon as she could reach the gun. It lay in its usual place behind the second pillow, the lace-covered one she had propped up to lean against while she read herself to sleep.

As her eyes adjusted to the bright light, she saw that the one who held her arms was a fleshy, round-faced youth in his twenties, French, by the look of his heavy nose and the sloppily cut suit and open shirt favoured by local working men. He forced her arms apart, causing her exposed breasts to jut forward. He looked like a typical Marseille street hood, stupid, but smart enough to wait for orders from the second man who was watching her with an expression of gloating anticipation. She took in his clothing, and meeting his eyes, for the first time felt fear.

He was the direct opposite of the man who held her. He was very tall, so lean as to be skeletal, his face a mask of hard, straight lines unsoftened by any excess flesh. Glittering dark eyes held hers in a brutal gaze. His clothes – trousers, jacket, roll-neck sweater, shoes – were all black. He wasn't French. There was an oriental look to his face, but Lady Janet couldn't place a nationality. He carried a black wooden cane with a knob of carved ivory as white as his face.

He spoke. The accent struck her ears as Slavic.

'Where is Grandzau?'

Again she felt fear. They weren't house robbers. Nor were they here by accident. Not if they knew about her and Grandzau. But what a foolish question. If they knew about Grandzau and knew his code name surely they knew the answer.

'Grandzau is dead.'

The man in black spoke again, as if he hadn't heard.

'Where is Grandzau?'

'I've told you, he's dead.' Lady Janet's voice, with its accent of upper-class English ease and privilege, grew insistent. 'Will you instruct your man to let my arms go? He's hurting my wrists.'

'Where is Grandzau?'

The man's long fingers left the ivory head and travelled down the cane. He was wearing black leather gloves and in the silence of her bedroom, Lady Janet thought she could hear the creak of leather as his fingers moved along the black wood. The grip on her wrists was as tight as before. She'd been trying to edge closer to the pillow, but she was still too far from the gun, and since she was held from behind, she hadn't enough leverage to break the man's grip on even one wrist.

The man in black shifted the cane in his hands, took hold of the ivory head. The movement caused his jacket to open slightly and she caught a glimpse of a Baretta in a shoulder holster. She'd get only one chance for her gun.

'Where is Grandzau?'

'Grandzau died three years ago,' she insisted. 'He died in a car wreck in the Alps. He's buried in a churchyard just south of the Italian border.'

'You are lying to protect him,' said the man in black.

'I can't protect a dead man.'

'You are lying.' He twisted his hands. The head of the cane turned with a sharp click. He drew his hands apart, separating the halves of the cane. Lady Janet's belly clenched. It was not the sword cane she had supposed, not a weapon, but a vicious instrument, a long, black leather riding crop.

He dropped the scabbard end of the cane, stepped closer to her bed, and reached towards her. Without a word, he caressed her with the whip. It tapered to a thin, flexible lash. He traced her breast, then her nipple, then her other breast.

She watched his glittering eyes as she felt the supple leather descend towards her belly, lazily zig-zagging across her taut, suntanned skin until stopped by the bedsheet. The man in black paused, the whip resting on her navel, reached out with one gloved hand, and flicked the sheet off her body and onto the floor. Then he resumed tracing the lines of her bare flesh, skirting her pubis, exploring her thighs. She drew her legs together as the whip sought to part them. The stiff, yet flexible lash continued its gentle exploration. She'd ridden with the kind; it had a bamboo core. Then he stopped, tapped her belly gently a couple of times, and asked, 'Where is Grandzau?'

'He's dead,' she said, struggling to keep her voice calm.

The man was changing subtly. She sensed a crescendo of emotion beginning to build behind his icy façade.

'You're lying.'

He lifted the whip and tapped her breast – a little harder, but soft enough still so that even though the second tap touched her nipple, she felt no pain.

'Where is Grandzau, Lady Janet?'

'He's dead. You can check it yourself.'

'You're lying.'

'I'm not,' she protested, determined not to plead.

The thin black whip rose high over her head. His eyes passed reflectively along her body. She stiffened for the stroke. Where would it land? Her breast? Her thighs?

'Turn her over!'

Her chance. The man holding her wrists hauled her around. She let herself go easily, building momentum, putting all her concentration into freeing her right hand at the crucial moment.

She twisted her wrist sharply towards her body, dragging all her strength against his thumb and fingers, pulling herself towards the pillow even as she loosened the weakest part of his hold. The Frenchman grunted surprise when his fingers slipped on her flesh. She pulled harder, gathering her legs under her to spring for the pillow, but his fingers closed like steel wire, bit into her wrist bones, and an instant later she was spread-eagled across the bed, her arms still pinioned, stretched apart, her naked back exposed from her neck to her ankles.

The man in black walked around the bed, drawing the whip through his fingers. Lady Janet twisted around and watched over her shoulder, terrified, sickened by her failure, her fear, and the helpless knowledge that she'd lost her only chance. She drew a breath and clenched her body as he raised the whip.

It descended in a blur, parting the air with a whistle, a

sharp cutting sound she knew from the hunt, from urging horses to take gates they were afraid to jump. The leather cracked like a gunshot straight across her buttocks. A sharp trail of pain made her body jerk convulsively and drew a strangled gasp from her clenched teeth and, an instant later, a scream, as the pain travelled into her thighs and up her back, coursing through her muscles like flame.

'Where is Grandzau?'

'He's dead,' she gasped, fighting to regain control before terror and panic ravished her mind. She swallowed hard and tried to order her breathing.

The gloved hand slapped her face.

'Open your eyes.'

She hadn't realized they were closed. The black glove was inches from her face. It held a sheet of paper, white, rough-cut at top and bottom. Letters swam before her eyes.

'Read it!' demanded the man in black.

It was printed in capital letters and she recognized a telegram:

YOUR BID IS EXPECTED AT – her eyes widened – THE PENDRAGON AUCTION. LANCELOT.

'Do you wish to continue lying?'

'But he's dead!'

The man in black twisted her long blonde hair around his free hand and jerked her head back until she was staring into his eyes. The pleasure she saw in them was terrifying. Nothing she could say would stop him from doing this to her. He lifted his other hand and Lady Janet flinched as she heard the whip cut the air again, racing to meet her naked flesh.

4

'What the hell is this supposed to mean?' glowered Alfred Cowan.

'Pendragon?' asked Helen Thorp, staring at the telex. Chamberlain got up and stood behind her, reading it over her shoulder.

'King Arthur,' he answered, touching the name with a large, meticulously cared-for index finger that looked slightly crooked as if it had been broken at least once.

'Head dragon,' Alfred Cowan agreed.

'What?'

'The Malory tales of King Arthur and the knights of the Round Table,' explained Cowan. He grinned at Chamberlain and added, 'Before television, my dear.'

'Who's Lancelot? And don't tell me he's a nice knight.'

Chamberlain said, 'I wonder how he got into our private telex?'

'Maybe he works for us.' Helen picked up the message and read it again. 'Who's Pendragon supposed to be? . . . Oh.'

'Head dragon,' Chamberlain nodded. 'Charles Hammond.'

'Oh, for Christ sake,' said Cowan.

'Is this supposed to be a ransom note?' Helen asked.

'Why would they send *us* a ransom note?' snapped Cowan.

Helen shook her head.

'Excuse me, sir,' said Chamberlain, 'but I think they sent a lot of them.'

'What makes you think that?'

'It says auction,' Helen answered. 'You invite a number of bidders to an auction. "Your *bid* is expected at the Pendragon Auction."'

'What kind of a nut plays dumb word games. Lancelot! For Christ's sake. Auction, ransom. They're still kidnappers. Bastards!'

'Maybe it's his way of saying who he is.'

'How?'

'A code name.'

'Well it doesn't make too damned much sense to send code to people who don't have the key. Right, Pete?'

'I think Ms Thorp has a point. He's using a code for a reason. He figures somebody will recognize it.'

Cowan glared at him, then turned back to Helen. 'Do you think Rice got one of these too?'

'There's one way to find out.' She picked up the phone, flicked on the desk amplifier, and dialled London. Chamberlain took the message and walked around the room reading it.

Alfred Cowan said, 'What makes you think Rice'll talk to you now?'

'Watch.'

The girl in London answered on the first double ring. 'All Seas –'

Helen cut her off. 'Lancelot calling Mr Rice.'

Cowan grinned and Chamberlain stopped walking in circles.

'Please hold the line.'

They heard a moment of whispered conversation, then Rice's French accent came on the line. 'This is René Rice. To whom am I speaking?'

'It's Helen Thorp at Comptel, René. We got one too.'

'What? Who –'

'Your bid is expected at the Pendragon Auction! Who else got one, René?'

44

'I have no idea,' Rice replied stiffly.

'But you do admit that Hammond was kidnapped.'

'You seem to have deduced that yourself, Miss Thorp. With the help of the media. Yes. Mr Hammond was kidnapped.'

'What are you doing?'

Rice sounded exhausted. 'Scotland Yard is investigating. Beyond that, what can we do but wait for their demands?'

'What other companies is Hammond dealing for at the moment?'

Rice hesitated. 'I can't disclose that information. We owe our other clients the same confidentiality we accord Comptel.'

'I'd like to suggest,' Helen said evenly, 'that someone, you or us, finds out who else got these messages. Comptel is considering contributing to a ransom fund, if other of Hammond's clients will too.'

'Like hell we are,' Cowan muttered at his desk.

'Do you want to call them, or shall we?'

Rice's accent grew more French, and less clear. He was practically mumbling when he finished saying, 'How can we be sure that they too received such a message?'

'By asking.'

'But what if they didn't?'

Helen was visibly controlling an impulse to shout. 'Then they didn't, René. It doesn't matter. They'll know by tomorrow anyway. Talk to your staff,' she added gently. 'See what they say. I'll call you in an hour with Comptel's contribution.'

Alfred Cowan glowered dangerously when she hung up. '*What* contribution?'

'Rice sounds terrible. I thought he'd handle it better. He's usually pretty cool.'

'*What* contribution?'

'We have to offer something, Alfred.'

'Why?'

Helen started to answer, noticed Chamberlain sitting in a chair, puzzling over the telex message. 'Listen, Alfred, why don't we discuss this while Pete . . .'

'Right,' snapped Cowan.

Chamberlain was already on his feet. 'I'll make some calls. If it's got a secure phone, I'd like the office next door.'

'Okay with you, Helen?' asked Cowan.

She nodded.

'Thank you, sir. Thank you, Ms Thorp.'

Chamberlain headed for the door. He wanted very much to hear their discussion, but at the same time he was relieved to be out of that high-powered room for a minute. It had been like reporting to the bridge on a flagship and finding the captain and the task force admiral waiting for your bright ideas.

Last year when Cowan had hired him away from the Agency, all smiles and promises in a DC hotel lobby, the Comptel president had been generous, sweetening the pot with a twenty-five K bonus for ransoming the kidnapped regional manager if Chamberlain would work for Comptel security. A guy like Charles Hammond ought to be worth a lot more than a regional manager. A *lot* more, if he played it right. And maybe for more than money, this time. Maybe a shot at getting out of security – a shot at getting in on top.

He locked Helen Thorp's door behind him and swept a tiny electronic receiver around the lavish room. The gadget lighted softly in his palm, confirming what a surreptitious sweep of Cowan's office had already indicated. Comptel's executive suites were bristling with electronic jammers and detectors. If he tried listening in on their meeting in the next room with the miniature eavesdropper he carried

46

in his pocket, he'd provoke a shriek from their anti-bugging alarms.

He paced around her office, snapping his fingers in frustration. She'd been a surprise, younger, more beautiful and tougher than company scuttlebutt had pegged her. Much tougher. She lived very well. Her handsome desk was tucked into an alcove, while the main body of the room contained two separate seating areas, one with a fur-covered couch, an elaborate stereo rig, and an antique bar made of wood veneers and leaded glass. Chamberlain shook his head, stymied for a way to listen in. As the international conglomerates operated further and further beyond the control and protection of national governments, they had to get tougher about their own security. Those that owned communications hardware subsidiaries were the hardest to crack. Comptel even had scramblers built into its top-level internal telephones, just like the KGB.

The bar! He selected a crystal highball glass and held the mouth against the wall between Helen Thorp and Cowan's offices. Then he pressed his ear to the bottom of the glass in time to hear Helen Thorp saying, 'But last year Hammond agented ten per cent of Comptel's business.'

Chamberlain moved the glass several inches until he located a wall stud that conducted the sound better than the insulated hollow part. He grinned and whispered *genius* to himself.

Alfred Cowan's voice rumbled through the wall like the belly of a large and hungry animal. 'Hammond's got too big a piece of our action.'

'It's a little late to worry about that now,' Helen Thorp replied. Chamberlain couldn't hear much of her tone, but the swift cadence of her reply had an angry beat.

'As a matter of fact,' rumbled Cowan, 'I've been worried about Hammond for some time now.'

'Alfred, for God's sake, do you want to do *less* business?'

47

Cowan's retort was so soft that Chamberlain could barely hear. 'Maybe I want *you* to do less business with Hammond.'

After a short silence, Helen said, 'And more business elsewhere? Is that what you're saying?'

'Maybe you've got stuck in a rut with Hammond. Maybe you should be expanding elsewhere.'

'This is a hell of a time to tell me.'

'Have you ever heard bad news at a good time?'

The silence that followed was so long that Chamberlain thought they had turned around and were speaking in the other direction. But when at last he heard Helen Thorp, he knew he hadn't missed a word.

'That bad?' she asked flatly.

'Yep. This just brought it to a head.'

'Alfred, how could I miss this? Why didn't you say anything?'

'You didn't listen.'

Again there was silence.

Chamberlain waited, alarmed that Charles Hammond was about to be dropped overboard and, with the deal-maker, Chamberlain's chance of getting in good with Cowan. Sure enough, Helen Thorp asked, 'Are you suggesting we forget about him?'

'Why not?' Cowan rumbled gloomily.

'Because if you are, it will cost us a lot.'

'We'll survive.'

'Four years' lost profit?'

'Three,' Cowan snapped too quickly.

'Settle for three,' said Helen Thorp. 'Will the board allow you that much time?'

'If I feed it to them a year at a time. Hell, our stock's up.'

'We can't pay bills with paper profits.'

48

'It won't be a happy couple of years.' The rumble took on a hard edge. 'But I'll be better off than you, sweetheart.'

'Yes, Alfred. I know that. I am utterly dependent on Hammond if I want to have your job when you retire.'

'Which you do.'

'Yes, Alfred, as we both know.'

Cowan laughed. 'You're in worse trouble than you think. If the board cans me, the last person they'd put in this seat would be my favourite protégée.'

'I'm aware of that,' she replied coldly.

'I wouldn't want that to happen,' said Cowan.

'Thanks. The question is what are we willing to spend to get him back.'

'I'd swallow the loss.'

'You won't, Alfred. Because it'll kill your expansion plans.'

Cowan snapped an angry retort. 'Why did that stupid son of a bitch get himself snatched? What about his security people?'

'He probably didn't listen to them.'

'That would be just like Hammond. Why in hell did I let you get me so tied up with him?'

'Because the arrangement worked. We're repeating ourselves, Alfred.'

'Why the hell can't we just have employees do what he does?'

'Because,' she replied patiently, 'any employee who has the ear of Egypt's defence minister, the chief of staff of Kenya's army's private phone number, and goes whoring with the prince who buys communications hardware for Saudi Arabia would be pretty dumb to remain an employee.'

'Screw,' said Cowan.

Helen Thorp's voice cut insistently through the wall and

swirled around the empty glass. 'Nor do we want Comptel employees paying *baksheesh*.'

'True.'

'If Hammond pays bribes out of his commission it's his own business.'

'So why the hell did he get himself kidnapped?'

'Moving right along, Alfred. Let's make a decision before it's forced on us. How much do we contribute to his ransom?'

'What do you need?'

'How do I know? It's an auction. They'll ask for the moon. What will Comptel contribute?'

'Fuck!'

'How much, Alfred?'

He answered quietly and Chamberlain wasn't sure he'd heard him say one million dollars.

'Not enough,' said Helen Thorp, and Chamberlain wondered what Comptel would pay for him if he were snatched. Thirty thousand dollars stuck in his head in a nasty way.

'Five! And that's it.'

Chamberlain whistled soundlessly. Raising five million cash, hiding the fact it was paid, and recouping it, would engage a platoon of accountants for the better part of a year.

Cowan's voice hardened, the pitch wavering as he apparently stood and walked around his office. 'But it's your job to get him back. No fuck-ups. That money goes nowhere until you know we've got him back. Clear?'

'You're doing the right thing,' said Helen Thorp. 'Shall I call Rice?'

'For five million he can pay for his own call.'

'Where are you going?'

'My ass isn't as far over the line as yours and seeing as

how there's no point in both our evenings being wrecked, Happy New Year.'

'What about Chamberlain?' she asked. 'Do I have to take him?'

'He's a hitter. Take him. You might need a hitter.'

Chamberlain shrugged angrily. He knew he hadn't made it into Cowan's plush office on ordinary talents, but the term, laden with more truth than he liked, gnawed a hollow space in his gut.

'But where's his head,' Helen persisted. 'What's he *like*?'

Cowan snorted. 'His head? He was a Navy demo diver.'

'Alfred,' she said exasperatedly. 'You know damned well I'm not a military groupie like you. What does "a Navy demo diver" mean?'

A hitter, thought Chamberlain.

'They've taken chances most of us haven't,' Cowan replied. 'It steadies a man.'

'Bullshit, Alfred. *Physical* chances. You take chances every day that would turn an ordinary person's hair white.'

'Let's just say Pete would be a nice guy to have along at a mugging.'

'Whose side?'

'Yours, if you want him. That's what we pay him for.'

'I don't know.'

'Happy New Year, dear. Call me if you need me.' The thin wall trembled as Cowan's door slammed shut.

Chamberlain filled his listening glass with Pelligrini water from Helen Thorp's bar, noting with surprise that it didn't bubble like Perrier. Then he dialled Langley, Virginia, on her private phone, which bore a hint of her perfume.

Cowan didn't matter any more. His big chance at Comptel had shifted into Helen Thorp's hands. Somehow he had to impress her and damned fast.

'Central Intelligence Agency.'

Chamberlain played it straight and gave the operator a short list of names, praying that it would be Arnie Fast that she managed to find on New Year's Eve. Arnie was one of the few people left who owed him one.

5

Something had changed. Something enormous, but indefinable. Her body still leaped and bucked and she still heard her voice shriek hoarsely, but after a while she realized she no longer heard the awful whistle of the lash, nor felt it add new pain to the agony that ripped her. She identified the pounding in her ears as her own heartbeat.

'Open your eyes.'

She opened them. The letters on the yellow paper swam before her. She cringed as the man in black touched the signature with the tip of his lash and tapped it again and again. Lancelot, Lancelot, Lancelot.

'Where is Grandzau?'

Through the agony that burned her whole body, her mind screamed that someone was using Grandzau's old Malory code.

'Do you wish to lie some more?' asked the man in black.

Who could know it? How could she convince him that Lancelot couldn't be Grandzau? The fat one holding her had shifted his grip. He held both her hands in one of his.

'Where is Grandzau?'

She wrested free and reached towards the pillow. The pain slowed her, contracted her body even as she tried to stretch. He caught her easily and forced her back on her belly.

'Where is Grandzau?' For the first time, he sounded impatient, and she realized again that he had beaten her for his pleasure. Now he expected the truth, but she had already spoken the truth.

'He's dead. I swear it.'

He raised the whip.

As she twisted around in another futile effort to escape she saw that the man holding her had opened his trousers.

'Later,' he promised. 'When she has spoken.'

New Year dawn broke behind the East River and laced cold, grey light into Helen Thorp's office at the top of the Comptel Building. Fifty storeys below, the streets were still dark.

It found Pete Chamberlain in quiet telephone conversation in one corner and Helen Thorp at her desk. He watched her cradle her phone with a satisfied nod and scan the single sheet of paper on which she had listed in a small, neat hand the night's conversations. Three cigarette butts sat in her ashtray, one for each two hours. She checked her watch and lighted a fourth, early, he noted.

He finished his call and headed her way. 'Okay, Pete. What have your "favours" told you about Hammond?'

'They nabbed him in broad daylight two blocks from Harrods. Very neat, including a phoney bobby and probably a planted chauffeur.'

'How the hell did they get inside Hammond's security?'

Chamberlain shrugged. 'I'll find out, eventually. But the important thing is they did it well and professionally, which increases Hammond's chances of survival.'

'Thank God for small favours.'

'Better than being taken by crazies. Who'd you get to on the ransom?'

'Everyone but Hans Streicher, which isn't surprising.'

'No. The arms dealers tend to be independent. He'll come around when he's sure he needs us.'

'Mishuma will match us. Lockheed couldn't find anybody who was allowed to say yes, but they want to. Same with Texas Instruments. They don't want their hands dirty so I think they'll let us represent them. British Hovercraft is another proposition. They're very comfortable working with military types, so they'll probably stand alone.'

'Will they join you when it counts?'

'Of course,' said Helen. 'It's to all of our advantage. A couple of smaller companies will also come in for smaller amounts. Some of them are in a lot worse trouble than us because Hammond handles the majority of their sales. They'll do what we tell them to. Also, the Paris office says the French government has approached us quietly. I think Hammond was selling Mirages.'

'They really kidnapped the right man,' said Chamberlain.

'They sure did. Everyone wants him back safe and sound and capable of finishing his jobs for them.' She bent her head back and stretched her neck. Massaging it with her fingers, trying to rub out the kinks, she asked, 'And what else did your favours tell you?'

'Two things. I finally located a guy who knew about the Malory code.'

'Did he know who uses it?'

'Sort of. A German named Karl Grandzau was selling secrets to both us and the Russians back in the late sixties and middle seventies. He had a small network in NATO and another one in East Germany. The kind of operator who every time you're ready to kill him for screwing you, comes back with some good dope from the other side. And speaking of dope, he was trading a lot of the narcotic kind on the side, heroin out of Marseille, until the Chinese in Amsterdam took over the business. Each of Grandzau's contacts had a code name from the Arthurian legend. Really corny. Grandzau's code name was Lancelot.'

'So we'll buy Hammond back from Grandzau.'

'Except Grandzau died three years ago.'

* * *

Lady Janet lay still, her body no longer able to flee the lash. The whip had never strayed from her buttocks, but the pain was everywhere. Sometime after the whip stopped cutting its song in the air, she heard the man in black talking on the telephone.

'She doesn't know. Perhaps he tricked her too.'

There was a pause. Then he said, 'Yes, I'm sure. I'll have to try the one in Bern.' He hung up the phone. Then she heard him say, 'Take care of her.'

'I'll be a while,' said the fleshy one.

Lady Janet sensed movement and watched through slitted eyes. She was still on her belly, the sheet soaked with her perspiration. The man in black passed into her range of vision, the whip still in his hand, and slipped it into the cane scabbard with a regretful sigh. The instrument clicked shut. He twisted the knob to lock it and walked out of the room.

She heard his heels clicking on the polished marble stairs. She waited, gathering her will. From behind her she heard the rustle of cloth, the double thud of heavy shoes, the clink of a belt buckle. The fleshy one removing his clothes.

She didn't know if she could move at all. Her body still coursed with pain. Her arms felt like lead. She tried to orient herself, to see where she lay on the bed, to figure where the pillow was, to fix exactly the way her arms and legs lay.

He grabbed her ankles and shoved her legs apart. From the window came the sound of a starter motor, then the distinctive rumbly clatter of a Citroën-Maserati. She forced herself to lie quietly while the man behind her arranged her body for his assault.

He was breathing loudly now, a deep and slow inhalation. His hand brushed her wealed buttocks and the resultant pain compressed her will. If she could only move, the moment was coming. She concentrated on the forward lunge. It had to be perfect. He was too big to fight at close quarters. This was her last chance. He was going to kill her after he had raped her.

The bed sagged as he knelt between her spread legs.

She leaped forward, sliding her hand under the first pillow, desperately burrowing for the gun behind the second. He bellowed surprise. She got her hand under the second pillow, but he grabbed her legs and pulled her towards him. Her fingers hit the hard shape of the gun, but he dragged her away from it. She kicked out like a swimmer, straining forward, pushing her hand back under the pillow.

She got her hand around the gun. In a practised motion, she flicked off the safety catch as her forefinger slid through the trigger guard. Twisting onto her side, nearly blinded by pain, she brought the gun around, sighting his meaty shoulder, squeezing the trigger.

He was naked, white as a drowned body. He gaped stupidly at the gun, then tossed a balled sheet at her with cunning speed. The shot exploded loudly in the big room.

Lady Janet fell back on the bed, weeping bitterly.

The man in black would pay for what he had done to her, but the sheet had spoiled her shot and now her best clue where to find him lay dead on her bedroom floor, a bullet through his heart.

6

'Dead? If Grandzau's dead, who is Lancelot?'

'No one knows.' Chamberlain stood up, stretched until his joints snapped, and walked to the glass wall. He stared at his reflection, which lay insubstantially over the grey city. 'But we have a worse problem. Much worse.'

'Pete, I don't like guessing games. Just give it to me quick and straight, without the dramatics. What's the worse problem?'

'My friends were a little too glad to talk. They were pumping *me*.'

'Of course the CIA is interested in Hammond.'

'Only because the Russians are.'

'Russians? No. Charles Hammond does not deal with the Russians.'

'*They* want to deal with him.'

She shook her head. 'Years ago they asked him to handle the grain trades; he got about a week into it and said, no way.' She grinned suddenly, surprising Chamberlain as her very beautiful face grew more beautiful in warm repose. 'Hammond says Russian bureaucrats make Arab cement traders look like bake sale ladies.'

'You like Hammond, don't you?'

He expected her to clam up, even jump down his throat again, but her grin drifted into a smile and she nodded, admitting, 'I like him a lot. Life moves right along when he's around. The man's got a flair about him.'

Abruptly serious, she was all business again. 'What did the CIA tell you about the Russians?'

'Minute the word was out that Hammond was snatched,

the KGB jumped in with all four feet. Tipped Scotland Yard to some IRA cells in London the bobbies didn't know about. Busted a Palestinian safe house with their own men. Thank God Hammond wasn't there. They're not exactly subtle. Now that they've heard about the telegrams, they're cosying up to Mishuma and Hans Streicher and God knows who else. They want Hammond and they want him bad.'

'For what he knows,' Helen breathed.

'Looks that way. Hammond knows a lot about a lot of armies, having sold them their best hardware.'

'What would they do with him?'

'Wring it out of him.'

'Oh God!'

'So it looks like we won't be the only bidder at that auction. We might work a deal with Mishuma and Streicher and surely Hovercraft, but the Russians will bid against us.'

'What will the CIA do?'

'Watch. Help us when they can without compromising other operations. And if it looks like the Russians will outbid us, they'll kill him.'

She sagged visibly, then brightened. 'But if they don't know where he is – '

'You better believe they're looking hard. When they find him they'll either kick the door down, or wait to see how the bidding goes. Either way, I wouldn't want to be Hammond.'

'Well . . . Will the Russians disrupt the auction?'

'Doubt it. Hammond's not likely to be present.'

'Why don't we make a deal with the CIA? Bid together.'

'Excellent, if we actually get to the auction. But the problem is the Russians are hunting Hammond already. They're not waiting for the auction.'

Helen Thorp nodded, chewing her lip. 'Right. And the CIA?'

'Watching the Russians. Ready to pounce if they get close.'

'All right. In other words, Hammond's best chance is to be found and rescued before the KGB or the CIA gets to him.'

'It's a helluva best chance.'

She stopped chewing her lip and hit him with the full force of her startling eyes. They shone, violet in the dawn, and her low, contralto voice harmonized with them, intent, demanding.

'Pete. What do *you* want?'

'Beg pardon?'

'What do you want?' she repeated. 'What do you want to get out of this?'

'I'm not sure I understand you.'

'My whole career's on the line with Hammond's life. Ordinarily, I'd handle this myself. But the Russians complicate my decision. So I need help. But I want to know more about Pete Chamberlain. What does Pete Chamberlain want?'

Chamberlain hesitated. He had heard Cowan say as much, through the wall. She was in trouble either way, but without Hammond, she was through. It sounded like the opportunity of a lifetime and his mind was chanting, *Don't blow it. Don't blow it.*

Helen Thorp shook her head, impatiently. 'Don't try to make up a right answer. Just tell me.'

He spread his hands wide, studied his thick fingers. If she had pulled a gun on him he would have snapped it away, faster than thought. If a pair of karate blackbelts charged, he'd paint the walls with them. But he felt slow and hopeless trying to promote himself. 'I want to get ahead.'

'So does everybody. The ones who succeed know why.'

Chamberlain looked away, out the window, still unable to come out and say, simply, that seventeen years of spook soldiering ought to lead to more than diddling the Wetlands Commission out of septic permits for his brother's condos.

She moved beside him. He felt her searching for his face mirrored in the glass. Down in the street, five hundred feet below where it was still dark, a clump of New Year diehards was waving forlornly for non-existent taxis. The sky was lightening rapidly and when he let their eyes meet it was in the dying reflection of the night.

Chamberlain opened his mouth and the words came out at last. 'You know what I want?'

'What?'

'I want to feel comfortable walking into Cowan's office.' It sounded stupid the second he said it, and yet it was exactly what he had been trying to explain all day long to his brother, and himself.

'Would you settle for my office?'

'What do you mean?'

'Get Hammond back alive and I'll guarantee you'll feel comfortable walking into my office. Any time. Any reason. Get him back, Pete. Blank cheque. *Get Hammond back!*'

7

'Chamberlain?'

He had already seen the blue-suited Englishman from the door of the Concorde and had tagged his knife-lean frame, grey moustache and unimpressed cop's eyes, Scotland Yard. The Brit extended his hand, both welcoming him to London and barring the way, and said, 'Alex Farquhar. Metropolitan Police.'

'Pete Chamberlain.'

'A chap at Comptel said you were coming. I told him I'd look out for you. If you've nothing in your shoulder bag Her Majesty's Customs Inspector would disapprove of, let's just slip by. Contraband? Live animals? . . .'

'No weapons.'

'Excellent. We found Hammond's security chief. I thought we might pop by the hospital, hear what he has to say for himself.'

'Wheeler?'

'Apparently he followed the kidnappers. A farmer found him twenty miles north of London crawling about a field with his throat slit.'

'Where did they go?'

'Wheeler started bleeding again and the doctors turfed me out before I could ask.'

'We gotta find out.'

'We will try.'

Wheeler was tubed and trached; the stiletto slit was pinched with black stitches. His face was dead white, his eyes cloudy.

'Can he talk?'

'No,' said the doctor.

Chamberlain opened his wallet, which had a notepad and pen. 'Can he write?'

'I'll give you two minutes. His life is in danger.'

'So is Charles Hammond's,' said Farquhar, leaning over the bed. 'Mr Wheeler. This is Inspector Farquhar again. We were starting to speak earlier, but you were bleeding. Feeling better? . . . No, I don't suppose you are. Can you remember how you got to the field where we found you?'

Wheeler moved his head, no.

'He crawled more than a hundred yards from where his car was stuck,' Farquhar murmured over his shoulder.

'He's one tough son of a bitch.'

Wheeler's eyes opened wider, he strained to see Chamberlain, who stepped closer. Then he reached for pen and pad, and when Chamberlain propped it before his hand wrote in a shaky hand, *Believe it*.

'Marines?'

Wheeler wrote, *Army. 101st*.

'How'd you lose him?'

'Blacked out.'

'What's the last thing you saw?'

'Birds.'

'Wheeler, you all here? You wrote birds.'

'Around the bend,' Farquhar said quietly.

'Shape up, Wheeler, Mr Hammond's counting on you.'

'That's quite enough,' said the doctor.

'Wheeler, what did you see?'

'I said stop that!'

Chamberlain shook him off. 'Come on, Wheeler. Screw the candy asses. What happened. Wha'd you see?'

Wheeler clutched the pen in his fist and drew five parallel lines, which he sprinkled slowly with black dots.

'Music?' asked Farquhar.

'He's lying on the ground,' said Chamberlain. 'Looking up.'

'Electric wires,' said Farquhar. 'Power lines.'

'What are those dots?'

'Birds. As he said. Crows on the wire.'

'Great. Must have lost so much blood he was hallucinating.'

'That's it,' said the doctor. 'Get out.'

'He's writing again.'

They watched the pen inch along the lines, forming a new shape over them.

'A plane! He saw a plane. Wheeler. Wheeler. Did it have numbers?'

Wheeler moved the pen as if it weighed as much as he did. He wrote three numbers. *Seven. Seven. Four.*

'What else?'

'He's unconscious,' said the doctor. 'Get out of here and I'll try to save him.'

In the corridor, Farquhar looked at the three digits and said, 'Thank God for computers.'

Six hours later, Chamberlain reported to Farquhar's Embankment office.

'Right,' said the Inspector, cradling his telephone with finality. 'The airports are all on it, and the radar chaps are tracing all of yesterday's intruder reports. Interpol is checking on the Continent. We'll turn up something, with luck. How did you do with Rice?'

Chamberlain slumped, exhausted, in Farquhar's visitors' chair. The Scotland Yard detective had a curiously bland office, a framed picture of his family the only personal object on his desk. 'Rice is not very helpful.'

'That was my experience too. I had to practically threaten to arrest him before he'd speak to me. Turned out to be a worthless little bugger anyhow.'

'I figured Hammond for having a ballsier second in command,' Chamberlain agreed. 'What if he gets sick in the middle of something big?'

'Or kidnapped,' Farquhar smiled.

'I started yelling,' said Chamberlain. 'Definitely the wrong move. Rice looked like he was going to cry. Unbelievable scene. Phones ringing, staff going crazy . . . Rice's secretary told me that Hammond's got twenty deals hanging fire and Rice is just sitting there with his head in his hands.'

Farquhar said, 'Some friends who've heard I'm with this case passed on some information about some of those deals.'

Chamberlain nodded politely. A highly placed cop usually had a couple of half-decent sources in the intelligence community, especially if he'd ever managed a favour like looking south when somebody ran north. 'Anything interesting?'

'Interesting *sounding*, but it's really little more than raw data. Charles Hammond does more than arrange bank loans, as I'm sure your employers have told you. What they might not have told you, however, is that Hammond has his fingers in some very strange pies in some even stranger places.'

'Like where?' asked Chamberlain.

'Mozambique. Hours after Hammond was taken, two Zimbabwe guerrilla factions sheltering in Mozambique launched a combined assault on a third faction that they suspected of kidnapping him to prevent their receiving arms.'

'Are you saying Hammond's a gun-runner?'

'Let's say he's been a go-between in arms deals. At the same time, in Brasilia, a colonel and a major got into a gun battle on the steps of the presidential palace. Hammond had met the colonel three times in the past month. The major shot him dead and was not arrested.'

'Sounds like he stopped a coup.'

'Yes, it does. My sources didn't know any more about it. Perhaps you can ask yours if it was a coup and if Hammond was involved.'

Chamberlain realized that it was time to offer something back. 'I heard that some of Hammond's friends in Madagascar headed for the hills when they heard he got kidnapped. They've got some kind of problem going on down there with elections.'

Farquhar nodded. 'Hammond has plantations on the island.'

'They were the one thing Rice would talk about. Them and some old French fortress he calls the Mountain House. Hammond's turned it into a palace. Gets down there about six weeks a year on vacation. Tough life.'

'What's your next move?' asked Farquhar.

Chamberlain hesitated. The Scotland Yard man was being very helpful and could continue to be so, but he was no dummy and he'd know right away if Chamberlain was holding back. He decided that Farquhar was definitely worth cultivating.

'Comptel is leading a consortium to buy Hammond. René Rice claims he can only contribute a million and a half dollars.'

'What?'

'Exactly. I'd like to find out why.'

Farquhar gazed at the picture on his desk as if he were viewing mug shots. 'Let me give you the name of a fellow in the City. Banking chap. Might know a thing or two about Mr Hammond's finances.'

Lady Janet tore through the villa, raiding the old caches for money, drugs, weapons and passports. Movement laced fire through her wealed flesh; she cried aloud, and kept hunting. Grandzau had hidden stuff everywhere, in wall switches, recessed lights, loose cellar bricks, hollowed books in the library, false-backed drawers. She found morphine, franc notes, US dollars, a smaller gun, British passports, all the familiar paraphernalia of sudden flight. When she found the syringes and the amphetamines, it was as if she had been sleeping these last few years and had now woken up to find herself back in that old, extraordinary life. Only a brief return, she promised, just long enough to kill the man who had savaged her.

He had gone to Bern.

Robert Fleming lived in Bern.

Fleming was one of two people in Europe, other than herself, who could have used Grandzau's Malory code. Fleming, herself and Daitch, all who were left of Grandzau's team. Comrades. Survivors.

She shot herself full of morphine – she could not travel without the drug, could barely move – forced herself to eat because instinct told her her body needed sustenance. She concealed a second charged needle and a gun in the small of her back, and flew from Nice to Bern, first class to minimize the risk of discovery by airport security and Swiss customs.

The pain retreated fitfully, moving across several dreamy acres until it crouched on the horizon, like a predator waiting for night. She floated on the plane in a doped haze, eyes closed, face veiled by her blonde hair, trying to think what had happened – stoned, like she hadn't been stoned in years. Before the plane landed, she drank coffee to clear her mind, and downed a third and fourth cup while she waited for her rented car. And again she ate, despite the need to hurry, bread and cheese for the strength to heal and fight.

The man in black had gone to Bern.

Grandzau's partner Fleming had retired to Bern.

Your bid is expected at the Pendragon Auction. Lancelot.

Lancelot. Grandzau. But Grandzau was dead. Dead absurdly, after a life of spying and smuggling, in a car crash, leaving her the villa, money, and freedom to do what she chose, a situation ironically like that she fled when she left her father's estate at eighteen.

Lancelot. From Grandzau's Malory code. Grandzau had been Lancelot. Fleming had been Pellinore. Daitch, Lionel. She was Guinevere. And when she protested that Grandzau should be her Arthur, the German had laughed. 'Such a Guinevere deserves a better Arthur than a gnome like me.'

Her beauty and her breeding had betrayed her. Until the day he died the little man, thirty years her senior, and light years from her class, could never believe how much she loved him.

Had Fleming gone back into Grandzau's secrets business? Had he somehow threatened the employers of the man in black? Who her tormentor served, she didn't care; he was her quarry. She was an English aristocrat – schooled in an ancient tradition of chivalric violence – and there wasn't a man in Europe she feared.

Her father, an aristocrat by birth and a powerful financier by talent and inclination, had been widowed without sons. But instead of remarrying, or sending her off to school, he had raised her in isolated splendour. Tutors had come to the estate, while he himself taught her to shoot, to ride, to wield a foil.

He was a demanding and gifted teacher and she had excelled. But where such skills might have made a young man secure, they provoked in Lady Janet a fearless hunger to embrace what lay beyond her father's gate. In her eager flight from horses and their dressage, Range-Rovers, tweedy plus-fours and stifling English certitude, Lady

Janet had rampaged beyond 'acceptable' student rebellion, deep into the Parisian underworld of drug traders, mercenary fighters, and freelance spies.

In a bar called '79' for the number on the narrow lane off the Rue de la Convention, she had, at nineteen, had her first absinthe, followed swiftly by her first heroin, her first man who paid – a mercenary fresh from Angola who had got full value for his money – and several more who had rejoiced in such quality at the customary low price until Henri Trefle put a stop to it. And finally Karl Grandzau. Her adopted mentors, either amusing themselves, or feeling they owned her, or perhaps recognizing a natural student, had extended her lethal repertoire to the knife, the *garrotte*, and her hands. But it had fallen to Grandzau, the secret seller, to render the ultimate refinement – employing her skills in defence of treachery.

She drove into Bern, across the city, and into a section of country-like houses on several-acre plots concealed by high stone walls. Fleming's gate was unlocked. She rang anyway, but no one answered.

Pushing the gate open, she got back in her car and laid her gun on the floor beside her seat. Then she drove into the macadam driveway between low walls of ploughed snow.

The place looked deserted. The immaculate snow-covered lawns bore no prints, but the walks were shovelled. Behind the house, glinting in the midday sun, were Fleming's greenhouses, the heated gardens he had often spoken of retiring to when Grandzau's schemes had paid off.

Lady Janet rolled down the window and listened. There was an eerie snow-damped silence. The walls blocked the noises of the city beyond, and the house, two storeys of white brick, was silent. Then she saw that the breeze had blown a fine film of powdered snow over the shovelled paths and that there were footprints on the path to the greenhouses.

She was wearing an unlined Burberry, too thin for the Swiss winter. She shoved her gun into the pocket, held it in her hand, and got out of the car. She left the door open and walked silently towards the greenhouses.

The sun was blinding where the snow met the white house, the glare like a blow to the face. She was exhausted and a small part of her mind, a rational piece not driven by hurt and humiliation, was clamouring to stop, to get back in the car, to go to a hotel and sleep until she could handle herself.

I'll have to go to Bern, the man who had beaten her had said. And Bern was where Fleming, one of the two who might have used Grandzau's code, lived. She kept walking, the gun rigid in her pocket, the barrel pushing against the cloth of the light raincoat. This was her only lead. She reached the greenhouse, hearing nothing.

Standing in the partial shadow of the greenhouse, her hand on the door latch, she thought she saw someone inside. She took the gun out of her pocket, opened the door, and stepped in. Ignoring the sight which greeted her first, she pressed her back to the door and shot glances to either side. Then, when she was sure she was alone, she approached Fleming.

His hair had greyed at the temples in the three years since she'd seen him at Grandzau's funeral on an Italian hillside. His fingers were caked with dried earth. He had started a new rose bed in a raised wooden planter. The homely scattering of trowel, pruning knife, basket and bone meal spoke as much for Fleming's innocence as the cruel marks on his naked body.

He was hanging by his bound hands from an overhead irrigation pipe, his wrists tied with a black silk handkerchief. The man in black hadn't struck him more than a dozen times, but Fleming was dead. His lips were blue. She guessed that the old man, with no information to appease his tormentor, had died of heart failure.

Fleming had always treated her with courtesy. Lady Janet cut him down with the pruning knife. He fell heavily. Still holding her gun, she covered his body with sheets of black plastic.

That left Daitch in Brussels. The only other one who could have used the code. Daitch the junior partner, Grandzau's bodyguard, the man who'd set up hideouts and boltholes so Grandzau could betray all sides and disappear until they gave up the search. Of the three, Grandzau, Fleming and Daitch, Daitch had been most treacherous, worse really than Grandzau, though he deferred to Grandzau's superior intelligence and brilliant imagination.

Lady Janet hurried to her car. If the man in black knew of him there was no time to sleep. Daitch was fully capable of killing him before she could. The pain was nudging through the morphine. She let it. It would keep her awake until she was on the plane to Brussels.

8

Peter Chamberlain lay chin deep in hot water. Through the rising steam he surveyed the striped marble bathroom walls of the Savoy Hotel. They were cream-coloured with natural black streaks at regular intervals, and in his exhausted state he dallied with the thought that someone had skinned a stone tiger.

A wall telephone between the toilet and the bidet rang loudly, echoing on the hard sufaces of the big, luxurious room. Chamberlain ignored it because he knew he was worthless until he got some sleep. He'd hung a Do Not Disturb sign on the front door, but he'd forgotten to tell the desk to leave him alone. It had been thirty-six hours since he'd reported to work at his Washington office. Since that morning he'd flown to New York, driven to Connecticut, helicoptered back from Connecticut, spent New Year's Eve and night on Helen Thorp's telephone, crossed the Atlantic Ocean, and run around London like a two-day package tour. Now it was midnight, London time, early evening in New York, and he was damned if he was getting out of the water to talk to anybody. The Scotland Yard man was tracing the plane Hammond might or might not have been taken away in.

The phone stopped ringing. Chamberlain went back to contemplating tiger stripes and the way his toes occasionally bobbed to the surface. He was so tired that the Scotch he'd taken into the bathroom sat on the edge of the giant tub, untouched.

He dozed for a moment, then summoned the energy to apply some soap. In the midst of slipping back under to

72

rinse his chest he thought he heard something outside the bathroom door. He stopped moving, waited for the sloshing, echoing water to quiet, and listened.

He felt the wet hairs on the back of his neck begin to curl away from his skin; his heart quickened and even though he knew his tired state was amplifying his reactions, he still felt fear. Someone was moving around the suite and he was lying naked in the tub in an unlocked bathroom. He wondered if he could get to the lock on the door, bolt it, and telephone for help without being heard.

Footsteps, muffled by the carpet, approached the door. Chamberlain wrapped his hand around a heavy, glass ashtray.

'Are you in there, Pete?'

He sagged back into the water. 'In the tub.'

Helen Thorp pushed the door open, gave the soapy bath water a single piercing look, lowered the toilet lid and sat down. She was wearing a dark blue cashmere dress and her hair down free, glimmering thick and black to her shoulders.

'Welcome to London.'

'What have you got?' she asked.

'The numbers on a plane they might have put Hammond on. And a lead on one of Grandzau's partners retired in Switzerland.'

'What else?'

'René Rice is an idiot and Hammond's broke.'

'What?'

'Neither of which makes sense.'

'Nor do you. What are you talking about?'

'Rice treated me like the enemy. He's got himself barricaded in the All Seas offices. He's not making any decisions and he's not supporting his staff. He's pretty lightweight for a chief of staff. Which means Hammond was an idiot for hiring him in the first place.'

'What do you mean Hammond's broke?'

'I talked to a banker. He's mortgaged up to his eyeballs on everything he owns. Everything. Which I think is one of Rice's problems. He knows he doesn't have any money for a ransom.'

'Hold it. Define broke.'

'No money. Maybe a million and a half in assets. For a guy like Hammond, that's no money. He owes on everything he owns. Even his Madagascar plantations. Wait till the kidnappers find out he's broke. Maybe they did. Maybe that's why they're making it an auction.'

'Wait. You say Hammond's broke because he's mortgaged?'

'Up to his eyeballs.'

'No. It doesn't work like that. For all you know Hammond went liquid to put his capital into barley futures. He stays on top of things and moves fast.'

'What if barley futures fell through?'

'It's not like personal finance,' Helen Thorp explained patiently. 'You're comparing Hammond to a Scarsdale doctor who's afraid to tell his wife that the kids have to go to a state school because he got burned in the market.'

'I don't get it.'

'Take my word for it. The fact that Hammond's company doesn't have cash for a ransom doesn't mean much.'

'But the guy must be worth millions.'

'Tied up, at the moment.'

'In what?'

'That's his business, Pete. You can't plan a financial strategy to include getting kidnapped. Now come on, get dressed. We have a meeting downstairs in ten minutes.'

'I've been up since yesterday. I'm going to bed.'

'Sorry, I need you. I've ordered coffee. Want some wake-up pills?'

'Christ no. How'd you get in my room?'

74

She dangled a key from its brass tag and dropped it into her handbag. Chamberlain closed his eyes and sank deeper into the tub, loath to leave the seductive warmth, much less dress and go downstairs. He wondered how she had talked his key out of the imperturbable desk clerk in tails and decided Comptel probably owned the place. Her perfume drifted over the water. He opened his eyes. It occurred to him that there was something he wanted more than sleep.

She returned his gaze, her eyes wide and guileless.

'What kind of meeting?' asked Chamberlain.

Helen Thorp fished a gold case from her bag, put a cigarette between her lips, made flame rise from one corner of the case, and inhaled deeply.

'A shareholders' meeting.'

'Comptel's?' He felt himself growing erect, but the deep, cloudy water hid him from her.

'Hammond's. I've got everyone together who's going to buy him back. People from Mishuma, Lockheed, TI, British Hovercraft, French Air, and even Hans Streicher.'

'How'd you manage him?'

'The same way I got the others. Comptel moved first, so it's our show and they're all hoping we'll get Hammond back for them.' She smiled, crinkling her eyes, and Chamberlain realized that she had slept since he'd seen her last. 'Basic rule of business, Pete. Everybody hopes the other fellow knows what he's doing.'

'There's another basic rule of business, Helen. Or maybe it's more a basic rule of life. If a lady walks in on a guy in a bathtub and she looks as good as you do he's going to ask her to join him.'

She crossed her legs and flicked cigarette ash into the bidet. 'You're too tired to be clever.'

'Are you referring to words or deeds.'

'I'm accustomed to both. I'll get your clothes.'

And a twice-defeated Chamberlain sank into the cooling water with the leaden knowledge that he had impressed the lady even less than the boss.

Ten minutes later, in the lift, she said, 'I'll fly commercial back to New York. You can keep the plane.'

'What range does it have?'

'It got me here from New York non-stop.'

'Thank you. Listen, do I tell these guys I'm going to kick the door down and hijack Hammond?'

'No. I just want to cover all bases. If you can't find him, these people will put up the auction money.'

'Do they know about the CIA interest?'

'They could. I don't know.'

'Marvellous.'

She led him down a hall to a hotel meeting room. 'Ready?'

Chamberlain took a deep breath and worked at straightening his shoulders. 'The last time I was this tired I was at the bottom of the South China Sea and a lot younger.'

'This'll go quickly. Then bed.'

'Are you here in the Savoy?'

'No. There's an apartment I usually stay in in London.'

She opened the door, leaving Chamberlain to wonder, with whom. Half a dozen men were waiting nervously. They stood and shook hands as Helen introduced Chamberlain. Then she said, 'Mr Chamberlain has worked for Comptel for some time. Last year he negotiated the release of one of our South American managers from leftist kidnappers.'

'Do you think these are leftist kidnappers?' asked a tall, grey-haired man who represented Lockheed.

'I don't think so, but it doesn't matter. The point is they've got Hammond and they're calling the shots.'

Chamberlain was too tired to bother remembering

names that weren't important. A man who looked very much like the first and who represented TI said, lowering his voice conspiratorially, 'My sources in the intelligence community suggest this Lancelot's been operating for some time in Europe. A kind of freelance spy.'

The Japanese man from Mishuma nodded agreement.

'I wish that were true,' said Chamberlain. 'Then we wouldn't have to worry about some crazy amateurs losing their nerve and killing Hammond. Unfortunately, our sources suggest that the freelance spy you're talking about died three years ago.'

This time it was the arms merchant, Hans Streicher, who nodded. Chamberlain gave him a small smile. He instinctively liked the bluff, hearty German. From what he had heard, Streicher was as decent a sort as you'd find in his trade. Of course, that wasn't saying much, but he might make a good ally if things got rough. He would look him up in the morning.

They asked some more questions. The gist of Chamberlain's answers remained the same. They would wait for the kidnappers to announce their arrangements. They would play by their rules. They would do nothing to risk Hammond's life.

'What if someone outbids us?' asked the Japanese.

'Like who?'

'Someone who doesn't want us to have Hammond.'

'Who would that be?'

'Mishuma has competitors who would gain by our loss.'

'I think that's pretty far-fetched,' said the man from Lockheed.

'It does seem a bit extreme,' said Helen Thorp. 'Besides, our pooled resources are enormous. Who could outbid us?'

The Frenchman from Dassault had not yet said a word. Now he spoke. 'The Russians.'

77

'What?' asked Hans Streicher.

'They made a clumsy overture to my aide this afternoon. They offered to bid with us. Back us. In return, they could help retrieve him. It was absurd. But it suggests that they have a reason for wanting Hammond and that isn't hard to guess.'

'He knows a lot,' said Streicher. 'Maybe too much.'

Helen Thorp rose from the table. 'Mr Chamberlain is aware of this and has had considerable experience in the area of intelligence and espionage. He is watching the Russians. Comptel has other employees similarly engaged.'

'No, no, no.' René Rice, Hammond's executive, finally broke his silence. He rose beside Helen Thorp, slight and not much taller than she, his dark face a wrinkled ball of frightened eyes, slash mouth, and narrow nose. Chamberlain had pulled an East African guide book from the Comptel Library for the flight over and he guessed that the Madagascan, like many of his island, was of wildly mixed blood – French, Indian, Arab, and native Malagasy. His accent was French. 'Mr Hammond knows many things, negotiating as he does for so many important people, but not the sort of information the Russians would bid for. Only the most secret weapons are unknown to the adversary governments; they number but a few, and would never be sold. So Mr Hammond would never be included in such a sale. The Russians have no reason to want Mr Hammond.'

Chamberlain and Streicher exchanged sceptical glances.

'We can't be sure of that, René,' said Helen Thorp.

'I know it,' insisted Rice. 'The Russians don't want him.'

'What about the Brazilians?' Chamberlain asked suddenly.

Rice looked blank. 'I don't understand.'

'Neither do I,' said Chamberlain. 'But a Brazilian colonel you people were talking to got shot right after Mr Hammond was kidnapped.'

Rice shrugged miserably. 'I know nothing of this.'

Chamberlain noticed that Kaga Nagumo, the man from Mishuma, was giving Rice a very hard stare. Helen Thorp glanced questioningly at him, too. Chamberlain looked around the room.

'Is anyone who might be on our side missing? You all know something about Hammond. Is there anyone else we should invite into this group?'

'Arabs!' said Streicher. 'Why are there no Arabs?'

'Good question.'

'He often helps me in the Gulf States,' said Streicher.

'Mr Rice?' asked Chamberlain. 'Can't you invite Mr Hammond's Arab clients to join the consortium?'

The Malagasy stared blankly and Chamberlain wondered again how Hammond could have hired such a lightweight.

'Mr Rice?'

'I'll try,' said Rice, doubtfully.

Chamberlain didn't believe him. 'This is no time to cover up, Mr Rice.'

'I'm not.'

'You're holding back. I guess you're used to giving your client discretion, but it's too late for that now. You know more about Hammond's business than any of us. You gotta stop blocking Ms Thorp and get us some more contributors.'

Chamberlain noticed that the others were nodding in agreement.

'Anything,' Rice said in a choked voice. 'I'll do anything to get Mr Hammond back. We must get him back.'

'Thank you,' said Chamberlain. 'Anyone who needs me, Comptel will know where I am. Good night.'

He headed for the door, relieved by the small approving smile on Helen Thorp's lips. She had liked how he handled Rice. He was back in her good graces, where he intended to stay, because this woman had the power to turn his life around – provided he got Hammond back.

Inspector Farquhar woke him an hour later by standing quietly beside his bed for the ten seconds it took his wearied senses to raise the alarm that he wasn't sleeping safely. He came out of it quickly, sagging back in disgust when he saw the light on the English police officer's face.

'Go away.'

'We found the plane.'

'Hammond?'

'No.'

'Please go away.'

'We found Grandzau's partner in Bern. Or the Swiss police did, I should say.'

'He's the kidnapper?'

'He's dead.'

'Marvellous.'

'Brussels.' Farquhar waited.

'What about Brussels?'

'Interpol think they've found Daitch.'

9

Buoyed by the extraordinary Scotland Yard assistance, Chamberlain felt an energizing second wind – or was it a third or fourth? – surge through his limbs as Inspector Farquhar bore him south over deserted roads in a high-powered police Rover. It was becoming clear that the Charles Hammond kidnapping was bigger than anything the CIA had ever sent him on. Miracle of miracles, his private-enterprise spook job had funnelled him into the big time. So much for amateur assholes, Arnie old buddy.

'So tell me about the plane?'

'We traced it north to Stornoway.'

'Where?'

'It's on the Isle of Lewis in the Outer Hebrides. Scotland. About six hundred miles from here.'

'Who was aboard?'

'Well, it didn't stay there.'

'Where'd it go?'

'Damned if we know. It seems to have flown directly there, refuelled and taken off immediately. The pilot filed a flight plan for Keflavik, Iceland, about seven hundred miles, but the Icelandics haven't recorded their arrival.'

'Meaning the plane was either lost or flew in another direction.'

'Most likely the latter, considering the circumstances. It was a twin engine Cessna with long-range tanks and extra wing tanks, so they have close to a range of twenty-five hundred miles.'

'What does a twenty-five-hundred-mile circle from Stornoway include?'

'Greenland, the Azores, Europe, North Africa, Scandinavia, and Russia.'

'Marvellous. When'd they leave Stornoway?'

'Yesterday afternoon.'

'So they're gone?'

'Interpol has sent out an alert for the plane. It will be found. The question is when.'

Chamberlain rubbed his eyes. 'I really thought we'd have something with the plane. The bodyguard living and following them wasn't supposed to happen. I hate to see a lucky break wasted.'

'Quite.'

'How's the bodyguard?'

'Still alive.'

'Yeah. He looked like a tough son of a bitch. Who got killed in Bern?'

'Fleming. The Englishman who was Grandzau's partner.'

'Oh yes.'

'He'd been tortured, according to the Swiss police.'

Chamberlain turned to Farquhar. 'Really?'

Farquhar glanced away from the road. When their eyes met, the policeman said, 'My people tell me that the CIA is afraid the Russians want Hammond.'

'How'd they get to Fleming so fast?'

'The CIA got there first, as a matter of fact. They put Fleming's house under surveillance. Photographed his visitors, tapped his telephone, the usual. But whoever killed Fleming slipped past them.'

'Let's hope they remember that when they find Daitch.'

The English police officer turned the Rover to the airport exit lane. 'As I understand my informant, Interpol located Daitch on its own and hasn't told the CIA, yet.'

'It won't take them long to find out. Interpol isn't very good with secrets.'

'I asked a fellow I know about those Malagasy who ran

off into the bush, speaking of secrets,' said Farquhar. 'Hammond's secrets.'

'Malagasy?'

'Madagascar. You mentioned that Hammond's friends on the island of Malagasy had –'

'Right. Same place. Where he has the plantations. His home. Sorry.'

'They've come back. They're campaigning again for the national election. It's an important one. Probably a change of government for the island.'

'How about the Zimbabwe guerrillas?'

'They're accusing the South Africans of murdering Hammond.'

Chamberlain laughed. 'Hammond really had a way with him, didn't he?'

'A Hong Kong gold trader killed himself this morning because Hammond disappearing ruined a deal he was set to sign with an Emirate sheik. And the major in Brazil who shot the colonel has vanished. They've arrested the colonel's wife. There's a rumour that she was having an affair with Hammond.'

Chamberlain laughed again. 'I'm sorry. I'm getting giddy, but Hammond sounds too important a guy to have an affair with only a colonel's wife.'

'Her family owns a fair part of the upper Amazon basin.'

'Oh . . . They think they might find oil up there. Interesting.'

Chamberlain looked at his watch. Two-thirty in the morning. Gatwick's deserted roads, quiet runways and empty buildings were ablaze with light.

'Can you recommend someone I should see in Brussels?'

'Say hello to Inspector François Aarschot.'

'Where do I find him?'

'He'll meet you at the airport.' Farquhar pulled up in front of the private craft terminal.

Chamberlain extended his hand. 'I think I owe you a few.'

Farquhar smiled wearily and Chamberlain realized he wasn't the only one running on no sleep. 'That's all right. You see they used our uniform to fool Hammond's bodyguard. We can't let that sort go unpunished, can we?'

They cranked up the Comptel jet's engines as soon as they saw Chamberlain emerge from the terminal. He trotted up the ramp, the door clunked shut behind him, and they started taxiing towards the runway.

Chamberlain glanced around appreciatively. The two grey-haired gentlemen piloting the thing looked as if they'd been through more than one war. The steward had the greying crewcut of a retired US Army lifer. He pointed at a bed with turned-down crisp sheets and said, 'You've got an hour if you'd like a nap, sir.'

He curtained off the area. Chamberlain was out of his clothes and between the sheets before the plane finished flinging itself into the sky.

The steward woke him with black coffee and some English tea biscuits. 'You've got time to have it in bed, sir. We're not into final approach yet.'

The coffee was excellent. The steward took the empty cup, showed Chamberlain the bathroom, and passed him his clothes when he came out. Chamberlain shrugged into his grey jacket, noticing that the steward had dispatched the worst wrinkles while he'd slept. Some brigadier had lost a fantastic aide when this guy retired.

The CIA had never treated him this well, nor had the Navy. But while he enjoyed the comfort, and the respect it implied, it frightened him a little. Particularly when so much was at stake. Daitch was a demo man, and there was no such thing as minor injuries when you went up against a demo man. Nor did explosives leave any room for error;

one slip and Charles Hammond would be very dead, as dead as Chamberlain's chances to come up a winner. There was nothing morally wrong with attentive servants and private aircraft, he thought as he sipped the delicious coffee and the needle-thin jet murmured towards Belgium, but you could lose your life if you started to believe in these trappings and ended up thinking that the button was the machine.

As they glided to a smooth stop in a quiet corner of the Brussels Airport, the Comptel steward brought him a mahogany box. Two guns were nestled in green velvet, a .38 Smith & Wesson revolver and a US Army .45 automatic that looked big enough to vaporize a Toyota.

'If you want to carry, sir, the company can work temporary permits.'

'No thanks. I'll be with the cops.'

François Aarschot was a short, pudgy man with slick black hair and a face that would have been taken more seriously had it a moustache. He looked, without it, petulant. He greeted Chamberlain with an irritable glare. His tight lips squeezed out a thick French accent.

'I could hardly refuse this opportunity to repay Inspector Farquhar's many favours all at once.'

Thinking he might have heard it wrong, Chamberlain smiled uncertainly.

Aarschot cleared it up for him. 'Monsieur. Permit me to mince few words. I dislike government spies intensely, and I like industrial spies even less.'

'You despise spies? Good. I'm not a spy.'

'I know who you work for and I know what you do for them. I promised Inspector Farquhar I would help you find this Daitch, and I will. This way, Monsieur.'

The Belgian police officer led Chamberlain to a small Mercedes-Benz and drove, without another word, into

Brussels, beyond the rich hotel district, into an older, poorer section not yet gentrified. Careening through a maze of narrow streets, they came suddenly upon a crowd of police vans.

White floodlights played on the front of a low, stone building. A small crowd of civilians in overcoats watched from behind the police lines. The police moved cautiously, ducking and crouching as they scampered behind their vans. Chamberlain spotted several sharpshooters on roofs in the gloom overhead. His breath puffed white when they left the warmth of the car. He jammed his hands in his coat pockets. He'd left his gloves on the plane and the cold was brutal.

Inspector Aarschot nodded irritably at the stone building.

'Daitch has barricaded himself in.'

'Does he have Charles Hammond in there?' asked Chamberlain, glancing nervously at the police firepower.

'No. He's constructed camouflaged pitfalls – what you call booby traps. He killed two of my men earlier this evening with a mine attached to the outer door.'

The remnants of the shattered door hung from twisted hinges. Chamberlain could see the burnt spot on the stone lintel where Daitch had attached the shaped charge. It was a neat job: the stone wasn't even cracked.

'How do you know he doesn't have Hammond?'

'We've spoken to him on the telephone. He hasn't uttered a word about Hammond. That is why. He is alone, Monsieur. I am sure of it.' He crossed his hands behind his back, rocked on his heels and glared defiantly at Chamberlain.

Chamberlain leaned on the Mercedes' roof and surveyed the scene with bleak regard. What if Hammond just happened to be in there? What if Daitch and the rest of his crowd were preparing for a last stand?

An armoured half-track clanked around the corner, forcing the bystanders to the narrow pavements. Chamberlain caught a glimpse of a startlingly beautiful blonde woman on the edge of the crowd. He stared at her, utterly distracted, until the half-track blocked his view. When it passed, she was gone.

It stopped, pointing at the door, like a rhino which had forgotten why it had started to charge. Typical police, Chamberlain thought gloomily. When in doubt bring in the heavy stuff. Poor Hammond.

'Inspector?'

'Oui, Monsieur?'

'How'd this all start? Were you trying to arrest him?'

'Of course not. We were obeying an Interpol directive to *surveille*. Suddenly Daitch killed a man.'

'Who?'

'Unfortunately, he was a member of the Soviet Embassy. An anti-personnel grenade exploded in the hall and moments later the man came tumbling out of the front door, dying. He fell there.' Aarschot pointed and Chamberlain saw the white painted outline of where the body had landed. It looked just about Aarschot-size, maybe a little chubbier. 'When my men went in to investigate, *poof*, the door exploded.'

'What was the guy from the Russian Embassy doing there?'

'We don't know. The Soviets took the body and said only that the man usually walked this way to work.'

'But what was he doing inside?'

'It's possible the Russian had a woman in a neighbouring apartment. She is away for the holiday, the neighbours tell us. These things will be resolved.'

'Do you have a floor plan?'

'What for?'

'I'd like to see the situation.'

Aarschot stared at him suspiciously. 'Very well. Come with me.' The Belgian darted from police van to police van, ducking in the spaces between. Chamberlain followed him, upright. A man who could set a charge like that on the door didn't need guns.

At the command post in the back of a communications truck, Aarschot introduced him to his fellow officers. Each in turn shook hands and accorded Chamberlain a quick nod.

They spread a building plan on a console and showed Chamberlain how Daitch occupied the entire ground floor. 'He may have access to the cellar,' said Aarschot. 'You can see over there how its front windows are bricked up.'

'Yeah, I noticed.'

'The back is unreachable. The building backs on to a solid wall. The way out is the only way in.'

'If it weren't, I guess Daitch would be long gone.'

'It is a last stand, Monsieur. From the look of the traps, he's been preparing his defences for a long time.'

'Why?'

The Belgian corkscrewed a fat finger in the direction of his brain.

'What set him off today? Did he see your men?'

'No! He did not, Monsieur. You have my word. No, I think he saw the newspaper stories about his former associate, this Englishman killed in Bern. He went berserk. There is psychology in this work, Monsieur, and in psychology you will find the answer to this riddle.'

'I want to talk to him.'

'Don't be absurd.'

'I have to talk to him.'

'What would you say that my men haven't already?'

'First I want to make damned sure that he doesn't have Hammond in there with him. And if he doesn't, I want him to tell me who does.'

'And how would he do that?'

'Hammond's kidnapper used an old code that Daitch once used. I want to know who else used it.'

'You can talk to him after my men have arrested him.'

'Inspector, you better get something straight.' Several officers looked curiously at him. Chamberlain lowered his voice so only Aarschot could hear. 'Nobody is going to arrest Daitch. He's an expert demolition man. And if he's even half as crazy as you think he is, he'll blow up the whole block before he'll let himself be taken.'

Aarschot rocked back on his heels. 'I have acquitted my debts to Inspector Farquhar. Good night, sir. A car will take you back to your plane. Or you can wait in a hotel, at your own expense, until we have Daitch behind bars.'

'Thank you,' said Chamberlain. He stepped out of the communications truck, slipped between two police cars and walked briskly across the narrow street to the floodlit house.

The Belgians were shouting at him and one cop even started after him, crouching low, until, with fearful glances at the windows, he turned back. Chamberlain mounted the front steps and an electronically amplified Aarschot shouted, 'Halt, Monsieur. Halt!'

Chamberlain went up the steps.

'Halt or he'll kill you, Monsieur.'

Chamberlain went into the foyer. Here, safe from being grabbed by a zealous cop, he probed the dark recesses with his pen light, climbed gingerly over a trip wire the Russian had been lucky enough to miss, and started into the dark hall.

The anti-personnel grenade had pocked the walls with shrapnel. It, or the door device that had killed the cops, had blown out the overhead lamps, so here he was totally dependent on his pen lights, of which he carried three.

Sleeplessness tended to sharpen his senses. He heard

better. Nonetheless, he swept the hall repeatedly with the light, crouching and holding it over his head in the unlikely event someone pegged a shot at it. He was convinced, however, there would be no shooting.

The hall was very long, longer than the beam of his light. He took a miniature microwave doppler horn from his pocket, set it securely on the floor, and turned it on. Movement within its projected waves would register, via a thin wire, a mild electric shock in his palm. There was nothing moving. He pocketed the device and started slowly down the hall.

He shied from a loose floorboard, started to step to one side, thought better of it, and inspected the walls. The right wall, opposite the loose board, looked clear at first glance. On closer inspection, Chamberlain saw a thin, seemingly rusty nail protruding at shoulder level. He moved close to the wall and stepped under it. Had he brushed against it while avoiding the more obvious trigger of the loose floorboard, he would have set something fatal off. It was overhead, in the ceiling. A Claymore mine. He swallowed hard. Daitch wasn't fooling around.

He traced the almost invisible trip wire leading from the rusty nail, up a groove in the wall, to the Claymore. He inspected it minutely, decided it was a simple, one-way trigger, and reached for it with the clipper blade of his customized Israeli Army knife. He'd modified the carbon-stainless steel instrument to suit his own purposes, most notably adding the powerful clippers – a wire cutter was a tool he'd found as scarce as it was indispensable at moments when it was needed. He'd never regretted sacrificing a blade to get the double slot necessary for the clippers, failing yet to find a good bottle of wine that far from a corkscrew.

He got the wire between the jaws of the clipper and bore down gently. He felt his mouth twitching a nervous, private grin; there always came an instant when you defused a charge when you had to ask, is this right? It was then you waited for the silent explosion. Veteran demolition men said you never heard the one that killed you.

If Daitch had hair-triggered the thing, he'd find the truth of the saying. He pressed harder. The wire parted with a loud snap. Chamberlain released a deep breath. The trap was defused. He crouched on the floor again, pointed the scanner down the dark hall, and waited for the tell-tale buzz in his palm. Nothing. He was still alone.

Behind him, outside, he heard loudspeakers. The police were bellowing something or other. Organizing a charge or threatening Daitch. He didn't know because he didn't understand French. He started down the hall again, casting his light from side to side, over the floor and up to the ceiling.

Suddenly, he stopped short. An odd little hole pocked one wall at waist level. He played the light over it. It looked manufactured, not accidental. He reached to finger it. The outer, dimmer glow of the pen light circle brushed an identical hole at ankle level. He jerked his hand back as if seared by steam.

His breath came short. He'd almost killed himself. He found a third hole at shoulder level. Then he turned the light to the opposite wall. He was not surprised to find a tall, narrow mirror. It was an old one, the edges bevelled, the plaster frame once gilded. It had been there a long time. Daitch, Chamberlain decided, was on the edge of brilliant. If he'd seen the mirror first, as he would have if the lights weren't out, he never would have noticed the holes opposite that emitted the invisible laser beams; then as he passed the holes and blocked the beams so they wouldn't reflect back from the mirror, he'd have broken an electrical circuit, tripping an electro-magnetic switch on yet another of Daitch's explosive delights.

91

Problem. They were spaced so that he couldn't crawl past.

He backed up, removed his overcoat, and transferred the contents of his suit jacket to the big overcoat pockets. Then he took off the suit jacket, donned the overcoat, balled the suit jacket into a missile the size of a soccer ball and hurled it down the hall. He flung himself back and to the floor.

The explosion was so quiet that he could hear the old mirror shattering. He got to his feet, puzzled, and moved forward cautiously. The mirror was slivers on the floor. A broad jagged line of broken plaster ran the full height of the wall where the holes had been. Whatever had exploded had come out of that wall. He bent down and retrieved his jacket.

The shredded cloth fell apart in his hands. The bomb had thrown a hundred steel lancets across the hall. He saw them now among the mirror slivers. A hundred tiny spears, as if the wall had erupted in a miniature nineteenth-century African war.

'*Daitch!*' The cry welled up in him, filled his throat, a primitive shout of victory. 'Daitch! Open up, you bastard, I'm better than you are!'

His voice echoed to silence and he stood waiting alone, the euphoria draining away, the adrenalin seeping out of him, feeling a little silly and vaguely frightened. Then, to his amazement, a wooden door at the end of the hall creaked open into a lighted room.

He approached cautiously, the hair prickling up his neck, until he could see inside. The man who had opened the door was returning unhurriedly to his chair in the centre of an over-decorated parlour. When he turned around and sat down, crossing his legs, Chamberlain could see he was a middle-aged man, who looked like a professor at home for a quiet evening with a book. He wore bedroom slippers and a woollen robe over trousers. He reached up and turned on his reading lamp and in the light spill his eyes were bright as marbles.

Chamberlain stopped in the doorway. 'Daitch?'

The man smiled sadly. 'Yes. Who are you?'

Daitch looked crazy. Gently, Chamberlain introduced himself. 'My name is Pete Chamberlain . . . Nice to meet you, sir.'

'You're quite good, Mr Chamberlain. Come in.'

Chamberlain took two steps.

'Mind the trapdoor!'

Chamberlain froze, but it was too late. He was caught flat-footed, smack in the middle of the throw rug that covered it. One of Daitch's hands rested easily on the arm of his chair. The trap release was more than likely under his finger.

Daitch chuckled. 'No, sir, you are *not* better than I. It's a twenty-foot drop to the sewer below.'

Chamberlain looked around, the balls of his feet tingling for the fall. He realized now that every potted palm, every bit of bric-à-brac, every writing box, every chair, table and settee was probably booby-trapped.

Daitch lifted his hand and motioned him off the rug. 'Come in. We've both made our points. Where did you learn your trade?'

'US Navy SEALs,' said Chamberlain, working hard at breathing normally.

'Ah, a diver? See, you could have swum to safety in the sewer . . . Now, what are you doing here?'

'I'm looking for Hammond.'

Daitch looked genuinely puzzled. '*Charles* Hammond?'

'Yes. Charles Hammond. The deal-maker.'

'Well, I know who he is. In fact I've met him in the past. Charming man. I read in the paper' – he nodded at a pile of newspapers on a tilt table – 'that he was kidnapped in London . . . Is *that* what this is all about?'

'I'm looking for Hammond.'

'What in the name of God would make you think that I had anything to do with kidnapping Charles Hammond?'

'We got an invitation to bid for him in the, quote, "Pendragon Auction".' – Chamberlain didn't like how surprised Daitch looked – 'It was signed, "Lancelot".'

Daitch's bright eyes narrowed. 'Is that why you killed Fleming?'

'I didn't kill anybody,' said Chamberlain, shaking his head. 'But someone looking for Hammond probably did,' he added lamely. It looked as if that idiot Aarschot had been right. Daitch was just an innocent basket case. A very lethal basket case, he reminded himself. But he still might know something. 'If you didn't use the Malory code and Fleming didn't, who do you suppose did?'

'Grandzau. Grandzau was Lancelot.'

'But Grandzau's dead.'

'Yes, isn't he?'

'Who else would use it?'

'Why would he use it would be a better question,' replied Daitch. He smiled vacantly.

'To identify himself,' said Chamberlain.

'Grandzau.'

'No. There must be somebody else.'

'There was no one else,' said Daitch. 'Just Grandzau, Fleming, and me.'

'It doesn't add up.'

A telephone rang, a startling noise in the quiet room. It sat on a tea table with an exquisite marquetry top. Daitch regarded it sourly. 'It's those damned police. Would you be so kind?'

Chamberlain reached for the receiver. 'Sure.' Then he stopped himself, stared at the telephone, looked for extra wires and scratches on the casing. But he wouldn't do it that way. It would be a very sensitive pressure switch, tripped by removing the weight of the receiver. He crouched down and inspected the table.

Daitch giggled. 'Not to worry. The telephone is quite safe.'

Chamberlain shrugged. It looked safe, and Daitch could already have killed him with the trapdoor. He picked up the receiver and heard Aarschot's prissy little voice. 'Now, Monsieur Daitch – '

'This is Chamberlain. I'm in here with Daitch and we're talking.'

'We're coming in,' Aarschot snapped after a shocked silence.

'No, you're not. Not till I'm done. I left one of his booby traps near the front. I'll disarm it when I'm through.'

'Remove it immediately!'

'Just sit tight.' He hung up. Daitch was smiling vacantly. 'Okay, Mr Daitch. Give me a guess. Who else would use the code?'

Daitch focused on him slowly.

'The Malory code?' Chamberlain prompted.

'Each of us retired in ways reminiscent of how we worked. Fleming didn't like the work. He despised the complex. He became a simple gardener. I who built the hideouts and protected the group from its enemies – of which we made many – became a recluse. A well-defended recluse, with my back to the wall and my flanks protected. And Grandzau? Grandzau loved secrets. He loved to find secrets. He loved to destroy them, by selling them. And he loved to construct them. Maybe when Grandzau retired, he created the ultimate secret.'

'Son of a bitch,' Chamberlain muttered. 'Okay . . . What if he did fake his own death? Where would he hide Hammond?'

95

Daitch's eyes grew hooded. He smiled. 'In a secret place.'

'Come on, Daitch. I don't mind kicking it out of you if I have to.'

'You've already breached my fortress. What else can you do?' His eyes clouded. Chamberlain stared, powerless to stop him from slithering over the brink of sanity. When he began to drool, Chamberlain turned and walked back down the hall, through the glass and lancets, under the defused Claymore, past the pocked walls; he cut the trip wire in the foyer, leaned out of the shattered door, and called to Aarschot.

The Inspector came running, followed by a phalanx of Belgian police in flak suits. Chamberlain led them down the hall into Daitch's room. They clumped behind him, boots pounding. The commotion roused Daitch from his stupor. For a moment his eyes grew bright with fear. Then he saw Chamberlain and he smiled.

'I don't know where Grandzau would hide Hammond because I always chose the hiding places, and I haven't chosen this one. If he were smart, he would choose a mobile niche. Not a foolish trap like I chose here.' He waved his hand scornfully at the room.

Aarschot signalled his men and they converged on Daitch's chair.

'Stay back,' Daitch shouted, his eyes burning into Chamberlain's.

Chamberlain was distracted by his own thoughts. 'Why would Grandzau fake his own death and kidnap Hammond?' he asked Daitch as the police gripped the seated man.

'Not for the money,' smiled Daitch, struggling to stay in his chair. He was holding the arms desperately. 'Not for the money. For the secret.'

Chamberlain shook his head. Two more cops shouldered

96

him aside and went to help. They began to tear Daitch's fingers loose, one by one. 'But he didn't keep it se – *Don't move him!*'

The room erupted in a sheet of white flame. The last thing Chamberlain thought as the flame turned black, was that it wasn't silent at all. The explosion from Daitch's final booby trap was the loudest sound he had ever heard.

10

Lady Janet was not surprised that Daitch's building exploded when the police went in. The only unpredictable event as she watched the long siege from the barriers had been that the American who had gone in first came out alive to signal them. But in the end, of course, it ended Daitch's way.

Cold and weary, she retreated from the flashing lights and ambulance klaxons, retracing her route from the centre of Brussels, and hurried into the railway station, debating where to go next. Amsterdam, perhaps, or Paris, to tap their undergrounds for information about the man in black. Both would take time and she was short of it.

She had learned outside Daitch's that she was not the only one hunting him. Interpol was hunting too; an officer had identified himself in an attempt to take her to dinner. She had already recognized the Russian who had tripped Daitch's door mine before the Belgian police had taken his body away – KGB in Amsterdam, years ago, a freelance running a little dope on the side, until the Chinese took over. Then came the American who had defied the Brussels police and survived in Daitch's booby-trapped house longer than he should have; such contempt for local authorities used to be a hallmark of the CIA.

She was sinking over a cup of coffee at an empty counter, wondering what did they want that the man in black wanted too, when the newspaper headlines she had been seeing with half an eye all day, suddenly leapt off the racks.

Charles Hammond Kidnapped.

Pendragon. The auction on the telegram. The deal-maker had to be Pendragon. But there was no one left to use the Malory code, no one but her. Fleming-Pellinore, dead this morning. Daitch-Lionel, dead tonight. Lady Janet-Guinevere, alone in Nice. Grandzau . . . Nor was there any reason to use the code, and by now the codes were no secret. They were virtually labels, now.

Identification . . .

She burst into sudden motion, flinging money on the counter, hooking her bag on her shoulder, moving, filling her mind, blocking her crazy thoughts. She bought a ticket to Paris. Only aboard the train – after another injection and three hours dead sleep stretched out in an empty compartment – did she allow herself to think about Grandzau.

Where is Grandzau? the man who had beaten her had asked. Not where is Fleming? Or where is Daitch? He knew where to find Fleming and Daitch. As he had known where to find her. But he had asked for Grandzau – not even Lancelot. Just Grandzau, over and over, long after his sadistic pleasure in torturing her had turned to a desperate rain of blows. Where is Grandzau? Where is Grandzau? Where is Grandzau?

Lady Janet stared at the French countryside flickering past the window of the high-speed express. The wheels made hardly a sound on the endless, seamless ribbon of welded track. Grandzau alive? Had he faked his own death in a flaming car?

A woman alone came down the corridor, wheeling a suitcase. Halfway in the compartment, she met Lady Janet's eyes and backed out, hurriedly.

But Grandzau wasn't a kidnapper. He had traded in words, facts, not bodies. Who else had reason to use the Malory code: 'Lancelot' had announced his identity.

Boasted of it. Grandzau had been vain. And he had often profited by *auctioning* information to competing services.

If Grandzau was alive these three years – faking his death as part of a scheme to kidnap Charles Hammond and auction him to the highest bidder – if he had done all that, what had he done to her?

The winter-brown fields began spinning beyond the window. She gripped a handrail, reeling from the enormity of what had happened. He had betrayed her in every way that mattered. He had tricked her. He had abandoned her to an empty life without him. He had cut her out of his grand scheme. With another woman? Jealousy evaporated as his cruelty hit her full force.

Grandzau had known they would come looking for the man who called himself Lancelot. He had exposed her to the savage interrogation she had suffered in the villa. The man in black had been Grandzau's instrument.

She wept, huddled in the train compartment, tears streaking her face, wetting her veil of golden hair. She wept as if no soul in the world cared if she lived or died. She wept, betrayed and alone, like an orphan.

Lady Janet registered at a quiet hotel on the rue de Bourgogne where she was not known. She shopped for a change of clothes and a warm coat, bathed, slept well past dark, and walked out into the city, her left hand grazing the edge of the gun in her pocket.

Fluent in French, she read the headlines in the news kiosks as she headed through the Fifteenth Arrondissement. Hammond had been missing for two days now and the papers were speculating that he had been taken by rightists, leftists, business rivals, or maniacs, but there had been no word from the kidnappers. Hardly surprising. The bidders Grandzau would invite to his auction would not bandy it about.

Consequently, with new news sparse, the French government's promise to aid its former colony of Madagascar should Indian Ocean tensions worsen had recaptured the leads. Right-wing newspapers approved arming the Island of Malagasy and also the formerly Portuguese Mozambique. Those on the left were caught between an anti-imperialist stance and a desire for the jobs that would be created by sending more planes and missiles to the Indian Ocean. Hints of increased Russian subversion in the area spiced the kiosk debate.

The Café '79' had been thirty-five years in a tired neighbourhood of narrow cobbled streets, brick walls showing through crumbling cement façades, rusted wrought-iron street lamps and peeling wood shutters. A big Citroën plant squatted on the Quai André Citroën a few blocks away. Here and there ageing post-war apartment buildings stood between the lower, older slums. Those who worked built cars and were implacably leftist. They mingled easily with the gangsters and mercenaries who frequented the '79'.

Lady Janet hadn't been there in years, but it was the sort of place that never changed until the *gendarmerie* had finally had enough, arrested the *patrons*, and bolted the door. Crossing the Seine at the Pont de Mirabeau, and proceeding into the dark lane, Lady Janet saw that hadn't happened yet. A single red neon sign announced the number, shining through the wire mesh that covered the single small window. Someone had tossed a grenade at that window during the Algerian war. It had missed the opening, but the *patron* went to wire mesh regardless.

Entering the smoky front room, she raised her head and her pulse quickened with the old excitement of being where she should not be. She sat at a table with a dirty red-and-white checked cloth and ordered white wine. One of the more prosaic things she enjoyed about France was that even a dive as awful as this one had a good wine if you had the price. She sat for several hours, smoking, sipping the wine, brushing off the attempts to pick her up. The room was rich with memories of the ways she had lived and the ways she had changed.

Absinthe had had a romantic connotation for a wealthy, sheltered girl who had known little more than a childhood of bucolic splendour on the Isling Gloucestershire estate and a year of grotty and thoroughly boring student rebellion. The bitter, potent liqueur had been her first eager step into the alluring depths below and beyond country hauteur and English dignity.

But too energetic and impatient in those days to wait for absinthe's apparition, she had switched quickly to wine – whites and burgundies, never the claret of her father's table – and heroin – for why wait for the Green Fairy when heroin delivered its visions with the speed of light. Heroin – the best from Marseille – was its own depth and her occasional companion for a decade; but though it often seized her remorselessly, her wealth had shielded her from the addicts' plagues of bad dope and dirty needles. The morphine she was injecting for her pain was the first drug stronger than aspirin she had had in a year.

Whoring at the '79' had earned her a thousand francs – charging the minimum – before Henri Trefle let it be known her customers would answer to him. A thousand francs, which she mailed to her father with instructions to invest it in something 'suitable'. Tonight she was unmoved by the stares and leers her beauty drew from the men at the bar. She had whored for the excitement and to spite her father. It, and he, had long since died.

But she needed Henri again, needed him to help her. He might. Not for love, God knew, but for hate.

She got a shock when Trefle walked in. At first she didn't recognize him. He'd deteriorated in the last four years, put on forty pounds and acquired a blotched face that was vivid proof he'd surrendered to his old enemy. Lady Janet watched him order it at the bar. The barmaid poured Algerian red. So he was broke as well. Now she noticed the threadbare bush jacket, no coat despite the cold, the filthy beret, the rundown jump boots, the faded trappings of a failed professional soldier.

Trefle drained the glass and rapped it on the bar to demand more. Turning around to observe the bistro with a sour scowl, he deliberately jostled a big man beside him – a very big man, larger than himself – and sneered at his protest. Before the man could take it further, his companion grabbed his arm and forcefully led him to the door, his drink unfinished on the bar.

Lady Janet sat back, relieved by the incident. Despite appearances, it seemed that Trefle hadn't lost his reputation as an expert guerrilla with the appetite of a psychotic killer. He stiffened when he saw her and stared in mild surprise. Lady Janet smiled and shifted painfully to the next chair. Trefle never sat with his back to a room or a door.

Taking his second glass and the bottle, Trefle left the bar and crossed the room to her table. Fat, and half drunk, he still walked like a cat. He had cat eyes, too – knowing, uncaring, quick and cruel.

'Bonsoir, Henri.'

'Bonsoir.' There was something new in his eyes, something that she had hoped to see, a bitter shadow that hadn't been there four years ago, a shadow connected to the twisted downturns at the corners of his fleshy mouth. She smiled again. He would do.

'Sit down.'

He sat heavily and sloshed Algerian red into her white Burgundy, staining her glass pink to the rim.

'Merci,' she said with an ironic nod. She knew what he

103

liked, knew how to play his admiration for her breeding and spirit. Raising the glass, she met his eyes. 'I *thought* I would find you celebrating.'

He slurred his words. 'I just wish I had been the one.'

'Ah, but you wouldn't give him back. No matter how much they paid.'

Trefle blinked slowly. He was drunker than she had thought. He muttered, 'I hope they kill him.'

'They won't.'

The cat eyes leapt to her face. He didn't want to hear that. 'If it goes wrong, they will kill him.'

'It won't go wrong.'

'Kidnappings usually go wrong,' Trefle insisted in a dogged slur.

'Not this one,' Lady Janet bored in. 'I know.'

Trefle blinked again and shook his head. She waited for him to ask how she knew, but Trefle shifted to another facet of what he wanted to believe.

'I should have killed him myself, while I still could.'

'I've brought you a second chance,' said Lady Janet.

Trefle hadn't heard. 'Hammond betrayed me,' he said.

She knew. It was why she had come here. Trefle had told her immediately after it happened, four years ago, when she had lied to Grandzau and pretended to visit her home in England, and had returned, instead, secretly to the '79', looking for action and excitement and had found Trefle, unexpectedly back from East Africa. Trefle had been wounded and he'd bled in the night and she'd left his blood on her body until she returned to the south of France, as some crazy proof that she could still be perverse even though she loved Grandzau.

'Hammond betrayed me.'

Lady Janet listened patiently. *Betrayal* was a serious word in the mercenary fraternity – as important a part of

104

their view of life as oiled weapons, spare ammunition, courage, and fear.

Trefle shook his massive head and hunched his great shoulders over the table. One hand toyed with his glass. The other gripped the edge of the table – gathering the checked cloth, threatening the wine – as if he were preparing to hurl the table across the dark room.

'What happened, Henri?' she prompted softly. 'What did Charles Hammond do to you?'

He recited the story like a litany. It was a short, clear, angry account, obviously oft-repeated, and just as obviously the source of a deep, bitter obsession.

Charles Hammond had hired Henri Trefle to raid Mogadishu, the capital of the East African/Indian Ocean state of Somalia. Trefle's mercenaries were to seize the government radio station and the president's palace – the first vital steps in a Hammond-engineered political coup. It was staged from a secret base in Kenya.

'I put my men in three unarmed transports – French, English, and German officers: *nègre* soldiers. We took off from Patta Island, north of Lamu, the moment Hammond radioed that the way was clear. It was understood that Hammond would bribe the Somali airport defence units. There were Russian ships in the Indian Ocean. So we flew at wave top, under their radar so they couldn't report us. When we reached the Mogadishu airport, the Somalis Hammond was supposed to bribe opened up on us with all they had.'

Trefle spat into the corner. He was staring at the table-cloth as he continued. Lady Janet sat still and attentive, bent forward to better hear his whispered voice. Each word was the same as the night he had bled on her breast.

'Hammond changed his mind. The way wasn't clear. The anti-aircraft shot down the planes following. My plane was in the lead and the pig Somalis weren't fast enough to

105

hit us. We headed back to Kenya. Behind us you could see the other two planes burning on the ground. The Somalis scrambled a jet from the runway. Again we flew darkened at wave top, but the jet found us anyhow. I think the Russian ships might have tracked us.'

He emptied his glass, refilled, ignored hers, and spat again. 'He was a trainer plane. All he had was a couple of light machineguns for target practice. Well, he practised that night. He couldn't shoot us down. We were too sturdy and the gun was too light. But he tried. He made run after run, lacing the fuselage again and again and on every pass more of my men died. My pilot dodged and twisted but the bullets kept tearing through our plane until the bastard ran out of ammunition.

'When we got back to Patta Island, there were twelve of us alive. I forbade them to touch a single dead man. I carried every body off myself. Even the pilot was gone, dead a moment after he touched her down.

'Had I seen Hammond that moment, I would have butchered him.' He touched his chest, over his heart, and Lady Janet saw he still carried his long glass knife. It was tempered glass in a fibreglass sheath and no airport X-ray would ever spot it.

Lady Janet waited silently.

His cat eyes landed on her face again. 'I've told you this before, the night I returned to Paris and you were here and came to my bed. Why do you pretend you've never heard?'

Lady Janet hesitated, struggling to meet his gaze. She'd let his drunkenness lull her into forgetting how quick he really was. 'I just thought . . . you wanted to say it.'

'What are you doing here? What do you want?'

She recovered quickly. 'Can we go to your room?'

Trefle inspected her piercingly. Then a slow, lazy, sensual smile rambled over his face. 'You still want it.'

'I want to talk.'

'Sure you do. Just like last visit . . . Pay the bill!'

He stood up quickly, and brushed past her as she fumbled for her money. Lady Janet twisted slightly to one side and kept her free hand out of her pocket, in case he was checking to see if she had a gun.

She followed him to the door, and walked beside him up the rue de la Convention, then into a side street, through an alley, and into a courtyard. Now she went ahead of him, climbing circular stone stairs several floors up in a crumbling brick *pension*. An open door revealed the turkish toilet that served the floor. Trefle unlocked his door, and ushered her in with a mock bow.

She entered quickly, crossed the room, which was dimly lighted by an overhead bulb, and whirled, drawing her gun, halting his rush. Trefle stopped, a drunken smile on his face, his eyes bright and hard.

'Stop,' she said. 'Back up.'

Trefle came a slow step closer.

'You taught me that the single advantage of a gun is its longer reach. And you said never surrender that advantage. I'll kill you if you come a step closer.'

Trefle stared, then shrugged. 'What do you want?'

'Back up.'

He backed to the wall.

'Good. Now hear me out. Grandzau kidnapped Charles Hammond.'

Trefle spat. 'Grandzau's dead.'

'He faked it.'

'So what?'

'Grandzau won't kill Hammond. He's auctioning Hammond to the highest bidder.'

'Yet another reason I wish I was rich.' He brightened. 'Maybe somebody will buy him for what he knows. Maybe they'll drag it out of him and then kill him.'

'There'll be others bidding to keep him alive . . . Tell me something, Henri. Why didn't you go after him?'

Trefle snorted harsh laughter. 'Money. How does a man like me even track a man like him. He's in Europe one day, Africa the next. Private planes, guards, helicopters. It wasn't possible.' He spat again. '*Merde*. If they get him back, they'll treble his security.'

'Would you like to find him right now?'

'Shut up, woman. You talk too much.'

'I'll finance the hunt.'

Trefle stared. 'You'll pay for me to kill Hammond. Why?'

'After you kill Hammond I will kill Grandzau.'

Trefle laughed. 'Because he fooled you? You're crazy.'

'I'll kill him and I need you to help me. I'll give you Hammond.'

'I don't believe you.'

'Move over there. Into the corner. Move!'

Trefle went reluctantly.

'Look at me!'

She shrugged out of her coat, smoothly shifting the gun from one hand to the other. Then she stepped between Trefle and the big mirror. She kept her eyes on his, her gun trained on his chest; she reached back, felt for the switch, and turned on the light by the mirror. Then she bunched the hem of her skirt in her hand and slowly raised it to her waist.

Trefle wet his lips.

'*Look in the mirror!*'

He tore his eyes from her beautiful legs and looked at the cloudy glass. The weals that criss-crossed her bottom and thighs had turned blue-black.

'Grandzau knew this would happen. He *made* this happen.'

Trefle wet his lips again. His eyes flickered between the mirror and her legs and back to the mirror. He smiled.

108

'They say that a woman learns to enjoy the whip.'

She shot him and Trefle went down with a scream.

She stood over him, holding her gun in one hand, her skirt in the other, and watched him writhe on the floor. She listened to footsteps on the stairs. They paused, then descended unhurriedly. It wasn't the sort of building where a single shot drew attention.

Cursing and moaning, Trefle struggled to a sitting position, spread aside his bush jacket, raised his dirty pullover, and inspected the bloody furrow her shot had ploughed through the roll of fat around his waist.

'You crazy woman, you could have killed me.'

'You're not the only man who can help me, Henri. Just the most convenient.' She released her skirt and smoothed it over her legs. 'Get up. I've booked the midnight sleeper to Marseille.'

11

'No, I'm not dead . . . Yes, I know I should be . . . Arnie, I got a headache and my ears are ringing . . . Goddamnit I know the Belgians are pissed and I don't give a fuck. It was their fault anyway.' Chamberlain put the phone down and held his head with both hands, trying to remember something Daitch had said about Hammond and Grandzau. Something secret.

He was holed up in a telephone booth at the airport, sipping coffee from a china cup. The steward from the Comptel plane rapped discreetly on the glass door, opened it at Chamberlain's nod, and refilled his cup from a pot he was holding. He could see the Comptel plane outside the building, pilot and co-pilot sunning themselves on the boarding steps, awaiting his orders. Where next, now that Daitch had proved a dead end?

'What's your name?'

'Kreegan, sir.'

'Thanks, Kreegan. Please tell the pilot to crank up.'

The phone squawked, solicitously. Arnie had done yelling, pleading now that he wanted to help. Just as in New York, the night Hammond was snatched, his friends at the CIA were being uncharacteristically giving. Even Arnie's bitching about blowing up Brussels had sounded *pro forma*. He didn't give a damn. None of them did. All they cared was that Chamberlain was well enough to chase Hammond. Which he was, despite his headache, because the Belgian cops had absorbed the brunt of Daitch's last charge, permitting Chamberlain to walk away with a ringing in his ears and a bump on his head.

110

He picked up the phone again. Yelling had made his headache worse, and touched off a secondary pain, like an earthquake aftershock.

'Yeah, Arnie, sorry. Listen, I appreciate your taking my call, considering. I really just want to know if you had any word on the plane that took Hammond.'

'Farquhar in London is on that. He's playing it close to his chest, but I don't think he's got anything, yet.'

'If he hasn't, I'm not sure where to go next.'

'Try Marseille.'

'What the hell for?'

'That's all I can say.'

'Come off it, Arnie. What's going on?'

'Bye, Pete. Glad you made it.'

'Goddamnit, what are you telling me?'

'Pete. You ask where. I say Marseille. You say *why*? You think Lewis and Clarke would have found the Pacific if they asked that bird lady *why*?'

'Arnie.'

'You think Tony Curtis would have got away from the Vikings if he asked that old woman with the magnet *why*? She said, north. He sailed. Go for it, Pete. Don't ask dumb questions your friends can't answer.'

Chamberlain weighed the abruptly dead phone in his hand like a suspiciously light melon. If that was the game they wanted to play, it didn't bother him as long as he got his information. Maybe they were making him their stalking horse or point man on this operation; he ignored a nasty little voice which was chirping in the back of his headache that he might have a problem getting out of the way when they changed their minds.

He dialled the operator and asked to be connected to Scotland Yard in London. The ringing in his ears was doing funny things to his memory. He knew he had Inspector Farquhar's number, but he couldn't remember

111

the number or whether he had written it down, and if so, where.

'I think I've used up your favours in Brussels for a while,' he told Farquhar.

'Not to worry. How are you?'

'One piece. Have you found the plane?'

'We're making progress,' said Farquhar.

'What sort of progress?'

'We're pretty sure it didn't go to Norway, Sweden, Denmark, Middle-Europe or Algeria.'

'Leaving Greenland, the Azores, and Russia?'

'Quite.'

'Plus anywhere they could have gone after refuelling at one of those places.'

'I rather doubt they'd have refuelled in Russia.'

'We gotta get that plane,' said Chamberlain. 'It's the only thing in their plan that went wrong.'

'I understand you spoke with Daitch,' Farquhar said matter-of-factly.

'Sorry,' said Chamberlain. 'I didn't mean to hold back.' He related the entire conversation.

'Interesting,' said Farquhar. 'It certainly does seem as if Grandzau is alive. Perhaps your friends at the CIA can persuade the Italians to exhume him. What's your next step?'

'Get out of here, get on my plane and go someplace, though frankly I don't know where.'

'Why don't you try Marseille?'

'Marseille?' mused Chamberlain. 'I guess it would be a good town to put together a little snatch team . . . Especially if you used to know people down there in the heroin trade.'

'Not to mention the information business. Remember, Grandzau often operated in Marseille. However, I must

112

point out that you're not the only one thinking along these lines.'

'Oh?'

'My friends at MI5 tell me that their friends at the CIA tell them that the KGB boys are already in Marseille, pulling off doors all over the waterfront.'

'What's with the Russians?' Chamberlain asked irritably. KGB. So much for Arnie's friendly help.

'Ask *your* friends at the CIA. I hear they're dogging the Russians' tracks.' Farquhar chuckled dryly. 'I think they're still hoping your little ransom consortium will bail them out.'

'Nice to know they'll be so close by if I need them.'

'Yes, I imagine you *will* find yourself in the cross-fire. Best of luck, old boy. Do check in when you get a chance.'

And Farquhar's friendly help too. The Brit was getting a free ride just like Arnie.

'I'll be sure to,' said Chamberlain. Fine with him. They could help all they wanted, so long as he got the reward. For whatever their goals, he knew his, which was to please Helen Thorp.

12

Marseille was warm. After snow in Washington, snow in Connecticut, bitter cold in New York, damp cold in London, and an icy North Sea wind in Brussels, it was blessedly warm. It smelled of spice and gasoline exhaust, tobacco smoke, the salt sea, and tropic heat.

Comptel had a house overlooking the Mediterranean. There was a bowl of fresh fruit on a table in his bedroom window, and beside it a telex machine buzzing out a message from Helen Thorp.

GLAD YOU'RE ALIVE. RECEIVED 2ND LANCELOT INVITATION. TEXT FOLLOWS. QUOTE. PENDRAGON WELL. AUCTION JANUARY 7. SITE TO BE ANNOUNCED. LANCELOT. END QUOTE. WE HAVE FIVE DAYS. REPEAT. FIVE DAYS.

Ms Ultra Cool sounded a touch panicky. Chamberlain leaned over the keyboard and typed a reply.

I'M HERE. I'LL LOOK AROUND. I'LL DO WHAT I CAN.

He waited for an answer, but she was apparently not near her machine. Kreegan bustled after him, arms heaped with paper boxes. 'You gotta have clothes, Mr Chamberlain. It's hot as hell.'

He lowered his voice conspiratorially. 'I got a Frenchie tailor waiting, but first I thought you might want this.' He produced a shoulder holster, pulled a short, heavy revolver from it and showed Chamberlain one of the shells.

Chamberlain inspected the bullet and the weapon. 'A *shotgun* revolver?' he asked dubiously. 'What's the trade-off? Whenever you fiddle a machine to get more of one thing, you get less of something else. What *won't* this thing do?'

'Well, it don't pack much wallop after ten yards. The shot spreads real quick 'cause the barrel's so short. And it's noisy.'

'I'll bet. Like artillery.'

'Also, don't try and reload too soon.'

'Heat?'

'Burn your hand off. Still, it's kind of handy in a back-alley town like Marseille.'

'Where the hell did you find this?'

'Modified it from an old Colt. I'm a bit of a gunsmith, sir.'

Chamberlain hadn't been sure he wanted to carry the thing, but the old guy was so proud that he said, 'Thanks. Thanks very much. Ought to come in handy for asking questions.'

Kreegan grinned and rubbed his crewcut. 'Use it in good health, Mr Chamberlain. Want your clothes?'

'Quick.'

Briskly, Kreegan tore the boxes open and unfolded a pair of tropical-weight suits, a beige and a dark blue. Chamberlain put on the beige. Kreegan strapped on the shoulder holster and brought the tailor running with a piercing whistle.

An hour later, after a swim, a shower and a shave, Chamberlain's headache had subsided, though his ears were still ringing. The tailor helped him into the altered suit and stood back, pursing his lips as Chamberlain dealt with the usual problem he had in summer clothes – where to put his tools so they wouldn't bulge through the light cloth pockets. The shoulder holster made things worse. The tailor had allowed for its bulk, but it still restricted the amount of equipment he could put in his left breast inside jacket pocket. Eventually he got things equitably distributed. He no longer bulged like a shoplifter, but the tailor still clucked at what he had done to the lines of the suit.

'*Portefeuille*?' he suggested plaintively.

'He means like a pocketbook,' said Kreegan. 'Guys carry 'em over here.'

'This guy doesn't – Okay, thanks for everything. I want you back on the plane in case I got to beat it out of here quick.'

All this bustling was distracting. Chamberlain waited, watching the Mediterranean, until the front door closed and cars pulled away. Then he went out himself, walked down to the old city and started looking for the Russians who were looking for Charles Hammond and Karl Grandzau. He wandered all the afternoon, but by nightfall he had seen nothing. He returned to the house, with a disappointed feeling that he'd been searching the streets of a city that didn't wake up until well after dark.

It was time to think and what he thought was that if Karl Grandzau had faked his own death and kidnapped Charles Hammond, then he had better find out everything there was to know about Grandzau. It was all very well to fly to Marseille because Grandzau had operated here, and because mercenaries were available and a kidnapper might use them to organize a snatch team, but for all he knew, Chamberlain realized, the German, who might or might not be dead, had a deeper love for and knowledge of Wisconsin and had stashed Hammond in a cow barn ten miles from Milwaukee.

Not for the money, Daitch had suggested. *For the secret*. That's what he had said the second before the explosion, Chamberlain remembered. *For the secret*. Whatever the hell that meant. It was frustrating because his single connection to Hammond's kidnapper might be a smoke-screen, someone else using the dead Grandzau's code to distract the pursuit. Five days. He had five days before the auction.

He telephoned Arnie Fast, who wasn't around, and got passed smoothly through some low-level types until a woman with a honey-soft Virginia accent said, 'Yes, Mr Chamberlain. Mr Fast said to expect your call.'

'Did Mr Fast say I could ask you to quizz the computer.'

'He said give you everything but my home phone number.'

Chamberlain laughed dutifully and said, 'Karl Grandzau. German. History. Associates, friends, and enemies.' He gave her his computer terminal number, the model – so she could transmit in the proper mode – and a one-hour deadline.

Then he telephoned Helen Thorp. The Comptel executive operator tracked her down at The Four Seasons where she was eating lunch.

'Sorry to drag you away from all the fun, but as long as I'm going through hell in this villa I'm going to make life miserable for the rest of you.'

She laughed and he found himself thinking of the line of her neck as she threw her head back. 'They're taking good care of you?'

'Kreegan should have been somebody's mother.'

'He's a treasure. What's your next move?'

'I need access to the Comptel computers.'

'Sorry. I can't authorize direct access.'

'Yeah, okay, I understand you can't open 'em just like that, but give me somebody who has access. I want to search for any info on Grandzau.'

'What can Comptel do?'

'How many branch offices do we have in Europe?'

'Thirty-eight.'

'And that's just Europe. We could have dealt with him at some time, sold him something, bought something from

117

him, who knows. I asked the Agency for the dope on him. As soon as I get names of companies he's owned and worked for, I want to run them through Comptel's computers. You know what I mean?'

'Right. I'll do it. There's only a few of us with complete access. And if you can't get me for some reason, go straight to Mr Cowan.'

'Thanks. Enjoy your lunch.'

'Wait. Did you get my telex?'

'About the new Lancelot message? Yeah.'

'Pete, we're running out of time.'

'We are.'

'Well, what the devil – I mean what are you going to do now, aside from tapping computers? What's your next step?'

'I hear Marseille is swarming with KGB types. I ought to have a chat with one of them.'

This time they were out in force and easy to spot, munching fried fish and dressed like a Russian tourist's idea of how a Marseille gunman looked. What gave them away more than their black shirts and white suits – an outfit some of the locals still wore – was their size. They looked like a pair of Ukrainian ploughboys. Back home in Connecticut, they would have been recruited for pro-ball in their junior year of high school.

Spotting them was one thing, dealing with them another. He'd already seen one back-alley bar they'd reduced to splinters, the stunned patrons stacked like cordwood in the corner. Now they lounged with their backs to the fish stand, surveying the pavement with open contempt. Across the busy street their back-up squad waited in a black Peugeot. In the unlikely event that someone they'd assaulted called the gendarmes, the Peugeot would decant a middle-level Russian Embassy official with diplomatic immunity for the hitters and a fistful of franc notes for the cops.

Chamberlain lounged in the door of a tobacco shop, working hard at looking French. The beige suit and the open-collar light blue shirt helped, but the *pièce de resistance*, the device that transformed his persona as well as his nationality, was the syrupy, perfumed hair tonic with which he'd slicked his hair down tight to his head. It felt like telephone wire, but if anything could make him look southern European – maybe even like a French cop – it was this glossy head. He'd tried to complete the effect with black, wraparound sunglasses, but had given it up at nightfall because he couldn't see out.

The KGB heavies finished their dinner and started swaggering down the crowded pavement. Chamberlain waited until the black Peugeot started after them before he followed. They walked aimlessly for a while and Chamberlain began to get nervous. Street work wasn't one of his strongest points. The Navy had taught him to hide in the water, emerge to wreak havoc, and hide again. The CIA had honed his aptitude for small things that worked and made him conversant with computers. At Comptel he'd been trying to learn to deal with powerful people and large organizations. But he had little practical experience in street work.

Had they made him? Were they strolling along looking for a quiet hole in the wall to beat his head in while the black Peugeot stood watch? Why weren't they moving with the purposefulness they'd reportedly been tearing up Marseille with?

He hung further back. There had to be some way to separate the two gorillas from the car, and then one from the other, long enough to ask one simple question. Two questions, actually. What were *they* asking the people they were leaning on? And what had they learned?

The Peugeot's horn trilled insistently, cutting through the street noise of cars and motorbikes, music from the bars, and the click and shuffle of hundreds of night-time walkers. One of the Russians ran to the car; he leaned on the roof, watching the street, listening intently to the back-up squad.

His partner slowed down and scrutinized the pavement. Chamberlain ducked into a boutique, picked up a sweater, and watched through the window. The Peugeot had a two-way radio antenna, and he guessed they had received new information.

The Russian nodded, pushed off from the car, and caught up with his partner. They broke into a brisk walk. The Peugeot overtook them. Chamberlain followed. Half a block along, the car stopped at the mouth of an alley. The KGB gorillas turned into it, running.

Chamberlain hesitated. The KGB was on to something, but to follow them he had to pass the back-up car. He pretended to study the posters outside a burlesque house, hoping it would drive forward, but it stayed at the kerb, its four occupants ignoring the angry horn-blaring and shouts of the drivers behind who had to swing out into oncoming traffic to pass it. Every second he waited, the KGB men were moving further away, closer to the target to which they had been directed.

He couldn't do it. He couldn't pass the car. A woman's laughter drifted across the street, a happy noise which distracted him. He saw two couples, arm in arm, strolling into a club, young, carefree, enjoying a good time. The music, which seemed to come from everywhere, was suddenly beautiful. What if the Peugeot crew had spotted *him* and the advance into the alley was set up?

He was afraid to pass the car.

Not afraid that he would lose his opportunity if they spotted him. Not afraid he would lose Charles Hammond.

But afraid he'd get hurt. It had to come sometime, and here it was – fear, like an iron grille fence he could see through, but couldn't pass.

He felt a little sick in his stomach. He had never questioned the theory that you had to be crazy to be a demolition diver; you couldn't do such work dwelling on what might go wrong. But now he realized that if it was true, he was no longer crazy.

The Russians solved the dilemma for him. They started their car and drove away. Chamberlain looked for a back-up squad, saw none. He ran to the alley. It was dark several paces in and it didn't look promising. One wall was the side of a porn theatre. A fire escape ran up it into the black sky. The near side was lined with dark doorways. He stepped around a pile of garbage cans, and crouched down behind them, blocking his silhouette against the lighted street he had just left. Listening for the sound of the men in the car following him, he swept the alley with the microwave scanner, felt nothing, and started rapidly in, cupping it in his left hand.

He came to the end abruptly and much sooner than he had expected. There he found a single wooden door, ajar. He turned around, faced the street, and swept the area. The scanner showed no one following. He pushed the door open, scanned the darkness. Nothing. He hesitated. The scanner was capable of reporting only a moving presence. An infra-red scanner might respond to a waiting attacker's body heat, but he didn't have one. He had a flashlight, but he was afraid to draw fire.

He slipped through the narrow space between the door and the frame, sidled along a wall for several feet, then stopped, trying to figure out what seemed wrong. A pinprick of light, high overhead, gave him the answer. He was still out of doors. He'd entered a courtyard. His eyes adjusted to the darkness and he saw the irregular crenellations of varying heights of walls against the slightly less dark sky. Several buildings surrounded the courtyard and which the KGB men had disappeared into it was impossible to guess.

He heard a loud crash, and a startled cry, quickly muffled. Closing one eye to protect his nigh vision, he flicked his flashlight for a second in the direction of the sound. In the brief moment of light he saw an open doorway and steps beyond. He ran to it, dodging a pile of flowerpots he'd seen between himself and the door.

He went up the stairs fast. The noise had come through an open window a floor above. The struggle in the dark was going on at full fury. He heard the thunk of fists slamming into bodies, the crash of bodies hitting walls, breath sucked in hard with pain or exertion. A whistling, swishing sound was followed by a scream.

Electric light blazed on, painting a battered, shabby room stark white, half-blinding Chamberlain. One of the Russians lay still on the floor, blood oozing from his throat. The second was locked in combat with a man as big as himself who was fighting to free his wrist from the Russian's grip. The Russian was holding on for his life. The man had a long shiny knife, wet with the fallen KGB man's blood.

None of them had turned on the light. Chamberlain whirled to face the rush from behind. What he saw looked impossible. There was a man sitting in the corner, but he hadn't turned on the light because his hands and feet were bound to the arms and legs of the chair. Chamberlain gaped. He had seen the stunningly beautiful woman who was swinging a gun at his head on the street in Brussels outside Daitch's house.

He was still trying to untangle the impossible from the obvious when her gun met his temple with a ringing crunch and a vicious blue stab of pain drove him to his knees. The last thing he saw as the pain shattered the light was the man with the knife breaking free and swinging his shiny weapon with lightning speed. It cut the air with a whistle and it gleamed like a long, thin shard of broken glass.

13

'I need a drink,' Trefle gasped.

Lady Janet looked away from the wheel of her rented Renault for a moment. The coast road was an unfolding black band ahead of the speeding car. In the dim glow of the dashboard lights she saw that the Frenchman's hands were trembling.

'There's brandy in my bag.'

Trefle pawed into it, extracted a silver flask with an exultant cry, twisted off the top, and tipped it into his mouth. His neck worked as the brandy poured down his throat. At last he lowered the flask. She took it from him, swallowed quickly and handed it back.

'Finish it.'

'I intend to.'

'Why did you kill them?' She knew it was stupid to ask even as she spoke.

'So they wouldn't kill me.'

'They were Russian, weren't they?'

'Sounded that way,' said Trefle.

Lady Janet concentrated on a series of bends in the road. They had been questioning the old Legionnaire who ran the rooming-house on the courtyard in Marseille when the Russians had interrupted them. The Legionnaire provided lodging for mercenaries down on their luck, in between jobs.

She felt Trefle's eyes on her and when the road straightened she returned his gaze. The brandy had calmed him; the muscles in his cheeks were no longer twitching.

'They were stronger than me,' he said. 'Not as quick, but stronger.'

His confession startled her. Not that he admitted their superior strength, but that he would bother explaining why he had killed them. He wasn't through: 'I don't have the strength any more. I drink too much. Maybe I've aged. But I have the will. And I know how. Better than any of them.'

Lady Janet found it difficult to imagine Trefle in a weakened condition. 'Perhaps you should get a gun.'

'Perhaps – stop there!'

A cluster of lights marked a small inn with a few cars parked by the bar entrance. 'We haven't time.'

Trefle seized the steering wheel and aimed the car at the inn. His grip was strong and Lady Janet had the choice of ploughing into the parked cars or braking. They slid to a halt.

'Henri.'

He lurched out, into the bar, and reappeared with a bottle. 'Drive.'

She pulled onto the black road as he struggled with the cork.

'Please don't,' she said, placing her hand on his thigh, spreading her fingers like lace.

'I thought we hadn't time,' he leered.

'Maybe later, when we rest. If you're not drunk.'

Trefle took a slug from the bottle. 'When we were lovers, I often thought my last sight on earth would be you plunging a knife into my heart as we came.'

'Charming,' she said in the cool way she knew pleased him. 'Why did you continue. Were you suicidal?'

'It seemed a small price for the pleasure. Remember how you would scream?'

'When you pleased me.'

125

'Maybe I should pull you into the back seat and please you now.'

'Let's just concentrate on Charles Hammond, shall we?'

'Don't worry, I'd lend you my knife.' He laughed, started to raise the bottle again, pressed instead against her fingers. 'That's nice,' he said dreamily. 'You know, Janet, if I did rape you, I bet you'd hold off on the knife until I'd got good and started. Yes?'

'Maybe if you were sober,' she said with a smile. And to her great relief, he jammed the cork back in the bottle and laid it on the floor, where it rolled to and fro as the car swayed on the mountain road.

They had done well in Marseille, until the Russians barged in. Charles Hammond's kidnapping was a subject of great interest among the mercenaries. Many remembered his betrayal in Somalia. Others were fascinated by the audacity of the plot. None had heard of the Pendragon Auction, and no one had any idea that Grandzau was alive. They speculated freely about Hammond's captors, and many claimed to know men who'd been in on it. Everyone wanted to have a former comrade in a big deal. Hard pressed to sift reality from fantasy, Lady Janet and Trefle weighed the teller's reputation and the nature of his speculation. Those who claimed a friend was in the hire of politicians or business rivals they ignored. Those who knew for sure that Hammond had been taken by terrorists they'd passed by, searching for someone who knew some plausible detail of Grandzau's plan.

Then they'd happened upon a mercenaries' brothel that the Russians had invaded. They hadn't killed anyone but some of the men had been badly knocked about. Trefle started in on them, while she had questioned the women. They learned it wasn't the first place the Russians had attacked. The Russians were tearing up Marseille asking the same questions they were. Where was Grandzau? Who had gone to work for him? A frightened prostitute, a nineteen-year-old Greek girl sniffling for heroin, told Lady Janet that a group of soldiers staying in the rooming-house in the courtyard by the porn theatre had been hired by Grandzau. She'd neglected to add that she had told the same thing to the Russians.

Trefle and Lady Janet had got there first and Trefle had just begun to threaten the Algerian veteran who ran the place when the Russians arrived. The man had started to talk and what he told them had them driving to Lyon. They would have taken a plane or the train, but the dead men they'd left behind would have been discovered by the police whose klaxons they'd heard as they'd fled, and the Marseille airport and railway station would be swarming.

The Marseille police attacked the case of the murdered Russian KGB agents on two fronts. Forensic teams, laboratory technicians, narcotics detectives and *Deuxième Bureau* operatives scrutinized the room where they were found for fingerprints, weapons, blood types, scuff marks, nail parings and hair samples.

At the same time, a pair of Corsican-born homicide detectives dragged Peter Chamberlain into an interrogation room at the back of their precinct house, woke him up with a bucket of ice water, and suggested he would save himself a lot of anguish if he confessed to the double murder. Chamberlain shook his head to clear it. Vaguely he wondered what cumulative damage there would be from the explosion in Brussels followed by a strong woman bending a gun barrel over his head. He saw the man who poured water on him wind up and throw an open-handed blow. He was too groggy to avoid it, and it crashed against his cheek.

It snapped his head back, but the sting cleared his brain.

'Okay, guys,' he said, raising his hands to protect himself. His hands were chained together in front of him. They had him seated in a straight-backed chair under a bright light. They were yelling in French, but when he looked blank, they switched back to the English they'd started with. He felt in his pocket, but his passport wallet was missing. So they knew his name, his nationality, and who he worked for. This was no time to be a lone hero.

All his pockets were empty. He spotted their contents on the window-sill. Gesturing carefully at the pile of paper and gadgets, he said, 'May I have my wallet?'

The cop who had hit him raised his hand, but his partner eased him aside. Both wore shiny grey suits and dark blue shirts. Both were short men, compactly built, and both looked perfectly content to slap him around until he confessed.

'What?' asked the cop.

'Can I call my company? They can vouch for me.'

'Vouch you're a murderer? We already know that.'

'If I'm a murderer, who laid me out on the floor?'

'Your second victim struck you just as you slit his throat.'

'Wait,' said Chamberlain as the second cop came closer to hit him again. The cop kept coming.

'Wait! The guy in the chair. He saw what happened. Ask him.'

One cop hit him, the other grabbed his hair and leaned close to his face. 'He said you tied him up and beat him and killed the Russians when they interrupted you.'

'What?'

They hit him again. Chamberlain tasted blood in his mouth. They closed in and slapped him back and forth between them. A deep and unusual anger rumbled to life inside him. The fact that these clowns spoke English meant they weren't just a pair of weirdos having their private idea of fun. They had their orders to get a confession.

Chamberlain exploded out of the chair, swinging his handcuffed hands like a club, felling one detective with a single blow he had begun at the floor, then kicking the other in the groin even as he lost his balance and fell heavily to the concrete. The first detective lunged groggily for him. Chamberlain rolled aside and levered himself back onto his feet.

The one he'd kicked lay coiled and writhing, but the first detective was coming for him again, climbing to his feet, pawing a blackjack from his pocket. Chamberlain tried to guess which way he would swing. He'd lost the initiative. All he could hope to do now was minimize the damage.

Lady Janet shivered in the cold mist that rose from the Rhône and settled in the river streets of Lyon. It was three in the morning and she was waiting in the car while Trefle jemmied a lock on a warehouse across the street. He waved. She slipped out of the car, closed the door soundlessly, and ran to him.

Trefle slid the door aside and squeezed into the dark interior. Lady Janet followed and fanned out to the right, drawing her gun, covering Trefle while he closed the door. She was reminded of the final days of Grandzau's drug business, when the Chinese merchants were tightening their grip on the market and sending strong-armers to close down independent operations. Grandzau had resisted as long as he could, turning a profit every day, until they fled for their lives. More than once, she'd flattened her body to a wall and raked the hostile darkness with her gun.

She heard a sharp click-click and narrowed her eyes. A second after the warning, Trefle flicked on a flashlight. It was a low-ceilinged room stacked with cardboard-boxed wine bottles stored for shipment to overseas markets. Lady

Janet recognized the label, an indiscriminate mix of non-vintage *vin rouge* no one would drink locally. She exhaled her trapped breath. They were alone. Having seen from the outside that the windows were shuttered, they turned on the lights.

They searched the room, found nothing but the boxes, and moved on, Trefle investigating the low cellar while she ascended steep stairs to the first floor. She had just entered a narrow corridor between stacked wine cases, when Trefle shouted.

Down the stairs, two at a time, across the ground floor, and a quick drop into the cellar, landing crouched and silent. Trefle pointed at a solidly built cabinet. The doors were open and there were gun racks inside, empty but for a single weapon.

'They've gone.'

'Bloody hell.'

The arsenal cabinet had held six guns. Trefle pulled out the last and inspected it with professional delight. Lady Janet recognized the M76 submachinegun that Smith & Wesson hadn't built in years. It was fast, accurate and light. With the stock folded it was twenty inches long. Disassembled it would fit into a medium-sized handbag.

She found a couple of boxes of 9mm Parabellum cartridges in the bottom of the cabinet. 'Break it down,' she told Trefle. 'I'll take it.'

'The *patron* is a good man.'

Lady Janet laid a pair of thousand franc notes on the empty rack and closed the cabinet doors.

The door to the Marseille precinct interrogation room slammed open and a white-haired plain-clothes inspector flanked by uniformed cops burst in. He took in the scene with a quick glance.

Chamberlain took a step back. The detective he had

kicked struggled painfully to his feet. The other detective put his blackjack back in his pocket and nervously saluted the senior officer. The uniformed men rushed Chamberlain and held him from either side.

The white-haired inspector spoke in rapid French. When he was through, the detectives shook their heads. 'Non.'

Chamberlain guessed that they'd been asked if he had confessed.

'Can I call my company?' he asked loudly.

The white-haired man looked at him. Chamberlain met his hostile gaze, his heart sinking. This was no saviour. Then he saw Kreegan's crewcut head through the open door. The steward pushed his way into the room. The white-haired man turned to him and it was obvious they had talked before.

'You're not permitted here.'

Kreegan ignored him. 'That's Mr Chamberlain. Can I take him with me?'

'You don't understand. He is going to be charged with murder.'

'You're kidding,' Kreegan scoffed cheerfully. 'Pete wouldn't hurt a fly. Now I've got the American consul coming down here from a nice party, just to tell you people that Mr Chamberlain is a respectable American citizen.'

The white-haired man was unmoved. He said coldly, 'My answer to the American consul will be the same as my answer to you. This man is to be charged with murder. And no force but a French court will free him from our custody.'

'Come on.'

'Get out.' He snapped his fingers and two more uniformed cops sprang into the room and grabbed Kreegan. 'Goddamnit,' said Kreegan. 'You're making a lousy mistake.'

'I'll arrest you next.'

Kreegan faced Chamberlain for the first time. 'I'm sorry, sir. They're being real pig-headed about it.'

Chamberlain had a sudden thought. 'Call the guy at Dassault.'

'Right!' cried Kreegan, and the white-haired man raised his brows. Stroking his nose thoughtfully, he watched the police escort Kreegan from the interrogation room. Chamberlain watched apprehensively as the Corsican reached for his blackjack.

The white-haired man stayed him with a gesture.

'Dassault?' he asked Chamberlain.

'Yeah. You may have heard of them. They built the Mirage, France's mainstay in the arms trade. Our companies are in partnership.'

Again the white-haired cop stroked his nose. 'We shall see,' he said. He gestured and the Corsican detectives left the room. The others followed and closed the door, leaving a grille open. Chamberlain sat down and waited alone, watched through the grille by a uniformed cop.

It was a long wait. After a while, he stretched out on the hard floor and tried to nap. The clanging door awakened him and he saw grey dawn light spilling through the windows of the outer room.

The interrogation room filled rapidly. The white-haired inspector was back, as were some uniformed officers, and Kreegan, looking pleased. A very young and angry-looking Frenchman, wearing a dinner jacket, came in. He gave Chamberlain a single look of utter contempt, loosed a torrent of shouted French at the white-haired inspector, then waited with crossed arms while Chamberlain's hands were unchained, his possessions, including the shot revolver, returned and Kreegan allowed to lead him away.

'Wait,' said Chamberlain.

'Let's go while the going's good,' said Kreegan, propelling him through the door.

'Back off,' snapped Chamberlain. He brushed past the inspector, and said to the man in the dinner jacket, 'You're with Dassault?'

'I am,' came the tight-lipped answer. 'Paul Gallitan.'

'Thanks for getting me out. Now I want to know what these clowns got out of the old guy tied to the chair.'

Gallitan's eyes rolled skywards. 'I want to go home, Monsieur.'

'Me too. There was a guy tied to a chair in the room where the Russians were killed. Where the cops found me. The cops probably have him here. I want to know what he told them.'

'Monsieur.'

'Mister, if your boss can send you down here to spring me he can boot your ass across the Pyrenees if I ask him to.'

The elegantly dressed man shrugged and raised his open hands high in a what-do-you-want-from-me pose, but he spoke to the inspector.

'*Non!*'

'*Oui!*' the young man bellowed. '*Immédiatement!*'

It was the inspector's turn to shrug. He snapped out orders until officers brought him a carbon copy of a typed sheet of paper. It was in French. Chamberlain glanced at the inspector's stony expression and decided he had pushed him as far as he could.

'Thank you.' He turned to the man from Dassault. 'Come on.'

Kreegan led them out of the station house and into a waiting limousine. Gallitan protested.

'We'll drop you as soon as you translate this thing. Get in.'

133

Kreegan drove. Chamberlain sank gratefully into the plush velour seat and said, 'What does it say?'

The Frenchman scanned the paper. 'This is an official confession form. The witness claims that a man and a woman came to the pension he runs, tied him to a chair and threatened bodily harm if he didn't respond to their questions. He told them he would comply. They asked if five men who had been staying at his *pension* had left suddenly. He said they had. They asked where they had gone and he said Lyon.'

'Where in Lyon?'

'He didn't tell the police.'

'Would he tell me?'

'Not without a serious bribe. You see these veterans and *colons* and mercenaries all know each other and of course stick together. They wouldn't have told him exactly where they were going, but he might have guessed. At any rate, he didn't tell the police.'

'What else does it say?'

'He told the police that the five were all marksmen.'

'When did they leave?'

'This morning.'

'Are you sure?'

'Yes.'

'That doesn't make sense. I'm assuming they were hired by Grandzau – the man who kidnapped Charles Hammond – but that was three days ago.' He looked at the early morning sunlight splashing the tops of the houses. 'Four days ago,' he corrected, half to himself, half aloud. 'Oh, for Christ's sake. Is this whole thing a wild-goose chase?'

'I don't think so,' said Gallitan. 'Karl Grandzau's name appears several times in this confession.'

'What?'

'The Marseille police know what you and the Russians were looking for. They've been watching the KGB and the

134

CIA for days now. So they asked. The veteran claimed that Grandzau visited his building last week.'

'Kreegan. Stop at a phone!'

Kreegan pulled up. The Frenchman opened the door. 'I'll take a cab.'

'You stay where you are. I'm going to make a call. Then we're going to go see that old guy and you're going to translate.'

'Monsieur, I left a lady – '

'My boss at Comptel will be very grateful to your boss at Dassault. Give you something to celebrate with your lady tomorrow.'

Chamberlain dialled London, direct, and got through to Farquhar, who sounded very pleased, considering the hour.

'We have the plane in Iceland.'

'Hammond?'

'No passengers. The Icelandic authorities are holding the pilot, but he swears he was hired to deliver it from Stornoway to Reykjavik. There are indications that he's telling the truth.'

'That means Hammond got off in the Hebrides.'

'Probably. We're searching Lewis and Harris right now.'

'Should I come up there?'

'I don't think we'll find him here. Even though there are many remote places in the islands, the folk all know each other. It wouldn't be such a safe place to hide. Hammond could be on an outlying croft, but much more likely he's been spirited away on a fishing boat.'

'Could he have flown out?'

'Not from Stornoway, though he might have been picked up by helicopter from an outer island.' Farquhar paused, then added, reflectively, 'I think we can assume he's in our general territory.'

'England and Northern Europe.'

'Admittedly a large area. However, there's something else that might interest you. About your partners. Mr Nagumo departed quite suddenly for Rome, at the invitation of the Japanese Embassy there. And your arms merchant, Mr Streicher, left for Germany, where he promptly disappeared.'

'So?'

'They had dinner together before they left.'

'Oh.'

'It sounds likely to me they've learned something about Hammond and have made new arrangements.'

'Sounds that way,' Chamberlain admitted glumly.

'I understand you had trouble in Marseille.'

'Not as much trouble as the Russians. I'll talk to you soon. I think I'm on to something.'

The old Algerian veteran looked as if he'd been indoors a long time. He had the leathery skin and the glare-narrowed eyes of a desert campaigner, but his complexion was dead white. It was as if he had fled the sun the day he was mustered out and hidden indoors ever since. He uttered a weary protest when he saw Chamberlain, Kreegan and the man from Dassault waiting in his spare, neat little apartment.

Gallitan had his instructions. He spoke kindly in French, telling the man that Chamberlain wanted to know only what he had already told the Marseille police. He hastened to add that the *Américain* bore no ill feelings about his false testimony concerning the death of the Russians that couldn't be forgotten in exchange for a quick and honest response. He warned that the *Américain* already knew much of what he had told the police so that a false answer would likely be recognized. Such a response would be regarded as hostile and would prolong the presence of these three strangers in the lodgings of a man who doubt-lessly wanted to do nothing more than go to bed.

'*Où est Grandzau?*'

The Algerian veteran stared at Gallitan for a long moment. His answer ran long and angry and when he was through, Gallitan translated it for Chamberlain.

'He says, how would a simple *concierge* know the whereabouts of the man who kidnapped the great Charles Hammond?'

'He said more than that,' said Chamberlain.

Gallitan hesitated. 'Uh, yes. He said that you are as stupid as the stupid police. He asks us to leave.'

'Find out when Grandzau was here. How many times. And who he hired.'

Gallitan spoke in French.

The veteran shrugged and replied irritably. Chamberlain watched his angry eyes, looking for the involuntary narrow-ing of a lie, wondering what sort of a soldier he had been thirty years ago. He might have served in 'Nam in the early fifties when they still called it French Indochina and the Vietnamese hadn't yet formed the world's deadliest heavy infantry.

Gallitan translated. 'Grandzau came here twice. A week ago, and a month or so before that. The first time, he hired five men. He took them with him. Last week he came back and hired five more, but they didn't leave until yesterday when they heard that the Russians were searching for them. He doesn't know much about the first five. They weren't here long. The second group he got to know. They were all great marksmen. Twice a week they would drive to the country and practise. He went along once to watch.'

'What weapons did they practise with?'

'He says they had a rifle and several handguns.'

'What kind?'

137

'He said that it is time for you to either leave or start paying for information.'

Chamberlain nodded at Kreegan who produced a fat roll and peeled off a hundred francs. The veteran stuffed the bills into his shirt pocket and answered the question. '9mm pistols and a Uzi automatic rifle,' said Gallitan. The Frenchman spoke again. 'He wants more money.'

'Give it to him,' snapped Chamberlain. He'd lucked with this guy and he wanted all the man had. Kreegan passed him a couple of hundred francs.

Gallitan translated. 'They went to Lyon to get more weapons.'

'Where?'

The veteran didn't know. He licked his lips, watching Kreegan's roll, and Chamberlain could see that he wished he knew the location of the arsenal in Lyon.

'What kind of weapons?'

The Frenchman's reply was animated. He was reaching for the money when he finished. Kreegan gave him a hundred francs while Gallitan tried to translate. Uncertainty made his own accent stronger.

'Smith & Wesson,' he said, distorting the Smith with a long *ee* sound. 'Submachinegun?'

'Right.'

'M76. He said 9mm.'

Chamberlain raised his brows. A beautiful weapon. But why were they only now going into action? Four days after Hammond was kidnapped. The first crew did the kidnapping. Was the second for protection during the auction?

'Was Grandzau alone when he came here the first time?'

'He was with a Maltese,' Gallitan translated. 'Both times.'

'Where were the others going after they got guns in

138

Lyon?' he asked, with little hope of getting an answer. To his surprise, the veteran answered, 'Brest.'

'Brest,' said Gallitan.

'I got that,' said Chamberlain. Brest on the northwest tip of France where the English Channel met the Atlantic Ocean. 'Why would they tell this guy that?'

The Algerian veteran grinned and reached for Kreegan's money. Chamberlain nodded and Kreegan peeled off several more large bills.

'They made many long distance telephone calls to Brest this past week. They kept asking him for change for the telephone. Then he heard them make hotel reservations.'

'What hotel?' Chamberlain snapped. Gallitan asked.

'He doesn't know.'

'Screw!'

Why would Grandzau keep the two groups apart? Easier to work with a small group the first time? Easier to get away with a small group? Or maybe it was like bringing in fresh reserves. The second group was saved the tension of the kidnapping and the immediate aftermath. And why Brest? He needed the long distance telephone records from here to Brest to trace the hotel. But he needed it done discreetly so he'd get there ahead of the French police, Interpol, the CIA and the goddamned Russians. Comptel probably had good connections with the phone people over here. He'd drop this in Helen Thorp's lap.

There was something else. The veteran was watching him, awaiting another question, eager to dip into Kreegan's roll again. 'Ask him who the man and woman were who slugged me and killed the Russians.'

The eager expression faded abruptly. The veteran said he didn't know. Chamberlain didn't believe him, but the sudden terror in his eyes promised that neither bribes nor threats would get the truth. Maybe he didn't know. Maybe it was just a healthy fear of the kind of man and woman who could slaughter a pair of KGB heavies and flatten an ex-US Navy SEAL in less time than it took to think about it. Despite himself, Chamberlain grinned at the veteran. Franc notes of enormous denominations blanketed the man's lap and stuck from his pockets like florid lettuce.

'You better get to the bank, old-timer, before somebody mugs you.'

Gallitan dutifully started to translate, but Chamberlain was already out the door, motioning him and Kreegan to follow. He had no doubt that he'd milked Marseille dry, but by now there should be answers at the Comptel house to the questions he had asked the night before.

The teleprinters had heaped data paper onto the bright tiled floor of the bedroom overlooking the pool and the sea. The CIA, Comptel's information centre, and Helen Thorp had all transmitted.

He called the CIA and had a long talk with Arnie Fast, whose information was fresher than Inspector Farquhar's. Both Streicher and Nagumo were on the move again. Worse, so were the Russians. While they talked he read the computer printouts answering the questions he had put to Comptel, and to the Agency. When he was done with Arnie, he read the last page in the printer, which was from Helen Thorp.

A teletype machine's full caps typeface always exaggerated a message's importance, but Helen Thorp's communiqué had the impact of a three-line, seven-column headline on the front page of the New York *Times*. Beginning, WHAT THE HELL DO YOU THINK . . . it blamed Chamberlain for destroying the agreement among the companies to buy back Hammond, and ended, AND COMPTEL NEVER HAS NOR EVER WILL AUTHORIZE ITS EMPLOYEES TO COMMIT MURDER.

Chamberlain turned on the transmitter and typed, I DIDN'T DO IT.

A minute later he picked up the ringing telephone.

'I certainly hope that's true,' said Helen Thorp.

'The Marseille cops believe in me.'

'The Marseille cops believe in the Mirage. Where is Hammond?'

'A short boatride from Brest.'

'What? Brest, France? Are you sure?'

'Reasonably.'

'How do you know?'

'I don't *know*, but everything seems to point to Brest. The CIA tells me that the Russians are heading there. The mercenary soldiers I just missed here in Marseille were heading for Brest – with a stop-over in Lyon for guns. At the same time, Comptel tells me that a corporation that Grandzau used to use to buy equipment purchased a whole pile of microwave power units from our French subsidiary.'

'What the devil do microwave power units have to do with kidnapping Charles Hammond?' demanded Helen Thorp.

'Listen, lady, I've been up all night and people have been hitting me with disturbing frequency, so would you let me just finish the good stuff?'

To Chamberlain's amazement, she was contrite. 'I'm sorry, Pete. I get very tense sitting around here not being able to control what's going on over there. Please go ahead.'

'I don't know what Grandzau needed microwave power units for, but he needed them in Brest. That's where the order was shipped!'

'Oh.'

'In addition, a friend in London – '

'Inspector Farquhar?'

'Yes – tells me that Hans Streicher and Kaga Nagumo had dinner at the Savoy last night. Together. Then Streicher flew to Essen and Nagumo went to Rome. So I called friends of my friendliest friend at Langley who informed me that Hans Streicher left Essen late this morning, about the same time Nagumo left Rome.'

'Do you understand what that means?' she asked sharply.

'Maybe they're on to something.'

'Maybe they are. But they're not sharing it. They're breaking with the consortium because of that fiasco in Brussels. They're playing into the auctioneer's hands. We'll end up trying to outbid each other while the Russians waltz off with Hammond. Goddamnit, Pete. Where do you think they're going? Brest?'

'Maybe. I'm told that Streicher's in a chartered plane. He didn't file a flight plan for Brest, but he's heading in that general direction. Nagumo's flying to Paris. He doesn't have a reservation, in his name anyway, on the connecting flight to Brest, but there's a train that's almost as fast.'

'Well, what the hell are you doing in Marseille?'

'Waiting for the plane's landing gear to get fixed.'

'*What?*'

'Relax. Everything can't work right every time. They're fixing it and I'll still get there faster than commercial.'

'But that's insanity,' she shouted. 'We're paying them to do a job!'

'Everything can't work right every time,' Chamberlain repeated soothingly, as Kreegan handed him the message from the airport with a doleful glower. Helen Thorp made an exasperated noise on the telephone and Kreegan pounded his fist into his cupped hand like a centre fielder who'd dropped an easy fly in full view of the television cameras.

'Good-bye,' said Chamberlain. 'I'm going out to the airport. If they don't get it fixed I'll buy a new one.' He started to hang up, then remembered the hotel. 'By the way, Ms Thorp. Do me a favour. Get somebody big in the French phone system to trace the calls from this number to Brest in the last month.' He gave her the number of the phone in the *pension*. 'There should be some calls to a hotel. But try to keep it quiet. I think it gives us a leg up over the rest of them.'

'Pete,' she said softly.

'What?' Was she going to tell him to be careful?

'You really fucked up.'

BOOK II

14

Events, Helen Thorp worried, were lunging out of control.

Chamberlain had sounded weary and thoroughly beaten on the phone. God knew what would happen next. Groggy herself, from a long, hard night and a hideously early wake-up call, she went out for a walk in the cold to clear her head. She headed up Sixth Avenue, sinking deliciously into her warm sable. She had Hammond to thank for the magnificent, hooded coat. Indirectly. As she had him to thank for so much else in her life.

It occurred to her that Hammond must have looked like Pete Chamberlain when he was in *his* thirties – athletic, broad in the shoulders, and not particularly tall. A solid chest and a light step. She shrugged the thought away. Aspects of other men, associates, even strangers on the street, often reminded her of Hammond. For Charles Hammond was not a man who gently left the mind. It meant nothing. The differences were soon more apparent than the similarities.

Charles Hammond pounced into rooms, as if to devour the occupants. Chamberlain entered warily, eyes quick and alert, like a medium-size predator ready for the deadly defence if it couldn't escape.

She had first laid eyes on the dazzling spectacle of Charles Hammond 'doin' business', as he called it, five years ago across a conference table in the Elysée Palace. The French Government was underwriting a microwave communications net in Mozambique. Comptel had bid to build the amplifying stations. Alfred had hired Hammond, the deal-maker, to broker with the Mozambique government and had sent Helen as his representative, her first major job for Alfred, she recalled. Her career-maker.

Hammond took her breath away. Nearly twenty years older than her, he radiated sexual energy. He had hazel eyes and ginger hair and an intriguing mouth half-hidden under a bristly ginger moustache. He had pounced into the room and at the table had unleashed the lightning mind for which he was legendary. A pirate, she thought, a brilliant, hungry, sensual pirate – utterly dazzling, so self-assured that his very confidence shimmered erotically.

Making the deal was exacting work, under the eye of the French who were extending their influence into east and southern Africa, and Hammond had handled it beautifully, garnering additional subcontracts for Comptel's Paris subsidiaries in the process. Throughout the subtlest complexities of the negotiation, his bright hazel eyes rarely left hers, and she quickly realized he was making extra points off the French solely to please her.

He asked her to dinner. She was twenty-eight years old and terrified, for the first time in her life, of a man. Hammond was too powerful for her to handle. He would demolish the vital barriers she had erected between her business and private life. He had the power to devour her, to take her hand and leap with her into a vortex of sensation. She knew it as surely as she knew that she could not afford to be devoured by anyone. For she already had her goal – chief executive officer of Comptel before she was thirty-five – and to protect it she chose her sensations carefully, and took her pleasures in portions she could manage.

She refused his invitation, boarded the Concorde as soon as she drafted Comptel's letters of agreement, and fled to New York. Courting – she recalled with a smile – was too tame a word for Hammond's pursuit. He came

148

after her like an army, in motion everywhere, omnipresent, exotic and implacable. Shortly after Paris Alfred had cornered the supply of a new silicon chip, which Mishuma Inc. wanted badly. Alfred sent her to Tokyo to see how badly. Poor Mr Nagumo had put her up in a beautiful cottage in a garden in the centre of Tokyo while they negotiated. Hammond telephoned, inviting her to dinner again. She refused, again, though by then images of him were daily stirring her mind and body. She caught him climbing over the garden wall with a silk bag filled with orchids. And she had let him stay for tea.

Soon afterwards, Comptel was working a three-way deal with Decca and the Indian government to build satellite ground stations in the north. Decca had the Indian contacts, Comptel a brand-new easily maintained receiver, but for some reason details were going badly. Alfred sent her to London to pry things loose. She boarded a mysteriously empty first-class section of the Pan Am Clipper, and when she climbed the staircase to the upper-deck dining room, Hammond was waiting alone, at a single table set for two.

He rose, resplendent in white tie. 'Champagne?'

'I don't like being trapped like this.'

'I won't stay without your permission.' He pressed a call button and a grinning stewardess appeared with a parachute, and helped him strap it on.

'Wait,' Helen laughed. 'Where are all the other people?'

'On the regular plane. I chartered this one.'

'The whole plane? Business and economy, too?'

Hammond shrugged. 'We might want to take a walk after dinner.'

'Pan Am conspired to put me aboard?'

'They owe me a couple. Listen, before we eat. Your Decca deal. They're pissed off. They're not used to being number two to anybody in high tech, and they certainly don't want to be embarrassed in front of their Indian clients. Work out something face-saving and you're home free – champagne?'

As they ate, that night over the North Atlantic, he was as exciting and charming as any man she had ever met. He seemed as delighted by her as she was captivated by him. They talked for hours at the table, walked the great empty ship, watched the dawn from the cockpit, and returned to the dining room for breakfast. He seemed to know her deepest thoughts and though he never touched her more than to take her hand, he seemed to know every yearning in her body. Back in New York, the Decca deal complete, a gift was waiting – a crystal and gold mirror in its own rosewood travelling box. 'Look how lucky I am,' said his note. 'See what I see.'

Then the coat. She had agreed to lunch on a business day, not for the mirror, but for his beautiful note. He took her to Barbetta and everything she had feared had happened.

She tried to explain how she knew he would consume her, but it came out confused and she heard herself sounding like any woman trying to convince any man that she had a career as important and as brilliant as his.

'It needs all of me,' she concluded lamely, miles from her meaning.

'Brillianter,' Hammond smiled, stroking her palm, making her shiver and wish it was her breast in his hand, her nipple between his fingers, her mouth on his smile. 'When I was your age I was a lot less impressive. You've got the stuff to do it both, have it all. You can have Comptel and be happy with me too.'

'Not with you, I couldn't. I would drown.'

He seared her hand with pleasure and all that saved her determination to protect her career was a meeting with an assistant secretary of state that she could not cancel. That night Revillon had delivered a Norwegian silver fox coat. She sent it back, took two years of bonus money out of a rising market, and bought the sable by herself. She had won a victory more symbolic than real. Because for Hammond, she knew well, there was never defeat, merely delay, and he conspired to be always near, thrilling her in a hundred ways.

Helen trembled, recalling the joy of his final 'victory'. Her 'defeat'.

They bumped heads getting into a limousine. She had actually opened a scratch on his thin, Celtic skin and she leaned close to wipe the red spot with her finger. He kissed her throat. Intoxicated by his nearness and his scent, she seized his face in her hands, forced her mouth over his. They flew to an island, someplace. Probably the Caribbean, because it was close. She literally could not recall the unimportant details. He chartered a boat. He was a satyr and she was more than ready to take him on and had, in fact, she remembered, her body jelly just thinking of it, devoured him as surely as he had devoured her.

'Marry me?' he asked bluntly when they finally hit New York like a tangled something the tide had flung on the beach. But she had said, wisely, Hammond seemed to understand, 'Give me five years.'

Who could have guessed, she thought sadly, that at the end of those five years Charles Hammond would be a prisoner and that Helen Thorp would be one of many invited to bid for his life?

Chamberlain flew commercial from Marseille to Brest after repeated delays in repairing the Comptel jet. Kreegan flew with him, shared his disappointment that the mercenaries had already left their Brest hotel and took care of renting a car while Chamberlain checked in with Comptel and the Agency's Brest station.

Comptel relayed a message from Helen Thorp. For what it was worth, she wanted him to know that René Rice had come up with a five million dollar contribution to the consortium's ransom fund. She added a zinger, 'Maybe you should have gone into barley futures, too. They sure beat condos,' and he regretted mentioning his brother's offer the long night they had tracked Hammond from Cowan's office.

The CIA turned out to be more helpful and less sarcastic. For openers they told Chamberlain that Hammond had made five secret trips to Brazil last year and had at least twice conferred at length with South African security forces. While the Brest station head was conveying this information a call came in from one of their field men. Kaga Nagumo had driven from Paris and rendezvoused this morning with Hans Streicher in a fishing village on the Channel coast.

Kreegan rented a Citroën. Chamberlain observed the way he drove out of the city, concluded he could do a lot better, and took the wheel when they reached the countryside. Seeming relieved, Kreegan unfolded some maps and navigated as Chamberlain headed north towards the Channel coast, driving faster and faster as he mastered the technique of making the front-wheel drive pull the massive car around the numerous twists and bends.

'Oughta see her any minute,' said Kreegan, jabbing the map. They topped a rise and the land dropped away to the grey Channel curtained indistinctly under low-hanging cloud and notched in the near distance by a French harbour village.

The buildings were stone, their roofs slate. They were clustered around an English Channel tide slip – a miniature artificial harbour formed by a pair of rock jetties that thrust out into the Channel, enclosing the natural basin, and protected by a massive steel tide gate. There was room inside for two or three small coastal freighters.

The harbour looked empty, but as they barrelled down the slope Chamberlain noticed the tide gates were swinging open. He floored it and the Citroën tore down the hill. He wove into twisting streets, blaring his horn at old cars and muddy farm trucks, and rounded a low, stone warehouse which had hidden the harbour quay from the road. Tied to the quay beside a squat crane was a sleek, narrow English-built wooden motor torpedo boat. Grey as the clouds and the Channel itself, it looked of World War II vintage, similar to an American PT. She was a pretty sight, but the amphibious tank sitting beside her on a flatbed truck was not.

'Jesus Christ,' said Kreegan, 'that's a Mowag Piranha 6 x 6.'

Chamberlain got out of the car, eyeing the cradle fitted on the boat's fore deck to hold the Piranha and the tubes on its turret – six Oerlikon 80mm rocket launchers.

'Wait here,' he told Kreegan, and hurried past the French dockers and fishermen who were watching with amusement the furious action surrounding the tank and motor torpedo boat.

Hans Streicher, his vast bulk encased in a steaming ski sweater, was bellowing instructions at a gang of husky young Germans struggling with a tangle of chain slings that hung from the rusty, steam-powered crane, which puffed and creaked ominously. Little Nagumo, neat in a blue suit, trailed the arms dealer like a robot, his own steps dogged by half a dozen Japanese bodyguards.

An ancient Frenchman in blue overalls lounged at the crane controls, one eye squinted against the smouldering cigarette affixed to his lip, his face a mask of doubtful expectation. He nodded occasional agreement with remarks called out by the watching dockers, and sneered when the Germans glowered.

'*Dumkopf!*' Streicher loosed a torrent of invective, yet as Chamberlain drew closer he saw that the German was struggling to hide a grin and that despite the chaos on the dock Streicher appeared to be very happy. He spotted Chamberlain, as did Nagumo. The Japanese frowned and said something to his bodyguards.

'*Bonjour*, my friend,' Streicher bellowed. 'What a morning.' A broad gesture with a massive hand laid exuberant claim to the rising sun, the blueing sky, the grey Channel and the green hills of France.

'Morning,' said Chamberlain. 'Good morning, Mr Nagumo.'

Streicher grinned at the tank. 'You see my idea?'

'I think I get the general drift.'

Streicher nodded vigorously. 'The boat's been converted to a motor yacht. They stripped her guns and replaced her Rolls Royces with smaller diesels to save fuel.' He grinned again at the vehicle on the flatbed truck. 'But that is going to give her some teeth again.'

'Where the hell did you find the Piranha?'

Streicher's good humour faded. 'I have *four hundred* of them corroding on a dock in Rotterdam, where they are stuck until Charles Hammond is free to complete negotiations with the Emirate sheik who promised to buy them.'

'Where's Hammond?'

'Ah, yes, but that's a secret,' Streicher smiled.

'We agreed to work together, Mr Streicher, Mr Nagumo.'

Nagumo drew himself up primly. 'That was before you ran amok in Brussels, Mr Chamberlain. We had to question your stability.'

Chamberlain was catapulted back to grade-school when he was banned from a birthday party for playing too rough.

'*My* stability? Your latter-day Axis is going to stick this tank on the boat and go shoot 'em up someplace? Grandzau sees this thing coming he's going to freak. Hammond's going to end up dead.'

'He won't see us coming,' said Nagumo, nodding at the Germans trooping aboard the boat with boxes stamped *Fragile*. 'ECM gear. Jammers to block his radar.'

'Grandzau's on a ship?'

Streicher said, 'My people traced a large purchase of anti-personnel mines to a freighter chartered by a paper French corporation which Grandzau used to use to buy equipment and rent safe houses. An old ship, which has to hug the shore. Mr Nagumo learned that a Japanese radical sold Grandzau powerful radar jammers, apparently to render the ship electronically invisible. His government has provided countermeasure gear to get through.'

'What makes you think it's near here?'

'Your CIA thinks it is.'

Chamberlain felt his gut drop. Arnie hadn't told him about a ship. What the hell was going on? 'What are the mines for?' he asked.

'Final defence,' Streicher answered cheerfully. 'Booby-trap the ship.'

'But Hammond –'

'Grandzau won't blow *himself* up, or Hammond. Charles Hammond's his ticket to safety.'

'You're going to get him killed.'

'You worry too much.'

'Goddamned right I worry.'

'It's too late for that, Mr Chamberlain,' Nagumo said. 'You've had your chance and failed.'

'I'm coming with you.'

'No.' Nagumo nodded and two of his guards moved

close to Chamberlain. 'You'll remain with these gentlemen until Mr Streicher and I have Hammond.' Chamberlain catalogued their stance, their hands, and bulging torsos. He figured he could probably take them, at the cost of a week in hospital.

'Even if you somehow outfight Grandzau without killing Hammond, you'll lose him to the Russians.'

'Not if we get there first.'

'I thought the CIA knows also.'

'They don't know as much as we do,' said Streicher, turning back to the crane.

Nagumo uttered Japanese. Chamberlain's guards indicated he should return to his car. The others removed their blue suit jackets and their ties, rolled up their shirt sleeves, and addressed the tangled chain slings. Streicher told his men, 'Get everything else on board.'

They began loading food, water and ammunition, while Nagumo's men strung the slings under the Piranha. A heavy truck with a hydraulic back lift rumbled onto the quay. Streicher paid the driver with a stack of franc notes. The driver lowered rows of thirty-gallon diesel fuel drums to the cobblestones, where, cursing the weight, Streicher's men rolled them up the gang plank onto the boat.

Shouts on the quay and a confident snort from the steam crane drew them on deck. The Japanese had swathed the Piranha in chains and the crane operator had just tried an experimental tug. Streicher's soldiers and the French loungers watched expectantly. Nagumo moved away from the cradle, but Streicher scrambled onto it and resumed bellowing orders, directions to the crane operator augmented by vast and enthusiastic arm signals. The lifting cables tightened and slowly the amphibious armoured vehicle's six wheels rose from the flatbed truck one by one until the Piranha hung in the air, its wheels drooping like wet pigtails.

156

To Nagumo's eye, the vehicle, which looked as if it weighed nine or ten tons, was tilting ominously. One of his bodyguards seemed to be of the same mind; the young man's brows were knitted with concern. The other bodyguards were smiling broadly, however, proud of their handiwork with the creaking chains, and the crane operator appeared monumentally unconcerned. Pointedly ignoring Streicher's shouted signals, he lifted the Piranha several feet higher and swung it slowly off the truck, over the quay, over the foot of water between the dock and the motor torpedo boat, over Streicher on the cradle.

For the first time, he removed his cigarette from his mouth. Then he thrust his head through the open window of his cab and hissed loudly enough for the entire quay to hear, '*Raus!*'

He threw a lever and the Piranha plummeted to the deck of the motor torpedo boat like a toppling castle. Streicher scrambled off the cradle, grinning mightily, and clapped his hands together when his weapon landed dead-centre, its wheels nestling into their waiting chocks. The boat settled deeply in the water.

'Like a baby in its momma's lap,' he called to the Frenchman. The Frenchman lighted a new cigarette and smoked while the Japanese loosed the chains and snaked them out from under the Piranha. When they had done and the Frenchman had secured his crane and shut down the boiler and strolled away, the tide had risen to cover the rocks near the harbour mouth. Streicher took a long look at the rocket-bearing weapon astride the sleek and low-lying boat, then ordered it to be covered with canvas.

'We might alarm the French Navy,' he shouted laughingly. He strode over to Chamberlain and slapped his shoulder with a consoling grin. 'Don't look so sad, my friend. There are plenty of fights in the world. You'll find another.'

Then he leaped into his boat, scrambled up to the flying bridge, scanned the instruments, checked that the twin gear levers were in neutral, and hit the port starter switch. Exhaust rumbled astern. Streicher jabbed the starboard starter and the second engine burbled into life. Chamberlain listened to them warming at eight hundred rpm. The German and the Jap were nuts; overloaded and underpowered, the boat would be lucky to make twelve knots. Streicher shouted. His men piled aboard, paratroop boots clunking on the decks. Nagumo stepped aboard and joined him on the bridge. Another shout and they cast off the lines.

'Your shot revolver is under the seat,' Chamberlain said to Kreegan. 'Show it to these clowns. I'm going on the boat.'

'Right behind you,' said Kreegan, scooping the gun off the floor and waving it in the face of the nearest guard.

'No. Get some air support. See where we go.' He hit the cobbles running. The harbour gate was wide open, letting a low swell into the basin. Streicher looked back, saw Chamberlain running, and reached for the gear levers.

He was thirty feet from the boat, which was drifting from the quay, when Hans Streicher threw both engines into forward. The motor torpedo boat erupted in a sheet of flame, rolled on its side, and sank like a stone.

15

'I should kill you for that,' snapped Lady Janet. Her hand was deep in her raincoat pocket.

Henri Trefle gave her an owlish leer. 'No, you shouldn't. You need me.'

'I needed you in there, you bastard, and where the blazes were you?' She jerked her thumb at the grimy hotel across the street from the bar where Trefle was drinking. A sea chill crept into the low-ceilinged room. It was late morning in Brest.

'Was that your idea of a joke?'

Trefle shrugged. 'I heard you tell the hotel manager that you would screw him if he told you where Grandzau's men went.'

'I assumed you would have the sense to get me out of it once we had the information.'

'I've given up trying to guess your tastes,' Trefle replied with an innocent smile. 'What was he like?'

A red dot of anger glowed high on each of her tanned cheeks.

'I had to break his arm.' Her blouse was wet where the pig had slobbered on her breast. He'd torn some buttons and left marks on her skin. Her gun filled her hand in her pocket and a red rage was pushing her to shoot Trefle, but he was right. Now she needed him badly. She was shooting morphine for the pain and amphetamines to stay awake and they were making her crazy.

'What did he tell you?'

'A taxi took them down the coast last night and left them at a country inn.'

Trefle put down his glass. 'Let's go.'

She followed him out the door to their car. She drove. Trefle dozed until they were out of Brest, heading west. When he awakened, she said, 'The manager told me that two Americans were there before us, also looking for Grandzau's men.'

'CIA,' grunted Trefle.

'It sounded like the man from Belgium I hit in Marseille.'

'Did he offer to screw the hotel manager?'

'Don't push me, Henri.'

The glass knife seemed to leap from his arm. Fast as she was, there was nothing she could do. The car was moving at a hundred kilometres and the road twisted right and left. His knife lay across her throat.

'I'll do what I please to you.'

She sat as rigidly as she could, neither slowing nor accelerating the car, moving only to shift the steering wheel. She'd been a fool to let her anger get the better of her. There was no defence. What did a crazy man care for the speed they were travelling?

'What shall I do to you?' he asked softly, pressing the knife until a sudden burning told her he had broken the skin at her larynx.

'Wait until you have Hammond,' she breathed.

'I don't need you any longer. We're close.'

'What if we're not? What will you do for money?'

'We're close. I can feel it.'

She said nothing. Denying what he believed might sound like a threat. He was crazy. She'd been crazy enough at times in her own life to know how close she was to death. He would do exactly what he wanted. And he would do it suddenly.

'Henri. There's an intersection ahead. I'm slowing the car. I have to stop for the traffic signal. It's turned red.'

'Don't slow down.'

She felt a thin stream of blood trickle down her throat. It tickled. She held her foot steady on the accelerator as they closed swiftly on the intersection. It was empty. Then she saw a tanker lorry approaching from the right, followed by a stream of cars the slower vehicle had backed up on the narrow road. Henri didn't seem to notice. But when she nudged the accelerator to try to cross ahead of the tanker, he smiled and shook his head.

'No. Don't go faster.'

They were seconds from the intersection.

'Henri. Please.'

He stamped on her foot, driving pain through the bones and the accelerator to the floor. The car leaped through the crossroads, missed the blaring tanker by inches, and shot down the coast.

Trefle took his foot from hers and his knife from her throat. He settled back on his side of the car, smiling to himself. Slowly, her breathing returned to normal. She dabbed the blood from her throat with her handkerchief, then pressed the cloth to the cut until the bleeding stopped.

After a while he stirred. He slipped the glass knife back into his arm sheath. When he spoke, he sounded sad.

'I want Hammond as much as you want Grandzau. I want to kill Hammond much more than I want to kill you. But I wanted to see you afraid.'

Lady Janet stared at the road and said nothing.

'Did you beg when they whipped you?'

'No.'

'I didn't think so. But this time you begged. I wanted that very much.'

They passed a sign pointing down a side road which seemed to lead to the sea. 'Three miles, Henri.'

'Drive for two and a half. I can't run like I used to.'

They put the car behind a hedgerow and walked until

they saw the inn at a quarter-mile distance. It was just past noon. If the men were there they might be at lunch. It was a good time to attack.

'Where were you going?' Chamberlain asked one of the Japanese bodyguards. The man stared at the water.

'Mr Nagumo did not say where they were going. Only he and the German knew.'

Chamberlain tried to figure what to do next. Kreegan returned.

'None of 'em knew, boss.'

'Who'd you talk to?' asked Chamberlain.

'Krauts. Commando types. They'd worked for Streicher before, riding shotgun on gun shipments, that sort of stuff. They did what they were told and they didn't ask questions. What do you suppose it was? Bilge fumes?'

'No. She was diesel.'

Back in the car Kreegan glanced in the rearview mirror. 'Cops.'

Chamberlain had already heard the klaxons approaching the village. 'Let's get out of here. I need a phone.'

Kreegan waited until the police vans drove past them onto the quay, then turned the car and left quickly.

'First hotel you see,' said Chamberlain. 'There. Perfect. Drop me and get some diving gear. Tanks and wet suit.'

Arnie Fast had offered the Brest station number when he had called him from Marseille. Chamberlain had checked in with them when he had arrived. But now a different voice asked for a code word and hung up when he used the word Arnie had given him earlier. A transatlantic call to Langley elicited a new code word, but when he called Brest again he got no answer, at first, and then a recording. Kreegan came back at that point and took over the telephoning, while Chamberlain checked out the diving gear.

'What? That's crazy. I told you we talked to them this morning. Twice. A couple of hours ago . . . Oh. Right. Thanks.'

Making an obvious effort to control himself, he gently cradled the telephone. 'It's disconnected. Just like that. They got a new number, but it's unlisted.'

'Give me the phone.'

Chamberlain called Langley again, but Arnie's secretary said that Arnie was in conference.

'When should I call?'

Her voice was as flat as a blackjack dealer's. 'He'll be in conference late into the evening and then he's going directly to dinner.'

'Tell him I understand.'

He hung up and stared at the ceiling. Kreegan had the good sense not to ask. After a while Chamberlain swung his feet off the bed, stripped, and worked his way into the wet suit. Kreegan helped him on with the jacket. Chamberlain zipped up and snapped shut the crotch piece. Then he put his overcoat and shoes on over the wet suit, while Kreegan put the tanks and regulator and the rest of his clothes in the suitcase he brought the gear in.

Chamberlain looked around the rented room, checking that he'd left nothing behind. He was trying to think of how he felt. Lonely.

'You know what happened?' he asked Kreegan.

Kreegan seemed embarrassed by the intimacy. 'I guess I can guess.'

'I've been cut off.'

Kreegan said, 'Do you mind me asking, sir? Do you still work for them?'

'No. I really did retire. I work for Comptel. My old friends there do me a favour, I do them a favour. It's a good deal for them too, having a friend in a big multi-national. It works both ways. They get a lot of information from ex-guys like me.'

'So why'd they cut you off?'

'I don't know.'

He did know, but the sense of caution was flowing steadily now. He was alone. For the first time since he'd joined the SEALs.

'It doesn't make sense,' Kreegan objected. 'Why'd they change their mind on you?'

'I don't know,' Chamberlain said. He spoke shortly, to shut Kreegan up. He knew exactly why they'd cut him off. And it had nothing to do with changing their mind on him or losing trust. They had stopped helping him with the Comptel operation for the simple reason that they had started their own.

He'd been their stalking horse. The only reason to desert a stalking horse was to draw ahead. Using him and trailing the KGB, they'd found Grandzau. He felt a little stupid. He'd probably given them the clue and he hadn't known it.

All he could do now was try to catch up. If they got there first and got in a jam Charles Hammond was dead. They could be trusted to put together a crackerjack operation. They weren't the dummies they led the newspapers to believe. But what if the KGB was drawing the same bead? There'd be a regular little war, with Charles Hammond in the cross-fire.

Exactly what Ms Thorp had hired him to prevent.

So he had to get Hammond first. With no help from the short-lived consortium, or Arnie Fast at the CIA. And Grandzau, it appeared, had teeth in the form of an agent on the ground, for the explosion had been no accident. Helen Thorp had relayed Grandzau's latest message:

HERR STREICHER AND HERR NAGUMO HAVE WITHDRAWN THEIR BIDS FROM THE PENDRAGON AUCTION – LANCELOT.

16

Chamberlain's rented Citroën bumped to a stop on the sand ripples at the edge of a narrow beach. A quarter-mile up the coast was the gated harbour where Streicher's boat had blown up. Offshore, an anchored fishing boat rolled violently. The sun was low, and dulling rapidly behind thickening cloud; the Channel was rough, and the wind had a cold bite.

He had had some rest at the hotel, while the police activity died down; hours later their emergency lights still flickered faintly on the dark stone walls in the village, but he was afraid to wait any longer.

He closed his coat over his wet suit, got out of the car and pointed at the last of the long rock groins that guarded the harbour mouth. 'I'll put my gear on over there. When I'm gone, stroll down and get my coat and shoes. Then turn the car around. I'll come out right behind you. Be ready to move in case the cops are after me.'

Kreegan looked at the cold grey water. A sizeable swell was smacking the beach. 'What are you going down for, sir?'

'Streicher and Nagumo were headed close enough to Hammond to get killed for it. I'm hoping his chart didn't burn.'

He carried his gear in his right hand, to keep himself between it and the village. Crouching behind the groins, he donned tanks and flippers. The fishing boat hadn't moved, but he saw no one aboard. The beach itself was deserted and the nearest houses in the hills were dark. He took a bearing on the harbour mouth and another on the end of the groin, which extended, he estimated, a quarter-mile off shore. Then he entered the water and swiftly disappeared.

It felt cold, but the long swim in the insulated suit warmed him quickly. He rounded the groin and headed for the harbour. It was damned near dark in the choppy water. He checked his watch and compass repeatedly, and adjusted for the surge, and felt proud of himself when he turned his flashlight on and saw the steel harbour gate ahead. It was closed again, because the tide had fallen. He felt his way under it. Inside, when the surge stopped, he broke surface to observe the quay on the other side. There were still police there but no diving support equipment that he could see. The last thing he wanted was to meet a police diver under water.

Estimating the distance at a little under three hundred feet, he took another compass bearing, went down again, and swam for the wreck. The water was less rough out of the surge and swell and he could see about ten feet. The harbour deepened as he neared the quay which was built on the original, natural basin, so that when he found the shattered motor torpedo boat, its hull lay in a surprising forty feet of water.

It was lying on its port side; he could see the starboard side, the side that had been facing the quay. It had borne the brunt of the explosion and much of the plywood hull was simply obliterated. The gaping holes made access easy. He swam between two splintered ribs, careful to avoid fouling, and found himself in the engine room. The low compartment seemed relatively unscathed, and the unexpectedly small diesel engines were still bolted to their beds.

Then he found a tangled mess of pipe and wiring and a big hole torn out of the bottom and both sides. It was practically amidships and was obviously the place the

166

explosion had started. He swam out of it and over the hull and examined the armoured 6 x 6 that had been under the canvas. It had slipped off the boat and some idiot had left the hatches unlocked because otherwise it should have floated. It stood on the harbour bottom, up to its wheels in mud. All six rocket launchers looked in perfect shape.

Chamberlain swam back into the explosion area for another look. It looked as if somebody had smuggled a big charge aboard Streicher's boat. How had he exploded it? Timer, probably, but it was a funny coincidence to blow just as the boat sailed. The explosion amidships had sunk the motor torpedo boat and it had nothing to do with the rockets on the amphibious armoured vehicle.

Back in the engine room, Chamberlain studied the diesels closely in the murky gleam of his diving light, pondering how he would have blown the boat. He found what might have been an extra electrical wire attached to the generator which had been powered by belt drive from the diesel engines. He traced the wire, hand over hand. It had been stapled to the underside of a longitudinal brace and ran back to a thicket of vertical and horizontal brass rods. The rods ran up to the deck and along the bilges to the reduction gears. Chamberlain was amazed. The guy who'd set the charges had gone to a lot of trouble to wire them to the gear linkages and guarantee that they would blow only when the boat was leaving the dock. Instead of using a battery, he'd drawn his electrical power from the generator, forestalling the possibility that they'd blow early if somebody was just fiddling around with the bridge controls. Why go to so much trouble? he wondered. It was a good way to ensure killing everyone involved including Streicher, but the same could have been achieved with a timer set for later in the day.

Chamberlain shivered as a deep chill rippled across his

back. The explosion wasn't an accident. Charles Hammond's kidnapper was practising an aggressive defence. Grandzau had come out of hiding to attack his hunters. Which meant he was stalking the stalkers – watching.

He had hit Streicher with a vengeance the moment the arms merchant had come too close. Had he hit the KGB too? The Russians had dropped out of sight since Marseille. And what about the CIA? Were they charging into a trap?

Chamberlain floated motionlessly inside the exploded hull, weighing the possibilities. No, he concluded with a taste of bitterness. That was one of the reasons the CIA had cut him off; they'd realized instantly that Grandzau was on the attack and they decided, rightly it turned out, that Chamberlain would take a long time to figure it all out by himself.

Was he next? Was Grandzau watching him too?

Absurdly, he poked his head out of the hull and looked around the murky water. You did things like that underwater. Fear was compressed in on itself until it reached a critical point a diver couldn't handle. He pushed it away.

He thought of Kreegan alone in the car. What if they got Kreegan and waited calmly on the beach to shoot the first head that surfaced? He decided to take a look from the groin before he approached the beach. But first, he swam to the bridge, where he hoped to find Streicher's charts.

He glanced at his watch. Twenty minutes of air left. He glided out of the hull, through a hole in the deck and swam through a cabin towards a narrow passage which would be the companionway to the bridge. He thought suddenly of the woman he'd seen in Brussels. The woman who had laid him out in Marseille. Son of a bitch. Grandzau's agent? Hadn't the German secret-seller had a woman partner? Was she his eyes among the hunters?

And then it began to make sense. Grandzau's agent. She

had ordered the boat to explode at the dockside so everyone would know it had been done. They wanted the news to spread to the others. It was a threat. A threat from weakness instead of strength. Grandzau couldn't attack them all, so he attacked one. The one with the least resources. He probably hadn't expected Nagumo to be along with Streicher, but it didn't matter. Streicher only represented himself. Nagumo represented Japan. They'd have a new man on the scene in hours. So Grandzau had lost little and gained much.

Chamberlain swam through the companionway and into the space of the open bridge when he saw the first body. The explosion had burned the man's clothes off. He lay sadly naked, his hair burned away, tangled in the twisted remains of a chair bolted to the deck behind the helm. Another dead man was pinned aft by a fallen timber.

Chamberlain searched for cubby holes where charts might be rolled, hoping the explosive flames hadn't burned them. He turned on his light and thrust the beam around the dashboard. If he was right in his conclusions, Kreegan was safe. And by the time he found any charts, the CIA would probably be debriefing Hammond in a Washington hotel room.

He bumped into the dead man in the helm chair and had the creepy experience of accidentally looking into his dead eyes. Streicher. Of course. He'd been at the helm. Something fluttered beneath him. Gently, careful not to tear the water-soaked paper, Chamberlain eased Streicher's body away from the seat of the chair and retrieved the chart that the German had been sitting on while he had manned the helm. The arms merchant's body had protected the paper from the flames.

Chamberlain swept his light over the paper as it drifted in the water. It was a British Admiralty English Channel Chart – an overview that showed the western end of the

169

Channel and a portion of the Atlantic. It looked as if courses had been pencilled in, but he couldn't tell for sure in the dull light. He folded it, took a final look around and checked his compass for the swim across the harbour.

A fourth body appeared suddenly in his vision. By the time he realized it was alive, he could see its mask and air tanks. He cursed his stupidity for staying on the boat too long. The police divers had finally arrived.

Chamberlain snapped off his light and lunged off the boat seeking the darkness. Then the diver made a quick motion and Chamberlain realized he had been wrong; a police diver wouldn't be coming at him at full speed with a twelve-inch knife in his hand.

Chamberlain twisted around and grabbed the diver's wrist and discovered he had made his third miscalculation in as many seconds. He had chosen to stand and fight a man twice as strong as he. The attacker wrenched his arm free, as effortlessly as if Chamberlain were a child, and feinted with the knife. Chamberlain dodged the blow. The diver was waiting for him. He wrapped his other gigantic arm around Chamberlain's torso. Chamberlain was crushed against the man's chest and now the knife was descending at his back.

He tried a knee, missed, but the giant's defensive reaction gave him an instant's respite. He twisted sideways a couple of inches. The knife clanked off his air tank, glanced through his rubber wet suit and burned across his ribs. He felt it scrape bone. The pain arched his back convulsively. Both his hands were trapped between his and the diver's body, crushed near his neck. He thrust up with all his strength and ripped off the man's face mask, pulling it down over his air regulator and mouthpiece. The diver panicked in the rush of cold water and let go.

Chamberlain lunged away, lost in the dark, afraid of crashing into the quay, desperately trying to read his compass. A hand fastened around his calf like a monkey wrench and yanked him backwards. The diver was trying to retrieve his knife which was dangling from his other arm by a wrist thong. He had replaced his face mask, but it was still full of water.

Chamberlain went with the yank, pulled the man's mask off again, jammed his fingers into one of his eyes, and ripped his air regulator from his mouth. The guy stopped pawing for his knife, and scrambled for his regulator, tightening his grip on Chamberlain's leg at the same time. Incredulous, and more than a little frightened by the diver's inhuman determination, Chamberlain clawed his pry knife from the sheath on his other leg.

The diver found his mouthpiece, blew out the water, and grabbed his knife. Chamberlain plunged the tip of his blade into the man's hand and tore loose. He kicked the diver's mouthpiece out again with a lucky thrust of one of his flippers and swam madly for the dark, fleeing in near terror, heedles of obstructions.

He gained control of himself, looked back, saw nothing, and swam further. Then he stopped and when he was sure he was alone, he checked his compass. The harbour gates were in the opposite direction. Detouring widely around the motor torpedo boat, he swam across the harbour as fast as he could, taxing his dwindling oxygen supply, not caring for anything but getting away.

It had happened so fast he hadn't had time to react, but when he'd pulled the diver's mask off, he'd recognized one of the KGB heavies from Marseille, one who'd ridden in the Peugeot, but whose face he had glimpsed when the car had stopped to give orders to the goons on the street. He increased his speed. The diver must have come off the fishing boat beyond the groin. Had they sent another killer after Kreegan in the car?

He surfaced for a split second, raising his head as far as

his eyes, and found the harbour mouth fifty yards to his left. The steel gates must have foxed the compass. He went under and headed for them. Ten feet away, he stopped dead in the water, braking with his hands.

The Russian was waiting under the gate. He had fixed his mask and regulator and was holding his knife again in his good hand. He was staring ahead and Chamberlain, coming in from the side, was out of his line of vision. If he had enough air, Chamberlain would have waited him out. The guy had to be wondering if Chamberlain had beaten him under the gate. But he didn't have the air and the quay was swarming with French cops who'd spot him if he tried to go overland. On the other hand, the cops could cover Kreegan and Mirage would probably come to his rescue as they had in Marseille. It made a lot more sense than tangling with the Russian who had him out-weighed and, if not out-classed, out-determined. He started to back away. The Russian swivelled his head, spotted Chamberlain, and came after him like a torpedo.

Chamberlain dodged and ran for it, slithering under the gate, banging his tank on the steel. At that moment, his air started turning awfully thin, awfully fast. He reached back, flipped the five-minute reserve and swam with all his strength.

The Russian was simply too fast. His enormous legs, long and thick as telegraph poles, drove through the water at an unbelievable rate. He caught up in seconds, and Chamberlain was reminded by a sudden weariness that he was no longer a twenty-three-year-old underwater demo man, but closer to thirty-five and tiring rapidly.

He turned to fight, pulling his knife from his sheath, and the Russian, caught by surprise, hurtled past. He recovered quickly, but his overshot had given Chamberlain a second to set up. Slowly, Chamberlain backed away. Overhead, the swells were crashing into the harbour gate.

Twenty feet down, they created a surge that raised and lowered the divers and whipped up the mud on the harbour floor. At a distance of eight feet, the Russian was an insubstantial shadow.

Chamberlain backed up, very slowly, watching as the Russian stalked him, readying his lunge. He thought his air was going thin again. He backed further away. His flipper brushed the steel harbour gate. He stopped.

The Russian's shadowy form hung in the water, eight feet away, rising and falling as he did. Chamberlain pointed his flashlight at him and turned it on. He flicked the beam from side to side, up and down, as if searching. All the while he watched the shape of the Russian's form. Suddenly it elongated and Chamberlain knew the man was making his run. The knife came first, then the big head, shark-like in its rubber hood, and the thick neck and giant shoulders.

Chamberlain felt the surge start to push him down. He brought his cupped hands sharply up from his sides and dropped under the Russian's charge. Then he kicked up with all his might, rising rapidly to ram his knife into the diver's stomach.

There was no need. The Russian hit the steel wall head first. By the time Chamberlain got to him he was floating limply, his mouthpiece dangling, his neck bent at an awful twisted angle.

Chamberlain felt a moment of regret that he hadn't taken the guy alive for questioning, and then his air ran out. He grabbed the Russian before the surge could take him away, and took air from his mouthpiece. Then he detached him from his tanks and let him sink, while he swam slowly around the groins and towards the beach, dragging the Russian's tanks with one hand. He landed a hundred yards beyond the car and lay in the surf, unmoving, scanning the beach, the water, and the car.

The beach and the groins were still deserted. The day had turned greyer, and undoubtedly cooler, though he couldn't tell that in the water, and it made it unlikely that anyone would be out walking. He saw no sign of Grandzau's woman or anyone else watching the car. Kreegan seemed all right. He was sitting at the wheel, unmoving, but at a natural angle. The fishing boat was still anchored off the groin and still looked empty. But he knew they'd be looking for their diver and they'd see him cross the beach. He crawled out of the surf into deeper water and swam underwater down the beach until he was immediately behind the car. Then, lying in the surf again, he slid out of his tanks and flippers, gathered his gear in his arms, and, leaving the Russian's in the water, shambled up the beach.

Kreegan flipped the passenger door open, just as he reached the car. Chamberlain shoved the empty air tank on the floor and fell into the passenger seat, drained.

Kreegan smiled tightly. 'I caught a Russian, sir.'

17

Chamberlain turned slowly. The Russian was slouched low in the back seat, a wiry man in a dark pullover and knitted sailor's hat.

'Only thing is, he wanted to keep his gun.'

The gun was pointed at the back of Kreegan's head. It shifted quickly towards Chamberlain's face. The Russian held it like he knew how. His expression was impassive, his eyes alert.

Kreegan spoke again, in the same light, brittle tone. 'I tried him out. I don't think he talks English. I thought if I waited for you, we might be able to take him alive. He's just been sitting here like he's been waiting for somebody to tell him what to do. I've been talking and talking to him and myself so he's used to the sound of my voice. There's a gun under my seat and a gun under your seat and what do you suggest we do?'

Chamberlain watched the Russian's eyes.

'Where did he come from?'

'A guy brought him in from that fishing boat in a rubber dinghy.'

Chamberlain's hands started shaking. He was exhausted. The fight had taken its toll in shock and fright. His back throbbed painfully, and he felt his entire body surrendering, craving rest, oblivion. He heard Kreegan's voice as if he were calling from the beach.

'Are you all right, sir?'

Chamberlain shook his head violently, trying to clear his mind. 'How'd he get the drop on you?'

Kreegan sounded insulted. 'I *let* 'im, sir. I pretended I

was sleeping.' He hadn't once taken his eyes from the rearview mirror since Chamberlain had sat down in the car.

'Why?' muttered Chamberlain, his head reeling.

'So we'd take him alive and he'd tell us what his crowd is up to.'

'But he doesn't speak English.'

'I didn't know that. But don't worry, sir. We'll get a translator. The company must have a couple in Europe. Right?'

'Right. Where'd the guy in the dinghy go?'

'Back to their boat.'

'Great big huge guy?'

'No. Little feller.'

'That means there's at least two of them.'

'Three,' said Kreegan. 'I think I saw a diver go over the side. I've been watching the water in case he comes up on the beach.'

'He's dead,' said Chamberlain. The Russian took no notice. He sat placidly, as remote as a stranger sharing a cafeteria table.

Kreegan glanced at Chamberlain. Chamberlain tried to gesture him to keep quiet, but the steward's open face dropped in amazement.

'Jesus! You're bleeding like a stuck pig.'

Out of the cold, salt water, Chamberlain's knife slash had opened up. The car seat was puddling with blood. 'Don't let him know.'

But the Russian had picked up on Kreegan's alarm. He sat up straight, his nostrils flaring, his eyes growing narrow, and waved them forward against the dashboard with his gun. Then he leaned over the back of the front seat and saw the blood.

He went white for a long moment, then red. Gesticulating angrily, he pointed at the car keys until Kreegan

176

removed them from the ignition and passed them back. Training his weapon on them, never lowering it for a beat, he backed carefully out of the car, moved around to the front, and sighted them through the windscreen.

Kreegan wet his lips. 'What's he going to do?'

'He knows I killed his partner, you damned fool. What do *you* think he's going to do?'

The Russian aimed through the windscreen at a point midway between Chamberlain's eyes.

'You want I should go for my gun?' asked Kreegan. 'It's right under my seat.'

'No, for God's sake. The man's five feet away.'

'He can't see my hand.'

Chamberlain felt his lips go numb with fear. Kreegan was tensing beside him – an amateur second-guessing a pro.

'*No!*'

'He's gonna shoot us anyhow, sir.'

'He could have done it in the car. He got out for a reason. Now sit tight, for God's sake, before you spook him.'

'Why's he just standing there?'

'I don't know,' Chamberlain said evenly. Kreegan was still balled-up, ready to jump. 'Don't get us killed, Kreegan.'

Kreegan edged forward on the seat. 'Did you notice his weapon?' he asked. 'SIG P-220. Very interesting pistol. Double and single action. Cheap weapon – aluminium and pressed metal. But it's got a real cute automatic safety catch on the firing pin instead of – '

'Shut up. He sees you talking and he thinks you're planning something.'

The Russian rocked the car slightly as he braced his knees against the front bumper. His pistol stayed aimed at Chamberlain's head.

Kreegan swallowed. 'I'm sorry, sir. I'm really, really scared.'

Chamberlain broke eye contact with the gun barrel and glanced at Kreegan. 'Just be quiet,' he said gently. 'Please.'

The Russian raised his other hand over his head and waved from side to side. Chamberlain sagged against the back of the seat. 'He's signalling his partner. It buys us time.'

Kreegan sighed.

'Don't go for your gun. The steering wheel's in your way and you'll never make it. We'll wait for a better chance.'

'I'm sorry about all that talk, sir.'

'Just relax,' said Chamberlain. He felt light-headed and didn't know if it was from blood loss or a nervous reaction. He wanted to look back, out at the water, to see who was coming from the fishing boat, but he was afraid to turn his head, afraid to spook the Russian.

Chamberlain watched him, waiting for him to glance towards the man in black, waiting for the instant the Russian dropped his guard. There had to be a moment when he felt safer because his boss had arrived. Chamberlain would kill him in that moment.

'Halfway here,' muttered Kreegan. 'Twenty feet. Funny, he's not using the cane. Just carrying it.'

Chamberlain stared through the glass into the unblinking, unwavering gaze of the man aiming a gun at his forehead.

'Ten feet,' said Kreegan.

Chamberlain was on the verge of motion. *He'll look now*, he thought. *Now.* He sensed that the man in black was coming up on Kreegan's side of the car.

'Oh, shit,' breathed Kreegan. 'He drew his gun.'

Chamberlain sank wearily against the back of the seat, feeling the blood squish in his wet suit. He felt cold. 'Forget it,' he muttered to Kreegan. 'No way.'

178

'Yes, sir.'

Chamberlain noticed that the Russian was still staring at him. He'd never shifted his eyes.

'He wants in, sir.' Kreegan nodded where the man in black had rapped his cane on the side window. All Chamberlain could see was the man's wire-thin torso, and the cane and gun he held in black leather gloves.

'Roll down your window,' said Chamberlain. 'See what he wants.'

Kreegan rolled it down and Chamberlain, despite the angry seething in him over the way Kreegan had got him into this mess, admired his gutsy, irreverent, 'Yeah?'

The man in black bent over until his skeletal face filled the window opening.

'Where is Grandzau?'

18

Lady Janet hadn't seen Henri Trefle so pleased with himself in years. He dumped his captive face-down on the back seat of the car, removed one of the man's bootlaces, and used it to tie his thumbs behind his back.

'Is he alive?' asked Lady Janet.

'Sure,' grinned Trefle. 'I just gave him a little tap on his neck.'

She remembered to smile back to encourage his good mood. 'Nicely done, Henri.'

They scanned the fields and trees, making sure no one saw them in the darkening afternoon light, then drove the car out of the hedgerow and sped inland, putting distance between themselves and the mercenaries they had surprised in the hotel by the sea.

Trefle chuckled, congratulating himself. 'It was perfect. They fled in every direction – one even went over the cliff – and this one, of course, came into the streambed, as I knew one would. He dived into my arms, thinking I was a rock, perhaps, that would shield him from your bullets. Some shield.'

'Some rock,' said Lady Janet.

Trefle laughed. 'Some rock.'

Several miles inland, she started driving down narrow dirt roads. Twice, she ended up in barnyards, and drove quickly away. The third time she found what they needed, a deserted barn beside a tumbled-down stone cottage.

She stopped the car and turned off the lights. Trefle reconnoitred the area on foot. Lady Janet stayed behind the wheel. The prisoner stirred on the back seat, tugged at his bound hands and tried to sit up. Lady Janet touched the cold muzzle of her Smith & Wesson to his head.

'Don't.'

From the corner of her eye she saw Trefle's shadowy form return from behind the buildings and enter the barn. A moment later he came back to the car.

'Drive inside.'

She eased the car in by the glow of the parking lights. She waited until Trefle had swung the sagging doors shut before she turned on the headlights. It was a small barn and smelled wet, abandoned so long ago that the hay and straw had rotted to dirt and mud.

Trefle dragged their prisoner out of the car. He was in his late twenties, a hard-looking Pole or Czech – the sort who had escaped the Communists and found all he knew how to do was fight. He blinked angrily in the headlights, and made a lightning fast move to escape. Trefle hit him in the solar plexus and while he was doubled over, Lady Janet helped Trefle hang him upside down from a rafter.

He was suspended a couple of feet off the barn floor, his eyes level with the blazing headlights. His face turned red as his blood rushed down into it. Lady Janet knelt beside him and held her gun to his forehead.

'We won't hurt you if you tell us where you were meeting Grandzau.'

He said nothing.

She repeated the question in French. He understood and spat in her face.

'Henri.'

She stepped aside and wiped her face as Trefle knelt beside the man. Trefle drew his knife. The glass glittered like diamond. He smiled into the man's eyes and turned his face so the man could get a better look at him. He smiled grotesquely over the razor edge of his blade, offering it.

'Do you know who I am?' he asked in French.

The question startled the soldier and riveted his attention. He focused on Trefle's splotched and bloated face, then the knife. Abruptly, his eyes widened.

'My name?' asked Trefle.

'Henri Trefle,' the soldier muttered.

'I can't hear you.'

The man cleared his throat. His face was very red now. He answered loud and clear. 'Henri Trefle.'

Trefle smiled again, leaned closer into the man's face and held the blade to his throat. 'I ask you once. *Where were you meeting Grandzau?*'

'On a ship.'

'What ship?'

'I don't know.'

A chilling growl rumbled inside Trefle. He clamped a huge hand around the back of the hanging man's neck and started to saw the blade across his throat. The mercenary screamed.

'*Wait, wait.* A launch. He is picking us up at the harbour with a launch.'

'When?'

'Tonight. Midnight. I swear it.'

'What harbour?'

'Below the hotel. We're to assemble on the quay at midnight.'

'How do you know that you're going to a ship?' asked Lady Janet. 'Why not across the Channel, or down the coast, or to an island? I think he's lying, Henri.'

'No, no. No, I tell the truth. They told us we would be on a ship.'

'Why would they bother?' Lady Janet asked Trefle. 'He's lying.'

'No,' shouted the prisoner. 'He made us prove we had been on ships so we wouldn't be seasick.'

182

'Where is the ship going?'

'Please.'

'Where?' snapped Trefle.

'Please. I don't know.'

'Henri,' said Lady Janet. 'Come here.'

They retreated to the furthest corner of the barn. The prisoner's ragged, frightened breathing echoed in the dank space. Trefle seemed anxious to get back to him. Lady Janet watched him swinging slightly. Outside, she thought she heard snow striking the thin walls.

'What do you think the others will do?'

Trefle shrugged. 'By now they've figured how we did it to them and that we're probably only two or three in number. If the money's good, they'll go to the quay earlier, set up a strong perimeter, and try to board the launch.'

'They'll be taking a terrible chance.'

'They're fighters. If the money's good, they'll take the chance. I would.'

'What will they tell Grandzau?'

'They might tell him that this man deserted. Especially if Grandzau isn't there personally at the launch.'

'And he wouldn't be, would he?' she mused.

'No,' said Trefle, eyeing the hanging mercenary with anticipation.

Lady Janet tried to form her next question and realized, suddenly, how tired, cold and hungry she was. They had driven most of the night and had begun canvassing the Brest hotels at dawn. Her whole body ached from holding it stiffly against the pain of the beating. And it looked like a long night ahead.

'What duties were you hired for?' she called across the barn.

Distance made the mercenary brave. 'We were not told,' he said sullenly.

Henri Trefle bounded across the barn and pressed his

183

knife to the man's throat. He broke the skin, as he had Lady Janet's earlier in the day, and watched with satisfaction as a thin trickle of blood travelled up the man's throat and dripped from his chin.

'My friend, you had better guess.'

The sudden attack destroyed the mercenary's last resistance. His words poured out in a torrent of fear. 'Grandzau told us we would work for only a few days. A week at most. A thousand francs a day per man. He promised there would be no heavy weapons, no artillery, no tanks, no other soldiers. He promised a simple job. We asked, how simple? He said, only guard duty. We would keep order, he said. Keep order. The money was good, you know that, Colonel Trefle.'

Trefle smiled faintly at his one-time rank.

The mercenary clung to the smile. 'We didn't mean to offend, *Mon Colonel*. We, I, didn't know this was your fight. I would not have taken such a job. I would not serve against Colonel Trefle. But I didn't know. The money was good, the jobs are few, surely *Mon Colonel* understands . . .'

Lady Janet listened from the corner, but the man had ceased to make sense. He was babbling, terrified what would happen when he stopped. She looked at her watch. Five o'clock. They had to get some food and rest and plan what to do at the quay.

She sensed that Grandzau was about to slip away. The fact that this mercenary team had been hired for guard duty was very significant. It meant that Grandzau was abandoning his present force – the men who had executed the kidnapping – which probably meant he was leaving his present hiding-place. That this new team was hired to keep order indicated that Grandzau was positive that no force could attack him. This team would protect him against the unlikely event that someone invited to the auction tried to pull something during the proceedings. The fact that Grandzau didn't expect an outside attack meant that he had an intricate, complex and foolproof plan to protect his Pendragon Auction.

'Henri. Cut him down, tie him up, and let's go.'

'He'll talk.'

'No I won't. No I won't, *Mon Colonel*. I swear it.'

'Tie him well. It will take him a day to free himself. We'll be gone by then.' She got into the car and reached for the key.

Trefle sighed, stood up, and backed away. He gripped the rope from which the mercenary was hanging and raised his knife. As Lady Janet turned the ignition key the starter murmured hesitantly. 'Damnit,' she muttered, flicking off the headlights to get more power from the overburdened battery. That's all they needed, to be stuck in a cowbarn in the middle of nowhere with a dead battery. She hit the key again and, relieved of the headlight strain, the starter kicked the engine to life. She raced it a moment and when she was sure it wouldn't stall, she turned the headlights back on.

Her stomach twisted. The mercenary hung limply. His head was below her line of vision, but the blood on Trefle's knife told what he had done. He smiled into the headlights, his eyes a mad glitter, and wiped his blade on the dead man's clothes.

Chamberlain wished he had taken the risk of going for his gun, even though the set-up had been suicidal. There was a mad, frightening note in the Russian's voice. He weighed the new odds. This wasn't going to get better unless he did something, but the odds were lousier than before. The gun of the Russian in black was inches from Kreegan and the first Russian was still drawing a bead on his head. Worse, they were unquestionably both pros, while he and Kreegan added up to one out-of-shape pro and one amateur who happened to like guns.

Before Chamberlain could say anything, Kreegan tried to tough it out. He replied with another question.

'Buddy, you think we'd be sitting here talking to you if we knew where Grandzau was?'

The man in black waited two or three seconds. Then, in a move so fast that even Chamberlain didn't see it coming, he broke Kreegan's nose with his cane. The steward yelled in pain, clutched his face, and bent forward. Chamberlain thought he was going for the gun under his seat, but Kreegan just moaned, the fight smashed out of him.

'Where is Grandzau?'

'We don't know,' Chamberlain said quietly.

The man in black reached through the open window and switched on the car's interior lights. He gazed at Chamberlain over Kreegan's bowed head.

'You dived to learn where Streicher was going. What did you find?'

'Nothing.'

The man's gaze was chilling, as if he knew he was going to do something terrible and was stalling, savouring the anticipation.

'My diver is still down there. What do you suppose he found?'

Chamberlain knew there was no sense lying. The wound on his back was condemning. He kept his voice neutral, his manner inoffensive. His gut was clamouring alarms, warning that this Russian was deadly. He tried to ignore Kreegan's agonized groans.

'Your diver broke his neck. He ran into the gate.'

'I never knew him to be a careless diver.'

'I got lucky,' said Chamberlain, trying to find a way to defuse the man. There was a turmoil building in him, a molten centre of emotion promising to explode.

'Then you must report what my diver would have reported. Where was Streicher going? Where is Grandzau?'

186

'I don't know.'

Kreegan's breath rasped miserably through his mouth. He was still crumpled forward, still holding his face in his hands.

The man in black glanced at Kreegan, then said to Chamberlain, 'Get out of the car.'

He covered him as he opened the door and stood up. The man in front of the car shifted his gaze to Kreegan. The man in black made Chamberlain walk round the car and stand with his back to him. Chamberlain sensed him examining his knife wound in the dim glow from the car's interior lights.

A bitter wind was blowing off the water and slicing through his rubber suit. It was insulated to keep body heat in when submerged, but in the air the wet suit was a sieve. Chamberlain shivered uncontrollably. The cold pebble beach froze his bare feet. He thought his bleeding had stopped, but he felt faint.

The man in black stepped in front of him, his gaunt face eerily white in the light from the car. He held his cane in one hand, his Baretta in the other. His emotional seizure appeared to be rising to a peak, but he was careful to stand out of his partner's line of fire. Chamberlain braced for a blow from the cane.

'Where is Grandzau?'

Chamberlain said nothing.

The man in black nodded at his partner, who turned his full attention towards Chamberlain. Then he twisted the cane and withdrew a whip, a riding crop almost as long as its scabbard. Chamberlain wondered if anyone in the harbour village could see the dimly lighted car on the beach.

'Where is Grandzau?'

'I don't know.'

The man in black checked that his partner had Chamberlain covered, then slipped his pistol back into his shoulder holster and said, 'Remove your diving suit.'

'Now hold on,' said Chamberlain, not quite believing that

187

this was happening. 'I don't know where Grandzau is and hitting me with that thing—'

'Shut up!'

'All I'm saying is, it isn't going to change the facts,' Chamberlain insisted calmly, keeping a wary eye on the crop.

The man in black returned a dead look. 'I haven't the time to argue with you. We are not fooled by your charade. We want Hammond and the CIA isn't going to stop us.'

'I'm not CIA.'

'Remove your diving suit,' he repeated, passing the whip through his hand. 'Or my man will shoot you.'

Chamberlain saw that he meant it and complied. He unsnapped the crotch strap and pulled down the jacket zipper. The man's hands were trembling, as if with excitement. He supposed he was a freelance operator. It wasn't like the staid and humourless KGB to employ psychotics.

'Stop!'

Chamberlain froze, to show he wasn't pulling a weapon.

'Hands behind your head!'

Chamberlain raised his hands and stood shivering, defenceless. The Russian reached into the open folds of the wet suit and gingerly removed the sodden chart Chamberlain had taken from Hans Streicher's sunken boat. He spread it on the bonnet of the car, pasting it down by its moisture, and lighted a pen light.

Chamberlain watched from the corner of his eye. There *was* a course pencilled on the chart. Streicher had been heading northeast towards the Channel Islands. The line stopped short of Sark, about two hundred miles from Brest.

The Russian looked up from the chart and out at the dark where his fishing boat was anchored. He made a deep, guttural sound, which, Chamberlain knew, had to be a curse. The boat was useless – too slow for the distance. The Russian

188

needed a car. A car first, and then another boat. He snapped a command and gestured at Kreegan.

Chamberlain started to back away, his hands still behind his head. It didn't take knowledge of the Russian language to know that the KGB men intended to take the car and kill them. The man in black straightened up from the map and angrily sheathed the riding crop. His dark eyes flickered towards Chamberlain and noticed he had moved. He drew his weapon as fast as a snake tongue and raised it to fire.

His partner opened Kreegan's door and yanked him out by the lapels. The Russian cried out, seconds too late. Kreegan's shot revolver boomed like a dynamite explosion, flinging the Russian into the dark. Blinded by the flash of the weapon, Chamberlain threw himself to the sand and crawled frantically around the car. He heard the swift *crack, crack* of the Baretta, Kreegan's yell, and a second *boom* from the shot revolver.

In the muzzle flash Chamberlain saw the man in black running towards the water. He yanked open the passenger door, pawed the gun Kreegan had left him out from under the seat, and fired in the direction the Russian had run. Again, the muzzle flash lighted the beach like a flashbulb. He had missed. The Russian had veered to the right.

Chamberlain fired twice, bracketing the area he'd run to. Two shots from the Baretta told him he had missed. He raised his weapon. From the other side of the car, he heard Kreegan gasp.

'Get out of here, sir. You haven't got the range. He'll pick you off from a distance. Get in the car.'

'Can you drive?' Chamberlain whispered, acutely aware that the interior light was still on and the switch was on the other side.

Kreegan uttered a forced laugh. 'Drive?' he choked. 'I can hardly hold my weapon.'

'You hurt?'

189

'Go, sir. While you can. You don't have the range.'

'Hang on,' Chamberlain called under the car. He crawled around the back and lunged in the open driver's door to douse the interior lights. He found the switch, then shut the door to keep them off. A shot snapped from the water and a bullet clanged off the door. Ricochet, which meant he'd hit the side from a shallow angle. He was close behind the car.

Chamberlain felt his way in the dark, crawling over sand and pebbles to where Kreegan lay on his stomach, holding his shot revolver in two hands, aiming towards the water.

'Don't move me, sir.'

'I gotta get you in the car.'

Kreegan shook him off with a moan. 'I'm dead, sir. No point making it hurt worse than it does already.'

'You're not dead, yet. I'm taking you to a hospital.'

'Sorry I screwed up.'

'Don't be an idiot, Kreegan. I'll have you there in an hour.'

'Thanks for letting me come along, sir.'

'What?' Chamberlain couldn't see Kreegan's wounds in the dark. He played his hand gently over his back, but he'd been hit in front and the Baretta slugs apparently hadn't exited.

'I mean I just wanted some fun, like I used to in the Service.'

'Where are you hit?'

'Thanks, sir.'

'Hold on, Kreegan. We're getting out of here.'

Kreegan didn't answer. Chamberlain touched him, but he lay still. He reached for his arm and tried his pulse. He felt none and when he put his ear to Kreegan's chest he heard nothing but the surf and the occasional noise the Russian made circling closer on the pebbly beach.

Chamberlain found Kreegan's gun and fired several shots towards the noise. The blinding muzzle flashes lighted an empty beach. Somewhere close the man in black was hugging the ground. Chamberlain slipped into the car, started the engine, and floored the accelerator, slamming the door shut by the forward lunge.

He heard the crack of two shots over the engine roar. A bullet tugged at the side of the car, low down near the wheels. The Russian was shooting at his tyres.

Then he was out of range. He turned on the headlights. A stone wall leaped in front of the car. Chamberlain slewed around the sharp bend in the road, missed the wall by inches, and raced through the harbour village, driving badly.

He felt himself going under. He'd opened the wound by crawling around the car and he was still bleeding. He felt his strength and will seeping out of his body.

He clenched the wheel and forced his face partially out of the window into the cold slipstream. The car speeded up, drifting from side to side of the narrow road. Dully, he knew he had to make Brest. He needed help badly, but Kreegan was dead.

He had to make it to the airport. With luck they'd fixed the Comptel plane in Marseille and flown to Brest. They'd get him a doctor. And then they'd fly him to the Channel Islands. If he didn't pass out before he made the airport.

He was stopped in the Citroën at a traffic light halfway through Brest when a blue Renault rounded the corner and sped off in the direction from which he had come. The blonde woman driving was the one from Brussels and Marseille, the woman he thought was Grandzau's partner.

Chamberlain hauled his wheel around and tried to pull out of the line of cars waiting for the light to change. The knife slash in his back burned angrily. He'd torn the damned thing open again. He gritted his teeth and backed and filled madly. Knowing it wasn't deep didn't make it hurt less. Or bleed less either.

191

The streets were clogged with homebound evening traffic and it seemed that no French commuter worth his salt gave an inch to a rich man's Citroën. Chamberlain finally got her facing the other way, but he couldn't risk speeding in the city streets because the gendarmes would put too many questions to a man driving in a wet suit. His clothes were on the back seat where Kreegan had put them. The Russian had pushed them to one side, but he'd seen they were all there, including his wallet.

He thought he saw the Renault's lights stopped at an intersection, but when he got closer, he saw that though it was a Renault, it was not blue, but red, and driven by a priest. He looked left, right, and ahead. There were cars everywhere and he realized he hadn't a chance of finding her, so he drove round a block and headed once again towards the airport.

He donned his clothes in the car and went to the private aviation counter, walking as steadily as he could, aware how bad he looked when he combed his hair in the rearview mirror. The woman on duty eyed him nervously.

'Where is the Comptel plane?'

'Ah.' She sounded relieved. '*Oui, monsieur.*' She directed him in pidgin English and with precise gestures.

Chamberlain went out to the apron and found the jet where she said it would be, its windows lighted, its boarding ramp down. He hauled himself up the steps and banged on the hatch, which was closed against the cold. The co-pilot opened up and peered out at the dark.

'Chamberlain.'

'You all right, sir? The company's been trying to get hold of you.'

Chamberlain had both hands wrapped round the ramp rail and found he couldn't move. 'No. I need a doctor. And I'm afraid I have some bad news for you. Kreegan's –'

'Hey, who the hell –'

Chamberlain got halfway round as a man stormed out of his hiding place under the jet, scaled the ramp, and shoved him and the co-pilot through the door.

19

'Hey Pete! You look a little ragged, fella.'

'Arnie!'

Chamberlain untangled himself from the terrified co-pilot and stared at Arnie Fast. He was a big guy, balding, with a tough face and a good smile. Like Chamberlain, he had the odd scar scattered about his sharp nose and high cheekbones. His parka was open, revealing winter combat fatigues and a big pistol on his hip. He looked tired, and Chamberlain had known him enough years to see he was just a little drunk.

'Nice little plane you got here, Pete. Happen to have a bar?'

'That way.' He propelled Arnie towards the main lounge, closed the curtain, and turned to the co-pilot, who was staring at Chamberlain's blood on his hands. 'Get me a doctor,' he ordered quietly. 'I need food right away. Hot and a lot of it. Him too. And I'll need to make a call to New York.'

'I'll try, sir. Kreegan runs the galley.'

'Find somebody to take over for Kreegan. But first the doctor.' He glanced at the curtain and whispered, 'Tell the captain we're moving out tonight. Tell him to find a landing strip in the Channel Islands. Sark, if they've got one. Otherwise, Cherbourg. And tell him both you guys are up for bonuses as soon as we hit New York.'

He brushed through the curtained galley, and the little cabin where Kreegan had made him sleep the night he boarded in London, and into the main cabin. Arnie was leaning on the bar. He waved a glass. 'Belly up, fella.'

'Fuck you!'

Arnie grinned. 'We meet for the first time in a year on foreign shores and you say to me, "Fuck you"? That's the thanks I get for helping you all week?'

'You set me up as a stalking horse. You used me to get close to Hammond.'

'In case you don't know it, the average American tax-payer can't call up his local CIA man for the latest information in the old computer.'

'Thanks a lot. As soon as I got close you cut me off.'

'What off?'

'This morning the Brest station yanked their phone out of the wall. When I called Washington, your secretary made it pretty damned clear you'd be in conference most of the year.'

'That was this morning.'

'What are you doing here?'

'To tell you the truth, I was in the neighbourhood.' He picked up a Scotch bottle and tilted it towards Chamberlain, but the banter quit his voice, abruptly. 'Cherbourg, to be exact.' He ignored Chamberlain's sharp look. 'So I thought I'd stop by and see how you were doing down here in Brest. Only a couple a hundred miles.' He gave the posh cabin an appreciative once-over. "Course, I fly commercial, unlike some of my retired old buddies who bailed out of the Agency when the Agency needed them most.' He tipped his glass to his mouth.

'I didn't bail out. I just moved on.'

'You know, Pete, semi-pro espionage is sort of like semi-pro ball. A lot more semi than pro.'

'Arnie, I'm cold, I hurt, and I'm tired. What do you want?'

'Anything new about Grandzau?' He pointed the Scotch bottle at Chamberlain again. Chamberlain nodded. 'No ice.' They touched glasses. He drank deeply for heat and release. It burned like heaven. 'I might have a thing or two to tell you, but seeing as how you cut me off this morning, I want you to answer a couple of my questions, first.'

He freshened his own drink and sat down.

'Make it quick. Let's quit fucking around.'

'Fine with me. I think Grandzau has an agent on the ground. A woman. Beautiful. Blonde. Looks about thirty and rich. Who is she?'

'Sounds like Grandzau's old girlfriend. English woman. Lady Janet Isling. Some lord's daughter. Rich and loony. We tried to find her when the Pendragon cables started, but she'd disappeared from her house in the south of France. Seen her?'

'She knocked me cold in Marseille.'

'Sounds like her style. She was running dope for Grandzau when he was fighting the Chinese dealers. Used to hang out in Paris with French mercenaries. Knows how to handle herself. I figured she was dead on junk by now. That type usually are.'

Chamberlain wanted to try his theory. 'Or maybe she's dogging our various tracks for Grandzau.'

Arnie didn't seem impressed.

Chamberlain said, '*Somebody* nailed Streicher and Nagumo.'

'True. What's your second question?'

'A possible KGB agent. Russian or middle-European. Thirties or forties, hard to tell. Tall, bony. Very weird. Carries a riding crop in a cane scabbard and likes to use it.'

'Sounds like fun, but I never heard of him.'

'Ask your computer.' He buzzed the co-pilot, who told him the doctor had arrived. 'Good. Send him through to the aft cabin and set up a call to Langley, Virginia.' He handed Arnie the telephone. 'Back soon. I'm going to get patched up and into some dry clothes.'

'I have people watching the plane.'

'Great allocation of resources.'

Chamberlain opened the door to the doctor and led her past Arnie into the aft cabin. She was a handsome, stern French matron with large hands. She helped him out of his shirt and stripped off the wet-suit jacket. He lay face down on the bed while she examined the knife slash. She gave him a couple of deadening shots around the cut and started sewing.

'Did you bleed much?' she asked in English, when she had finished.

'Yes.'

'Turn over carefully.'

She produced a couple of plastic blood packs, beaded with condensation from recent refrigeration, and administered a transfusion through a vein in his left arm. 'Your blood type was in the company records.'

'Do you work for Comptel?'

'Of course.'

'How bad's my back?'

'I'm sure it feels much worse than it is. You'll have to move carefully for a couple of days.'

'I'm freezing. Can I take a hot shower?'

'I'll put a water-tight tape over it.'

Twenty minutes later the doctor helped him into his grey suit jacket, freshly cleaned and pressed, and asked how he felt.

'Not bad. Thanks a lot.'

She straightened his tie, and left with a smile.

When Chamberlain joined Arnie in the main cabin, two places had been set at a portable dining table, and a white-jacketed steward was waiting to serve soup. Arnie lowered his sherry glass.

'You look better.'

'What did you find out?'

'There's no record of anybody with that description in the KGB's European ops. We'll keep looking.'

'I had a feeling he'd be freelance,' said Chamberlain. He drank his soup quickly and told the steward to bring the main course immediately.

'My turn,' said Arnie. 'What do you know?'

Chamberlain had been wondering since he'd boarded the plane what to tell him about Streicher's chart. His first inclination was to go to Grandzau's island alone, but the Russian knew about it too and he wasn't in any position, tonight, to tackle his and Grandzau's people at the same time with no preparation. The Russian team had lost four men since Marseille, so the man in black would have his own troubles and even with the rest of KGB-Europe backing him up, it would be several hours before he'd be able to do anything like launch a night attack on a rock in the English Channel.

He looked Arnie in the eye. 'You know damned well I don't want you blundering into this and getting Hammond killed, but I gotta tell you that it's likely the Russians'll attack Grandzau in the morning.'

'Where?'

'He's on a little island in the Channel, west of Sark.'

'Shit! That's all you know?'

'That's what I think.'

'Yeah, well think about this, Chamberlain. I lost an entire assault team on that fucking rock this fucking afternoon.'

Chamberlain gasped. 'What? . . .'

'We put the pieces together, including a few you didn't know about, and reconned the thing from the air. Weather socked in and something played hell with our air support's radar, so we couldn't back up the assault team.'

'He bought radar jammers from a Japanese radical.'

'Wonderful to hear that now, Pete.'

'And how the hell was I supposed to tell you?'

Arnie stared, his eyes deep with fatigue. 'Anyhow, Grandzau had laid on quite a welcome. Sowed the fucking beach with anti-personnel mines. Had some nicely situated automatic weapons. So they lost their asses. Some of your ex-SEAL buddies . . . Naw, you wouldn't know 'em. Young guys . . .'

'Hammond?'

'Do you think I'd be here if I had Hammond?'

'Why are you here?'

'On the slim chance that you'd found something we didn't already know.'

'A frontal assault sounds pretty stupid, Arnie. It's a kidnapping, not a war.'

Arnie got up angrily. 'You any closer? Grandzau's vanished, gone, missing. Goddamned kraut made a shambles of all of us. Even the KGB is lost. Everybody's lost.'

'I'm sorry we didn't connect about the radar jammers.'

'Yeah, me too.' Arnie shoved past the new dining steward, out of the door, and down the ramp. He waved angrily at several shadows that materialized into men and they trooped after him into the terminal. Chamberlain finished his steak, reached across the table, and ate Arnie's. The intercom buzzed and the co-pilot told him he had a line to New York. Chamberlain sighed, and failed to cheer himself with two more shots of Scotch. At least Hammond hadn't been killed. And when he got done telling Helen Thorp about the latest screw-ups, he could go to bed.

'Fools,' said Henri. 'Everywhere but where we are.'

They had hidden their sleek, low boat under a dock that commanded a clear view of the quay and the rock jetties that formed the mouth of the anchorage. There was barely

199

room to stand and since the tide was coming in they'd twice had to adjust their lines on the dock pilings, but they were deep in shadow, invisible from the quay.

Lady Janet had almost despaired of stealing a boat in January on this north coast. Only fishing craft were in the water this time of year and they weren't fast enough to trail the kind of launch Grandzau would send. Then Trefle had hit upon the idea of stealing a pleasure boat from a winter storage shed.

They had broken into a yacht basin in a Brest suburb. Between the cold, the hour, and the holidays, they'd had the place to themselves. They winched a fast, seaworthy runabout onto a trailer and fitted it with a pair of giant outboard motors. While Trefle checked the engines and hooked up batteries, she'd scouted around and taken a half-dozen extra petrol tanks. Then they hitched the trailer to the Renault, took on petrol at the shuttered marina's pumps, and drove to the Channel coast to the harbour next to this one. Launching in the dark, they'd made a cold, wet, bone-jarring run to this anchorage. Trefle had pushed it hard and the boat had pounded terribly in the choppy seas.

'What time is it?' he asked.

'Ten.'

'I'll spell you at eleven.' He fell asleep, snoring lightly.

Lady Janet scanned the quay again, saw that none of the mercenaries had changed position, and shifted her attention to the jetties. She strained her ears for the sound of Grandzau's boat. She was soaked from spray and freezing cold and her last injection was wearing off hours too soon. She gnawed hungrily at some cheese, tore off a piece of bread and ate it and stole a swallow of Trefle's red wine to wash it down.

She wanted another injection. She held off until ten-thirty.

Trefle awakened at eleven. 'Get some sleep.'

'I'm fine. I feel quite well.'

She couldn't quite see his face, but she felt his gaze and thought she saw the street lamp on the quay reflected in his eyes. He was looking at her.

'You're using a lot of that stuff.'

'I've been off it a year. It's just for the pain.'

'It always is.'

She passed him the binoculars and reclined on the cushions where he had lain. Sometimes, when she got this high it was hard to remember why she was hunting Grandzau. The cold and the pain and the hate were at a distance. She imagined the pain and hate sitting on the quay, put in a box, a crate, waiting to be picked up and sent to sea. Waiting with the mercenaries for Grandzau's boat.

She imagined standing up and looking at the quay and seeing the crate sitting there. She looked at it for a long, long time. Trefle shook her awake.

'Up! Something's coming.'

She sat up groggily. Trefle scooped a handful of water from the side of the boat and hurled it in her face.

'All right. All right.'

'Listen.'

She heard the faint mutter of an engine.

'Something's wrong,' she whispered. 'It's not coming from the water.'

Trefle cursed softly. 'Untie the stern.'

She threw the rope in the water. She felt Trefle's urgency. There wasn't time to untie it from the piling. Trefle slashed the bowline with his knife. Before the boat could drift out from under the dock, he wrapped an arm around the piling and sat down behind the steering wheel, his other hand on the starter key. Lady Janet slung the submachinegun over her shoulder and examined the quay through the night glasses.

'They're facing the street,' she reported. 'I don't think they know what it is, either. They've drawn their weapons.'

'Maybe it's just somebody out for a drive,' Trefle said doubtfully. 'I see lights.'

A pair of headlights crested the hill and descended quickly.

Trefle cursed. Lady Janet watched the mercenaries. The one on the roof had his weapon trained on the quay. The lights disappeared behind a building and reappeared an instant later on the quay.

The car swerved into a tight U-turn and stopped, facing back up the road. Someone shouted. '*Merlin!*'

'Go!' screamed Lady Janet.

'*Merlin! Merlin!*' Grandzau's old code word for all clear. His password. The mercenaries were running towards the car. The three from the doorways were sprinting across the open space.

Trefle hit both starters at once. He had the big, screaming Mercuries in gear and the boat flying across the anchorage in another second.

Lady Janet unslung the Smith & Wesson and levelled the perforated barrel at the car. Three of the mercenaries were already in it, and the last was sliding down the drainpipe.

She pressed the trigger and the gun began its smooth bucking.

Trefle knocked the barrel up.

'Don't kill the driver!'

He slewed alongside the quay, lost control of the speeding boat. It slammed hard into the stone. They were thrown to the bottom, tangling in the mess of lines, cushions, seats, and hastily rigged wiring. Lady Janet tore

202

loose first, hauling herself onto the high quay, dragging her weapon after her.

The car was rolling. One door hung open. The last mercenary chased after it, leaped. The others pulled him in and the car squealed towards the turn.

Lady Janet ran with all her heart, legs frantically pumping, gaining. The driver got second gear and it pulled away. She loosed a long, desperate burst at the tyres.

The car skidded into the turn. It rounded the building and passed from her sight. Seconds later she saw its tail lights climbing rapidly up the hill. Lady Janet ran a few more yards, then shambled to a halt in the middle of the street, her weapon trailing from one hand.

Lights flared on in the cottages and some doors opened tentatively. Oblivious, she stared up the hill, gasping for breath, watching the car escape. Hot tears blinded her.

'Come on!' Trefle yelled.

Lady Janet could not move.

She was vaguely aware of the lights in the windows and somewhere heard people shouting. She didn't care. Trefle came running. He had blood on his face.

'Let's get out of here.'

'We didn't think he would come by land,' she whispered.

'Later.'

'He pointed everyone towards the water.' The weapon slid from her hand. It clattered on the stones. A couple of men came out of a door. Big men. Made bold by the sight of a woman, a single man, a fallen gun.

Trefle snarled. He picked up the gun, threw Lady Janet over his shoulder, and carried her back to the boat.

He had to escape.

Charles Hammond was coming back to life. His mind was working again, working, chewing the problem, casting off the lethargy of drugs, shock, fear and confinement.

They'd brought him tea in a tin cup. He banged it loudly on the iron door.

Who had kidnapped him? Why? Where was this windowless room with an iron door? Someplace in the north. It was cold and damp and he had to stick close to the radiator which warmed his cell. He had been moved around repeatedly, but had been too doped to remember more than being carried in and out of planes, helicopters, trucks. But he knew nothing about his kidnappers. Bedouin revolutionaries or right-wing Chicago Poles, he didn't know. He didn't know what they wanted. He didn't know what they needed. He didn't know how they intended to get it.

Under better circumstances – ensconced in his Malagasy villa, say, basking in the perfumed warmth of his tropical gardens – the irony of Charles Hammond the deal-maker not knowing anything might have been funny.

Information, after all, was his life, his work, his skill and his talent. For to negotiate successfully, you first had to know what you wanted. And then who else wanted? Who needed? Who counted? He knew the right people – the ones who counted – a constantly changing band of winners, survivors and losers. He knew their wants. And most important, he knew their needs. But the joke was on him right now because he was the one who needed, and he didn't know what the hell was going on. All he knew was, *he had to escape*, because this kidnapping couldn't have come at a worse time, if God Himself had fingered him.

His guards were French. Correction, *spoke* French, with a variety of accents.

Maybe the French Foreign Legion had him.

The feeble joke pointed at a fact. Mercenaries.

He smiled and banged the cup harder.

He had a fact. And he liked it. Hired guns doing a job. Professionals who wouldn't panic or turn weird. He had been trying to ignore his fear. Now it slipped away like mist in the wind. For whoever had him weren't crazy. At least they weren't fanatics who'd kill him for a cause or parcel post his ears to prove they meant business.

Hired by whom? A dozen possibilities raced through his mind. He had a few enemies. Enemies were bad for business, nonetheless the very act of doing business could and occasionally did produce enemies. More likely, however, was the possibility that some of his clients had rivals who wouldn't mind seeing him on ice for a while. In fact, when he thought about it, some of his clients were engaged in negotiations so Byzantine that even *they* might put him on ice awhile.

But enemies would have killed him already. And there were simpler ways to stall negotiations than snatching the negotiator, for crissake. One could always say one's government was dragging its feet. Or, if one happened to represent a government, one could blame the bureaucracy. Which they usually did anyhow, Hammond thought sourly.

He banged his cup, hoping their motive wasn't the most obvious. Ransom could get very sticky. The door flew open.

And there stood his Maltese chauffeur, the little bastard who had sprayed him in the face. Hammond was curious whether they intended to return him alive, so he took a chance. He belted the Maltese in the mouth – which surprised him and made Hammond's hand hurt in a satisfying way – and started running down the stone corridor.

The Maltese recovered and loped after him. Ahead was a door. Unlocked. Hammond tore it open and found himself on a stone terrace overlooking a foggy sea. He heard the chauffeur running. Stairs. He turned to them, but the younger man caught him easily. His lip was bleeding and he was angry, but he didn't try to hurt him back.

Good. The guards had orders to keep him intact.

'I want to see your boss.'

The Maltese dragged him inside and started back to the room.

Hammond doubled over, convulsively clutching his chest. The Maltese went rigid. Then he raced down the hall, shouting for help, while Hammond writhed on the stone floor. The Maltese returned in seconds, followed by a short, gaunt, white-haired man in his sixties.

Armed guards hurried after him with a doctor's bag. The Maltese looked terrified. The white-haired man knelt beside Hammond, his face working, his eyes intent.

'Can you hear me? . . . Herr Hammond. Can you hear me?'

German accent.

'*Herr Hammond?*'

Scared silly.

'Hypodermic,' snapped the German. Expertly, he filled the needle from a vial of adrenalin. The guard unbuttoned Hammond's sleeve. 'I think he's stopped breathing, sir.'

Knows about my heart, Hammond thought. Organized. Prepared. Knows he needs me alive. Excellent. He sat up, grinning. 'I'm fine.'

The German expelled his breath. 'You would play games with me?' he asked stuffily.

'Unless you're here to rescue me from the kidnappers, you're playing games with me too, fella.'

'That was not a funny trick.' He squirted the adrenalin on the floor and handed the needle to the Maltese.

'Who are you?'

'Put him back in his room.'

The guards yanked him to his feet, a little less gently

than the Maltese had handled him, and dragged him down the corridor while the German walked the other way.

'I'll make you a deal,' Hammond yelled.

'You're in no position to make anyone a deal.'

'Like hell I'm not.'

'What do you mean?' The German turned around and Hammond, craning to see past the guards, knew he had him.

'Anybody with something to offer is in a position to deal.'

'You can't afford your ransom. You have no money.'

So it was ransom. But how in hell did the kraut know he had no money? 'I'm not talking about ransom.'

'You can't pay ransom. You have nothing. You're a man in a locked room, until I let you go.'

'Insurance.'

'What?'

'I can offer insurance.'

'What kind of insurance?'

'If you tell me who you are, and what you're going to do with me, I'll insure your scam against failure.'

The German approached him, intrigued. He gestured the guards should let him go. 'What do you mean?'

'Told you I had something to offer,' Hammond grinned. 'So let's sit and talk some business. You got an office?'

Ponderously, the German said, 'I like your audacity. Yes. Come.' He led him out of the corridor and upstairs to a worn, comfortable sitting room with a coal fire, and plush chairs – thirties' relics which, like the carpet and yellowed lampshades, had seen better days. Hammond caught another uninformative glimpse of the sea through a curtained window and took the chair the German indicated. The fire was nice, but his cell had been warmer and he asked for a blanket. The Maltese chauffeur brought and fitted it solicitously around his legs, after which the German told him to bring tea.

'Yes, I'm sorry about the cold. I'm sure you miss the warmth of your island this time of year.'

Hammond nodded. 'Since my heart attack I can't seem to handle the weather up here any more.'

'I had a by-pass myself, a few years ago. I do almost everything . . . except love-making's become rather frightening.'

Hammond grinned, boasting to take command of the situation. 'That's my idea of the way to go, if I have to.' He surprised himself, thinking suddenly and forcefully of Helen Thorp, and added, more seriously than he had intended to sound, 'Love-making's okay. Falling in love, or falling out, that'll kill you.'

The German shrugged. 'Now what is this insurance?'

'The premium is information. Who are you? What's your plan?'

'And what do I get in return?'

'Ransom insurance.'

'Ransom insurance?'

'Sure. If anything goes wrong with your scam – and we both survive – I'll pay you one million dollars within six months.'

The German stared. Then he laughed, his features growing wizened as laughter compressed his mouth and brow around his long, thin nose. 'Well, that's very clever, but your ransom will be much much more than one million dollars. I'm estimating something in the range of fifty million, perhaps more.'

'I should hope so,' Hammond shot back. 'Like most insurance you're better off if you don't have to collect. But one million dollars is a million more than nothing. And all it costs you is some information.'

'How do I know you will pay me?'

Hammond's expression hardened. 'If you know enough about me to kidnap me, you damned well know the value of Charles Hammond's word.'

'Yes. Quite.'

'So we have a deal.'

'Why not? I won't fail, but it's an amusing thought.'

'Who are you?'

The German introduced himself, smiling, enjoying Hammond. 'My name is Karl Grandzau.'

Hammond knew the name. An espionage hustler. A cheap little go-between and notorious double-crosser. Grandzau had played the East–West spy game with stolen middle-level secrets that were often out-dated before money changed hands. Then he dropped out of sight. In fact, Hammond seemed to recall he had died, but the smirk on his face suggested that was apparently and unfortunately not true.

Of all the silly people to get kidnapped by – and now, of all times – the worst goddamned luck in the world, just as he was about to pull off the deal of his life, the big one, the deal to end all deals. He had been a foot from paradise before this joker grabbed him. *He had to escape*.

'What makes you think I can't afford my own ransom?' he asked casually.

'You think very little of me,' Grandzau replied. 'You know all the facts and all the people who care about the facts. But I know secrets.'

'You think there's a difference between facts and secrets?' Hammond retorted, concealing his scorn until he concluded how to deal with this joker.

'Oh, there's a big difference between your facts and my secrets.'

'Like what?'

Grandzau started to tell him, in great detail, secret by secret. Hammond listened, aghast, and when the German was done, Charles Hammond was sick and trembling. For Grandzau had explained why it was no accident he had been kidnapped.

And there was no escape. All Hammond could hope for was that the right bidders won him in time at the Pendragon Auction.

'More tea?'

The Maltese had poured during the tale and left the pot under a stained cosy.

'Fuck off.'

'You're awfully edgy for a man who's supposed to be the calm one in the middle of the storm,' Grandzau said mockingly. 'Charles Hammond the negotiator. The great deal-maker. The cool go-between.'

'I'm sick of dealing and you know it.'

'Don't worry, Herr Hammond. It is not in my interest to disappoint your new friends.'

He raised his haggard face to his captor. 'Will you keep your word? Will you let me go in time?'

'Of course – provided anyone bids for you.'

'What? What do you mean?'

'Relax,' Grandzau said soothingly. 'I was only teasing, as you teased me before with your "heart attack". Of course they'll bid for you. They'll bid a king's ransom . . . As well they should for a man who would be king.'

BOOK III

20

YOUR BID IS EXPECTED AT THE PENDRAGON AUCTION SAVOY HOTEL. LONDON. LANCELOT.

'*London?* What the hell am I doing in New York?'

'Ms Thorp will see you now,' said her secretary. She took back the telegram she'd handed him when Chamberlain arrived, and led him into Helen Thorp's office. She was conferring with a young, Cardin-suited executive.

Chamberlain thought that the suit's upturned shoulders made the guy look as if he would fly away on little wings. He was in a lousy mood. Helen noted his arrival with a quick glance and resumed her instructions.

'Copy me up to two hundred and fifty thousand. Over that, tell me first.'

The guy's hands quickened. He asked, 'Can I go to a million?'

'Not without telling me.'

She stood up and rounded her desk, and walked him past Chamberlain to the door. The guy stared through him, visibly annoyed that Chamberlain had been allowed in before his meeting was over. Chamberlain watched Helen Thorp from the corner of his eye. She was wearing a dark pleated slit skirt and a pale blue silk blouse buttoned to the neck. Her thick dark hair swayed as she walked and when she reached for the doorknob, her breasts swelled attractively against the silk.

She smiled. 'If I'm out of town and it's urgent Mildred can reach me. Thanks for coming in, Brian. Mr Cowan and I think you're doing a damned good job.'

She closed the door and regarded Chamberlain coolly

through her long lashes. 'Which is more than I can say for you.'

'If you told your secretary to let me in early to show me how important you are, it worked. I'm very impressed.'

'It was to show you how important you are.'

'If I'm that important why the hell did I have to come to New York if the auction's in London?'

'Why?' she asked with ice in her voice. 'To keep you out of trouble between now and the time Hammond is auctioned.'

Chamberlain glared angrily and she glared back. 'Alfred Cowan was worried that you might crash the company plane into the Savoy, but I told him not to worry, that Hammond was safe if you were aiming at the Savoy because you'd hit the Dorchester.'

'If you want to fire me, fire me. But spare me the sarcasm.'

'Spare *you*. Did it ever occur to you that a little sarcasm is all that's preventing me from screaming my head off at you. Can you imagine what it's been like getting your reports these few days? Five groups were looking for Charles Hammond. You tied for fourth place with the Russians.'

'First, second and third got killed.'

She let go the doorknob and waved his objection aside. 'But number three, your *friends* at the CIA almost got Hammond killed with them, which was precisely what you were hired to prevent.'

Chamberlain met her angry gaze, then looked away. She wasn't the sort to waste time yelling at him if she was going to fire him. Getting Hammond back was still too good a chance to screw up by getting in a fight with Ms Thorp. He looked at his watch. Four o'clock in the afternoon, New York time. He'd taken off from Brest the moment she had called.

'You're right, Ms Thorp. The simple fact of the matter is that I'm no closer to Hammond than I was three days ago in this same office.'

'Almost four.'

'Four. Right now it's ten o'clock at night in London and I should be there.'

'I'm afraid we'll have to get bidding instructions from Mr Cowan, first. He's waiting for us. He said to bring you in as soon as you got here.'

'Is that why you brought me back to New York? To see Mr Cowan?'

'Yes.'

'I have a big mouth. I'm sorry.'

'Let's not keep Alfred waiting.' She led him through Mildred's office to Cowan's. Chamberlain followed sheepishly, feeling silly, and enjoying her perfume.

Cowan was in a conference call, sitting at his desk with his feet propped up on an open drawer, addressing a speaker phone. He nodded at Helen and Chamberlain. 'Sorry, boys, I gotta get off. Try to work it out and get back to me in the morning.'

He flipped the phone off and said, 'Have a seat. How you doing, Pete?'

'I've done better.'

'Didn't work the way we thought it would, did it?'

'No, sir.'

'What's your next step?'

'I guess that's up to you and Ms Thorp, sir.'

'You think we should bid?'

'You're asking my opinion?'

'Yes, damnit. I'm a bit busy for small talk.'

'Yes, you should bid. And I think you should put every effort into patching up the consortium so you can outbid the Russians. They want him very badly.'

'Why do they want him?'

215

'I don't know, sir. But they sure as hell do.'

'Helen?'

'Alfred, it just doesn't make sense. The more I think about it, the less sense it makes. But they want him.'

Cowan said, 'What about the CIA?'

'The CIA is going to be a real problem now. They'll probably take their defeat very personally.'

'What the hell for?' snapped Cowan. 'I thought they're supposed to be professionals.'

'They are, but several important people there are now responsible for losing an entire assault team. A clandestine assault team that isn't even supposed to exist and now a lot of people know about it. And those people are almost certainly going to decide that to clean *their* records, at least, they're going to have to pull off a major victory and the only major victory they can pull off that will mean anything will be keeping Hammond from falling into Russian hands.'

'Goddamnit!'

'There's possibly a bright side to it, Alfred,' said Helen Thorp.

'Yeah?' Cowan growled. 'Name it.'

'Grandzau, or whoever Lancelot is, has done a very good job of protecting Hammond so far. Perhaps he has a way to hold the auction safely, in which case we can buy him back. With the help of our partners.'

'What do you think, Pete?'

'She's right. He's probably got a damned good plan.'

'How the hell can he hold a ransom auction at the Savoy Hotel?'

Helen looked at Chamberlain. He knew that she was expecting him to answer, but he wasn't sure what to say.

'I mean that's the craziest thing I ever heard of,' Cowan added.

'Hard to tell,' Chamberlain said slowly. 'He might tell

us all where to go next from there. Or, and I suppose this is possible, he might hold an auction in a private conference room. They've got all kinds of meeting facilities, I'm sure.'

'All I know is last time I stayed there and changed rooms when my wife joined me, it took them eight hours to transfer my bags. Now are you telling me that they'd bring Hammond to the Savoy?'

'Very unlikely. They'd probably keep him someplace else and rig a telephone hook-up to prove he's alive.'

'I hope,' Alfred Cowan said ominously, 'that for Hammond's sake, that doesn't happen. Because you' – he pointed at Helen – 'are not taking any Comptel money to any auction where Hammond isn't. You're not taking a penny anywhere you don't have a guarantee you can buy him alive.'

'Of course not, Alfred.'

'Don't "of course not" me. I'm not making any exceptions on this. If Grandzau wants Comptel money at that auction he's going to produce Hammond on the spot.'

He looked at Chamberlain and Chamberlain nodded because there didn't seem to be any point not to.

Cowan pointed at Helen again. 'This thing has the potential to be a hell of a con job.'

'Except that Hammond is kidnapped,' said Helen. 'Surely you're not suggesting that a man of his talents and success would engineer his own kidnapping for a few million dollars?'

'Not likely,' said Cowan. 'But I want proof that he's alive before I pay a penny for him.'

Helen smiled. 'You're repeating yourself, Alfred.'

'For emphasis, dear. Emphasis.'

'How high can we bid?'

'I've been thinking maybe we should raise Comptel's contribution to ten million dollars.'

217

Helen Thorp stared at him. 'Thank you, Alfred. Thank you very much.'

'Just remember the conditions. And one more; I want you over there.' He turned to Chamberlain, who hoped his annoyance hadn't shown. All he needed was her dogging his tracks in London. 'Pete, I think you better play it defensively for a while. Watch the CIA and watch the Russians, but don't go for Grandzau. I think we better rely on his good sense. He's done pretty well so far, wouldn't you say?'

Chamberlain heard himself saying, 'Yes, sir. He's done very well.'

'Okay. Thanks for coming over so fast. Now, I think you better hop right back on that plane and head for London.'

'Yes, sir,' replied Chamberlain. He stood with a grin. 'You're spending more on my aviation fuel than my salary.'

Cowan looked at him blankly. 'Fuel's expensive.'

Chamberlain wished he'd kept his mouth shut. 'Yes, sir.'

'One other thing, Pete.'

'Yes, sir?'

'Keep an eye on Ms Thorp. I don't want her in any danger at all. I'm not kidding. As far as I'm concerned, she's more important than Hammond.'

'The stockholders might not agree with you,' said Helen.

Cowan ignored her. He held Chamberlain's gaze for a long time with hard, flat eyes. Finally, he lumbered around his desk, awkwardly patted her shoulder, and mumbled, 'Take care of yourself.'

Chamberlain spotted a KGB man. Thirty feet across the lobby a CIA operative was reading the Reuters News Service teletype printouts that the Savoy Hotel displayed for its guests. Buying the Paris *Herald Tribune* at the news stand, he sat down on a couch between them and when Helen Thorp found him there he had already concluded that both super spook agencies had changed tactics.

The CIA operative had the grey hair, the recent suntan, the horn-rimmed glasses and the casual houndstooth jacket associated with a retired midwestern businessman trailing his wife on yet another world tour. He wore a kindly, grandfatherly expression and though he might have stood with a touch more solid grace than the average grandfather, he could easily pass for a man who played squash twice a week with his doctor.

The KGB man looked equally benign, exactly like a middle-European university professor, with a light, wispy cloud of white hair swirling above a balding pate, wire-rimmed glasses, and a badly cut woollen suit. He looked a bit too shabby to belong in the Savoy, but he could have been attending a convention.

'They've pulled out the heavies,' he told Helen. 'They're both just lying back and watching. These clowns aren't even carrying coats. They couldn't follow us into the street.'

'Maybe the heavies are outside.'

'I already checked. They're not. No, they just decided to stop hitting.'

'Like us.'

'Right. Grandzau's intimidated all of us.'

'Good. Let's go.'

They walked the few blocks to the City where All Seas had its offices. René Rice, the receptionist informed them, was out for the day.

'But I had an appointment,' said Helen Thorp.

'Mr Rice asked me to apologize. He had to leave on a pressing matter.'

'I'm at the Savoy. I must talk with him. Let's go, Pete.'

Chamberlain followed her out of the door. When they

got to the street, she said, 'He's been ducking me. He can't handle this.'

She looked up and down the narrow street and checked her watch. 'Damnit. Okay, back to the hotel. We'll work on the others. Get a cab.'

Chamberlain hailed a taxi. On the ride back, she sat in one corner, staring out of the window, chewing her lip. She'd been nervous and irritable on the flight over and a night's sleep hadn't helped much. Chamberlain sympathized. Grandzau had the lot of them locked up in the Savoy, waiting.

'Shall we try the hospitality suite?' she asked when they got back to the Savoy.

Chamberlain knew it wasn't a question. He followed her up the stairs, thinking again that Grandzau was close to brilliant when it came to manipulating the people who were waiting for his auction. He had rented a suite on the second floor, in the name Pendragon Ltd, and stocked it with a bar and a waiter who presided over a sumptuous hors d'oeuvre table.

Bored and restless, the invitees to the Pendragon Auction gathered in the hospitality suite as they would at a convention and drank and schemed and speculated what would happen next. When Chamberlain and Helen Thorp arrived, the new representative from Mishuma was telling the man who claimed to have inherited Hans Streicher's business that a bell-boy had told him that Pendragon Ltd had rented an entire floor of the hotel starting in two days.

'The seventh, that would make it. He's holding the auction right here.'

The man from Dassault shook his head scornfully. 'Ridiculous. He won't hold the auction in the hotel. Five limousines are reserved early in the morning of the seventh. It will be done in some country house out in Surrey.'

'We say *down* in Surrey,' remarked the Englishman who represented British Hovercraft. 'Not *out*.'

The Frenchman stared, sneered, '*Anglais*,' then spied Helen Thorp and lighted in smiles.

'Ms Thorp. What have you heard? Where will the auction be held?'

'Not a thing, but I'm glad I found you all here. Now's as good a time as any to re-form the bidding consortium and finalize our commitments.'

She looked around at the dozen men in the room. Several, seeing her expression, put their glasses back on the bar. She said to the bartender and the waiter, 'Would you excuse us, please. That will be all for now.'

They trooped out.

'And you, please,' she added, when they had gone, nodding at the Russian who shrugged unhappily and levered his bulk out of the chair in the corner and lumbered out under the stares of the others.

'Is there anyone else who intends to bid for Hammond alone and not join in the consortium?'

Men looked from one to another and said nothing.

'Is there anyone else who should be here that anyone knows of?'

'There's a Qatari sheik who's bidding,' said the German.

'Has anyone seen him?'

No one had.

'It's probably a rumour.'

'What about Rice?' asked the Frenchman.

'I'll get to him,' said Helen.

'None of us have seen him,' said the Frenchman. 'Perhaps Rice is also a rumour.'

Several men laughed.

'I'm sure,' Helen Thorp replied icily, 'that Charles Hammond's own company will contribute handsomely to the auction fund that Comptel has started.'

The man from Dassault picked up his glass, and clinked his ice thoughtfully. 'Who's to say,' he asked no one in particular, 'that Comptel Incorporated is to direct the consortium to buy back Charles Hammond?'

'Any company contributing more than Comptel is welcome to the doubtful pleasure of managing the consortium.'

'Well, how much is Comptel contributing?' asked the Frenchman.

Helen Thorp stood where she had when she entered the room, several feet in from the door, her hands in her coat pockets, Chamberlain behind and to her right.

'If Grandzau didn't bug this room, then the KGB or the CIA or Scotland Yard probably did. Possibly all four did. Therefore, I suggest you write your contributions on a piece of paper and pass them to me and I will award the chairmanship of the consortium to the highest contributor.'

'Can we trust you to do that?'

'I will then pass the papers around and everyone can see. Then I'll take them back and burn them.'

Chamberlain found himself admiring her infinite patience. Nothing the Frenchman could say would ruffle her. She took off her coat, handed it to Chamberlain and sat down. She had a gold pen and she wrote briefly on a cocktail napkin. There was no other paper around, so the others followed suit. And while they were writing, Helen Thorp casually blotted her lips with her napkin. They brought them to her. She collected them in her lap and when she had the last, she shuffled through them, reading without expression. Finally she stacked them in a neat pile and stood up.

'Well,' said the Frenchman.

Chamberlain saw a small red spot rise to her cheek. She crossed the room and handed the napkins to the Japanese. The man from Mishuma bowed, glanced through the napkins and passed them to another man. He rose and cleared his throat.

'Encouraged by Comptel Incorporated, we as a group have raised a very large fund to ransom Mr Hammond. We at Mishuma are pleased to lead such a generous consortium.'

Someone started clapping and several others followed suit.

Chamberlain watched Helen Thorp. She clapped politely, as if at any ceremonial meeting. The red spot had gone from her cheek and he couldn't read what she was thinking, though he had the feeling that she had begun to relax.

Chamberlain watched the napkins go from man to man. Most read them eagerly. One or two looked chagrined, as if their companies hadn't contributed enough. Several looked in awe at the man from Japan. Something had been bothering Chamberlain, and now he got it. Most of the American companies had replaced the men they'd sent earlier in the week; with Kaga Nagumo gone, and Hans Streicher, this was a younger and more aggressive group. The first crowd had been a bunch of lawyers. This time, the companies were sending a different type, as if they had decided that their top young executives were better equipped to deal with the auction. Like the CIA and the KGB, the companies who wanted Charles Hammond were treating Grandzau more seriously. The whole event had taken on a more cautious tone. He watched them return to the bar and freshen their drinks.

Something about them still bothered him. There wasn't the panic here there had been before. He shook his head, wondering what made him think the fix was in?

21

'What'd they go for?'

They were walking quickly down a carpeted hallway. She seemed very excited.

'About sixty million dollars, not counting the Japanese.'

'And counting the Japanese?'

She turned to him, awed. 'The Japanese are contributing *thirty* million dollars. They must have government backing. Can you imagine what Hammond is doing for them to make him that valuable?'

'Ninety million bucks for one guy? He can't be worth that much.'

'Let's hope the Russians feel the way you do.'

'Grandzau's a genius,' said Chamberlain. 'Hammond can't be worth that much to any one group. But together –'

They had reached the lobby and she interrupted him. 'There's somebody coming your way.'

Chamberlain looked up. 'Hello. Inspector Farquhar, this is Ms Helen Thorp, my boss at Comptel. Inspector Farquhar's with Scotland Yard. He was *very* helpful right after the kidnapping.'

Farquhar took her hand, then shook hands with Chamberlain.

'Mr Chamberlain exaggerates. Actually, we helped each other.'

'How's Wheeler?' asked Chamberlain.

'Recovering nicely. Asking to be let out, but it will be a while. Hammond's bodyguard,' he explained to Helen.

'Yes, I visited Mr Wheeler earlier today.' Chamberlain looked at her, surprised. She hadn't said anything to him.

Farquhar turned to Chamberlain. 'I wonder if you might have a moment?'

'Sure.'

'I'll be upstairs,' said Helen. 'Call me when you're done.'

Farquhar watched her walk to the lift. 'Good God, man. Where do I sign up?'

'There's an opening in the London Office.'

'I'd prefer her office. Something to drink?'

'Sure.'

'My car's waiting. There's a nice little pub over on St Martin's Lane. Shall we?'

Chamberlain glanced around as they walked out of the door. Now the CIA and KGB men were watching him with interest. Farquhar's car was a regular Metropolitan Police car.

'I'd prefer leaving here in something less conspicuous,' Chamberlain remarked.

Farquhar laughed. 'Terribly sorry. This was all they had.' But Chamberlain noticed that Farquhar took pains to exit from the car before they reached his pub. Once inside, with beer in hand, Farquhar said, 'I'll get to the point. Two points, actually. The first is important, the second interesting.'

'What's up?'

Farquhar cleared his throat. He seemed embarrassed, but determined, and as he spoke, his determination hardened.

'I've traced your meanderings across the Continent with some concern.'

'How do you mean, traced?'

'Interpol followed you easily, shall we say. Hardly surprising, the general death and mayhem that accompanied your visits to various towns and cities. My concern, how-ever, turned to alarm when I learned you were headed back to London. Quite simply, old son, we can't permit that sort of thing here in England.'

'Fair enough. What's the interesting thing?'

'We won't permit it. I have my orders. We are not to interfere in the Pendragon Auction, but neither are we to allow wholesale slaughter in the streets. We will deport anyone, regardless of alliance, who participates in any violent act.'

'Do you think Grandzau will hold the auction here, at the Savoy?'

Farquhar smiled, obviously relieved to be done with his message. He scooped up Chamberlain's glass and got two more lagers from the sweeping double bar. When he returned to their round corner table, Chamberlain was watching the street through the curtains. He released the cloth and took the glass mug Farquhar offered.

'Cheers,' said Farquhar.

'Cheers. Do you think that Grandzau will hold his auction in the Savoy Hotel?'

'That's my interesting news.'

'He will?'

'No. You probably are aware that some of our Concordes were never put into commercial service. The poor things have been ferried about to wherever someone might buy one and occasionally, rarely, they've been chartered for private work.'

'Why bother?'

'I imagine the accountants are happy to enter anything on the credit side. At any rate, we've just learned that somebody who sounds awfully like Grandzau has chartered a Concorde.'

Chamberlain put his mug down. 'For when?'

'The seventh.'

'Where to?'

'That, we don't know. But he's requested pilots who know the Gulf States. Draw your own conclusions.'

'The Persian Gulf? Why the hell all the way down there?'

'Why not?' asked Farquhar. 'The Gulf area might encourage some of Hammond's Arab clients to participate. They'd feel safer on their own ground. He was heavily involved in some of the smaller states' arms purchases. He was virtually Hans Streicher's only agent in the Gulf.'

Chamberlain nodded. 'Sure. With the Shah gone, every sheik with a spare two billion dollars is building his own army.'

'Why do you think my government is so interested? Hammond has such marvellous contacts in the smaller states. We had concentrated too long on Iran and Saudi Arabia. Our arms people found Hammond could do a lot better for them than they could in places like Qatar, the Emirates, even Kuwait. They say he has a fine touch with the more primitive peoples.'

'But why would Grandzau hide in Hammond's territory?'

'He seems to have planned everything very carefully. Certainly there he doesn't have to worry about CIA and KGB attacks.'

'He's got to worry about the Arabs,' said Chamberlain.

'One would imagine he's made an arrangement.'

Chamberlain sipped his lager. It didn't make a lot of sense. 'Why the Concorde?' he asked. 'Can you imagine what that thing costs?'

'The figure I heard for the deposit alone would have kept an earl comfortable for a decade.'

'Do you realize what this whole kidnapping has cost Grandzau?' Chamberlain marvelled. 'The snatch, the plane, getting to that island – you heard about the island?'

'Oh yes. The CIA débâcle was cause for a certain amount of delight in European circles.'

'And now the Concorde? Money, money, money. Who the hell is paying for it?'

'Grandzau could have retired rather well off.'

'He'd have had to,' said Chamberlain. 'He must have a backer. A very rich one.'

'Possibly,' conceded Farquhar. 'But that doesn't help us.'

'Specially if he's sitting down in some Arab state right now waiting for the fun to begin.'

'He's done well.'

'I wonder why he bothered chartering a Concorde?' Chamberlain mused.

'Speed. It's a long flight to the Gulf.'

'Sure, but he would be better off putting us on a conventional plane so we get there exhausted and in no condition to give him any trouble at the auction. That's what I would do.'

Farquhar drained his glass. 'I would too, but then again, neither of us came up with the clever idea of kidnapping Hammond in the first place. I'm afraid I must be going. Can I drop you?'

Chamberlain lifted the curtain again and checked the street.

'Is that guy following me?'

Farquhar looked. 'Fellow with the cloth cap? Yes. Ever since you landed last night at the airport. I have men observing everyone at the auction. We're quite serious about minimizing the carnage.'

'I thought I saw him down by René Rice's office a couple of hours ago.'

'He's a new man,' Farquhar said dryly. 'Not yet as skilled as his partner.'

Chamberlain pulled a disgusted face, and Farquhar laughed. 'Sorry, old son.'

'Where *is* René Rice?'

'Up until two hours ago he was holding continuous telephone conversations with Madagascar. We've of course got taps on his telephones, in the event the kidnappers make direct contact.'

'What's he talking about?'

It was Farquhar's turn to make a face. 'Frankly, I haven't the foggiest. We can't locate a single soul in the entire British Isles who can understand his brand of Malagasy. It's polysyllabic, with a vengeance. They link scads of phrases which form single unpronounceable words of unbelievable length.'

'Like German?'

'Much worse. The French sent us a translator. It was their colony, you see. He was worthless. Rendered literal translations which bore no relationship to the intelligible. Rice must know we're listening and he's circumspect.'

'Could you tell how Rice sounded?'

'Agitated. Hammond's name popped up regularly.'

'Until two hours ago?'

'Yes. At that time the phones to Madagascar went dead.'

'Just like that?'

'It was expected. One of their political parties called a general strike to protest against electioneering irregularities. Candidates arrested, that sort of thing. At any rate, poor Mr Rice went home to listen to the government radio broadcasts on his wireless. The election is in two days. Same day as your auction, in actual fact.'

'Jesus. I want Rice concentrating on Hammond, not a goddamned election in Malagasy. Did you tap his house, too?'

Farquhar nodded. 'Complete surveillance. We arrested

229

some KGB thugs hanging about the All Seas offices and we're taking no chances that they grab Rice.'

'I'd like to talk to him,' said Chamberlain, 'if you have no objection.'

'None.'

'Where does he live?'

'I'll drop you. It's on my way.'

While Farquhar hailed a cab with his furled umbrella, Chamberlain approached the man who'd been following. He looked frozen. The thin sleet had dusted his cap and shoulders dirty white. Chamberlain caught his eye and circled to hold it as he turned aside.

'They closed Covent Garden market about eight years ago so you're the only guy in the theatre district wearing a cloth cap. Bad show.'

The young man reddened, but he had the sense to look blank before he hurried away. Chamberlain climbed into Farquhar's cab. 'Not bad.'

'I trust, therefore, that you gave the lad some encouragement.'

'Sure.'

They rode silently for a few minutes while Chamberlain mulled over the meaning of the chartered Concorde. An extravagance, unless speed was vital. But if speed were, why hadn't Grandzau sent the bidders where he wanted them now, instead of putting them on ice at the Savoy?

A big, hard-faced man going to fat opened Rice's door. Chamberlain recalled that Rice's secretary was former FBI. Before either could speak, Rice peeked around his secretary's shoulder and nodded. 'Monsieur Chamberlain. It's all right, Patterson. I'll take care of this.'

Patterson, expressionless, went back into the room. Over Rice's head, Chamberlain saw that the apartment was sparsely furnished with a few elegant, black lacquer

Chinese pieces. A single splendid carpet, bordered by pickled wood floors, coloured the middle of the room. A gas fire burned hotly in a small marble fireplace, beside which sat an armchair. On a table next to the armchair was a large shortwave radio. Rice's mournful eyes were half shut with exhaustion.

'May I come in?'

'What does Ms Thorp want?' His hands were trembling.

'I believe she wanted confirmation of the All Seas contribution.'

'I'll call her tomorrow.'

'Sir?'

'What is it?' He was already closing the door.

'Who did Mr Hammond visit the morning he was kidnapped?'

Rice answered without having to think about it. 'The morning he was kidnapped Mr Hammond had breakfast with the Japanese ambassador to Great Britain.'

'I mean who was he meeting where he was kidnapped?'

Rice hesitated.

'Did you tell the police who he met?'

'Oh, yes. You could ask them.'

'Or you could tell me.'

Rice shrugged. 'At this point, nothing really matters, does it?'

Chamberlain said nothing. A man in Rice's position would have deeply ingrained habits of discretion.

The Malagasy shrugged again. 'He was visiting an old friend. A Major Ramsey, who lives at the Overseas Club.'

'An intelligence officer?' asked Chamberlain, wondering if he should have gone into this earlier.

'Retired.'

'Oh. Did Major Ramsey and Mr Hammond ever do business?'

Again Rice hesitated. Did he regret opening the topic?

'Perhaps before my time. I've only served Mr Hammond eight years.' His face began to crumble. 'It was just an ordinary morning. He was late, as usual, and I phoned ahead with explanations. Then Patterson and I went to the airport to ready the plane. We had UN meetings in New York on the second.' His voice mirrored the breakdown of his face. 'One moment all was normal, the next, chaos.'

'Was Ms Thorp expecting you?'

'I don't involve myself in Mr Hammond's private life.'

When Chamberlain got back to his room, he knocked on the door that led to Helen's suite, gestured towards the bathroom, sat on the edge of the tub and turned the cold water on full blast.

'Privacy,' he explained over the roar of the tap.

'Aren't you overdoing it a bit?'

'Streicher's boat didn't blow up by itself. Grandzau's had somebody on the ground all along. Stashing the bidders in the same hotel just makes it easier to keep track of us.' He stopped talking and stared. She was wearing a silk robe, a silver-grey clinging garment that set off her beautiful eyes and jet hair. He blurted, 'Jesus Christ, you are gorgeous.'

Her brow furrowed in surprise and annoyance. 'Get off it, Pete, I don't have time for that.'

'Sorry,' he said, wondering, Does she sleep with Hammond? She seemed to worry more about what his kidnapping was doing to her job than to his health. Maybe they were all business. He also wondered why it seemed so important to him. When he had first seen her he hadn't cared who she slept with as long as she had room for another. Now, it occurred to him that in the midst of all this insanity, he was falling for the woman. It also occurred to him that he would probably wait for the dust to settle before he made a move. Yes, she was gorgeous, but she happened to have a serious hold on his future. And his future, at the moment, was Charles Hammond. He gave her an easy smile, and said, 'It just sort of slipped out.'

'Well, put it back. What did Farquhar say?'

'He thinks that Grandzau's rented a Concorde to fly the bidders to the Persian Gulf tomorrow.'

'The latest rumour around the hotel is that Grandzau is sending us to Scotland on the train. I like yours better.'

'I've got another one that's even better.'

'What?'

'This is just my idea. I haven't told anybody.'

'What?'

'How about, Hammond set up his own kidnapping?'

She nodded calmly, and it occurred to Chamberlain that she might have had the same thought. Obviously she knew Hammond very well. How well he could only guess from Rice's oblique comment on Hammond's private life.

'How,' she asked, 'of all the possibilities, could you have come to that conclusion?'

'I added up what the kidnapping must have cost. Somebody's put a fortune into it.'

'And because Charles Hammond is heavily mortgaged you assume that he spent his money on faking his own kidnapping. Is that your *only* reason?'

Chamberlain began to feel uncomfortable. 'No. Holding the auction in a Gulf state is another. He'd feel safe there among his Arab friends.'

'Anything else?' she asked coolly.

'I found Rice.'

'And?'

'First of all, it still bothers me that he's such a lightweight. It's like Hammond doesn't trust somebody smart around him.'

'Ridiculous,' said Helen.

233

'Anyway, Rice told me that Hammond visited a retired spy a few minutes before he was snatched. Supposedly it was a social call.'

'So?'

'Funny coincidence. Funny sort of friend for a busy guy like Hammond to have. A social call in the middle of the day. How many do you make?'

'Purely social? None. But that's me. I don't really have friends. But it was the holidays, and perhaps he stopped to make a courtesy call. People do that around the holidays. Hammond would do that. Stop by and see an old man alone in his Club for Christmas.'

'What got this started in my mind was what Mr Cowan said about the kidnapping and the auction having great potential for a con.'

'Anything else?'

'Yeah. I doubt Rice is in on it. He seems too broken up.'

'Anything else?'

'No . . . you don't sound convinced.'

'I don't agree or disagree. I'm just being devil's advocate. I want to think about it and I think I better talk to Alfred.'

Chamberlain started excitedly for the door.

'Where are you going?'

'You talk to Mr Cowan. I'll check out Ramsey at the club.'

'No. Don't do that.' She stood, the robe shimmering from her breasts.

'Why not?'

'Because I want you here with me when Grandzau makes his move.'

'That's not till the day after tomorrow.'

'We don't know for sure. Farquhar's guessing about that Concorde. Grandzau's completely unpredictable.'

'But he's not going to start the auction without everybody.'

'Pete,' she said flatly, brushing past him and out into the suite. 'I want you with me.'

Chamberlain followed her, exasperated. 'Ms Thorp, this could mean something.'

'Like what? We've already decided to stop hunting Grandzau and do what he wants.'

'What if it's a con?'

'It's not,' she said angrily.

'May I suggest something?'

'What?'

'To protect the company. To protect ourselves. It won't hurt to have a couple of your analysts try to sort out Hammond's finances. And it won't hurt for you and me to go see this Major Ramsey. Those are two decent leads. We'd be crazy to pass them up.'

Her eyes had turned cold and very hard. He'd seen that same look in Alfred Cowan's eyes when the company chairman was issuing a direct order. It was a detached look a professional fighter got after he'd made his decision to kill.

'You're right,' she said. 'I'll call New York. Then we're going over to see that man.' She grinned. 'It'll beat hanging around this dumb hotel.'

'I'll get some dry shoes,' said Chamberlain. He stopped, halfway through the door that connected his room to her suite. She was already reaching for the telephone.

'Hey, thanks,' said Chamberlain. 'Thanks a lot.'

'For what?' she asked, eyebrow soaring.

'For listening to me.'

Helen Thorp looked at him, held him with her steady gaze. Then she grinned again. 'I'll meet you in the lobby. Ten minutes. Next to the KGB spy.'

She took his arm as they rounded Harrods and walked into the quiet neighbourhood behind the giant department store.

235

'Do you mind?'

'Not at all.'

The snow was glazing the pavement and her leather-soled boots were sliding on the ice. He could feel her fingers through his coat.

'I'm so glad we came,' she said. 'I can't stand sitting around.'

Chamberlain glanced at her as they crossed a street. She looked as happy as she sounded. Despite the storm, which was driving afternoon shoppers off the streets, she'd insisted on leaving the cab on Knightsbridge and walking the last few blocks. The cold air had flushed her cheeks and snowflakes lay like stars in her black hair.

'Do you walk a lot?' Chamberlain asked.

'Oh, yes. I hate having to exercise, and I'll be damned if I'll jog around town in a sweatsuit. I'd much rather put on some decent clothes and take a good long look at a piece of New York. Where is this place?'

'Right around the corner, I think. There it is, Herbert Crescent.'

They followed the curving street until they came to the Overseas Club, identified only by its number, midway in the row of Dutch façade town houses. The street continued a couple of hundred feet to a small garden surrounded by a black iron fence. Through the fence and the bare trees could be seen another street of town houses.

They climbed the steps of the Overseas Club. Helen rang the bell. Chamberlain had a look up and down the street. 'Eerie, isn't it?' said Helen. 'They took Hammond right there.' A couple of little English cars were parked where the limousine must have sat.

When the hall-porter opened the door, he led them politely into the foyer before he asked their business. Chamberlain noticed a bulge in his morning coat which might have been a gun. Helen asked if they could see Major Ramsey.

'Have you an appointment?'

'I'm afraid we don't. But if you would be so kind as to tell Major Ramsey that I am Helen Thorp and a friend of Charles Hammond, I think the Major might see us.' The hall-porter went in to ask.

'You're acting awfully English all of a sudden,' Chamberlain remarked.

'When in England . . . It worked for Hadrian and it's working for me.' She gazed about the foyer, inspecting the paintings on the walls, quietly enjoying herself, until the hall-porter returned. The Major would probably see them in the front sitting room. Chamberlain thought that the foyer, which was much smaller than most clubs he'd been in, looked very easy to defend, an asset in a home for retired spooks.

The sitting room was dimly lighted, and tomb silent – a large room filled with leather chairs on a drab carpet, heavy draperies, and oil portraits of men from the 1940s on the walls. Major Ramsey sat by a coal fire. He rose when he saw Helen Thorp, shook her hand, and then Chamberlain's, and invited them to sit by the fire.

Chamberlain thought Ramsey must be seventy-five if he was a day. A neat and trim man, with a little bristly moustache and a pink scalp. He had tiny, bright eyes and a clear voice.

'How do you know Charles Hammond?'

'He has managed business deals for the company I work for, Comptel Inc.,' said Helen. 'Mr Chamberlain works in our security division and is assisting me in our efforts to get Hammond from the kidnappers.'

'Any new word on the auction?' asked Ramsey.

'How do you know about the auction?' Helen asked, glancing in alarm at Chamberlain.

237

'Come, come. I can ask old friends a favour now and then. They know how worried I am about Charles Hammond.'

'No new word since we've been summoned to the Savoy.'

'Why did you want to see me?'

'We wondered if you could tell us what Charles – Mr Hammond came to see you about just before they kidnapped him?'

Ramsey glanced into the fire and answered softly, 'He came to say Happy New Year.'

'Is that all?' asked Chamberlain.

'It meant a lot to me.' He waved Chamberlain's objection aside. 'No, no. I understand your meaning. I'm sorry. It was purely a social call, with no connection with the kidnapping, except for one thing.'

'What's that?'

'It was on his schedule to see me that morning. So the bogus chauffeur was able to tip off his henchmen. I want to help get Charles back, but I can't. I have nothing to add.'

'What did you talk about?'

Ramsey looked at Chamberlain. 'CIA?'

'Was.'

'Quite . . . We talked, like friends talk.' Suddenly he brightened. 'Do you know what?'

'What?' asked Helen. She'd been regarding him with a smile while Chamberlain asked the questions. Now she leaned forward, warmly and attentively. 'What did Charles say?'

'He invited me to come and live in Madagascar – Malagasy. You see I worked in East Africa for many years. Long before your time, Mr Chamberlain. Before your CIA knew precisely where East Africa was, as a matter of fact. He knows how the cold troubles me in England.'

'That's wonderful. Are you going to go?'

'I told him I would. But now – yes, I'll go, if Charles survives this. He said I could live on one of his plantations. Or in Tana. Or both. He's retiring there, too, you know. Very – '

'He's always talked about that,' Helen said. 'Well, thank you for seeing us and – '

'He said he was through dealing. "No more deals," he said. "I'm retiring."'

'Charles Hammond retiring,' Helen laughed. 'I find that hard to believe.'

'So did I.'

'Just talk I think. Good-bye, Major.'

As they started down the front steps of the Overseas Club, Chamberlain stopped suddenly, Helen slipped and had to grab his arm. 'What's wrong?'

'There. Across the garden.'

Through its bare trees and bushes, which were accumulating snow on their branches, he saw a man almost obscured by the glistening sleet. 'What? What's wrong?'

'See the guy walking on the other side of the garden? See, he just turned into it, heading this way.'

'In the black coat. Yes.'

'He's the KGB man who killed Kreegan.'

22

'What's he doing here?'

Chamberlain cursed himself for not bringing a gun. He'd taken the shot revolver from the plane, but he'd hidden it in the hotel room. London was no place to be caught carrying without all kinds of licences and Inspector Farquhar had made it only too clear how little support he'd be if Chamberlain got into trouble.

The man passed from sight, then reappeared. He was heading towards Herbert Crescent and now it was unmistakable that he was dressed entirely in black and carrying a short cane. Chamberlain looked at Helen. She couldn't run in those boots, but he had to get her out of his way. He looked up the street, from where they had come. Too far.

'Quick. Get back inside the club.' He walked her, protesting, back up the stairs to the Overseas Club. 'Go sit with Ramsey again. I'll get back to you as soon as I take care of this clown.'

'What are you going to do?'

'What you pay me to do. Please get inside.'

'Wait a minute,' she said, irritated.

'You're putting me in a dangerous position. Will you please get inside?'

'It can't be the same man. What's he doing here?'

'That's the first thing I'm going to ask him, if you will just get out of my way.'

She rang the door bell. Chamberlain started back down the stairs as the door opened.

He heard the hall-porter invite her in out of the snow.

Too late.

It had taken too long to get rid of her. The man in black had already emerged from the park gardens and was well onto Herbert Crescent, flicking his cane against his leg and nervously eyeing the street. The instant he saw Chamberlain coming down the stairs of the Overseas Club, he turned and ran.

He had a thirty-yard lead. Chamberlain tore after him, astonished and elated. The guy was running because he didn't know that Chamberlain wasn't carrying and he didn't know that Chamberlain was alone. Which meant *he* was alone. And maybe wasn't carrying either.

The man in black ran like a scarecrow, the tails of his coat flapping, his heels kicking comically high. But he fled over the slippery ground, gaining with every gangling step, and when he had reached the end of Herbert Crescent he had increased his lead to forty yards.

Chamberlain pumped after him, slipping and sliding, encumbered by his own overcoat, panicked by the guy's uncanny speed. The Russian turned hesitatingly left when he reached the gardens. Chamberlain rounded the turn seconds later, ignoring a clamouring voice in his brain that screamed that his quarry could be standing ten feet past the turn aiming a gun at his head.

He wasn't. He was running still, his lead greater. The distance between them had grown so that the sleet and snow partly obscured Chamberlain's view of him. When he turned the corner the wind hit his feet, driving the stinging sleet into his eyes, burning his cheeks. He thanked his good luck in having bought slip-on rubbers while waiting for Helen in the lobby. They gave him some traction. Still, he rounded the corner wide and had to slow for a second to regain his balance.

He sprinted ahead again, forcing his knees high against his coat. The Russian turned left again. By the time

Chamberlain rounded that corner, he was almost out of sight, up a long, narrow street that ended at the road that ran behind Harrods.

Chamberlain tore at his buttons, flung off his coat.

The Russian jinked right when he reached the end of the narrow street. Chamberlain ran blindly until he reached the corner. Slithering right, again ignoring the chance that he'd be gawking down the Russian's gun barrel, he raced round the corner and searched desperately for a sign of him.

Harrods took up the entire left side of the street, a tall brick wall with dark windows. No one was out in the thickening snow. Street lights glowed dully in the dusk. He ran. A car horn sounded behind him. He flung a glance over his shoulder. A taxi cab. Chamberlain kept running.

Ahead was Sloane Street, cars and buses lined up and moving slowly on the busy thoroughfare. If the Russian made it there he would never find him. A flutter of black suddenly darted through the snow, crossed the street and vanished inside Harrods.

Chamberlain reached the door seconds later. Bursting through the foyer into the main store, he found himself suddenly in a crowd. He worked through it, breathing heavily. It was warm in the store. The snow melted instantly on his shoulders.

He rose on tiptoe and tried to see over the heads and hats of the shoppers. The man in black was crossing an aisle almost a hundred yards away. Chamberlain started after him, sprinting across empty spaces, then elbowing through clusters of customers.

He veered away from cash register areas as he plunged deeper into the store. Twice he lost sight of the man in black, only to spot him again, trapped as he was among jostling crowds. They were concentrated around lifts and stairways and Chamberlain realized that it was almost five o'clock, near closing time. He lost the man in black again. He climbed onto a display counter a salesgirl was covering with a muslin cloth and despite her perplexed inquiries scanned the giant store.

The man in black was running down a staircase. Chamberlain leaped from the counter and charged after him. He descended the low stairway two steps at a time and found himself in a white tiled fish and meat room. The butchers were storing their wares and boys were scooping ice from the empty fish trays. Two customers were left, paying at a cash register, but the man in black had vanished.

Chamberlain saw two exits. He darted from one to the other. The Russian could have gone either way. He chose the door that led to the busiest part of the store, and began searching faces among the departing shoppers. He had seen nothing by the time he was back outside. He looked up and down the street. The pavements were mobbed with people heading for the Underground.

He took a chance and went into the station and down the long escalator to the trains. There were several turnings the Russian could have taken. Chamberlain walked the crowded platform, scrutinizing faces and clothing, but when two trains had come and gone, he realized it was hopeless. Wearily, shivering now as his perspiration dried in the cold air, he made his way up to the surface and walked up Sloane Street and around Harrods, back towards the Overseas Club.

He found his coat where a thoughtful citizen had draped it over an iron fence and got into it gratefully. His hair was soaked from the snow and he buttoned the coat to his neck as he walked quickly towards Herbert Crescent. The snow was filling the long, skidding footsteps he and the man in black had made on the street.

The hall-porter remembered him.

'Mr Chamberlain, yes. I'll tell the lady you're back.'

Helen Thorp came out in five minutes. She greeted Chamberlain with a small smile. 'Where's your dangerous captive?'

'I lost him.'

'You certainly were dramatic about it.'

Chamberlain said nothing. He rose while the hall-porter helped Helen into her sable. The hall-porter offered to telephone for a mini-cab, but suggested they would have better luck on Sloane Street because it was rush hour.

Helen Thorp said they would walk a while, but when they got down the steps and into the full force of the now-blowing snow, she decided otherwise. 'I guess we better get a cab.' She took his arm again as they started slogging back the way they had come.

'Ramsey tell you anything more?'

'No.'

'Anything more about Hammond retiring?'

'Not really. I think Charles might have said that to encourage Ramsey to accept his hospitality. You know, he might have said he would be lonely down in Malagasy and Ramsey would be doing him a favour. Sorry, Pete. I was hoping for a little better, too. But it was just a holiday visit.'

'Are you sure he's telling the truth?' Chamberlain asked doggedly. An experienced agent would find it easy to play the role of a half-dotty old man. But Helen was sure.

'He's just a nice old guy who was happy to have a visitor.' She squeezed his arm so Chamberlain turned to her. 'Do you know what he did?' she asked with a grin.

'What?'

'Took me up to his room on the pretext of showing me his collection of African masks and patted my bottom.'

'You must have made his week.'

'I stood still long enough to make his month. Hey, are we getting a cab or not?'

'As soon as we see one.'

'What's wrong with you?'

'Nothing that catching that Russian son of a bitch wouldn't have cured.'

She stopped and appraised him with her arresting dark eyes. 'You look cold and you're wet and I know a better cure. Come on, I'll buy you a drink.' They were in Sloane Street, caught between hordes of shoppers streaming towards the Underground and other hordes fighting for taxis.

'Fine by me,' said Chamberlain, looking around for a pub.

'Not here. Come on, cross the street, we'll go down there and over to Motcomb.' They walked for five minutes on streets that grew quieter and quieter until she turned into a pub nestled among houses and small shops. Inside, the air was thick with cigarette smoke and the subdued roar of a drinking crowd that lined the bar and filled every table.

It was a neighbourhood place for men and women of all ages stopping off on their way from work. It was warm and friendly and it told Chamberlain that Helen Thorp knew this part of London very well. He wondered again whose apartment she stayed in when she came to London.

She ploughed through the people around the bar, exchanging smiles and remarks with those she jostled, and returned to Chamberlain with two glasses.

'Double whiskies. Hope you like 'em.'

'Perfect. Thanks.'

'Cheers.'

'Cheers.' He met her eye for an instant, marvelling at this side of her he hadn't seen – her ease and pleasure at the busy bar and her warm delight at being alive. He reflected that he had met her under the worst conditions, right after Hammond was kidnapped. And he wondered again, for the fortieth time, what their relationship was.

'Have you lived in London?' he asked.

'Bits and pieces. Several months at a time. Have you?'

'No. New York's my only city.'

'What about Washington?'

'That's no city.'

She laughed. 'True. Actually, I think every real New Yorker needs a country house in London.'

Chamberlain smiled at her smile. She had a beautiful full mouth.

'Where'd you grow up?' she asked.

He told her a little about Connecticut and his first, curious visits to New York City and how he had settled in Greenwich Village for college.

'NYU? You must have been bright. The Business School was my second choice after Wharton. It was tough to get in.'

'I think they had a quota to balance the student body so they let small-town Service types like me in if we could read and write. The crunch came when they asked me to think.'

'Would you like another drink?'

'Sure. Let me get it.'

The crowd began to thin out at six-thirty and by seven o'clock the pub was almost empty. Helen said, 'There's a nice place in Covent Garden for dinner. Just around the corner from the hotel. Care to join me?'

'Sure. Thanks.'

'It'll be fun. Let's go back and change.'

It was still snowing and the streets were empty. They walked to Belgrave Square and found a cab which took them slowly and cautiously across London. Chamberlain felt happy, looking forward to dinner with Helen. What if he could pull this thing off? The kidnapping had already drawn them closer than he could have ever hoped with a powerhouse exec like her. Maybe her needing him now would extend beyond his hitter talents, maybe they could somehow work together. Or, and he certainly hadn't started out looking for it, *have* something together. It could just happen . . .

As was customary at the hotel, when the Savoy doorman opened the cab door, he said, 'Good evening, madam. Good evening, sir.' Then he added in a barely audible mutter, 'The police are waiting in the lobby, Mr Chamberlain. For the lady.'

Chamberlain caught up with Helen inside the revolving door and whispered into her hair, 'We've got cops, I don't know why.'

She turned her face to his, as if to kiss him, and whispered back, 'Inspector Farquhar is sitting on the couch. Do you want to run for it?'

'What?'

'I'm kidding, you idiot.' She kissed him on the mouth. '*That* ought to give him something to think about. Let's go see what he wants.'

She pushed through the revolving door and Chamberlain followed, thinking that the taste and softness of her lips was giving him as much to think about as the sight of her kissing him was giving Farquhar.

Farquhar got quickly to his feet. Chamberlain spotted two of his plainclothes back-up men moving casually closer. The KGB and CIA observers watched almost openly. Farquhar's polite smile was nowhere in evidence. He looked one hundred per cent cop. One hundred per cent angry cop. He said hello, with a chilly glint in his eye, and got right to the point.

'Ms Thorp. I'm afraid I'm going to have to ask you a

few difficult questions. Shall we go to your suite or would you – '

'My suite would be fine, provided you tell me what this is about first.'

'This is about the murder of Major Donald Ramsey in his rooms at the Overseas Club this evening.'

Chamberlain looked at Helen, but she showed nothing. She was as cool as she was behind her desk in New York, and she said just what he was thinking. 'Murdered?'

'He was found after you left.'

'Are you suggesting I should have a lawyer while you ask your questions?' She glanced once at Chamberlain and he wondered, how hard is she? As hard as this act of hers? Or is it an act?

'That's your decision,' Farquhar replied.

'I'll take Mr Chamberlain to witness.'

They rode silently up in the lift. Chamberlain thought that the entire exchange in the lobby must have looked like a simple business meeting to anyone who could not hear the words. He thought that Farquhar was being a bit theatrical, but supposed it was his way of softening up a witness. Were it anyone without the balls of Helen Thorp. How Farquhar could suspect her was beyond belief, or certainly would be if he had heard her talking about the old man the way she had.

A third plainclothes officer was standing outside the Comptel suite, hands clasped behind his back at parade rest. Farquhar nodded to him and he stood aside, as they entered the suite and closed the door. Helen sat in an easy chair, her back to a corner.

'All right, Inspector, what is this all about?'

Her no-nonsense tone infuriated Farquhar. The British inspector reddened visibly. He made no effort now to hide his feelings. Mimicking her tone with devastating accuracy, he said, 'This is about a fine old gentleman, a patriot, a war hero, a devoted public servant, being murdered in cold blood in the club he chose to make his final home. And it is about the fact that you were his last visitor.'

'Was he seen alive after I left?'

'No.'

'Then why are you subjecting me to this nonsense instead of arresting me?'

'I'm very tempted . . . If I had one more shred of evidence –'

'But you have none,' Helen shot back.

'Wait,' Chamberlain said. 'Wait a minute, both of you. Farquhar, did you know Major Ramsey personally?'

'I had that honour.' Farquhar drew himself up ramrod straight.

'I'm sorry. And I'm sure Ms Thorp is sorry, too. But she certainly didn't murder him. You know that, Farquhar.'

'I am sorry,' Helen said quietly. 'It's extremely upsetting.'

'Yes, it is,' said Farquhar. 'Extremely. Perhaps I should apologize too for letting it colour my actions.'

'What can we do to help?' asked Chamberlain.

'Tell me why you visited him?' asked Farquhar.

Helen Thorp stared at the floor. At first Chamberlain thought she was thinking, then he realized that she hadn't heard. 'Helen?' he asked gently. They'd shifted easily to first names at the pub. 'Ms Thorp?'

She shuddered and when she raised her eyes they were filled with tears. 'Excuse me.' She stood up and walked to the bedroom. Farquhar and Chamberlain exchanged glances. So she wasn't so hard. It just seemed that her first reaction was to stay tough. Later she let go when she thought she was safe.

'She'll be back,' Chamberlain said quietly. 'I can answer the question, if you want.'

'Please.'

'Hammond was kidnapped right after meeting with him. We wanted to know what they talked about.'

Chamberlain waited for a response, but Farquhar said nothing. He paced a few steps, back and forth, then went to the couch. The two men sat silently for several minutes, until Helen Thorp came back from her bedroom.

She had dried her eyes and evidently fixed her make-up, but she was deathly pale and seemed to be struggling to maintain control. Chamberlain noticed the depth of her upset, and recalled again how animatedly she had described Ramsey taking her upstairs to see his African masks. The old major must have struck a very deep chord in Helen Thorp.

'Excuse me, Inspector. I'll answer your questions now.'

'Would you care to sit down?' asked Farquhar.

'I'll stand.'

'Mr Chamberlain has told me why you went to see the Major.'

'Yes. Pete felt we might learn something about Hammond's recent activities which might be helpful. It seemed worth a try.'

'Well, could you tell me, briefly, what you and the Major discussed.'

Chamberlain got up and walked to the window. He moved the thick curtain aside and looked at the snow. The Russian must have doubled back and entered the club through a back way or window and surprised the old man in his room, about the time he and Helen were at the pub.

When Helen finished telling Farquhar the things she had told Chamberlain, the Inspector asked a few brief questions, then said, 'Thank you for your co-operation.' He rose from the couch and faced Helen, who had remained standing throughout. 'Ordinarily,' he said, 'I would ask you to remain in London until my investigation was complete, but I realize that in this instance you may have

250

to leave hurriedly to attend your auction. I will accept your word that you will return immediately if, and when, I need you.'

'You have my word,' said Helen Thorp.

'Thank you. Ah, Peter, I wonder if you would accompany me for an hour or so?'

Chamberlain looked at Helen, although Farquhar's question was more a demand than an invitation. 'Are you all right?'

'Yes. Go ahead. I'd just as soon be alone.'

'You're sure?'

'I'll see you in the morning.'

'Can I bring you anything?'

'I'll get something to eat from Room Service. Good night, Pete. Good evening, Inspector Farquhar.'

Out in the hall, after Farquhar had dismissed the plain-clothes man and they were walking to the lift, he said, 'I gather this falls in the midst of an otherwise very pleasant evening.'

'I've seen better timing,' Chamberlain admitted. 'What can I do for you?'

'I warned you not to mess about in London.' He stabbed viciously at the lift button and Chamberlain saw that despite his gentle treatment of Helen Thorp, the inspector was still seething.

'We were curious,' said Chamberlain. 'We just went to talk to the guy, that was all.'

The lift came and they got in. Chamberlain looked for the plainclothes man, but he had apparently taken the stairs. The doors closed and Farquhar exploded angrily.

'And then you went chasing a man through the streets and dashing around inside Harrods like a pack of cheeky schoolboys. The management telephoned a complaint. Why didn't you open fire on him? There couldn't have been that many shoppers about at that hour.'

251

'I don't carry a gun.'

'You bloody well better not, or I'll have you in Dartmoor till the Second Coming.' He patted both sides of Chamberlain's jacket with quick, expert strokes and seemed disappointed he found no weapon. Chamberlain wondered how he would get the gun in his room back aboard Comptel's plane. The lift doors opened on the lobby and he followed Farquhar outside, into the snow.

When they had walked beyond earshot of the doorman, Farquhar asked, 'Where the devil do you think you are? Some banana republic where you entertain the natives with spy adventures? Who were you chasing?'

'A Russian. Probably KGB. He shot a guy who was working with me in Brest. Yesterday.'

'An employee of your firm?'

'Yes.'

Farquhar stopped on the corner where the Savoy drive met the Strand. 'And you were intending to wreak revenge in the streets of London?' he asked disgustedly.

Chamberlain shivered. The wet snow was melting on his bare head, starting to soak his hair again. He said, 'I'm looking for Charles Hammond. I wanted to know what the hell this guy was doing outside the Overseas Club.'

'And what do you think?'

'It seemed like a hell of a coincidence, but I guess he had the same idea at the same time that Ms Thorp and I did.'

'What idea?'

'To check out what Hammond was up to. I guess he's grasping at straws just like us.'

'Do you think that he went back and killed Ramsey?'

'Was Ramsey beaten?'

'There was a single mark on his face,' said Farquhar, looking at Chamberlain sharply. 'We weren't sure what caused it.'

252

'Did it *kill* him?'

'He was shot.'

'A Baretta?'

'Yes. Apparently Ramsey was going for his own revolver, but he was too slow.'

'This guy moves like greased lightning.'

'The Major used to,' said Farquhar, staring at the snow.

'Did he get off a shot?' asked Chamberlain.

'No,' said Farquhar. 'Not this time.' He raised his hand and further down the Strand a dark Jaguar with a long radio antenna parked in front of Simpsons turned on its lights and skidded away from the slush-filled kerb.

'How'd you happen to know Ramsey?' asked Chamberlain.

Farquhar hesitated. 'Well, as a matter of fact, we met in Kenya. I was doing a stint with the colonial constabulary and he was a captain then, somehow attached to MI5. He was doing counter-insurgency work against the Mau Mau. Rather successfully, too, as it turned out. I came back to the Yard, but he stayed for years, even after independence. Tremendously knowledgeable fellow. There wasn't a thing about East Africa he didn't know.'

He took Chamberlain's arm as the Jaguar slid to a halt in front of them. 'Tell me more about this Russian.'

Flushed pink, Helen Thorp stepped out of a deep bath, dried with a towel warmed on the steam-heated rack, removed her shower cap, and shook out her long, dark hair. Then she wrapped herself in a thick terry robe and stepped into her bedroom.

The man in black was waiting in the armchair beside her bed. He held a gun in one hand and his cane in the other. She said, 'Who –'

And he asked, silkily, 'What did Major Ramsey tell you?'

253

'*What?* Who are you?'

A pulse beat in his bony temple. He sat with one leg draped casually over the other, but his entire frame was rigid with tension.

'I've run out of time,' he snapped. 'I won't be misled by the CIA.'

'I'm not CIA!'

He ignored her protest and fixed her with his glittery eyes. 'I will kill you if you don't tell me what Major Ramsey told you.'

'He didn't tell me anything.'

The man in black raised his gun.

'You can't shoot. Everyone will hear.'

'The walls are thick. No one will hear. And if they do, what happens to me won't alter the fact that you are dead.'

Helen Thorp went white. 'He didn't tell me anything. He just talked about his past.'

'You're lying.'

She bolted towards the sitting room. He thrust his cane between her legs and leaped on top of her as she sprawled. Clamping a powerful hand over her mouth, he silenced her scream and forced her to the floor, pressing his forearm against her throat, crushing her windpipe until she was pinned flat on her back, fighting to breathe.

'I have no time,' he muttered. 'No time.'

She kicked, which caused her robe to ride up her legs. His gaze fixed longingly. 'No time, no time,' he mumbled again, but even as he uttered the urgent words, his eyes were possessed of a fierce glow, sexual and utterly mad.

He lifted her off the floor, one bony hand still clamped over her lips, and threw her on the bed so hard that her arms and legs flew like pinwheels. Swiftly, he forced her onto her belly, ramming her face into the bedspread, sat on her buttocks, and tied her hands behind her with the belt from her terry robe. When she arched her back

254

and tried to scream, he jerked a perfumed handkerchief between her lips and tied it tightly. She rolled over and levered her knee into his groin. He grunted and fell off her. She kept rolling towards the telephone.

He got there first, forced her across the bed and back onto her stomach. Then he snatched her panty hose from the dresser top and tied her ankles. He stepped back and stared, she drew deep, shuddering breaths.

'What did Ramsey say?'

He picked up his cane. She lay, breathing hard, watching him. He twisted his cane's ivory handle, and, smiling, separated the handle from the cane, unsheathing his long thin riding crop.

Helen Thorp's eyes widened in disbelief.

'What did Ramsey say?'

She shook her head. He drew the whip through his fingers. 'You may nod when you are ready to talk.'

He raised the whip, swished it sharply through the air, then seized the hem of her robe and lifted it slowly. A spasmodic shiver rippled the flesh from her head to her toes as he slid the terry cloth up her legs. 'For your sake, I hope he told you something.'

She shook her head violently.

He smiled, his teeth as white as his awful bony cheeks.

'A shame. I ask you once more. What did Ramsey say?'

He raised the whip towards the ceiling, and slowly, inch by inch, bared her skin.

23

'He'll be terribly disappointed if you tell him,' Lady Janet drawled mockingly from the door.

The man in black froze with Helen Thorp's robe in one hand and his whip poised high in the other. Only his eyes moved and when they found her long blonde hair, Lady Janet's pale lips parted in a smile over her gun, which she held in both hands, trained at his head.

'Turn around. Very slowly.'

The man in black let go of the robe and started to face the door.

'Completely round. And raise your hands higher. *Both* hands.'

Henri Trefle hulked beside her in a new overcoat and a broad-brimmed hat pulled low over his blotchy face. He grunted a warning.

The man in black exploded into motion. One moment he was still standing beside her bed with his hands high in the air, the whip still firmly between his fingers. The next instant he was flying over the bed. His free hand leaped inside his jacket and pulled out his Baretta while he was still in the air.

Lady Janet tracked him, and as his weapon cleared his jacket she fired twice, and twice again – four muffled bangs no louder than a door slamming – and when the man in black hit the floor on the other side of the bed, his gun fell from his hand and bounced on the carpet.

Henri crossed the bedroom in two giant strides and knelt by the body, his hands poised.

'*Mort.*'

Lady Janet pocketed her weapon, went to the body, and stared down at it, her face working. She was running too long on uppers to feel much, and Karl Grandzau was still her real quarry. But this was more satisfying than she had imagined, for this monster who had tortured her so cruelly had felt fear, and had died knowing she had taken her revenge.

Henri waited, saying nothing.

Finally, she bent over Helen Thorp and removed her gag.

The American executive babbled her relief. 'Thank you. Thank God, thank you.'

Lady Janet surveyed her coolly. 'You are a lucky woman.'

'Oh I know. I know. Thank you . . . Could you . . . undo my hands, please?'

'Where is the auction?'

'What?'

'Where is Grandzau's auction?'

Lady Janet swept an impatient hand through her hair, and Helen Thorp gazed stupidly up at her, as if unable to believe that this saviour wouldn't untie her.

'Henri!'

He was running the fallen riding crop through his fingers. Smiling at Helen, he murmured, 'Sad we haven't the time for a lengthy interrogation.' He tossed the whip on the bed, rolled Helen on her back, pulled his long, transparent knife from the folds of his coat. He shifted it this way and that to show her the light glittering on its razor edge.

'Where is Hammond's auction?'

'Wait!' Helen cried, trying to shrink from the knife until Henri clamped his big hand around the back of her neck and pulled her to the blade. 'Wait. I don't know. They haven't told us yet. They just told us to come to the Savoy.'

Lady Janet watched expressionlessly.

Helen's frantic eyes shifted from the knife, to her, to Henri. 'We think it's still on the seventh. The day after tomorrow.'

'Where?'

'I told you, we don't know. They haven't said.'

'Henri.'

'Wait, please. Wait! The police. Scotland Yard. They said that the man holding the auction – '

'Grandzau.'

'Yes. They think he's chartered a Concorde to fly us to the Persian Gulf.'

Lady Janet looked incredulously at Henri, who shook his head.

'It's true,' Helen cried desperately. 'I swear it.'

'When?'

'Probably tomorrow night or the next day.'

'What airport?'

'I don't know what airport. This is crazy. Ask them. What airport do Concordes fly from?'

They looked at each other again.

'That's all I know,' Helen said wearily. 'Please untie me.'

'Let's go,' said the woman.

'What about her?'

'Somebody will come along. Let's go.'

'But she saw you kill him.' He nodded at the body on the floor.

Helen paled. 'No. No I didn't, I won't say a thing.'

'She'll never see me again,' said the woman. 'Besides, neither I, nor you, nor probably he, entered Britain through Immigration. I'll take the chance.'

'We must kill her.'

'No, Henri. It will just bring pressure. Leave her.'

258

'You go ahead,' said the giant, tapping the flat of his blade in his hand. 'I'll take care of this.'

'Oh, one thing,' said Chamberlain, as he climbed out of Farquhar's car in front of the Savoy. 'Helen Thorp mentioned that Major Ramsey was kicked out of Kenya by the new government when England left. But you said he stayed on.'

'It was rather sticky,' answered Farquhar. 'First they gave him the boot. Shortly thereafter they grew open-minded enough to realize they needed his sort of expertise so they invited him back. Are you sure you won't have a drink? There's a nice little American place in the next street. Theatrical, but I dare say they wouldn't deny a compatriot.'

Chamberlain wanted to see if Helen had waited up for him.

'I better pass. Tomorrow might be a long day.'

'Cheerio.'

'Good night.'

He entered his room from the hall, hoping to find that she had opened the connecting door to her suite. She hadn't. His room was dark, hot and stuffy. She'd gone straight to bed. He debated looking for the bar Farquhar had mentioned. Then he noticed the light under the connecting door. He started to knock, then thought better of it. She might have gone to sleep and left the living room lights burning.

He thought of the phone. But if she'd forgotten to alert the switchboard, he'd wake her, which wouldn't be a good idea, considering how upset she'd been earlier. Best to leave her alone.

Then he heard voices. A man's low tones rumbled through the door. 'Son of a bitch,' Chamberlain muttered, wondering if it was the guy she usually stayed with in London. So much for her upset.

A woman spoke, insistent, persuasive. It didn't sound like Helen. Then he heard her voice. He pressed his ear to the door. He couldn't hear the words, but she sounded frightened. The voices were distant as if they were talking in her bedroom.

Chamberlain pressed an electronically amplified sound pick-up against the door and listened closely. He slipped it back in his pocket and gently turned the key, concentrating on turning the latch without a click. Softly, he opened the door and peered into the living room. It was empty and the voices were coming clearly from her bedroom. The man and the woman were arguing. She sounded English, he, French. Upper-class English.

He thought of Grandzau's agent, Lady Janet Isling, and crept silently back to his closet where he had hidden Kreegan's gun. Then he slipped into the living room and glided cautiously towards the voices. He was halfway across when Helen Thorp gave a fearful cry. Chamberlain abandoned caution and walked straight into her room.

Helen was huddled on the bed, partly clad in a bathrobe, her hands and feet bound. The man who had knifed the KGB agents in Marseille had his blade to her throat. Dead, at his feet, was the Russian in black. Three bullet holes occupied a six-inch circle in the centre of his chest. That left Lady Janet Isling with the gun.

He felt her rush from the left, stepped under her swing, grabbed her arm and twisted it sharply behind her, bending it high to force her to drop her gun. He pinned her tightly in his arms and put his shot revolver to her head. Then he told the man with the knife, 'Back off!'

260

Helen gaped at him in astonishment. But the big guy with the knife touched the edge of his blade to her throat, and gave Chamberlain a bloated smile.

'Perhaps, Monsieur, I care less for my lady than you do for yours.'

24

Chamberlain squeezed Lady Janet tighter and thrust his hip into her buttocks so she couldn't kick him in the groin. 'Back off,' he repeated, walking her to the side, edging towards a clearer shot at the gun.

The Frenchman pivoted with him, holding his knife to Helen and keeping her between him and Chamberlain. 'No, Monsieur. *You* back off. She means nothing to me.'

'Maybe not, mister, but after you cut my lady and I shoot yours, I'll still have my gun and you'll only have a knife.'

The Frenchman eyed him fearlessly. 'I have taken revolvers from men your size before.'

'This one fires buckshot.'

That shut him up for a moment, and Chamberlain was relieved to see that if he didn't give a damn about the woman's life, he at least cared for his own enough to think about it.

'Henri,' the woman hissed. 'Hammond. Remember. Remember Hammond.' What the hell was she talking about? wondered Chamberlain.

'*Alors?* For that scum I should merely *back off.*'

'*Yes!*' she commanded, shuddering with effort. 'Do as he says, Henri. *Remember.*' She shook in Chamberlain's arms like a taut steel cable. The Frenchman wasn't buying it.

Chamberlain watched him helplessly. He couldn't fire the shot revolver so close to Helen.

'Henri Trefle does not *back off*. It is a question of honour.'

Chamberlain cursed himself for getting the guy's back

up. He shouldn't have threatened his pride. 'It's a Mexican stand-off,' he said, soothingly. 'The best way out of a Mexican stand-off is we *both* back off. You look like a pro, Mister. Why don't we both get out of this thing professionally?'

The guy peered at him owlishly and Chamberlain realized he was half-drunk. The woman took up his point, relaxing in his arms to communicate her agreement.

'Yes, Henri. The man is right. You are both professionals.'

Henri said nothing and didn't move. He loomed over Helen like a puzzled bull. He made no expression when Lady Janet tried again to persuade him.

'We just want to get away, Henri. It doesn't matter what happens here.'

Chamberlain shot a glance at Helen. She was starting to shake. Another minute and she'd be unable to remember that her life depended on not moving a hair. He looked back at Henri. Nothing. The blotched face was unfathomable.

Then Chamberlain felt his own concentration waver. The source of distraction was Lady Janet. Since she had stopped struggling to indicate that she supported him in the matter of Henri, her body had transformed itself from tensed, hostile bone and muscle to soft breasts and gently swelling hips.

It was crazy. He'd get killed that way. But her odour was electrifying and despite the fact that her gun lay close by on the rug and she might be throwing him off guard, Chamberlain remembered that the smartest woman he'd ever slept with had told him that harmonious smells fuelled the richest sex.

Crazy. He kicked her gun farther away. Then he felt her tremble. It lasted a single, unguarded instant and he felt

263

her steel herself against a repeat. She'd felt it too. Then the moment was gone.

Helen Thorp started trembling violently. He couldn't wait any longer.

'I'll make the first move,' said Chamberlain. 'I'll step away from your lady.'

'You have a gun,' Trefle complained sullenly. 'What does "stepping away" mean with a gun?'

Chamberlain released Lady Janet and backed up two paces, training his weapon on her.

'Pick up your gun.'

She found his eyes before she reached for it. Her pupils were black pencil points. A drunk and a junkie, thought Chamberlain. What a combination. 'I won't shoot,' he promised. 'Pick it up.'

She picked it up and pointed it at him. 'All right, Henri. You can let her go, now.'

Henri Trefle said nothing. She glanced at him, wetting her lips. 'Henri!'

Helen tried to jerk back from the knife. Trefle clamped a huge hand around the back of her neck and pushed her forward to his blade. Lady Janet fumbled in her coat pocket and lifted some red pills to her lips.

Chamberlain shook his head. 'Not now, lady,' he muttered, despairingly. 'Please not now.'

Helen whimpered. He could hear in her voice that she was flaking out beyond caring.

Lady Janet stared at her pills.

'We need you whole,' said Chamberlain. 'Please don't.'

Lady Janet looked at him slowly, tipped her hand and let them fall to the floor.

'Thank you.'

'Henri! Let's go!' Her order carried a new intensity that cut through his resistance. He backed away from the bed and sheathed his knife in a swift, liquid motion. Then he

264

swaggered towards the door, pointedly ignoring Chamberlain, but stealing a glance at the revolver that fired buckshot.

Chamberlain and Lady Janet looked at each other. He would have given years of his life to know what she was thinking.

'I'll stay here,' he said. 'You just go.' And then he added, softly, 'I'll cover,' to which she replied, 'Thank you.'

They backed out silently, through the sitting room and into the hall. Helen broke into muffled sobs. When he heard the door click shut, Chamberlain sat beside her, covered her beautiful legs, and untied her hands and feet.

'Oh, my God,' Helen moaned. 'Oh, my God.'

'It's over.' He drew her gently into his arms and held her, pulling the bedspread over her to keep her warm, stroking her back to comfort her. Gradually her sobs lessened and when she no longer trembled with them he poured her a neat Scotch from the bar in the living room and held it to her lips until she took the glass and sat up and drank by herself.

'How do you feel?'

'Awful. Please hold me some more.' Chamberlain embraced her until she stopped shaking.

'Do you want to talk about it now? Or after I call the police?'

'What for?'

'We've got a body in our suite.'

'Call them now. I want it out of here.'

He telephoned Farquhar at Scotland Yard and got the sergeant who answered to agree to call him at home. Farquhar arrived at midnight, by which time Helen had recovered enough to change into her clinging silk robe, brush her hair until it shone and apply some make-up. She sat in the armchair, quietly sipping her second Scotch while Chamberlain outlined what had happened and an angry Inspector Farquhar studied the body.

'I gave you a clear warning,' he said to Chamberlain.

'I didn't kill him,' Chamberlain protested. 'The woman did.'

'Yes, and who was this woman?'

'I don't know,' Chamberlain lied. He felt a debt to her for helping them out of the stand-off with her partner. 'She was blonde and had a thick German accent.'

Helen Thorp looked into her glass.

'Would you like to explain the sequence of events again?'

Chamberlain repeated what Helen had told him. Then Farquhar turned to Helen and asked her to explain what had happened. She related the same story.

Farquhar listened, tight-lipped, then made a couple of telephone calls and, a short time later, admitted to the suite several detectives and the Savoy's night manager whom he engaged in a whispered conversation. The detectives photographed the room and everything in it, then took the dead man's fingerprints and fed them into a portable facsimile machine they attached to the telephone.

The night manager left, looking worried, and Farquhar glared impatiently at the facsimile machine.

'You won't find his fingerprints filed in the Yard,' said Chamberlain.

'I'm not asking the Yard,' replied Farquhar.

'MI5?'

'Why don't you mind your own business, old son?'

'You won't find him there, either.'

'What makes you so sure of that?'

'I already told you, the CIA doesn't have a file on him and they share that kind of info back and forth with your intelligence people. You know that.'

'Perhaps we file our "info" differently,' Farquhar replied dryly. 'Now tell me more about this Frenchman.'

'Big man. Two-fifty at least. Stones? How many stones is two hundred and fifty pounds? I don't know. You figure it out. Very big. I saw him in Marseille for a second swinging his glass knife. Tempered glass. He looks like a drunk, but in Marseille he moved awfully fast for a drunk.'

'Go on.'

'The woman called him Henri. He referred to himself as Henri Trefle as if his name meant something special. Big rep, I guess. I figure him for a merc.'

'Certainly sounds likely. And the woman with the French accent?'

'German.'

'Ah yes.' Farquhar placed another telephone call and spoke at length. Chamberlain sat beside Helen. She reached for his hand and held it tightly while the police stenographer wrote down her answers to Farquhar's men. When Farquhar hung up, Chamberlain asked, 'Shouldn't she have a lawyer?'

'It's all right, Pete,' said Helen. 'I'm fine.'

'You're welcome to one,' said Farquhar, 'but you can be sure this isn't going to be any sort of trial. MI5 has sent the word down through the Foreign Office. They've identified the dead man and they'll slap a D notice on the whole affair.'

'Who is he?' asked Chamberlain.

Farquhar flashed a snapshot of Lady Janet. 'Could this have been the woman?'

'I don't think so,' said Chamberlain.

'It's rather a clear photograph.'

'It's not her.'

'Ms Thorp?'

Helen glanced at it. 'I'm sorry, Inspector. I hardly remember a thing about her. I was too frightened.'

'Have another look, Peter.'

Chamberlain dutifully inspected the picture. It was of

professional quality. She looked younger, was wearing riding dress and a sullen smile. She'd become more beautiful since then.

'It's not the woman I saw.'

'Strange. She's supposed to have spent some time with Trefle. You're right, incidentally. He's a mercenary soldier. I'll have more on him shortly. The thing is, this woman was also involved with Herr Grandzau.'

'You're kidding?' said Chamberlain, beginning to wish he hadn't involved himself in the lie. But he was in now and there was no point in screwing things up with Farquhar by admitting it. 'Who is she?' he asked, continuing the charade along logical lines.

'Lady Janet Isling. A very confused young lady. Her father was a baronet and one of the very few of the landed gentry who actually increased his holdings under the Labour governments. The old boy had an uncanny knack for parrying Socialists.'

Chamberlain knew most of it already from Arnie Fast. The important thing he'd learned tonight was he'd been wrong about Lady Janet being Grandzau's agent. 'But why were she and Trefle looking for the auction?'

'Haven't the foggiest, old son. Don't you want to know who the fellow on the floor is?'

'She knew him,' Helen Thorp interrupted. 'And he knew her. He was terrified when he heard her voice.'

'I rather doubt he was ever terrified in his life,' said Farquhar.

'What's his name?'

'Ivor Peitscheski.'

'Never heard of him. KGB?'

'Not exactly. He'd been given *carte blanche* with their European support facilities, men, cars, weapons, money, but he was just visiting. This wasn't his territory.'

'What was?'

Farquhar had seemed to enjoy his role as dispenser of information. But now he looked genuinely puzzled.

'East Africa.'

'Like Ramsey?'

'Like Major Ramsey.'

'I don't understand,' said Helen Thorp.

Farquhar waved an empty, ignorant hand. 'Neither do I. According to my sources, Peitscheski's enemies shipped him out to Africa years ago because he was too dangerous to keep around the Kremlin. But instead of getting his throat slit in a tribal dispute, as they had hoped, he thrived. He's engineered coups and committed assassinations in every state on the Indian Ocean.'

'But why would the KGB choose *him* to nail Hammond?'

The telephone rang and a detective passed it to Farquhar. While he was talking, his men wheeled in a laundry cart, dumped Peitscheski's body in it, covered him with sheets, and trundled him out. Helen stared disbelievingly when Farquhar, listening intently on the telephone, gave Chamberlain a grave wink.

'Just like that?' Helen asked quietly.

'Guess Farquhar takes the Foreign Office at their word.'

'Get rid of him,' she whispered. 'I want to get into bed.'

'Right away.'

When Farquhar hung up the phone, Chamberlain intercepted him and steered him out of Helen's bedroom into the living room.

'Can we kind of wrap this up? My boss is beat.'

'Of course, old son. Almost done. I do think, however, that I'll post a man at her door. At both of your doors. Best for all concerned, what?'

'Thanks,' said Chamberlain.

'Incidentally, I've learned some more about Trefle.' He shuffled through the notes he'd made on the telephone. '*Colonel* Henri Trefle. French mercenary. Foreign Legion veteran of Indochina and Algeria. Congo veteran. Angolan veteran. Rhodesia, South Africa, Somalia.' He paused and looked quizzically at Chamberlain. 'There's a widely believed rumour, but unsubstantiated, that his force was annihilated during a failed coup in Somalia four years ago. Seems he was betrayed by a certain Mr Charles Hammond.'

'Hammond was involved in a coup attempt?' Chamberlain heard his voice echoing stupidly.

'Organized it – or at least that's what they all say. Who knows, but the East Africa coast is a regular cauldron of coups and counter-coups because the superpowers are always taking sides. Sea lanes, you know. Down the East African coast, through the Mozambique Channel. Oil tankers to Europe have to pass along the East African coast. Europe's pipeline as it were . . . Or lifeline, if it's squeezed.'

25

Chamberlain glanced past the bedroom door at Helen
Thorp. A dozen questions rocketed through his mind, but
he couldn't ask them of Farquhar. Some because they'd
undermine his lie about Lady Janet. Others because Farquhar's behaviour tonight had confirmed what Chamberlain had suspected since morning. Farquhar had too much
access to too much information for a simple Scotland Yard
detective. And far too much clout. Special Branch was
more like it, or one of the myriad super-secret M agencies.

He said, 'Don't bother putting your guys on the door. I
can take care of things here.'

'No trouble, old son,' Farquhar smiled.

'Thanks,' Chamberlain smiled back, wondering how the
hell he'd sneak out of the place without being tailed. 'I can
use the peaceful sleep.'

'Good night, old son.' Farquhar ordered his squad out.
A cluster of chambermaids surged in from the hall and
hastily straightened the room under the stern eye of the
night manager. While they worked, Chamberlain dialled
the telephone.

'Who are you calling?' asked Helen Thorp.

'Friend at the agency,' he replied, noting it was nearly
one in the morning and wondering where Arnie would be
in Washington at seven o'clock in the evening. As it turned
out, he was at his desk and sounding friendlier than he
had in Brest. 'What can I do for you?'

'I'll do for you,' said Chamberlain. 'Figure I owe you a
couple. Remember the Russian?'

'The cute one with the whip?'

'A certain lady we've discussed shot him in my boss's hotel room.'

'Dead?'

'Very. His name was Peitscheski.'

'Oh, damnit, of course. Ivor the terrible. He's been shoving a chunk under the corner in Africa for as long as I can remember. About time somebody nailed him. But what was he doing in London? Wait a minute. He's the guy the Russians sent after Hammond. That makes no sense at all.'

'Did Hammond ever work for you guys?'

'Fat chance,' snorted Fast. 'We should be so lucky.'

Fast couldn't be expected to admit it on an open line, Chamberlain reflected as he hung up, but his denial had been so spontaneous that it sounded like the truth.

'Why'd you tell him that?' asked Helen.

'I might need another favour.'

Through the bedroom door he saw a charwoman scrubbing the bloodstains from the rug. A hall porter covered the soapy residue with a towel and covered the towel with a beautiful Chinese rug. The night manager inspected the suite, repeated his apologies to Helen, and shooed his staff out. A quiet descended upon the rooms and it seemed as if the night's terrors had never happened.

'Like another drink?' asked Chamberlain.

'Please.'

When he brought them back to her room, she was sitting up in bed, her legs under the blankets the maids had turned down.

'How do you feel?'

'Much better. Why did you ask if Hammond had worked for the CIA?'

If Farquhar hadn't bugged the suite before, he most certainly had by now. Chamberlain leaned closer and whispered, 'Come into the bathroom again. I'll tell you something.'

She shook her head. 'I can't move,' she whispered back. 'Come here.' She touched her ear.

Chamberlain sat on the bed beside her. She pulled him close.

'Something crazy is going on.' Chamberlain whispered beside her ear. 'Remember that Peitscheski operated in East Africa?'

'Yes.'

'And Ramsey worked in East Africa.'

'Okay,' she nodded, stifling a yawn.

'Now get this.' He told her what Farquhar had said about Trefle and Hammond.

She considered it for a moment. 'First of all, it's just a rumour. Second of all, it wouldn't surprise me that much if it were true. Charles is into everything. Who knows the connection. What was Trefle really doing? What was Hammond doing? The real question is, what does that rumour have to do with Hammond being kidnapped by Grandzau?'

'Everything's pointing to East Africa,' said Chamberlain. 'Are you sure that Major Ramsey didn't say anything else about Hammond's business there when you went back?'

'Positive,' she said sleepily.

'Farquhar told me that after the Kenyans kicked him out, they invited him back.'

'That's not what he told us.'

'Which is it?'

'I don't know. And I don't see it matters. Peter, I feel so strange. I'm surprised to be alive. Peter . . .'

Chamberlain pounded a light rhythm on his knee. 'East Africa, East Africa, East Africa – I'm going back to that damned Overseas Club. Maybe some of the old guy's friends knew what he was doing with Hammond.' He

273

stood up, glancing around the suite. 'Farquhar left a couple of watchdogs in the hall,' he whispered. 'I gotta get around them – hey, are you all right?'

Helen nodded, but her eyes were welling.

'What's the matter?' he asked, sitting down next to her again.

'I'm so scared.'

'It's over. Peitscheski's dead and the other two won't be back. Besides, Farquhar's got people all over the hotel. I'm going to have to lose them in the street.'

'Could you please hold me again?' she asked, raising her face beseechingly to his. Her tears dispersed in the fine lines under her eyes. Her mouth trembled. 'Please?'

Over her black hair he watched the mirror picture of Helen crumpled against him, him holding her awkwardly, unsure what was expected, what was needed.

He held her for ten minutes. Gradually, her breathing steadied. When he thought she was asleep, he turned out the beside light, extricated his arms, laid her gently on the pillow, and started to draw the blankets up to her chin.

'I'm cold,' she whispered.

'I'll get you another blanket.'

'No.'

'What?' he whispered.

'Come in with me.'

Chamberlain laughed his surprise. Very tempting, but not this night. 'I'm too wet for that,' he replied lightly. 'Farquhar's almost as bad as you are about tramping around in the snow.'

She opened her eyes. 'I mean it.'

'Helen, you don't want that. You're reacting to your fright. Give me a raincheck for when you're feeling better. I'll sit right here until you fall asleep.'

She looked up at him through a veil of jet hair. And when she spoke he saw her smiling in the near darkness.

'Do I have to telephone Alfred Cowan to order you into my bed?'

'I wouldn't want him to think I'm insubordinate,' Chamberlain smiled. 'But are you sure? I mean you've been through a lot.'

'Jesus Christ! Yes, I have been through a lot. But I happen to find you attractive and I enjoyed the afternoon talking and damnit I want to sleep with somebody and I'd just as soon it was you.'

'Now there's an invitation I could hardly resist.'

'I want to be held. But not by somebody in wet clothes.'

Chamberlain took them off and slipped in beside her. She turned to him and nestled into the crook of his arm, kissed him warmly, closed her eyes, and pressed closer. He let her lead. Sometimes after a frightening action he felt dead inside. Other times relief at being alive ignited enormous sexual desire. He would go slow until he was damned sure which it was for Helen Thorp.

Her body was surprisingly lush, possessed of fuller breasts and thighs than her tailored skirts and blouses had led him to imagine. She moved softly against him, but she was terribly awkward, stopping and starting fitfully, fluttering to excitement, only to drift away, floating alone, a sporadic passion stalled by the terror she'd had. She closed her eyes tight and strained against him as if trying to crush the fear.

He tried to nurture her excitement and when she cooled, he filled the dead places with tenderness, smoothing the low spots, building the high. Slowly, she responded. He became very detached observing her needs, and several times Lady Janet drifted across the skyline of his consciousness.

He brought her, at last, to a small orgasm, an internal sigh, and continued to hold and kiss her with gentle care. Feeling slightly superior, and duly proud of his talents, he waited for her to plunge deeply into a satisfied sleep. When it seemed that she had, he tried to climb out of bed, carefully, so as not to disturb her. 'Where are you going?'

'Overseas Club,' he whispered. 'Go to sleep.'

'You've earned a night off,' she whispered back, and without another word, she slid down his body and took him determinedly in her mouth, jolting him out of detachment, arching his back with pleasure, ripping a cry from his lips . . . He came with staggering force. She stayed with him, drawing him out, demanding more, until he was quivering weakly and then she licked and stroked him hard again and made him come a second, long, convulsive time.

Still she kept him. Shaking from head to toe, his breath ragged, his mouth dry, he reached for her face, begging her to stop, so intense was the electric pulsing of her mouth.

Helen removed his hands and pressed them to his sides. 'You can't move them,' she whispered, but this time when she had caressed him to hardness, she freed him from her mouth and slowly mounted him, drawing him into her with successive gasps. She retrieved his hands and pressed them around her bottom and shook convulsively. Chamberlain bucked under her, revelling in the fullness of her flesh and she pulled him deeper inside and came with him in long, rippling waves, that shook the bed and blotted the light from his mind. Seconds, minutes, years later, he awakened, hardening in her hands, turning with her, sliding on top of her, melting into her, crying with her.

He knew next that she was sitting up, cross-legged, wrapped in blankets, caressing his feet, watching his face, and sipping brandy. She took his eyes and held them a long time. 'Tell me,' she said.

He told her all he remembered and she listened with a

half smile. Then she extended her brandy. 'We'll sleep late, tomorrow.'

He drank. Nothing had ever tasted better. She took the snifter back, downed what remained, and set the glass aside. Chamberlain watched her every move, awed. He was utterly drained. Her travel alarm said it was morning.

'Go to sleep,' she said.

He reached to touch her breast, and failed, his arm dropping limply at his side. 'Yeah. Gotta get up early. Check out the club in the morning.'

She whispered softly while he dozed and he heard her gently mocking him. 'So many theories. So many theories. Now they're all from East Africa. Before the blonde woman was Grandzau's agent. But she can't find the auction. Then Hammond staged his own kidnapping because he was broke.'

'Not because he was broke,' Chamberlain mumbled drowsily. 'He went broke setting it up.'

'Go to sleep.'

Her fingers moved ceaselessly. He was astonished to feel himself grow hard again, and then he was awake, and the sun was streaming through a crack in the curtains, and Helen Thorp was dressed, sitting in the armchair, sipping a cup of aromatic coffee, and reading a yellow telegram.

26

The night surfed into his mind and slid away.

'Good morning.'

'From Grandzau,' she replied, waving the telegram. 'The waiter brought it with the coffee. We leave London tonight.'

Chamberlain drank in the soft curves of her mouth and eyes and found it hard to imagine anything urgent. 'Good morning,' he said again. 'Or afternoon.'

She leaned over him, kissed his face. 'Read it. You better get dressed. We'll have to talk to the others and go to the City.'

She dropped the telegram on his chest, with another kiss and a cosy smile. 'It was great. It was the kind of great people get married for.'

Chamberlain stared, a smile grabbing his face. 'Yeah.'

'Now get dressed. We have tons to do.'

It was the longest, most detailed Pendragon message by far.

PENDRAGON AUCTION BIDDERS WILL ARRANGE TO TRANSFER FUNDS TO BANQUE ET SOCIETE DE SUISSE ZURICH. ASSEMBLE HEATHROW PRIVATE AVIATION LOUNGE 6.00 P.M. TONIGHT. BIDDING WILL BEGIN 8.00 A.M. GMT. RECESS 9.00 A.M. GMT TO INFORM PRINCIPALS. AUCTION RESUMES 10.00 A.M. GMT. CONCLUDES 10.30 A.M. GMT. PENDRAGON AVAILABLE 12.00 NOON GMT. TRANSPORT PROVIDED – LANCELOT.

'Why's he making such a big deal about the time?' asked Chamberlain.

'Specifics are reassuring.'

Chamberlain climbed out of bed and padded into the living room where the breakfast service was laid out. He poured himself coffee, grabbed a hot croissant in a napkin, and came back.

Helen watched him shyly. 'I wanted to ask you last night, but we didn't talk much. What happened to your back?'

'Just a gouge. I ran into a KGB shark in Scuba gear.'

'It didn't seem to slow you down.'

Chamberlain put down his coffee and croissant and kissed her. She clung to him, running her hands on his skin, but when he nodded at the bed she said, 'Raincheck. We have just a few hours to move a lot of money into Zurich.'

Chamberlain quickly drank the coffee, ate the croissant, dressed, and re-read Grandzau's cable. He read it several times. Finally he realized what was bothering him.

'You know something? This is a *private* message.'

'Of course it is. They all were. Alfred is still going crazy trying to figure out how they slipped them into the Comptel private links.'

'Yeah, that's a cute trick, but that's not what I'm talking about. This message is really private. It's really intended for only one of the bidders.'

Helen stopped dabbing perfume behind her ear and looked at him curiously. 'What do you mean?'

'It's reassuring, like you said, but only in terms of time. Grandzau doesn't promise that Hammond is alive, which you'd expect a kidnapper to do. You know, send a lock of hair or a finger.'

'Stop it,' she shuddered.

'Sorry. And he doesn't promise that the bidders will be safe, which is a natural worry. And he doesn't make any threats – you know, come alone, don't bring guns and knives.'

'He's taking for granted that he's dealing with a sensible

279

crowd. We're business people. I'm not going in with a gun and neither is Mr Nagumo.'

'Mr Nagumo is dead.'

'You know what I mean. His replacement, Mr Soma.'

'But this message makes one promise very clearly. He'll spring Hammond at noon, Greenwich Mean Time.'

'More theories, Pete?'

'And deliver him by Concorde. To me that can mean only one thing. Grandzau knows that somebody needs Hammond immediately. At a specific time and place. And they'll pay anything to get him there. You and I don't give a damn what time we get him tomorrow, just so long as the auction goes smoothly and nobody gets hurt. But somebody needs him at noon for some very special, specific service. Something only Hammond can do only at noon or on a Concorde flight from noon. It's not like you and Mr Cowan needing him because he agents ten per cent of your business. It's much –'

'How did you know that Hammond negotiates ten per cent of Comptel's business?' she asked sharply.

Idiot. He'd been so excited over his idea that he'd let slip what he'd learned eavesdropping. 'I listened in from your office when you and Mr Cowan were talking.'

'You couldn't have. The entire top floor is electronically secure.'

'I held a glass against the wall.'

A broad smile lighted her face. 'Did you really? I had no idea you were so . . .' She faltered.

'Clever for a hitter?'

'No,' she said, colouring slightly. 'Cunning.'

'I'm not cunning. But I've been taught a lot of initiative. Sometimes it works.'

'Well, you're not supposed to know that about Hammond and Comptel, so keep it to yourself. As for your latest theory, I don't see what it's all about.'

'What got me thinking about this, originally, was I was talking to Farquhar about the Concorde that Grandzau's chartered. There was no need to pay for that dinosaur unless Grandzau was making a point of promising speed. Why speed? Why noon? What time is that in the Persian Gulf?'

Helen shrugged. 'Three or four.'

'The hotel knows.' He telephoned the desk and the clerk answered as if that particular question was raised daily at the Savoy. 'Okay. It's four p.m. there when it's noon here.'

'I have to go, Pete.'

'The point is, don't you see, if anybody needs Hammond that badly at that time, they might need him for a long time. They might never give him back.'

'Yet another reason for you and me to make sure our consortium buys him instead.'

She tossed him his coat with a grin. And in the lift she kissed him suddenly on the mouth, as she had the first time in the doorway, yesterday, and said, 'We're going to have to figure out someplace neither you nor I have ever been.'

'How come?'

'Well, once we've rescued Mr Hammond, we're going to deserve a vacation.'

Chamberlain looked at her, his heart soaring. 'I would love that.'

She told him where to meet her that afternoon. 'Call me there if you are held up.'

'Right.'

'Hey?'

'Yes?'

'Thanks for a nice time.' She kissed him, slowly and passionately on the mouth, then strode out the door. Her sable coat hid all but the tilt of her head and the wind twirling her thick hair.

Chamberlain watched until her cab pulled away. Then he let loose his breath. He found a telephone booth with a comfortable armchair and asked the hotel operator for the Langley number, wondering if Arnie would talk to him. Fast's secretary was so cordial that when she said that Fast was out of town, Chamberlain believed her.

'Did he happen to leave a message for Pete Chamberlain?'

'Yes, he did. I assume it will mean something to you.' She proceeded to read the message in a flat monotone. 'Grab your robe and grab your burnous.'

'Right. Thank you.'

He hung up and pondered a moment. The CIA had bolted for Arabia. The KGB couldn't be far behind. How many airports could they all cover? Or would they track the plane *en route*? That seemed the more likely, but it also seemed an odd flaw in Grandzau's plan. Neither the KGB nor the CIA would have any trouble tracking a Concorde across Europe. Even the Swiss could do it.

He dialled another number. 'Good morning, Inspector. Pete Chamberlain.'

'It's afternoon on this side of town,' replied Farquhar and Chamberlain wondered if he'd listened to last night's tapes from the bugs in Helen's bedroom.

'We got telegrams from Grandzau.'

'Thank you. Actually, I've already read one.'

'Just thought you'd like to know.'

'Kind of you,' Farquhar said coolly, obviously still put out about the death of the Russian agent. 'Can I do anything for you?'

'Yes. Is it still the Concorde?'

'Very much so. Don't ask me how we know, but they've laid on a secret landing at Abu Dhabi.'

282

'Not much to go on,' said Chamberlain.

'Not in Abu Dhabi,' Farquhar agreed. 'Herr Grandzau could auction Hammond on the runway if the Arabs permitted and there'd be damn all we could do about it. I think you better resign yourself to something, old son.'

'What's that?'

'You're going to an auction.'

He had time to kill before meeting Helen so he settled on a walk in the sun. It was almost warm and last night's snow was gone from the pavements. He left his coat open and headed slowly down the Strand.

He noticed a lot of bobbies. There were several in the area of the Savoy and it seemed that every time he turned around he saw a big, uniformed man patrolling the street in solemn, measured steps.

Farquhar, he guessed, was taking no chances. Just a few more hours and the Pendragon menagerie would be flying east and Scotland Yard and MI5 could go back to their daily business of worrying about the Irish. Until then, however, Farquhar had evidently blanketed the streets around the Savoy.

He went into a travel agents and studied the big world map they had on the wall. Somalia, Kenya. What the hell did Hammond want in Somalia? And Kenya? It was hard to imagine two more different countries, the Kenyans having developed into a prosperous and independent version of the rich English colonial outpost it had been, while the Somalis were turned inside out by civil war and Ethiopian invasions stirred up by a modern guerrilla version of imperialist Russians and Cubans. Another talk with Major Ramsey could have been very interesting. And there off the coast of Africa sat Malagasy, the other side of the Mozambique Channel. Chamberlain felt old. When he'd studied geography, his seventh-grade teacher had called it the Straits of Madagascar.

It was getting late. He left the travel agents and hurried into the Temple Gardens. It was quiet, the walks deserted. Yesterday's snow had melted in patches revealing wet and impossibly green grass in the fields of white. Many of the red buildings were in shadow, the winter sun having settled early behind the taller buildings of central London.

Chamberlain paused under a brick archway, temporarily lost, and checked the address Helen had given him. The paths split in several directions. Ahead was a small white green-patched lawn. A tall London bobby rounded a corner and headed towards him. He'd ask the cop.

'Pete!' He heard her calling from another direction and he turned to the sound, his pulses soaring more than he would have predicted. She was running towards him, her coat flying open, her hair blowing. She waved and slowed to a quick walk. Her cheeks were flushed.

'I thought I saw you.'

'Just in time. I got a little lost.'

'Come on, we're late.' She took his arm and steered him down one of the paths, past the tall London bobby who nodded gravely as he might to any lovers. Chamberlain was shaken by the intensity of his feelings. He thought he would never forget for the rest of his life the way she looked in the cooling afternoon in the still gardens in the middle of London.

They went through a painted wooden door and up narrow stairs, through a foyer lined with unruly bookshelves heaped with briefs tied in red ribbon, and into a small dark office. An old clerk looked up, as if expecting them, and led them into a larger back room where were gathered the other members of the consortium which had been formed to buy back Charles Hammond.

They took the two seats left at the back of the room. The

284

Japanese man from Mishuma was addressing the group. 'He called the meeting secretly so Grandzau wouldn't know everything,' Helen explained quietly. 'It's a pep rally.'

'Kind of putting one over on Grandzau?'

'Exactly.'

The consortium had expanded to nine members and as each, like Helen, had an aide, there were seventeen men and one woman in the room. Soma, Nagumo's replacement at Mishuma, was talking about the need for solidarity, on which they had all already agreed, and then about the need to ask their companies to be prepared to bid higher if necessary on the second round, which made most of his audience squirm uncomfortably.

Soma had done his homework, running the details of half a dozen pending financial deals and the political manoeuvres in the Middle East that would be affected. 'Essentially, gentlemen, nothing is getting done while he's a prisoner. Nothing. The resultant chaos will be on our heads.'

Chamberlain slumped in his chair and stifled a yawn. Idly, he wondered if the Japanese had stumbled onto something. Was the Russian pursuit of Hammond merely another part of an obstructionist foreign policy? Would they put Hammond on ice just to queer Middle East politics? It could take a long while to pick up the pieces of all of Hammond's deals.

He sank lower and dealt with another yawn. From this new angle he was able to frame the Japanese speaker in the right eyeglass lens of the aide sitting in front of him. Oddly, there was *no distortion*. The lens looked like ordinary glass!

Helen stirred impatiently. He wondered how difficult it must be for her to play second fiddle to the Japanese. Their lovemaking had left him as awed by her as before and even more mystified. He counted himself lucky to have known two or three women who were capable of complete abandonment. She was less abandoned than determined. The wild ones were sometimes crazy in the morning, as if fantasy remembered changed to nightmare, but Helen Thorp stayed determined, a promising link between day and night.

He hadn't felt so good in a long time. Funny, if he got Hammond back and things worked out that he ended up with a new job *and* in love with the boss. Funnier still, if she was in love with him too. It was a little early for adults to be in love, he reminded himself. On the other hand, few people in love stayed adult very long, so it was debatable. What wasn't debatable, however, was that until Charles Hammond was returned intact, no one at Comptel, Helen included, was rewarding Pete Chamberlain for anything.

'I'll be back,' he whispered to Helen. He eased quietly out of the room, found the old clerk and asked for a telephone. The clerk let him into the solicitor's private office, but made a point of leaving the door open. The solicitor, host of the secret meeting, was nowhere to be seen. Chamberlain gripped the phone, thinking furiously. Even if Fast's secretary would agree to send a message to Abu Dhabi, it would take too long.

Chamberlain shrugged and dialled Farquhar's office.

'Inspector, this is Pete Chamberlain.'

'Again?'

'This is about a favour, but I'm not sure if the favour is for me or you.'

'Perhaps I should be the judge of that.'

'I'm going to give you a message concerning the Pendragon Auction and I want you to pass it on to your counterpart in the CIA.'

'Whatever are you talking about, old son?' Farquhar laughed jovially. 'I haven't any *counterparts* in the CIA. I'm a policeman.'

'Cut the crap, Farquhar. If he happens to be Arnie Fast, tell him I'm really pissed off. But, whoever he is, tell him to pull his plants out of the auction.'

'Plants?' Farquhar barked. 'What plants?'

'I counted five, maybe six.'

'Give me your number, I'll call you back.'

'333 8080.'

Chamberlain waited by the phone and wondered what the old clerk was thinking. Fucking agency never stopped trying. Nice trick, though, and they'd done a damned good job of making the hand-to-hand guys look like businessmen who pummelled tennis balls at weekends. If they pulled it off, Grandzau would never know what had hit him. But if Grandzau's mercs tumbled, and it took one to know one, then there'd be a real mess and a dead Charles Hammond.

He watched the clock on the wall. It was an old ticker, with Roman numerals and a sweep hand that chopped each minute into sixty ponderous seconds. He watched it for ten minutes and began to think of calling Farquhar back, when the phone rang.

'For me,' he called to the clerk, and picked it up. 'Chamberlain.'

'Hey, old buddy. I told them they couldn't fool you, but nobody listened. I'm not one bit surprised. Sometime you got to tell me what tipped you!'

Chamberlain thought he heard a satellite echo on the line, and presumed that Arnie Fast was in Abu Dhabi, but he didn't care.

'Get 'em out or I'll blow the whistle.'

'Hold on, Pete.'

'I don't work for you, Arnie. I work for people who are

287

paying me to get our man back in one piece. You're risking his life.'

'Now you listen to me –'

'Don't give me any crap about loyalty to the old company. I retired, legally, fairly, and I haven't broken any agreements.'

'I'm talking about loyalty to your country.'

'You're calling it that, but you're talking about loyalty to the agency. And to you, to get you out of that mess you made in the Channel.'

'No. Listen. I can't give you the whole story, but it's vital that we get him back.'

'I'll get him back.'

'I don't think you can handle it, old buddy.'

'I'm doing better than you are so far.'

'Where would you be without my help? Probably just pulling into Marseille.'

'Probably,' Chamberlain admitted. 'But now, we're going to play by Grandzau's rules and get him back alive. So get your guys out.'

'Pete. Please, listen. They're just a precaution.'

'Precaution? And what happens when we win the bidding and your phonies can't deliver their share of the money?'

'They can. It's legit. The outfits they represent are pledged to give the money, just as if they were their own people.'

'How'd you talk them into that?' Chamberlain asked suspiciously.

'By appealing to their patriotism.'

'Arnie.'

'The companies were glad as hell not to risk their own people. If the auction goes well, my guys'll never make a move. They'll just pony up the money like everybody else

288

and ride shotgun until he's home free. They're on your side, Pete. Insurance in case something goes wrong.'

'I don't like it. What if they go off half-cocked?'

'Come on, Pete. They're good guys. The best we have.'

'You can't throw a good team together in one day.'

'You think this is their first job? Tell you what. I'll set up a meet with the team leader. You check him out yourself. You'll see what I mean.'

'We're leaving in three hours.'

'He's going to check with me right after that meeting you're in is over. I'll tell him to talk to you. Pick a spot.'

'The Cheshire Cheese.'

'How corny can you get?'

'It's close by and busy enough to be private and safe.'

The meeting had broken up and Helen Thorp was swept past him on a crest of attentive colleagues. Chamberlain followed. He caught her up on the narrow path outside the solicitor's door. She was looking around.

'There you are. Listen, it's three and we have to leave the hotel about five. Why don't we have a late lunch?'

'I promised to meet a guy.'

'Is it important?'

'Let me fill you in later.'

'Are you going back to the club?'

'No, no more theories.'

'Do what you please, but it seems silly to me.'

'I'm not going to the club. Can you get back to the hotel all right?'

'I'll share a cab with the Japanese,' she said, smiling through the group to Soma, the man from Mishuma. They parted on the Strand, Helen hailing a cab with the Japanese and his aide, Chamberlain hurrying towards Fleet Street. He debated whether to tell Helen if he went along with the CIA. The fewer in on the secret the better. It annoyed him that he was tempted to go along, take the insurance, if the team leader looked good.

The team leader looked very good. So good that Chamberlain hadn't recognized the tweedy Lockheed lawyer as a plant. He surveyed the Cheshire Cheese with the happy eye of an Ivy League English professor on a Christmas vacation pilgrimage to Dr Johnson's favourite pub. He gave the television above the bar an appropriately pained look and winced again when his gaze fell on the jukebox.

Beautiful, thought Chamberlain, a real pro. A little fat and middle-aged until you took very close notice of his hands and feet where years of training had created physical clues that weren't easily erased. He stood slightly pigeon-toed, balanced and ready to spring from the balls of his feet. And there was a tension in his hands, an inclination towards motion.

He crossed the room and joined Chamberlain standing at the bar. His cover name was Doug Pickert and he said there was a real Doug Pickert in Lockheed's legal department. He knew how to talk in a clear, quiet voice that was easily understood, but wouldn't carry. Chamberlain passed him a Newcastle Brown Ale.

Pickert thanked him politely. He took out a briar pipe and began stuffing it with tobacco and Chamberlain wondered how many times he'd rammed the stem through somebody's eye and strolled innocuously away before the body hit the floor.

He got it lighted without incident and spoke, probing with merry, soft eyes. 'We support you fully in your desire to retrieve the subject without violence.'

'With a gang of hand-to-hand killers?'

'Think of us as a precaution,' Pickert replied mildly.

'Insurance?'

'Exactly,' Pickert beamed. 'That's a perfect word.'

'It's Arnie Fast's word.'

Pickert sighed indulgently. 'Pete – you mind if I call you Pete?'

'Get off it,' snapped Chamberlain.

'No, you get off it,' Pickert shot back. 'You've got your back up for no reason. And I know you know it. You're just being a pain in the ass for the hell of it. We're the A team, Pete. The best. We don't fuck up. You can count on it. So if Arnie *says* we're insurance, he *means* we're insurance.'

'I'll tell you what I told Fast. You can't throw an A team together in two days. I don't care how good the guys are.'

'I've been drilling my guys since two hours after Hammond got snatched. And don't you tell me, sonny, that I can't put together an A team in six days.'

'I've been around a while,' said Chamberlain. 'How come I've never seen you or any of your guys before?'

'You really want to know?'

'Yeah, I want to know. I want to know who the hell you guys are. How come I've never seen you?'

'Because the Agency doesn't make guys like us work with sluggers like you.'

The best Chamberlain could muster was a sarcastic, 'Were you in on Fast's classy little op in the Channel Islands?'

Pickert was unruffled. 'Good God, no. Fast is as bad as you are, waltzing around the world looking for battle ribbons. If you'd just stop and think about it, you'd see the safest way to get Hammond is spring him from the auction itself, and then, only if necessary . . . Can I tell Fast that you're with us?'

Chamberlain cast bleak eyes on the dirty floor. 'I'm not against you.'

'Trust us.'

'Sure.'

'Great, Pete. Really great. Share a cab back to the hotel?'

'No. No thanks. I think I'll walk.'

'Well, see you on the plane.'

Chamberlain watched Pickert wander out of the Cheshire Cheese, beaming and swaying like a tourist high on history and stout English ale. A few minutes later he made his own melancholy way out to Fleet Street. Considering the doubts the agency might have about him, he wouldn't have risked the close space of a cab with a man of Pickert's skills even before the slugger insult.

Listlessly, his mind lumbered through the things he could have said, but no words he knew could have erased the bitter hurt. It was his own damned fault. He'd done it to himself. He'd hit a pro and the pro had bloodied him back. A real pro, not just a hitter.

He walked west along Fleet Street towards the Strand as darkness fell. Office workers were filling the pavements, flooding up from the City and pouring out of the newspaper buildings. Chamberlain wallowed blindly among them, his eyes on the pavement, the hurt burning the more he tried to ignore it.

Kreegan surfaced suddenly on his thoughts – Kreegan and Wheeler, Hammond's brass-balled bodyguard. Endowed with guts, a measure of common sense, and the patience to stand guard in other people's cars and foyers, they occupied the lower levels on the scale of hard men upon which Pickert had found him wanting.

Chamberlain walked slowly, thinking of the qualities that separated him and Pickert. At the bottom of Pickert's scale of hard men were the property guards, three-dollar-an-hour security men, lobby guards, elevator starters, floorwalkers, bank guards, Brinks drivers, Pinkertons, airport security, most cops, feds, Treasury agents, Scotland Yard, Interpol. People-guards were a notch higher, private bodyguards to the Secret Service, rated by the value of whom they protected, the penny ante ones like Kreegan doubling as bag carriers, the special ones like Wheeler weaving elaborate precautions.

Idea guards held the high ground on the scale of hard men, the defenders of the faith, the spooks and spies and saboteurs dominated by Pickert, maybe not because he knew more ways to kill with his bare hands, but perhaps because he owned enough brains to avoid the stupid mistakes he could expect of lesser hard men, sluggers like Chamberlain.

A double-decker bus splattered Chamberlain with icy slush from a flooded gutter at the corner of Chancery Lane. He jumped back from the kerb, too late, and spotted a tall bobby watching him over the heads of the rushing crowd. Chamberlain looked away, then quickly back, wondering if Farquhar had put a uniformed tail on him as a loud warning to be good, but the bobby was sauntering assuredly into the road, gesturing a double-parked taxi into motion.

The cab shot ahead and it occurred to Chamberlain that the policeman's determination to move the traffic was so obvious that the cab driver hadn't offered even token resistance. Pickert was like the bobby, not too smart to make stupid mistakes, but determined not to.

Sick of himself, and certain that the crowds who brushed past were aware of his limitations, Chamberlain crossed Fleet Street and cut into the nearest Temple alley. A detour through the deserted gardens would give him space to think. And he'd return to the Savoy via the quieter Embankment in better shape than he was now to deal with the night ahead. But by the time he had found a way into the Temple Gardens he still couldn't break loose from Pickert's insult.

He'd racked up a real bonehead list of stupid mistakes

in the last six days. Some were ordinary miscalculations, but others were colossal idiocies that a guy like Pickert would never have pulled.

Pickert would not have let an amateur like Kreegan pal around like an old war buddy while he tried to find Charles Hammond. Pickert wouldn't have lied to Farquhar because he liked the feel of Lady Janet Isling. Nor would Pickert have taken Helen Thorp to bed, or anyone else connected with the Pendragon Auction, before the job was over, unless it was to find out some specific information. All he'd found out in Helen Thorp's bed was that he wouldn't mind staying there a long time.

The Temple Gardens were dark, the walk illuminated intermittently by pale yellow pools of lamp light. Pausing in one of the pools, Chamberlain thought it might not be too late to undo some of the damage. He looked at his watch, his pulse quickening with the relief of going back into action. The hell with Pickert.

He'd just have time to check out the Overseas Club if he went directly on to Heathrow from there. Phone Helen Thorp and tell her to bring his clothes to the plane. A little role reversal. Leave the shot revolver in the room. Comptel could afford the loss and he'd had no intention of smuggling it past Grandzau's mercs anyway. Knowing he would never make it to Knightsbridge in a cab during rush hour, Chamberlain turned in a half circle, wondering which Underground line was closer.

A tall London bobby strode heavily through the light pool behind him, his whistle lanyard swinging rhythmically with his measured step. So Farquhar was following him after all. No wonder he'd been seeing bobbies all over town today. Fired up because he was moving again, Chamberlain flung aside the last vestiges of Pickert's depressing condescension and broke into a broad grin.

Screw all of them. Why not ask Farquhar's tail which Underground line was closer?

He hurried towards the approaching bobby and intercepted him in the near dark between the two lamps.

'Excuse me, Officer. Which way is the closest subway station?'

The guy was good, he had to admit. Didn't blink. Went to the offensive.

'Are you not aware, sir, that the Temple Gardens are closed to the public after dark?'

'Sorry, I didn't know that. I'm just taking a short cut. I'm looking for the subway.' Subway, to emphasize that he was a lost tourist. Charades within charades. Incredulously, he watched the bobby take a summons book from his pocket and begin to write.

'You're kidding,' said Chamberlain.

'Have you any identification, sir?'

Chamberlain gave him his passport. Despite the fact that it was so dark that his face was a white blur beneath his helmet, the bobby copied Chamberlain's name on the summons.

'You may answer this in any police station, sir, within forty-eight hours.'

'Sure.'

'Here you are, sir.' He extended the summons and the passport together, one for each hand, and Chamberlain took them, one in each hand.

The last pterodactyl, Lady Janet thought, must have looked as formidable as the first. And so with Grandzau's chartered Concorde, the needle-nosed supersonic jet liner perched in splendid isolation on a remote Heathrow apron. She and Henri Trefle had been watching for hours from the cold shadows of a transformer hut just inside the airport's chainlink fence, but she might have been in Gloucestershire for all the opportunity of boarding it.

When they had first breached the fence to slip aboard and hide, they found Grandzau's Concorde guarded by a pair of mercenaries under the watchful eye of a carload of Metropolitan 'Police. The guards stood under the ship, back to back. The police checked the identification of the crew of the ground power unit as it had rolled up and plugged in; they observed the same routine when a tanker piped jet fuel aboard. A lav-service van had arrived next, pumping chemicals, then a canteen van, with the bidders' meals, and then a swarm of mechanics who checked struts, tyres and flaps. A water truck topped off the tanks and a man came by in a cherry picker, raised himself above the nose, and wiped the windscreen.

'Soon,' said Henri, when an air-start cart parked under the engines and indeed, moments later, the flight engineer was delivered in a police car.

More guards. Lady Janet was desperate. There was no way aboard. She was going to be left behind. She racked her brain. At least she could think straight again. She had had a decent sleep, at last, in a quiet hotel, and she hadn't taken an injection or a pill in twenty-four hours. The pain was still there, a fierce reminder of what Grandzau had done to her and what she would do to him if only they could board the plane.

She pounded her gloved hand on the concrete where they lay in the lee of the hut.

'Henri! Do something!'

'Shall I make us invisible?'

Chamberlain never knew if it was Wheeler in his thoughts or the belated realization that the policeman couldn't have seen his name in the dim light when he wrote the phoney summons. All he did know was that the warning had come way too late.

The bobby thrust the stiletto underhand and the gleaming sliver leaped up at Chamberlain's belly, searching entry to his heart. He was a big man to use a stiletto, and a big man to take one away from. Filling his victim's hands was a deadly effective trick and the underhand thrust involved no unbalancing lunge that Chamberlain might have used to pitch him forward.

Chamberlain's single advantage was that Farquhar had told him about the trick played on Wheeler. He accepted the summons and his passport, side-stepped, dropped the flimsy summons, but wrapped his fist around his passport, curled it into a tight shaft and rammed the hard edge of the document into the killer's nose.

He gasped in pain and surprise and stopped in mid-thrust. Chamberlain gripped his extended forearm in one hand and his bicep in the other and used all his strength to break his elbow over his knee like a piece of firewood.

He screamed once and went down in a tangle, clutching his arm, bringing his legs up protectively. Chamberlain went for him in a frenzy, determined to find out why Grandzau's killer had come after him right after a meeting with the head of the team that the Agency was planting in the Pendragon Auction.

But before he reached him, the bobby did an incredible thing. He blew his whistle the way a real bobby blew his whistle to call for help. Chamberlain froze, astonished. Did the whistle mean he had partners nearby? Or was he a real bobby doing some freelance killing on the side? Or was he just a smart operator, all alone and bluffing with his whistle to frighten Chamberlain away? Another police whistle answered, thin in the distance. And then another, echoing shrilly in a nearby arch. Chamberlain knew it would take hours to talk his way out of police custody, hours even to persuade them to check with Inspector Farquhar. And by then Grandzau's Concorde would have taken off for Arabia with Helen Thorp aboard and Chamberlain out of the auction.

He looked frantically at the fallen killer, who was watching him through slitted eyes. He had to know who had ordered him killed. But the whistles were drawing nearer. He did the only thing he could do. He ran.

Not all the invited bidders waited for Grandzau's Concorde to take them to the Pendragon Auction.

Arnie Fast accidentally ran into his KGB counterpart in the sweltering lobby of a low-rent Arab hotel any civilized race would have shut down years ago. Neither man wasted time wondering why the other was there. Both knew that the routes around the Arabian princes lay in the back alleys of the bazaar.

'Comrade,' said Fast, as they edged warily past each other, each with a hand in his pocket, 'we're going to blow your ass away.'

The Soviet had managed a station on East Forty-fifth Street, half a block from the United Nations Secretariat Building and even closer to the American Mission to the

UN. By the time the CIA had figured out what he had been doing there he had changed his cover corporation and had moved, like any up-and-coming Manhattan entrepreneur, to a flashier address in the Citicorp Building. He gave Fast a tight smile and a reply in perfect English.

'Don't count on it, meathead.'

Outside, as he drove swiftly through the tangled alleys of the old dhow harbour, the Russian regretted that he had let the American goad him into speaking. In the hotel, Arnie Fast scratched his head and wondered for the dozenth time why they were so uptight about Hammond.

The bidders for the Pendragon Auction looked, at first glance, like any travellers stuck in the limbo of a boarding lounge – perched on uncomfortable chairs, faces washed out by over-bright lights, carry-on luggage at their feet, waiting for their plane to be announced. They eyed the jetway doors and ignored the rest of the terminal beyond the glass wall that separated the-soon-to-depart from the eventually-to-depart. Security looked tighter than usual, however, even for IRA-embattled Britain, with armed officers covering the entrance and the jetway exit. And the bidders themselves, who appeared unusually anxious-looking for seasoned business travellers, acted more like a group than an ordinary crowd of passengers, perhaps because they were eyeing each other speculatively, weighing the competition and calculating the likelihood of forming final-hour partnerships if the need arose.

Helen Thorp, wrapped in sable, was talking to the Japanese Soma, who had seized leadership of the business consortium. Soma was listening intently, nodding his head, smiling, gesturing agreement and slyly reaching for her hand. She glanced repeatedly at the empty seat beside her, and when a husky American lawyer approached she saved it with her carry-on bag and rescued her hand simultaneously, without skipping a beat, and the lawyer retreated to his similarly well-built colleagues.

Security officers came and went, reporting to the knife-lean Alec Farquhar, who stood at the front of the lounge, observing everything with a stern paternal gaze and issuing orders with quick economical gestures. He looked at his watch at regular intervals. Suddenly a tall berobed Arab wafted into the glass lounge from the main concourse, brushing past security, before Farquhar stopped him. A British solicitor was at his side, waving a Pendragon telegram, and Farquhar let them through. The Japanese hurried to greet them, smiling and extending a plump hand, which the tall Arab regarded with a sublime indifference.

Wearing an airport security uniform and a service cap low over his eyes, Pete Chamberlain watched through the concourse windows. He had stolen a trick from the bobby who had tried to kill him, trailed an airport guard into a gentlemen's on the far side of the vast terminal, taken his uniform, handcuffed him to the plumbing, and gagged him with his belt. Now he was trying to figure a way to board Grandzau's Concorde before whoever had set the phoney bobby on him in the Temple Gardens tried to kill him again.

Pickert's team seemed the most likely suspects, though it could have been Farquhar, for both the Briton and Arnie Fast – and only Fast and Farquhar – knew he had discovered the Agency plants. Grandzau was a remote possibility. True, Grandzau had used a bobby to kidnap Hammond, but suspecting him presumed three unlikely conditions: that Grandzau had a man on the ground who had overheard the suspicions he had voiced to Helen at the hotel (and he was not forgetting that Farquhar had the room bugged); or that he, Chamberlain, had somehow got closer to Hammond than he realized; or that the killer had

300

just happened to attack (coincidentally?) the instant he had discovered the Agency plants and met with Pickert. All in all, Chamberlain thought he would be safest on the Concorde guarded by Grandzau's mercs than among his 'friends'.

A policewoman bustled into the lounge and spoke to Farquhar, who called for the group's attention. Chamberlain edged nearer the door. The guards looked at each other, as if wondering why he was hanging around.

Farquhar said, 'If I might have your attention, Gentlemen and Lady? I should like at this time to announce the departure procedure. In several minutes you will be led downstairs and onto the tarmac where a bus will take you across the airport to your aircraft.'

The bidders began picking up bags and buttoning coats.

'Before boarding the bus you will be searched, electronically and by hand, for weapons. There are public conveniences at the back of this lounge and I strongly recommend that you divest yourselves of any objects that Heathrow Airport Security might deem inappropriate aboard an airliner.'

He paused, but none of the eighteen bidders left their plastic chairs.

'An arrest for weapons violations would obviously prevent the detainee from boarding Herr Grandzau's aircraft.'

Still, no one moved. Farquhar looked from face to face and issued a final warning. 'Make no mistake. Great Britain's primary interest is to see each and every one of you safely out of this country.'

Chamberlain observed that neither the boyish-looking Englishman who represented the hovercraft and tank manufacturers that depended on Charles Hammond to sell their wares in the Gulf States, nor the overweight City investment counsellors contributing a hefty sum from a

British bank and insurance consortium blinked an eye at the heavy warning.

'Very well. Once aboard the bus, I have been instructed, you are in Herr Grandzau's hands. His guards will search you as well. We have no reason to suspect you will be in danger, and yet, there will be little or nothing we can do to help, so I suggest you follow their directions to the letter. You must keep in mind that Charles Hammond's kidnappers have come too far to take any chances at this late date, and they have shown themselves willing, already, to kill.'

Chamberlain hurried along the concourse, down an escalator, and found a door that led outside. Planes roared and whined and the air was bitterly cold and reeked of kerosene. There was no sign of the bus among the blaze of airport lights and the scurrying ground vehicles, but he located the Pendragon departure lounge a hundred yards along the wall of the building by the security people posted at its downstairs door, and moved boldly towards them. His uniform allowed him close enough to see the bidders shuffle through the security bottleneck just inside the door at the foot of the stairs.

They were subdued. Soma was first. His Japanese aide, one of the CIA plants, followed closely. Then came the four English businessmen, two young, two middle-aged, all of whom were, as near as Chamberlain could tell, legitimate bidders. Then a fifth Englishman, who had come with the Arab, then the Arab. Three young American attorneys shoved their carry-on bags and briefcases onto the X-ray conveyor and stood still for the electronic wand and a hand search. All three plants, Chamberlain thought, did an admirable job of concealing their excess musculature. The Germans passed through, and a couple more Americans, Boston bankers representing the CIA. Then the Lockheed man whose overdeveloped neck had given the whole thing away, and then Pickert, offering his pipe for inspection with a jovial smile. The French, two men with long, pinched faces, sidled through the electronic passage. An alarm shrilled.

Farquhar's own men frisked both of them. Shaking his head in disbelief, Farquhar watched them extract a miniature derringer from the sleeve of one of the Frenchmen. His companion purpled, but was allowed to pass. Farquhar personally arrested the other and ordered him to be taken away. A uniformed sergeant took his arm.

'My embassy shall hear of this,' hissed the Frenchman.

'Come along, sir.'

Helen Thorp was last. She carried only a handbag, which evoked no response from the electronics. She held her coat open and let a policewoman frisk her blouse and skirt.

Chamberlain tensed. Farquhar was coming out, apparently to signal the bus. He faced him and spread his hands open at his sides.

''Fraid your boy's got a broken arm.'

'Peter! My God, what are you doing here?'

Chamberlain said nothing.

'Are you all right, old son? Was it you did that bloke in the Temple Gardens?'

'Yours?' Chamberlain asked coldly, watching his eyes.

'Good God, no. He's probably the same blighter who almost killed Hammond's bodyguard. I had a feeling it was you. Why'd you run away?'

'Would you have stayed?'

'Oh, I see what you mean. Of course not. Well, his trick backfired. Our patrols found him before he could get away. You didn't see his knife, did you?'

'No.'

'Too bad. He must have hidden it. Anyway, good to see you. Are you going aboard?'

303

'If you let me.'

'Come on inside then,' said Farquhar, taking his arm. 'We'll run you through the machines – see here, Ms Thorp, Peter is back.'

'So I see,' said Helen, who'd been watching from the edge of the milling group.

'Are you all right?'

'Fine.'

'Good. I was worried.'

'I'm sorry I got held up.'

Farquhar walked Chamberlain through the search, holding his arm throughout. He let him go at the door, whispering, 'I see you've agreed to go along.'

'I don't know if they believe me.'

Farquhar smiled. 'Stay out of their way and I think you'll be all right.'

'Who do you suppose sent the pig-sticker after me?'

Farquhar gave him a look that Chamberlain could only define as genuinely sympathetic. 'I have no idea, old son. No idea at all.'

He squeezed Chamberlain's arm, opened the door and stepped out into the night and returned with a young man in battle dress. The business-suited bidders gaped at the violent costume. He wore jump boots, jungle fatigues, twin ammunition bandoleers and a string of grenades around his waist. He had a dark beret on his head, a bright red silk scarf at his throat, and a vicious-looking machine pistol in his hand.

Chamberlain heard the bus.

'Incidentally,' said Farquhar, ignoring the soldier, his eyes flickering over his own men, cautioning them to stay calm, 'Where did you get that security badge? Who does it say you are, Constable McGeedy?'

'He's in the john on the other side of the building.'

'Unharmed, I trust.'

304

'Just tied up. He's fine.'

'What would you have done had I arrested you?'

'I would have assumed you were going to kill me.'

'And reacted accordingly?'

'Right.'

'I rather thought as much.'

The bus stopped next to the door with a squeak of scarred brake linings. There was a quick knock and the soldier opened the door. Two more soldiers, similarly attired and armed, stepped in.

'*Allez!*'

He motioned to Chamberlain first, frisked him professionally and passed him through the door to a fourth soldier who led him onto the bus. It looked like an ordinary airport bus with an open luggage hold underneath, except it had an electronic checkpoint built into the door in case airport security had missed anything. Chamberlain, assuming as much, had deposited his various pocket gizmos at the left luggage counter.

He walked to the back of the bus, as the soldier instructed and sat down and looked out of the window. The Concorde was nowhere to be seen in the blue, green, red and white-lighted distance of the giant airport. No surprise. Airports always shoved trouble to their outer edges. Grandzau's Concorde would occupy a lonely place on the rim of the lights.

He waved when Helen stepped aboard. She hurried back and sat beside him, wrapping her coat tightly closed. 'I'm freezing. Put your arm around me.'

'It's just terror.' Chamberlain held her, surprised by how violently she trembled.

'What's the TV for?'

Chamberlain had already noticed the screen above the driver's seat. 'No idea.'

'Pete, where were you?'

'I went to the Overseas Club.' He didn't want to talk about the attack in the Temple Gardens.

'And?'

'The old codgers were pretty shook up about Ramsey, so they're packing their service revolvers. The place looked like a genteel Dodge City; steely-eyed gang just hoping I'd make a false move. Unfortunately, Ramsey hadn't confided in any of 'em.'

'Too bad.'

'Doesn't matter now. I see Grandzau attracted an Arab. That ought to bump the bidding up. Who's the Brit with him?'

'He's a solicitor who specializes in Arab work.'

'Here we go!'

The guards trooped onto the bus. The last aboard drove. Gears clashing, the bus pulled away from the terminal, into the sea of lights. An airport vehicle guided it out of the terminal area, through a maze of taxi ways, stopping and starting to let airliners pass.

Attaining a road that seemed to circle around the runways, the guide dropped aside and the bus continued on its own. Chamberlain glanced back, but in seconds the truck lights were lost among the thousands of runway lights, glide pattern markers, flashing wing and tail lamps, whirling support-truck dome lights and the now distant but still bright terminal.

The bus reverberated from the almost-ceaseless roar of jets taking off and landing. Ten minutes after the guide truck had dropped off, the bus made a sharp turn and there, waiting in the distance, was the Concorde, its thin drooping nose pointed whimsically down the blue-light-lined runway.

Lady Janet saw the bus's headlights suddenly separate from the surrounding glitter. She had already calculated her moment to slip aboard. The police had left after the pilots were delivered. There were only the two mercenaries on the tarmac now and mechanics were busy connecting their air-start machine to the Concorde's engines, which began, just before she saw the bus, to whine. Now the first engine roared to life, shaking the ground. The mercenaries fled to the front of the slender plane and regrouped far ahead of the needle nose as a second engine fired up with a deafening thunder.

'*Now!*' she shouted. 'While they're watching the bus.'

She shot to her feet, to spring the short distance to the boarding stairs. Trefle yanked her to the ground.

'Impossible.'

And indeed, even as she clawed at his massive arm Lady Janet saw Henri was right. Guards who had boarded before she and Henri had arrived, hurried out of the plane, down the steps. Heavily armed mercenaries. Grandzau was taking no chances. Bitterly she watched them dog-trot towards the bus, which parked a hundred yards from the Concorde.

'Why so far from the plane?' Henri asked, as the bus's headlights went out.

Beyond the roar of the Concorde engines, her sharp ears picked up a familiar thudding sound and, almost simultaneously, a faint boom like a distant explosion. Before she could form an answer all the lights went out at once and dark descended on Heathrow Airport like an avalanche.

28

Lady Janet and Henri Trefle stared in disbelief. Where Heathrow had blazed with a million lights, the black night crouched over a vast plain, pocked fitfully by the wing, tail and belly lights of jet planes that were blundering blindly above the dark airport and milling on the runways like lost cattle. The Concorde's third engine had caught, but the thudding noise she had heard grew louder in the sky, and Lady Janet sensed a flourish of dim reflections settle in the dark space where the bus had parked.

Suddenly she knew what Grandzau intended. She ran, screaming, 'Henri! It's a trick! The bus, Henri. The bus!'

Chamberlain sat tight, betting when the driver doused his headlights that the airport power failure wasn't an accident. He wished he knew as surely what Pickert's boys were doing in the dark. At least he had his back in a corner.

The ominous whine of jets lumbering overhead in the dark was suddenly louder. Grandzau's mercs had opened the door. Then a new noise, the muffled beat-thump of a helicopter.

It was close and getting closer. Sounded like a big job. He could distinguish the separate beats of twin rotors. A big Chinook or one of the Sikorski sky cranes. It was over them in an instant, thunderous, turbines screaming, giant rotors swishing, beating the night, shaking the bus like a tent in a wind storm.

When it seemed that the brain-scrambling racket couldn't get louder, a dragging, ripping noise vibrated the bus like a big anchor chain roaring through a hawser pipe.

Seconds later all the noise diminished slightly. The mercs were back in the bus. They'd shut the door. Again he heard chain, jingling this time.

Someone cried out, an involuntary, frightened yelp of surprise. Chamberlain felt his stomach drop. Christ! They'd picked up the whole goddamned bus.

It hung still, for a moment, near the ground, then lurched forward, tilting slightly to starboard, and began a lunging, swaying, thunderous, struggling stair-stepping climb into the night sky.

Chamberlain looked out of the back window when the runway lights started blinking fitfully to life again. He caught a glimpse of the Concorde, still waiting. The lights flashed off, blackening the airport once more. The labouring helicopter gained speed and altitude, and soon all he could see was a scantly lighted snow-covered countryside.

The snow, less than a thousand feet below, sent up a pale backglow that illuminated, ghostly pale, the stunned faces of the bidders twisting in their seats. The soldiers watched passively. Two manned the door in the event, Chamberlain figured, that somebody panicked and made a crazy run for it.

He noticed several of the CIA plants shoot meaningful glances at Pickert as if asking, what now, sir? Pickert looked unperturbed. He stuffed his pipe absent-mindedly, then slipped it into a pocket.

Chamberlain listened to the wind racing past the bus. It had certainly never gone this fast in its life before. He guessed from the sound at one hundred knots. The rotor beat had eased considerably as soon as the aircraft levelled off. You could talk if you yelled. Chamberlain leaned close to Helen and yelled.

'Nicely done.'

'What?'

'Grandzau. You could almost like him if you didn't think about the jets trying to land.'

'Where do you think he's taking us?'

'Helicopter's probably got a five-hundred-mile range.'

'That's a lot of help.'

'Well, you know we're not going back to London.'

'Which direction are we flying?' she yelled back.

'South, I think. I don't know.'

An eerie blue light shone suddenly from the television, and brightened to a picture of a face. 'I am Lancelot,' a voice roared from loudspeakers, louder than the wind, the turbines, and the thrashing rotors. Everyone watched the television.

'Charles Hammond is safe at the auction site where we shall arrive in several hours.'

His silky, Germanic accent put Chamberlain in mind of the Red Baron radio commercials – the mild voice of the tame Hun. It didn't quite go with the gaunt, lined face, the hooded eyes, and the hard, greedy mouth.

'I am in the helicopter which is lifting your bus. Rest assured that you and I both are in far less danger than if the CIA and the KGB knew where we were going. The helicopter is capable of its task. The Americans named it the Jolly Green Giant in Southeast Asia, and they should know.' Deadpan, he added, almost as if reading from a script, 'In fact, I shouldn't be surprised if some of the corporations you represent actually submitted the low bids for its moving parts.'

Grandzau chuckled mechanically as the TV screen went dark.

The plants started eyeing Doug Pickert, chafing for orders. Chamberlain sympathized. It would be very satisfying to climb out of a window, up the side of the helicopter, and strangle the son of a bitch. Unfortunately, it was no way to find Charles Hammond.

The racing slipstream blew Lady Janet off the helicopter like a high-pressure firehose. She pitched backwards into the night, landed on the roof of the bus and slid over the side. Stunned by the impact and stiffened by the bitter cold, she clawed desperately at the rivet-studded metal, then hit one of the sling chains. She grabbed the heavy links with both hands and began climbing back up to the helicopter.

'Crazy woman,' yelled Trefle, crouching in the lee of the open luggage hold. 'Wait till they land.'

Lady Janet braced her rubber-soled boots on the links and went up the sling like a ladder. This time, when she reached the roof of the bus, she crawled aft, and hid from the wind behind one of the helicopter's wheel struts. She was not waiting for them to land because she knew that Grandzau would never have the confidence to leave an operation like this to subordinates.

Grandzau would be in the helicopter cockpit and she was going up there to kill him while his mercenaries were trapped in the bus. She'd seen them go in the bus seconds before the helicopter took off. The bus was already airborne when she and Henri had flung themselves into the luggage hold.

She smelled salt. The ground was no longer white, so she guessed they were over the sea. The rotor down-draught and the slipstream tore at her like living things. She started up the strut. She'd been ready this time for whatever Grandzau pulled. She had good gloves, boots, and several layers of tight-fitting warm clothes. She had a pistol under her breast and the Smith & Wesson 76 strapped to her back, set to full automatic.

311

Reaching the belly of the helicopter, she left the protection of the wheel strut and hauled herself inch by inch up the handgrips that studded the side of the aircraft. The sound of engines and rotors was as punishing as the beat of the wind. She headed for the point where the cable that held the steel girder sling-support entered the belly. It was extended several feet down so that she was able to stand on the steel supports while holding the cable.

The bus swayed back and forth so the cable moved inches forward and inches back, making the well through which she intended to enter the craft a dangerous place should the cable swing against her as she climbed up. She waited a few minutes, got used to the swing of the arc, and made her move.

She was up and through quickly, but the Smith & Wesson caught and she struggled to free it, knowing the cable was swinging back towards her legs with crushing force. She twisted violently to one side and was up into the hold of the giant helicopter.

She lay still, trying to see in the dark. They'd never hear her over the racket, but she'd never hear one of them either. It was a luxury to be out of the slipstream. Slowly, trusting to her black clothes to hide her, she worked her way forward, guided by a faint red light, until she could see the cockpit, and the silhouettes of the pilot and Grandzau, black against the glow of the instruments.

Though she'd known the truth nearly a week, it was still shocking to see him alive. She remembered the burial she'd arranged in the mountains for the blackened, mutilated body the Italian police had pulled from his car. She remembered how she had loved him. Then she eased the Smith & Wesson from her back, braced the sling around her arm, rose to one knee and flicked off the safety.

He turned to speak to the pilot and she saw his face.

312

She waited, deep in shadow, to feel something. Repulsion, love, hate. There was hate, a beautiful, contained force that would never leave her, but what flew through her mind, as odd as a summer bird in winter, was something her father had said shortly before she left home.

They'd stopped to breathe the horses on a ridge above the old village where once lived the grooms and gamekeepers – those shepherds of her childhood – long dead or moved to council housing. Her father had lighted a cigarette, a Senior Service, jammed it into his ivory holder, slipped the holder between his teeth and remarked of the London middle classes who were renovating the stone cottages for weekend homes, 'How have the petty risen!'

What, she wondered bleakly, had she ever hoped Grandzau would change in her life?

He'd aged markedly in the three years and looked as if he might have been ill, but mostly, he looked the same – the same pretentious, striving, treacherous and rather ordinary criminal he had always been.

She might forgive him the deception, she thought, but not his cruelty. The years alone had cleared her perceptions, purged the demon that sought places she didn't want to be. The very clarity with which she now saw Grandzau was proof of the debt she owed him. For whatever reasons, he had freed her. But the cruelty she'd suffered, the knowing, deliberate cruelty, she would never forgive; still, she lowered her gun. She wouldn't kill him. Now that she saw what he was, what he wanted, she knew a sweeter revenge.

The bus swayed in the chains, buffeted by gusty headwinds that slowed the big helicopter to eighty knots. It swung side to side in widening arcs that staggered the aircraft and sickened the passengers who were already miserable from the ceaseless racket and the bitter cold.

The cold, thick and damp and smelling of salt, was a frightening reminder of the black sea somewhere below. Occasionally they saw the lights of a ship and each time it seemed they were flying too low, much closer to the invisible water than would seem safe.

'Are you cold?' shouted Helen.

'Freezing,' yelled Chamberlain, beating his hands together. His gloves were useless and his feet felt as if he'd been wading in a brook.

'Put your hands in here.' She leaned against him and closed her coat around his hands. 'Better?'

'I'll tell you after the circulation starts. Thanks.'

She leaned closer and put her lips to his ear. 'Listen. There's something strange about Soma's assistant. Can you hear me? Just nod.'

Chamberlain nodded. Her lips were warm and soft as he remembered.

'I know Soma, slightly. I've met him at conferences, but his assistant is somebody new. He's a little strange. I can't quite put my finger on it, but he's almost not Japanese. He seems to have to remind himself how to behave with Soma. Am I making any sense?'

Chamberlain nodded.

'There's not enough respect. Do you know what I mean?'

Chamberlain nodded again. He was familiar with the elaborate rituals of deference that characterized Japanese corporate life.

'You wouldn't have noticed it,' she said, 'but Soma's been coming on to me, so they've been around a lot . . . What do you think?'

She turned her head and pressed her ear to his mouth.

'I think you're even smarter than you look. The guy is a CIA plant. There's six of them. Him, Pickert from Lockheed and his assistant and the eager beaver attorneys from the other American companies.' He felt her stiffen.

'Let me finish. Pickert's the boss. They're hand-to-hand guys. Elite squad.'

She tore away from him and screamed into his ear, 'Why didn't you stop them?'

'I just found out. I braced them but then I let them talk me into going along with them.'

'Are you crazy?'

'I thought they were right. And I believed them when they said they wouldn't make a move unless things went wrong. They said they were insurance and I bought it.'

'That's a pretty big decision to make alone, Pete. Too big.'

'I was alone. You weren't there.'

'Next time pick up the goddamned telephone. Jesus Christ, Pete. I hired you to protect Hammond, save him from violence and you let those, those *crazies* come along. I don't believe you. How dumb can you get?'

'Dumber than you think,' Chamberlain shouted into her ear. 'Somebody tried to kill me right after I met with Pickert. Did Hammond ever work with the CIA?'

'I don't know,' she said angrily. 'Why?'

'Because the guy who tried to kill me was a lot like one of the kidnappers. The fake bobby.'

'Doesn't that sound like Grandzau tried to kill you?'

'That makes no sense.'

'Neither do you. Goddamnit, Pete. Now what are we going to do?'

'We gotta go along. You'll start a war if you blow these guys. It's too late.'

'It's not too late. I can tell the guards right now.'

'Forget it,' said Chamberlain. 'Pickert's guys would fight.'

'But Hammond is safe.'

'And what if Grandzau gets shot or the goddamned helicopter crashes?'

'Why didn't you tell me?' she raged.

'It's easier not to give it away if you don't know.'

'Well, now I know, damn you.' She shoved his hands out of her coat and stared into the thundering dark.

Chamberlain shoved his hands into his coat pockets and craned his neck to look out of the back window, down at the black, invisible sea, wondering.

White light flowered in the darkness. The helicopter dropped towards it and Chamberlain made out a ship wallowing in heavy seas.

'Are we going to land on that?' yelled Helen.

'I hope not.' He could see the deck rising and falling fifteen feet on every wave.

The ship turned and ran with the wind. The helicopter skimmed the aft bridge house, dangled the bus in front of the white structure, then lowered it towards the heaving deck. The deck swooped up to meet them and the bus hit with a bone-jarring impact that flattened its springs, bounced it off the deck, and down hard again.

An explosion like a high-powered rifle sounded overhead and the passengers ducked reflexively. 'They're shooting!' cried Helen.

'Explosive bolt on the sling assembly. He winched us down and cut loose. Safer than trying to land with us.'

As Chamberlain spoke, the helicopter floated to the deck ahead of the bus with surprising agility. Men ran to it from both sides, dragging lines to tie it down. The rotors stopped turning, the lights went out, and the bidders sat again in darkness, until the guards turned on the bus lights and motioned them out.

Chamberlain and Helen Thorp reached the rolling, pitching deck last. The guards pointed them after the others, through a door in the bridge house, and down a central winding stairway, through a corridor and into the crew's dining room. The bidders sat at two long tables. On the thickly painted beige walls were advertisements for bags, caps and jackets which sailors could purchase with duty-free Marlboro cigarette cartons. It wasn't much warmer inside than it had been out.

Chamberlain smelled food and was suddenly hungry. It was almost midnight. The guards remained standing, one in each corner, and a couple of young men in dungarees and white serving jackets began placing large bowls of stew and jugs of hot coffee on the tables. They returned with bread and butter, served that, and retired. Everyone ate but the Arab, who sniffed disdainfully and asked the nearest guard if the stew held pork. The guard shrugged. The Arab, his black eyes fathomless, pushed the stew aside, buttered some bread and sipped black coffee.

Their host appeared after the stewards had cleared the table. Grandzau was wearing a heavy bridge coat and he stood just inside the door, saying nothing, watching, until everyone noticed he was there. A hard-looking merc stood beside him and Chamberlain saw the shadows of others in the corridor.

'I trust you've enjoyed the sailor's fare. Your cabins are ready. There will be a certain amount of sharing of the accommodation, with the exception, of course, of the lovely lady from Comptel Incorporated.' He nodded towards Helen. 'I was disappointed to learn that Mr Alfred Cowan would not join you. I have long admired his skills.'

A look that Chamberlain thought would split concrete flickered through her long lashes, but she said nothing.

'Where is Herr Hammond?' shouted the German who'd replaced Hans Streicher.

'Herr Hammond is asleep in his cabin.'

'We want to see him,' said the Frenchman from Dassault.

'You will see him in the morning.'

'No,' shouted the German. 'Now.'

Grandzau shook his head. 'You will see him tomorrow morning. You may examine him thoroughly before the auction to be sure that the goods are undamaged. Now, you will sleep. My men will take you to your cabins.'

Chamberlain lay awake in the top bunk of a two-man, junior-officer cabin. The ship was rolling ten degrees, slow and easy for a navy man, probably hell on the people who were used to crossing oceans by plane.

'You sure the pipe doesn't bother you?' Pickert called up from the bunk below.

'It's fine.'

'"Cause these days a lot of people don't like smoke anymore.'

'I kind of like it,' said Chamberlain. 'It reminds me of a professor I had in college. He smoked the same stuff.'

'Middleton's Cherry Blend?'

'I guess so.'

Pickert chuckled contentedly.

'What's funny?'

'I was just thinking of a fellow I know who's trying to do business in Arabia.'

'Funny coincidence we'd end up in the same cabin. You think the Hun's bugged the joint?'

'I'd count on it.'

'I almost got mugged on my way home this afternoon.'

'That a fact? London's not the town it used to be.'

'I suppose so. I mentioned our conversation to a couple of people.'

'I don't think much of a fellow who blabs bar-room confidences,' Pickert said slowly. 'Especially when they're true.'

'These people wouldn't say a thing unless I woke up with a terminal hangover.'

'My old sea legs tell me it's going to be a real calm night.'

'Glad to hear it.'

'Are you balling that boss of yours?'

'You're way out of line, Pickert.'

'Bimbo.'

'Pickert, if you rate her a bimbo I pity Lockheed next time you negotiate a deal with Comptel.'

'I wasn't talking about her.'

The guards brought breakfast to the cabins, coffee and a plate heaped with sweet rolls. At seven-thirty they ordered everyone down to the crew's dining room. In the confusion, Chamberlain slipped through an open cabin door for a look out of its ports, which faced forward. They were heading east, into the sun.

She looked like a ten-thousand-ton freighter. They'd covered the helicopter and the bus with canvas tarpaulins. From the sky she'd look exactly like any other freighter carrying deck cargo.

A guard noticed him in the cabin and, brandishing his machine pistol, ordered him out.

They'd removed the long tables from the crew's dining room and set up folding chairs facing the galley door at the aft end. There were many more guards. Four stood in the corners, watching the bidders, cradling their weapons. They'd changed from the bulky battle dress to black woollen pullovers and blue jeans. Each wore a woollen watchcap and carried a machine pistol. Two more guards waited by the galley door and another two stayed outside the other door.

Helen Thorp had saved him a seat. He thought that the dark circles under her eyes made her look beautifully dissipated. He asked how she had slept.

'Rotten. And I'm sick.'

319

'It's calming down. You'll be better.'

'Where the hell is Grandzau?'

When the electric clock on the bulkhead hit eight o'clock, Grandzau marched into the room, flanked by two more guards. That made ten Chamberlain had seen.

Grandzau faced the dour bidders. Most looked exhausted, battered by the helicopter flight and a largely sleepless night on the rolling ship. They eyed him with a mixture of disgust, impatience and hopeful anticipation.

Grandzau smiled back. He'd dressed with great care. A white carnation gracing the lapel of his three-piece, blue banker's suit proclaimed this was an occasion, a momentous day, despite the shabby room.

'Good morning,' he said formally. 'The Pendragon Auction will now begin. May I present to the bidders, Herr Charles Hammond.'

29

Charles Hammond pushed through the swinging galley
door, followed closely by an unarmed Maltese guard and a
sea-kitchen odour of steam, animal fat and strong soap. He
was dressed like a sailor in borrowed clothes, baggy blue
jeans and a ribbed black sweater stretched over his barrel
chest. Grandzau reached for his elbow. Hammond shook
him off impatiently and stared, chest heaving, at the people
who had come to bid for his life.

They stared back. Chamberlain thought he looked beat,
less the magnetic superstar dealer, and more like a man
who had had about as much as he could take.

Hammond's face was drawn. There were dark circles
under his eyes and his mouth sagged at the corners. His
ginger hair and the harsh fluorescent lights conspired to
give his pale skin an unhealthy pallor. He looked down at
his trembling hands and quickly clasped them behind his
back, as if to confine them. His restless eyes skipped about
the shabby dining room and fell on Helen Thorp.

'Hello, Helen.'

The folding chairs were crammed tightly together and
her shoulder had been touching Chamberlain's. He felt an
electric tension ripple through her body. She leaned
forward intently, and Chamberlain knew, with a curiously
sinking heart, what their relationship had been.

'Are you all right, Charles?'

The bidders exchanged worried glances.

Then a jerky smile lighted Hammond's weary features.

'Still worth bidding for.'

321

Ignoring Grandzau, he stepped closer to the seated bidders.

'I'm okay. They treated me all right – if you can treat anybody all right when you lock him up for a week.'

Hammond looked at his watch. Abruptly, he began pacing back and forth in front of the group, still ignoring Grandzau, nodding hello to bidders he knew, standing taller, pacing faster. Chamberlain sensed the fires that drove him, his love of action. Confinement must have been killing. Now he was moving again, and growing more animated with every word.

'We gotta get going. How 'bout those of you who know me personally telling those who don't that I look like my normal, healthy self. Then let the Hun here' – he jerked his thumb at Grandzau – 'get on with this so I can leave gratefully with whomever buys me.' He flashed a big smile that tried to circle the entire group in its nervous spirit. 'I truly don't want to be here any longer.'

It hadn't quite worked. They were still staring like a crowd at a bloody accident. Hammond snapped his fingers twice – a sharp, impatient, let's-go beat.

'Helen! Get this moving, sweetheart. Tell 'em you know me and I'm fine.'

Wait, thought Chamberlain. That sounds like *former* boyfriend talk. Too brusque for Helen to take from a lover. Helen Thorp jumped to obey. Casting Hammond a wry, intimate grin that an amazed Chamberlain read as you-haven't-changed-and-I-guess-you-never-will, she stood up and addressed the bidders.

'I've known Charles many years and there's no question in my mind that other than looking tired and fed up with being at the mercy of Mr Grandzau, Charles Hammond is his usual, very fine self. I've never seen him better or in more of a rush.'

Hammond gave her a wink and Chamberlain saw that he was the star his reputation said he was, high-powered, and ready to soar again as soon as a few functionaries like Pete Chamberlain did their job and set him loose. Helen turned to Grandzau. 'I think that if Mr Grandzau would please start the auction, we really should get going.'

Grandzau looked relieved to be given back charge of his own auction.

'I will state the rules of the Pendragon Auction,' the German began methodically. 'The item for purchase is Charles Hammond. He may be removed from this ship immediately upon verification of the winning bid being deposited in my accounts and moved successfully to another bank in another country. Two rounds of bidding will be divided by a recess during which you may communicate with your principals. I guarantee that Charles Hammond will be in the winner's possession before twelve o'clock noon. The winning bidder may leave the ship by helicopter. The Concorde at Heathrow will be at his disposal as part of the purchase price. The other participants will be returned to England aboard this ship, whose captain and crew are my prisoners.'

Grandzau took a deep breath.

'The Pendragon Auction has begun. What am I bid for Charles Hammond?'

A quiet settled over the dining room, a human quiet that allowed the drone of the ship's engine to fill the space left by voices. Heavy china clinked behind the galley door as the freighter rolled from side to side. The expressionless guards fingered their machine pistols, and Charles Hammond stared at the deck as if too modest to watch the bidders vie for him.

Grandzau licked his lips and watched them expectantly.

No one said a word.

Several members of the consortium looked at Soma, wondering if the Japanese would begin. But Soma sat stony-faced, waiting, perhaps, for the Russians. The Russians stared at the galley door. The Boston bankers bidding for the American government looked as non-committal as a pair of Brooks Brothers mannequins. The Arab examined his elegant rings, while his English solicitor studied his own, unadorned pink hands with equal interest.

Charles Hammond looked up with a grin. 'Somebody?'

'Five million dollars,' said the American bidder.

'Ten million dollars,' said the Arab.

'Fifteen million,' said Soma.

'Twenty,' said the Russian.

Stepping in increments of five million dollars, the bidding for Charles Hammond rose to fifty million dollars with the Russians maintaining their lead. There it stopped.

Chamberlain expected the Arab to drop out first. The Sheik neither had government backing, as did the Russians and the Americans, nor the awesome combined resources of the international conglomerates.

'Sheik Mādir?' asked Grandzau.

The Sheik's as-yet-silent English solicitor rose to his feet, bristling dangerously. 'May I remind you, sir, that Sheik Mādir is under no obligation to bid in any particular sequence whatsoever. Until you have given fair warning that you will accept a bid as final, Sheik Mādir remains a contender, with all the rights and privileges of the other contenders. May I suggest,' he added acidly, 'that you ask Mr Soma his intentions.'

Grandzau flushed and bowed stiffly.

'I stand corrected by the Briton.' He turned to Soma, then took the Japanese's glance as a warning not to make the same mistake with him. 'I have a bid of fifty million dollars from Comrade Petrov. I remind you that no final bid will be accepted until after the recess. Do I hear fifty-five million?'

'Fifty-five,' said Soma.

'Sixty,' said the Arab.

The Russian said seventy million, the Arab came back at eighty, the American bidder went to eighty-five, and Soma shot the consortium's bolt at ninety million dollars.

Grandzau beamed. 'Would a bidder care to close the first round at an even one hundred million dollars?'

Chamberlain followed his eye from one bidder to the next. Hammond and the Russians kept watching the clock. Suddenly he was sure that the Russians would keep the lead in this first round. They were here to win and the price meant nothing.

'Don't be shy,' teased Grandzau. 'Who will make it one hundred million dollars?'

'One hundred million,' said Sheik Mādir.

The Russians stared in disbelief.

Conversation buzzed among the chairs.

Chamberlain looked at Helen Thorp. She was chewing her lip and gazing at nothing. The enormity of the numbers sank slowly into Chamberlain's head. What in the world would the Sheik want him for? What were the others' limits? Why hadn't the Russians tried to top as he'd expected?

Hammond gazed at the Sheik, a puzzled expression clouding his anxious face. He saw Chamberlain watching him and looked away.

'All done!' said Grandzau.

Soma did a creditable job of feigning indifference. The American bankers traded smiles of bland unconcern but Chamberlain found them as unconvincing as the smile of a Chevy owner parked at a traffic light beside a new Cadillac. They probably had a hundred million limit with strict orders not to ask for more. They did not, after all, represent the entire United States, merely a small department in a single agency. The Russian bidders were undoubtedly in the same circumstances, though from the looks on their broad faces, their limit was still higher than a hundred million.

'This concludes the first round of the Pendragon Auction,' said Grandzau. 'Sheik Mādir leads at one hundred million dollars. The participants have five minutes to compose messages to their principals. I shall transmit them and the bidding will resume at ten o'clock.'

Hammond looked at the clock on the wall. Eight-thirty. Three and a half hours till his release into the hands of his buyer.

Grandzau snapped his fingers. Hammond's guard took his arm and marched him forcefully back through the galley door. Grandzau followed with two more guards and once again the dining room filled with the smells of the kitchen. Chamberlain watched the door flap, then looked at the clock which appeared to interest Hammond so much and wondered again about the Pendragon Auction's tight schedule.

Helen Thorp was already on her feet. 'Will you excuse us?' she asked the Russians. The Boston bankers were on their way to the exit.

'Nyet!' The Russian followed his answer with a long, slow, insolent look, until Helen Thorp turned to the nearest guard. 'Move seventeen of us to another room, or move them. Or I start yelling for Grandzau.'

The guard waved his machine pistol at the Russians. 'Raus!'

Moving with deliberate languor, they climbed out of their chairs and sauntered down the corridor.

'They're not sending any messages,' muttered Chamberlain.

'Bluffing,' she muttered back. 'All right, Mr Soma.'

'Thank you, Ms Thorp.' Soma faced the circle huddling hopefully around him. 'As Ms Thorp suggested yesterday, we've each arranged codes to communicate with our companies, even though most of us promised not to ask for additional contributions. The need is apparent. Would you each give me two pieces of paper? Your code message on one. And the additional sum you are requesting on the other.'

The consortium members retired to separate places, conferred with their aides, and scribbled their messages. Chamberlain watched Helen draw $10,000,000 in a clear, bold hand. She glanced at him. 'Alfred always says big numbers are the only way to get attention.' She handed it and the code message to Chamberlain who took them to Soma's aide, who, when he had received everyone's, shuffled the messages and numbers into two neat piles and brought them to Soma.

Soma read the numbers and brightened. He handed the messages to a guard who hurried from the dining room. Several minutes later, they heard the helicopter take off from the foredeck.

Chamberlain noticed Doug Pickert's small, appreciative nod. Grandzau had patched together an uncrackable communications net. Flying at a safe distance from the ship, the helicopter would fire a brief, almost-untraceable electronic message burst. A land receiver, waiting in England or France, would pass them on to the principals and by the time their answers were radioed back, both ship and helicopter would be a hundred miles from where the messages were sent. All to serve Grandzau's precision schedules. Why had Grandzau taken on the burden of promising such precision? It complicated everything, unless there was something much bigger going on at the same time as the auction.

Grandzau's mercenaries passed around mugs of strong, sweet tea. Helen didn't want any. Chamberlain sat beside her, drinking his, while she moodily chewed her lip and ignored his efforts to make conversation. He gave up and walked down the corridor to the central companionway. The other bidders stood around the various levels of the open stairwell under the scrutiny of the guards who had carefully stationed themselves from the bridge level down to the main deck.

Chamberlain jogged up to the bridge and back down to get the blood flowing. Pickert gave him a friendly wave, but didn't interrupt his conversation with the Boston bankers. The ship's gentle roll and its suburban playroom formica décor were the only things that made the recess of the Pendragon Auction look any different than any mid-morning break at any convention conference anywhere in the business world.

The helicopter returned in an hour, swooping over the bridge house onto the main deck, its big engines reverberating against the steel bulkheads. The bidders hurried down the stairs and gathered at the door to the main deck, awaiting the pilot with their replies. Grandzau bustled up, took them from the pilot as he opened the door, and passed the envelopes to their owners. The guards pointed down the corridor and the bidders hurried aft to the dining room to resume the Pendragon Auction.

Soma collected the answers from the consortium members, read them, and settled expressionlessly into his seat. 'How'd you do with Mr Cowan?' asked Chamberlain.

'He came through.'

The guards crowded back into the dining room, taking up their positions in the corners and at the doors. Grandzau reappeared from the galley, followed by Hammond and the Maltese guard. Hammond anxiously eyed the clock on the bulkhead. Ten o'clock. Two hours until the promised noon release. Time enough to transfer the money.

'We resume,' said Grandzau. 'The last bid was submitted by Sheik Mādir . . .'

'One hundred and twenty million dollars,' said the Russian.

'I have a bid for – '

'One hundred and twenty-five million dollars,' said the Boston banker.

'One hundred and thirty million,' said Soma.

'One hundred and fifty million,' said the Russian.

'One sixty,' said Soma.

'One seventy,' said the Russian.

After a long wait, Grandzau said, his voice barely in control, 'I have a bid from Comrade Petrov for one hundred and seventy million dollars. Do I hear one eighty?'

He looked at Soma. Soma did not raise his eyes. Grandzau looked at the Boston bankers. They sat with forced good-loser smiles on their faces and said nothing.

'Fair warning. I have – '

'One hundred and eighty million dollars,' said the Arab.

Grandzau looked at him sharply, and Chamberlain had a crazy thought gallop through his mind. *The Arab was a shill*. Grandzau had put a plant into the auction to force up the bidding.

Grandzau swallowed hard and paled visibly. 'I have a bid,' he began haltingly, 'for one hundred – '

'One hundred and ninety million dollars,' said the Russian.

The Arab opened empty hands.

Grandzau sagged with relief.

'Fair warning. Comrade Petrov bids one hundred and ninety million dollars. Fair warning.' He glanced from bidder to bidder. 'Fair warning at one ninety. Fair warning . . . Charles Hammond is – '

'Wait!'

Chamberlain surged to his feet.

The guards turned as one, levelling their weapons with startling speed. He'd forgotten them. He raised open palms. 'Wait.'

'What is it?' demanded Grandzau.

Some of the guards shifted their weapons to the rest of the room. Several guns continued to train at Chamberlain's head. 'Wait.'

'*Nyet!*' shouted the Russian. 'We won.'

'Not yet,' said Chamberlain. 'Grandzau, would you accept a combined bid from our consortium and the CIA bidder?'

Grandzau's eyes widened.

'*Nyet!*' the Russian yelled again. He and his colleagues were on their feet, angrily waving their arms and ignoring the guards who brought their guns to this new turmoil.

Grandzau bit his lips. He looked at the Russian, at the clock, and at Hammond who was holding his wrist and staring at his watch.

'Will you?' asked Chamberlain. He glanced down and saw Helen nodding approvingly. Soma had turned around to get her opinion. The Japanese didn't look convinced. Swiftly, he polled the other consortium members with his eyes. The Americans were nodding vigorously, but the Frenchman, the Germans and the English looked unalterably opposed to the idea of joining up with the CIA.

Across the room, the Boston bankers were smiling, as well they might. Unlike the consortium members, they had no reason to distrust the combination that Chamberlain had proposed. Chamberlain caught their attention, called loudly enough for all to hear.

'*We* take delivery.'

'Agreed.'

'Mr Soma?' asked Chamberlain.

Soma looked around once more. He nodded. Chamberlain turned to Grandzau. Greed was struggling with caution in the German's face. He too faced a risk. A serious risk compared to the sure thing the Russians were offering.

Grandzau said what was worrying him. 'I will not accept a new bid as a stalling tactic.'

'I'm proposing a legitimate combination.'

The German addressed the group, his face hardening as he spoke. 'Is there anyone in either the consortium or the CIA who objects to combining their bid?'

Chamberlain waited anxiously, but the only objections were the shouts from the Russians.

Grandzau nodded grimly. 'I will accept a combined bid on one condition. If either party fails to deliver, both parties will be executed.' He added, in the ensuing silence, 'Shot dead.'

'Comrade Petrov bids one hundred and ninety million dollars. Do I hear two hundred?'

Soma traded a long, searching look with the Boston bankers.

The Russians had stopped yelling.

Chamberlain sat down again. Hammond eyed his watch. The CIA representatives nodded to Soma. The Japanese glanced at his consortium partners and breathed deeply. Chamberlain sympathized. Matters had turned extremely personal.

'Two hundred,' said Soma. 'Two hundred million dollars.'

'I have a bid for two hundred million dollars,' said Grandzau.

This time the Russian bidder got to his feet. He raked the room with contemptuous eyes, found Chamberlain, and shook his head irritably. Chamberlain knew then it was all over. And he knew something else. Hammond meant much more to the Russians than a few secrets about Free World weaponry. Hammond was integral to an important Russian plan – some enormous goal. For this kind of money he had to be.

The Russian spoke, still conveying irritation more than any emotion. 'Your combined resources amount to two hundred and eighty-five million dollars. The Union of Soviet Socialist Republics bids two hundred and ninety million dollars.'

Soma paled. Helen Thorp gasped. Her fingers bit into Chamberlain.

Grandzau started to repeat the bid, his voice cracking. The Russian cut him off.

'You will get nothing if you fail to keep your bargain. There is no time for more haggling. *No more time.*'

'Fair warning,' Grandzau cried hurriedly. 'Charles Hammond is sold to Comrade Petrov for two hundred and ninety million dollars.'

In the absence of a gavel to end the Pendragon Auction, Grandzau smacked his fist gleefully into his open palm. His guards took the joyful gesture as a signal to surround the bidders, cocking their weapons with a simultaneous steel clatter.

Pickert and his men, starting to their feet, sank quietly back to their chairs, staring into the guns. Grandzau gestured the Russians to join him. They, the Maltese, an armed guard, Grandzau and a strangely relaxed Charles Hammond exited through the galley door and reappeared a moment later walking up the corridor outside the dining room.

'Where are you taking them?' asked Pickert.

'Radio room,' said a guard.

'What about us?'

'You wait.'

Pickert looked around at the nine armed mercenaries

pointing machine pistols at the seated losing bidders. 'Anything you say, fella.'

It seemed to Chamberlain that the guards were aiming mostly at Pickert's men. One, however, a lean Spaniard by the door, held his weapon trained squarely at Chamberlain. It was almost as if they knew about the plants. Chamberlain toyed with the thought that he should feel complimented that the guards figured he rated his own guard, but he wasn't complimented, he was worried. Grandzau and the Russians had the whole thing firmly under their control.

Chamberlain turned to Helen. She was huddled deep in her coat, her face expressionless.

'Hammond looked kind of happy.'

'Relieved it's over,' she replied without looking at him.

'He doesn't seem worried about the Russians.'

She shrugged, defeated. 'That was a nice move you pulled, Pete.'

'Too bad it didn't work.'

Helen said nothing. Chamberlain eyed the armed guards. He wondered if the extra ammo clips they had stuffed in their belts under their sweaters were a bad sign. He'd guessed right after all at the end of the first round. The Russians hadn't topped the Arab's bid then because they had known that they would win when it counted, at the end of the Pendragon Auction.

Helen Thorp had been wrong. The Russians hadn't been bluffing when they sent no message to their principals because they themselves were the principals. They had been arrogant, knowing they had no limits on what they could spend to buy Charles Hammond.

But Chamberlain had guessed they would win before the recess. How? he wondered. What had tipped him? Time. Hammond was frantic about the time. He couldn't keep his eyes off the clock and his watch. *No more time,* the Russian had warned, his meaning clear. Hammond had no value to them after a certain time.

Chamberlain wondered. Grandzau had promised release at noon.

Had Grandzau kidnapped half a partnership? Had Hammond made a deal with the Russians before he was kidnapped? A deal he had to close today?

30

A machinegun clattered loudly, firing short, clean expert bursts. Somewhere, high in the bridge house, a man screamed death.

Chamberlain threw his chair at the guard nearest the door and hurled Helen Thorp after it.

'*Run!*'

The guard was wrenching his arm free of the thrown chair and his gun was starting to fire, the bullets marching swiftly across the ceiling and walking down the wall. Chamberlain kicked at his groin, missed, but connected with his stomach. Soma, the Arab, the English solicitor and the Frenchman fled through the door and followed Helen Thorp up the corridor, away from the mêlée in the dining room.

Pickert's men had rushed the guards the moment the machinegun sounded. The advantage of surprise had allowed them inside the mercenaries' fire screen. The room was echoing with weapon fire, the thud of hands and fists and the cries of startling pain.

Chamberlain clubbed the man he had kicked with his bare hands until he collapsed to the floor. Reaching for his weapon, he saw a mad kaleidoscope of wildly swinging arms, legs, and guns. The guard had fallen on his weapon. Chamberlain couldn't get it out from under him and even as he tried, Pickert yelled, 'The galley!'

His team seemed to separate from the mercenaries and hit the swinging door *en masse*. Several had captured machine pistols. Pickert went through last, pausing to help a man shot in the leg and catching a bullet in the shoulder as the mercenaries regrouped and started to direct a blaze of gunfire at the swinging door. Pickert was slung backwards into the galley, shouting as he fell, 'Run, Chamberlain!'

Chamberlain was the last man who wasn't a guard in the dining room. The rest of the legitimate bidders had made good their escape up the corridor and all of Pickert's plants were in the galley, already returning the mercenaries' fire. He flung himself out the door and raced up the long corridor, weaving, smashing from bulkhead to bulkhead.

He heard the sharp, metal snap of a weapon being cocked behind him, heard the first bullet leaving the slip, cracking into the chamber, and flung himself face forward, hit the deck and rolled. Three slugs filled the space he'd been in.

He kept rolling into the stairwell, grabbed a post, and frantically tried to pull himself out of the line of fire. Two more shots whined off the hard linoleum, splattering hot chips in his face. Then the gunman shouted sudden pain, and the firing stopped.

Chamberlain scrambled onto the stairs and shot a glance back down the corridor. The gunman lay on the floor. One of his comrades was pouring fire further down the corridor at the outside door to the galley. Pickert's men inside and Grandzau's mercenaries in the dining room had bottled each other up. Chamberlain could hear them trading shots through the galley door. At the same time each group covered the corridor from its outer door, so neither could move from its position.

'You okay, Chamberlain?' Pickert was calling from the galley, the wound in his shoulder tugging at his voice like a beggar at his sleeve.

'Made it.'

'Get Hammond!'

Chamberlain ran up the square, open stairwell, up past

passenger and officer cabins, past the lounge where the other bidders hid fearfully, past the officers' dining room, the boat deck and the captain's deck. The shooting below crashed and echoed on the steel bulkheads and the noise smothered the thud of his shoes on the rough treads.

He stopped short, halfway between the captain's deck and the bridge deck, and quietly reversed. The unarmed Maltese guard and the other guard were sprawled, dead, at the top of the stairs. One of the Russian bidders lay moaning feebly outside the radio room. Charles Hammond was standing in the radio room, visible through the open door, his hands high over his head, his face taut with fear.

Chamberlain went down two levels to the boat deck, went out into the cold, and climbed the steel stairs up the side of the bridge house to the bridge deck. Helen Thorp was already there, pressed against the white bulkhead, peering through a port into the radio room. She whirled about, wide-eyed, awkwardly levelling a machine pistol at Chamberlain's belly.

'It's me. Where'd you get the cannon?'

'Thank God. What a mess. You won't believe this. Look.'

Chamberlain ducked under the port and peered in from the other side. '*What?* Where the hell did she come from?'

Charles Hammond, the other Russian, and Grandzau all had their hands in the air. Grandzau and the Russian were standing beside the ship's radios, big consoles which formed an L on the forward and inboard walls. Hammond was just inside the doorway, facing Henri Trefle who was holding his knife. Lady Janet Isling sat cross-legged on the radio operator's bunk, her back in the corner, and a machinegun in her hands.

Chamberlain stepped back from the port. 'Where did they come from?' he repeated.

Helen Thorp handed him the machine pistol. 'Stop them.'

She insisted on coming with him. All right, she might cover his back when Grandzau's guards made it past Pickert's outnumbered men. They raced down to the boat deck, entered the stairwell cautiously, found it still empty, and tore up the stairs. The fight below raged, staccato bursts of gunfire, shouts, yells, then followed by long seconds of ominous silence.

Chamberlain didn't have much time. He'd been on enough ships to know that Grandzau's mercenaries could find another way out of the dining room if they looked hard enough.

Stay, he motioned to Helen at the landing between the captain's and bridge decks. He climbed over the stair railing and swung across the pit of the stairwell until he could grab a railing on the far side. The ship rolled and he started to fall back, almost dropping the gun. Who, he wondered, was at the wheel, or had a frightened helmsman put her on auto-pilot and gone to hide?

He hauled himself over the railing, and crawled past the dead guards to the edge of the open door, which, he could see from here, was hooked open to a ring in the deck. The radios blocked his view of Grandzau and the Russian to the right. Lady Janet, Hammond and Trefle, all to the left of the doorway, were also invisible unless he stuck his head round the corner, in which case Lady Janet would have a perfect opportunity to blow it off.

He was inches from Trefle and Hammond, however, and could hear every word that transpired between them whenever the shooting below abated. Hammond sounded scared witless, Trefle implacable. Hammond was pleading that what had happened in Somalia wasn't his fault.

'They took everything I had,' he said. 'You must believe me, Colonel.'

'You betrayed my men,' Trefle said simply.

'*I* was betrayed. I lost a fortune.'

'My men lost more.'

Grandzau shouted, 'Janet. You can't do this. Stop him!'

'Shut up, Karl,' came the cool, even reply.

'You don't know what you're doing,' cried Grandzau.

'But I do, Karl. I most certainly – '

The crash of gunfire riddled the rest of Lady Janet's reply. When the shooting subsided, Chamberlain heard Hammond again. The deal-maker's tone had changed. He was still afraid, but he sounded hopeful, as if he'd worked up a plan.

'Colonel, listen to me. I can offer something much better than revenge.'

'Nothing can buy your life.'

'I'm offering to buy yours, Colonel,' Hammond replied boldly.

Chamberlain heard the heavy slap of Trefle's hand on flesh and saw Hammond sprawl to the deck. He shook his head and rose to a cautious crouch, his eyes gauging Trefle, never seeing Chamberlain kneeling beside the door.

'Colonel, I have an army. But I have no general.'

'An army like mine you shot to pieces?' Trefle asked dangerously.

'Ten thousand men.'

Lady Janet laughed. 'He's having you on, Henri,' she drawled.

'What army?'

'Colonel, will you be my general?' Hammond rose to his knees, as in prayer, supplicating, and offering. Proud of the sacrifice. He raised one finger as if to stop a second blow. Chamberlain saw Trefle's shadow darken over him. 'Listen, Colonel – '

'Don't!' shouted the Russian. 'Don't tell him.'

Chamberlain looked at his watch. 10.40. Still time to radio to transfer money by the deadline. He glanced down the stairs. Helen Thorp was angrily waving him on. *Do something*. She couldn't hear Hammond. Chamberlain raised a hand to still her, then pointed down. She was neglecting to watch their backs and the firing below decks had stopped. Then he realized that the wounded Russian was staring at him.

'Explain,' demanded Trefle.

Chamberlain stared back at the Russian, transfixed, waiting for him to do something that would give him away. Instead, he closed his eyes and lay still.

'Be careful, Henri,' Lady Janet drawled again. Chamberlain thought she sounded as if she was enjoying herself.

'Shut up, woman. Explain.'

Hammond was still the only person Chamberlain could see in the radio room. The deal-maker stayed on his knees. He spoke soothingly, slowly, as if to a wise child, as if no one else were listening, and calmly, as if his eyes weren't flashing up at the bulkhead clock and down to his wristwatch.

'She stands like the Colossus of Rhodes, Colonel. You know her. She dominates –'

Gunfire rattled through the ship, multiple short bursts that sent deafening echoes up the open stairway. Chamberlain couldn't hear what Hammond was saying, but before the shooting stopped he was damn sure that 'she' was Malagasy. And it wasn't too hard to fill in the space after 'dominates' either. The Mozambique oil tanker channel. Europe's pipeline. Lifeline, when squeezed.

'Insurgency? You want me to put down insurgency? You're crazy. The Americans will blow you off the face of the map.'

Not necessarily, thought Chamberlain. That depended upon who Hammond's partner was.

'It's taken four years,' Hammond said. 'Everything's falling into place. I've made the ultimate deal and I'll never have to make another deal again, for anybody. Now they'll come to me.'

'You're crazy,' said Trefle.

'Don't tell me I'm crazy,' snapped Hammond, rising scornfully, daring the mercenary to hit him. 'I don't want to rule the world, just a piece of it. It's all planned. The police, army units, radio station and an ally.'

'What ally?' Trefle asked suspiciously.

Russia, you dummy, thought Chamberlain. *Hammond made a deal with the Russians*. In the old days when Malagasy was still Madagascar, Russia didn't have a navy. But they did now, and they'd give a lot for a base on Malagasy. Maybe even two hundred and ninety million for a man who could offer them one.

'Henri, look out for him,' Lady Janet warned again. 'He's tricking you.'

'What ally?'

Shooting broke out again, but Chamberlain knew Hammond's answer. Russia would support a Hammond coup in Malagasy. A lot of pieces fell neatly into place. A lot of other pieces, on the other hand, fell right off the table, but one thing was sure, Henri Trefle was wrong. Hammond was not crazy. It was, however, almost unbelievably unlucky that he had been kidnapped.

'It was all set, then *this* happened. Help me, General.'

'How?' asked Trefle.

Incredibly unlucky. And so were the Russians unlucky.

Hammond's voice shook with suppressed emotion. 'Let this stupid, meddling, idiot German finish his goddamned auction. Let my ally pay the ransom they've bid. Come with me. They have planes waiting everywhere, don't you, my friend?'

'You talk too much,' the Russian said coldly.

'And you worry too much,' said Hammond. 'It's in the bag, isn't it, General?'

Perhaps Hammond was *too* unlucky, thought Chamberlain, recalling something Daitch had said about Grandzau before he'd blown his house in Brussels. *Not for the money. For the secret.* He was getting the money anyway, but what was Grandzau's secret? Hammond and the Russians were both obsessed with time. But so was Grandzau. Chamberlain had spotted his private message in the last telegram. Guaranteed noon delivery. Grandzau knew about Hammond's deal. Had known Hammond's secret all along. Had known how the Russians would fight to get Hammond back. Had defended himself at enormous expense.

'*Henri!*' Icy determination rammed the laughter from Lady Janet's drawl, but she had lost her tenuous hold on Trefle's will. Chamberlain saw the mercenary's thick, dark shadow lengthen suddenly like a springing cat. Wild reflections flashed across the radio room. Someone gasped in shock and Lady Janet gave a startled cry as Trefle's huge blade swished through the air like a long silver whip.

Hammond's eyes, locked to the blade's swift flight, suddenly widened. Lady Janet fired five times, then fired again, echoed by shooting elsewhere in the ship. Henri Trefle backed slowly out of the radio room and toppled over the wounded Russian. Blood bubbled from his riddled chest. He was still alive, as he fell. His dying eyes lighted with dim recognition when he saw Chamberlain crouched beside the door.

'Slow,' he murmured, imparting his reason for his death. 'Too slow.' One of Lady Janet's bullets had shattered his tempered glass blade. He held its crumbled stump in his dead hand.

In the radio room, Charles Hammond moaned relief. 'Thank you. That psychotic – '

'I'll kill you for what you did to him.'

'No, Janet,' pleaded Grandzau. 'Please.'

342

She sucked in a deep breath. Chamberlain held his own. She sounded badly shaken. Would she lash out and kill Hammond? He tensed, as if to charge into the radio room, but there was nothing he could do.

She took another deep breath. 'I should kill him, Karl, but I won't. I much prefer to watch your grotty little hands itching to use that radio. When is your deadline, Mr Hammond? Noon? One? It's a long way to Madagascar.'

Chamberlain pressed tight against the bulkhead because Hammond had started glancing at the door as if planning a break. *Don't*, Chamberlain prayed. *Don't tempt the lady*.

Then Hammond spoke and sounded easygoing and good-natured, only slightly baffled by the turn of events. 'Listen, dear. I'll level with you. I don't know who you are and I don't know what your problem is with Grandzau, but I have got to be in Tananarive when the polls close. We've got an election today and there's going to be some fraud, and some dispute and a little violence and I've absolutely got to be there to step in and smooth things over. The whole deal is planned, has been for months. You're obviously a woman of the world and you can understand that. It has nothing to do with you and Grandzau. Please, let him make his radio call. Let him collect the money my friend here has pledged. Then let me go and you can do whatever you want to Grandzau to make him tell you his account numbers. Have your fun with the little bastard *and* keep the goddamned ransom. Two hundred and ninety million bucks ought to be worth putting off making one dirty little kraut unhappy.'

Lady Janet laughed brittly. Shots echoed in the ship. 'Put your hands back in the air, please. All of you. That's better.'

'What do you say?'

'Terribly sorry, but I'm enjoying this arrangement immensely.'

343

Hammond's voice changed from conciliatory to threatening. 'Listen, sweetheart. You screw me up and you'll have the entire Russian KGB hunting your tail around the world. They're not going to take too kindly to losing a naval base on the Mozambique Channel.'

'You've tried bribery, Mr Hammond, and it didn't work. Now you threaten me, and I can assure you that won't work, either. What is left?'

'You dumb cunt!' Hammond yelled. Chamberlain glanced down the stairwell. Helen had heard that. She started over the railing. Chamberlain waved her back, but she kept coming.

Lady Janet laughed again.

'Insult? From a stranger? Impossible.'

Hammond sobbed in frustration. 'All right. All right. You name your price. What do you want?'

'You made me kill Henri. You betrayed him twice.'

Helen edged around the open stairwell, jumped for the railing out of Hammond's sight, and slipped. Chamberlain darted to her and pulled her over as she dangled by her hands. They crawled back to the radio room door. Gunfire coming up the stairwell was followed by screams, then silence.

'Janet, for the love of God,' pleaded Grandzau. 'This is madness. Why are you doing this to me?'

'Why did you leave me?' she asked. 'Why did you fake your death and leave me alone? And leave me out of your scheme? I would have helped you with this. I always helped you. Why did you trick me?'

'Because you went back to Trefle,' Grandzau answered tonelessly.

'What? I went once. I had to be sure. It wasn't to hurt you. You weren't to know.'

'Did you think you could keep that secret from me?' Grandzau asked with scorn. 'Keep a secret from Karl

344

Grandzau? I sold secrets, I bought secrets. You were a fool.'

'So you punished me with your secret?'

Grandzau's voice took on an intimate note. 'Janet, your revenge is crueller than the crime. I was hurt that you would go to Trefle behind my back. I couldn't stay with you any more.'

'So you punished me.'

'Punish is not exactly – '

'Karl, what that man did to me compressed a lifetime of pain and indignity into a single, agonizing, eternal hour.' The laughter, the drawl and music were gone from her voice. 'It will never leave me.'

'*I* didn't whip you,' Grandzau shrieked.

'Did you think that the KGB would discuss the whereabouts of my resurrected lover in the presence of my *solicitor?* You planned it so *they* would avenge my infidelity to you. You didn't have the courage to do it yourself.'

'But *I* didn't have anything to do with it,' protested Hammond. 'I didn't have anything to do with any of you people until this bastard kidnapped me. Why are you taking your revenge on me?'

'You were my device, Mr Charles Hammond. As Henri Trefle was yours. You recall you did have something to do with him even before your unfortunate kidnapping. You betrayed him in Somalia and again this moment, trying to turn him against me. You forced me to kill him. Perhaps this is my last gift to Henri . . . He was a kinder lover than you might suppose.'

'Kill her,' whispered Helen Thorp.

'She's doing us a favour,' murmured Chamberlain. 'The Russians have a deadline. The whole thing'll be over in an hour.'

'Kill her. Before she kills Hammond.'

'She won't.'

Helen shook her head violently. 'She's crazy. Listen to me, Pete. Hammond's got to get away from her. Do what I say.'

'It's not necessary,' Chamberlain argued. 'It's not worth the risk.'

Helen placed her hand on his arm. 'Look at me, Pete.' She drew him into her dark eyes. 'Save Hammond and you can name your price at Comtel. You can have a great job in the company, or you can take the money and run. Alfred and I have already discussed a two hundred thousand dollar bonus if you save Hammond. But it's really up to me and I can go a lot higher to show the company's gratitude. Save Hammond, Pete. Kill her.'

Chamberlain took the gun and climbed silently over the railing, down the stairs, and out of the door onto the boat deck. Two hundred thousand dollars – back to real-world numbers he could understand. Helen followed a few paces behind. It had been a while since the last shots were fired below decks and the silence threatened. The ship was trailing a curving wake in the grey waves. The sea, the small circle visible towards a hazy horizon, was empty, the ship alone.

She followed him up to the outside bridge deck. He glanced into one of the radio room ports, ducked under it, and looked in another. Helen ducked under both ports and surfaced behind Chamberlain. 'Can you see her?'

'Cover your face,' he muttered. 'I have to shoot the glass out first.'

Lady Janet felt very well, considering how close Trefle had come to killing her. She had her back wedged safely into a steel corner, her weapon comfortably in her hands, and Grandzau writhing in a dual agony of greed and dashed hopes.

She was sad about Trefle. She'd known the deadly risk when she'd first approached him for help, but with a drinker and a crazy man there was always a small hope, a wish, that he'd miraculously change. His knife had slashed a long, deep hole in the radio operator's mattress inches from her groin.

She didn't know who was fighting aboard the ship. She'd seen the mercenaries. Perhaps the crew had struck back. But she had stumbled onto the perfect revenge. Charles Hammond, Grandzau and the Russian had a single goal. To use the radio. It and the clock held all their attention. There was a perfect symmetry to it all. Hammond for Henri. The Russian, who might well have commanded the man in black, and Karl for her. She heard the port glass shatter before she heard the shots that broke it. She was still trying to raise her weapon when a second machine pistol burst poured through the port. The bullet stream seemed to flow forever, tremendously loud and longer, much longer, than such a weapon should be fired.

'You hit the radio!' screamed Helen Thorp.

'You're goddamned right I hit the radio. I blew it to pieces and now I'm going to get the one in the helicopter. Here. Take the gun. Safety's off. Cover me if they come up the stairs.'

'Don't, Pete.'

'Don't tell me how to do my job, goddamnit. Hammond's safe as long as Grandzau can't call the Russians. Cover me.' He started swiftly down the outside stairs, plunging like a sailor with both hands on the rails.

'Stop!'

Chamberlain turned and looked up into the deep black bore of the gun he had given her.

* * *

347

In the radio room, Grandzau, Hammond and the Russian gaped at the ruined radios. Chamberlain's bullets had riddled their aluminium cases, smashed the power dials, shattered the frequency counters and ravaged their inner circuitry.

'There's another radio on the helicopter,' Grandzau shouted.

Lady Janet laughed. The sound of her laughter frightened her. The sudden, unexpected, unknowable attack had thrown her to the edge of hysteria. The ports and the open door yawned dangerously, threatening new assaults.

She pressed her back deeper into the steel corner and fought for control. It lay in the power she held over Grandzau. 'I should imagine that whoever smashed this one is already on his way there, wouldn't you think?'

'Janet, I'll give you anything.'

'You already did, Karl, but you took it back. Close that door.'

'Are you pointing that at me?' asked Chamberlain.

'Yes.'

'Helen, what are you doing?' He started back up the stairs.

'Don't move.'

He stopped halfway up. 'Helen. If I don't get to that helicopter radio someone else on the other side will. It's the only way they can sell Hammond in time. Let me go. I know what I'm doing. It's the best for Hammond.'

'Fuck Hammond, you idiot.'

'Huh?'

'The Russians are buying Hammond from me.'

'I don't get it.'

'They're paying two hundred and ninety million dollars into *two* accounts. Half to Grandzau. Half to me. I'm the silent partner. I'm the money man. Who the hell did you think paid for all this? I'm the inside man. Who do you think planned the auction? Grandzau?'

Chamberlain stared at her. 'What are you going to do?'

'I'm going to shoot you and then I'm going to kill her.'

'She'll blow your head off, Helen. She's a pro.'

'For one hundred and forty-five million dollars I will take the chance.'

The sea wind blew her jet hair like silk. Her cheeks flushed, her nostrils flaring, she was, Chamberlain thought sadly, the most beautiful thing he had ever seen in his life. He looked past the gun barrel, into her eyes, and only felt sadder.

'You're taking too many chances, Helen. I'm a pro, too. Never point a gun at a hitter.' He started up the stairs. Her pupils narrowed decisively as she pulled the trigger.

31

The weapon filled her hands, heavy, mute.

Wearily, Chamberlain watched her work the unfamiliar safety and try again.

'I emptied the whole magazine into the radio.'

'You tricked me?' The wind was still blowing her hair and neither fear nor anger made her less beautiful.

'I'm sorry. I'd feel really guilty if you hadn't pulled the trigger.'

'Why?'

'I guess I wanted to see how dumb I really was.'

'You're not dumb.'

'Apparently not.'

The gun slid from her hands and clattered to the deck. Chamberlain stayed where he was, halfway down the steps, looking up at her. A single tear floated, balancing, on the rim of each of her dark eyes.

'Why is there a deadline?' he asked.

'I don't know.'

Chamberlain started down the stairs.

'Pete? Let's make a deal?'

He stopped and looked up at her again. 'A deal?'

'Help me. We'll share.'

Chamberlain shrugged. 'I guess I could learn to handle the fact that you just tried to blow my brains out. There's a lot of shooting going on anyhow. And I could joyfully forgive your taking me into your bed on the chance that Ramsey's cronies might spill something.'

'It was a *very* slim chance,' she smiled.

'Tipping off the KGB that we were going to the Overseas

Club was something else and I find it even harder to accept your sending Grandzau's killer-bobby after me. Much harder.'

She didn't deny it. 'I was frightened. I thought you were on to me. You kept asking all those questions . . . But I stopped him the first time. In the Temple Gardens?'

'For the first time I am grateful. But since you didn't stop him the second time, I feel that my best future lies with Alfred Cowan. He hasn't tried to kill me even once.'

She shook her head scornfully. 'Do you want to be somebody's employee the rest of your life? Or do you want to share one hundred and forty-five million dollars with me? Make up your mind, Pete. We don't have any time.'

Chamberlain sighed. 'Helen, you're making it hard to say no. I can't think of anything I'd like better than the opportunity to screw your brains out on a regular and loving basis.'

'I'll expect a touch more elegance of expression from you in the future,' she said with a smile. 'I'm very demanding.'

'Why are you lying about Hammond's Madagascar plan? You know damned well why there's a deadline.'

She went white. 'I . . . Why are you trapping me?'

'Why are you lying to me, Helen?'

'I don't trust you.'

'*You* don't trust *me*?' He started down the stairs. She followed.

'Where are you going?'

'*You* don't trust *me*? I haven't tried to kill you. I haven't lied to you.'

'Pete, please wait.'

He started down and she followed. When they reached the main deck, her heel slipped on the wet steel and she fell hard. Chamberlain knelt beside her. Single shots sounded sporadically from inside the ship. Pickert's men would run out of ammo first. Had Grandzau put a guard on the helicopter? It stood beyond the airport bus, far across a wide stretch of open, shelterless deck, but the dangerous approach wasn't what was holding him back.

He wished, now that he'd figured it all out, that he could be as sure as he was when he shot out the ship's radio. She was confused and scared and she'd hurt herself when she fell. He couldn't bear to see her vulnerable. He wanted reasons he could buy.

'How'd you get mixed up with Grandzau?'

'I had an affair with Charles Hammond.'

'I wondered.' She was trembling in his arms.

'Everyone wondered. We thought we'd kept it secret. Charles said that if people knew they would think I was acting for him instead of Comptel. He was the most exciting man. You have no idea the aura he projected. When he left a room it was empty. I thought we had invented love.'

She threw back her head and laughed bitterly.

'Grandzau approached me in New York. Like a dirty little man who bothers secretaries on the bus. He told me that Charles was using me to push phoney deals at Comptel . . . Since you figured out his plan you can figure out the rest.'

'Why'd Grandzau tell you?'

'He said that Charles was plotting a coup against the Republic of Malagasy, and supporting it with my deals. I was still young enough to feel more hurt than the fool I was. He told me because he wanted my help. The help of a brilliant woman scorned, as the little bastard put it. He's just smart enough to know his limitations.

'Grandzau had a great idea. Since the key to Hammond's coup was Russian recognition in return for a naval base on the Straits of Mozambique Grandzau figured that if he kidnapped Hammond the week before the coup, the

Russians would pay anything to get him back. And *do* anything. He couldn't figure a foolproof way to protect himself until he got the ransom. How could he fight the entire Soviet Union?'

'And you told him how?'

'I was devastated. But hurt changed pretty quickly to anger. I thought, okay, maybe Charles intends to take me in with him. He was the kind of man who would give me the Island of Madagascar as a love gift. I believed he might do that. So I went along with Grandzau. I knew I could stop him at any time. Right up until last week. But he never took me with him. Last summer we slowly stopped seeing each other and I finally had to admit that he did not love me. And probably never had. That he'd used me all along. Had courted me not for love, but as part of his plan, his ultimate deal.'

'So you had an auction.'

She tossed her head. 'It wasn't really an auction, as you guessed. Just a smokescreen to confuse the Russians. Everyone ran in circles and it dissipated the Russian heat, just the way I planned it. It would have worked perfectly if it weren't for that bitch in the radio room.' She shook her head. 'I can't believe that Grandzau's past had to come back now.'

'He brought it with him,' said Chamberlain. 'Why didn't you trust me. Because I wouldn't kill her?'

'No. I was worried about your reaction to the Russian connection. I'm international. I don't care what individual governments do as long as they keep the civil peace intact and corporate taxes negotiable.'

'But I'm ex-Navy and ex-CIA and you didn't know how I'd feel about planting a Russian Navy base on the Free World's oil lanes. You could have asked.'

'"Free World's oil lanes" doesn't sound as if you'd like it.'

'I don't,' said Chamberlain. 'But not for the reason you think. The last thing the world needs is a bunch of amateurs starting World War III. Because once the amateurs like you start fooling around, you bring in the hitters like me and Henri Trefle and pretty soon somebody's massacring a bunch of dumb natives, and the few of them that survive become insurgents, and it just gets worse and worse.'

'I was right. You're going to wreck the radio in the helicopter and destroy everything I've done.'

'I don't believe you people. Grandzau's just a weasel, but you and Hammond, you're businessmen. What are you starting wars for? You've got all the money in the world already and most of the power. Airplanes, hotels, good restaurants. What the hell else is there?'

'I knew you'd be this way. No one is starting a war, Pete. Hammond is just realigning things a little. Everything goes in cycles. Nothing matters for very long. You know that. All this is now is a magnificent opportunity for you and me to be rich and happy for the rest of our lives . . . Quickly, *we must get the Russian to the radio.*'

'Maybe you're right,' said Chamberlain. 'Maybe the US and the Russians would sort the thing out as usual. But you didn't hear Hammond plea-bargaining with Trefle. He knows there'll be resistance on the island to his coup so he offered to make Trefle – France's candidate for world psychotic of the year – General of the Armies of Madagascar.'

'I'm sure that was because Trefle was threatening him.'

'Events threaten the nicest plans. Then the plans don't stay nice.'

Helen stood up, pushing him away. 'So it boils down to having the balls to do something that counts.'

Anger gorged Chamberlain's throat. He didn't want to be reminded that refusing Helen's offer might not have been the smartest move, particularly if he'd been afraid to take the chance.

'I'll show you something that counts.'

Crossing the deck with long, hard strides, he headed for the giant helicopter. It was parked in the middle of the main deck, its long rotor blades drooping like the wings of a sunning dragonfly. Helen ran beside him. 'What are you doing?'

Chamberlain kept walking.

'Don't ruin the radio.'

'Not just yet.' He strode up the single open ramp, through the cavernous hold, and up to the cockpit.

'Stop right there, fella,' said the pilot.

He was American. He was pointing a .45 US Army automatic at Chamberlain and he looked scared. Chamberlain gave a quick look over the pilot's right shoulder, fracturing his attention long enough to hit him in the nose and take the gun away.

'Any more weapons aboard?'

The pilot held his nose in both hands and looked into the barrel of the .45. He was sullen, but co-operative.

'In there.'

Chamberlain opened the locker, scanned the contents of the mercenaries' arsenal, and selected a heavy-calibre sharpshooter's rifle. It was bolt action and fully loaded. Ignoring Helen, who was eyeing the radios, he said, 'Take off.'

'Where?'

'Up.'

The pilot wound up his turbines, got them going good, and said, 'Come on, buddy. Where you want to go?'

'Just pull alongside the bridge house. Nice and low. Starboard side.'

'Shit, I hope you know what you're doing, Mister.'

355

'I got the gun,' said Chamberlain, glancing at Helen. 'It doesn't matter if I know what I'm doing. Up!'

The helicopter rose hesitantly, put its head to the wind, and gained altitude.

'Alongside and lower,' said Chamberlain.

'This ain't exactly the most manoeuvrable son of a bitch.'

'Just get down there. That's right. Stay off about a hundred yards.'

'Pete, what are you doing?' asked Helen.

'Pickert's pinned down in there. See that port? That's the galley. See those two ports. They're the dining room where we had the auction. Grandzau's mercenaries are in there.'

'What are you doing?'

Chamberlain raised the rifle and shoved the barrel through a small window behind the pilot's head.

'Mister, I can't hold her like this. You got air currents coming off the side of the ship'll blow us ass up into the drink.'

Chamberlain was holding the rifle with one hand. He stuck the .45 into the back of the pilot's neck, glancing, again, at Helen. 'Do your damnedest to make sure that doesn't happen.'

'You're crazy, Mister.'

'Just making a point for the lady. Get in closer.'

He dropped the gun in his lap and opened up suddenly with the rifle. The booming concussions were deafening over the scream of the turbines. Glass flew from the ports in the side of the ship, glistening slivers that fell to the sea and scattered into the dining room.

The scope's cross-hairs jogged and slid around the shattered port, the exaggerated consequence of the helicopter's vibrations and the rolling of the ship. Most of the time Chamberlain saw only the welded plates. He had fired fast and indiscriminately until he'd scored a lucky hit on the glass. Now he tried to line up a harder shot.

The rotors flung salt spray through the window, wetting his face, ruining the pilot's vision.

'I can't hold her, Mister.'

'Give the lady a lifejacket.'

The scope passed over the port and he could see the mercenaries ducking for cover from this new assault. Two covering the hall door held their ground. Chamberlain zeroed in on them and fired six times as fast as he could work the bolt. Two of the high-powered slugs made it in the port and blasted through the barricade of tables they'd heaped around the door.

The mercenaries scattered. Chamberlain swung the barrel and bounced three shots off the hull nearer the galley. A signal. Then he sighted the port again, and waited. Movement flickered in the corridor. Pickert's men were slipping past the now-unguarded dining room door. Chamberlain waited until one of them charged onto the main deck and leaned over the gunwale, covering the dining ports.

'Okay. Take her back on deck.' He turned to Helen and met her level gaze. 'That counts.'

They landed. The pilot sagged in his seat, his hands trembling. Chamberlain returned the rifle to its rack. Then he fired the .45 into the radio, until the gun was empty and the radio was filled with holes.

'And that counts.'

Helen shook her head in disgust.

'Take off,' he told the pilot.

'Now where?'

'Anywhere. Just get out of here. If you're lucky they won't catch you.' He headed for the hatch. 'Going with him?' he asked Helen.

357

'Should I?'

'No. You're safer in your own world.'

She followed him off the helicopter and watched it thunder up and grow small in the sky.

'I assume you covered your ass at Comptel?'

'Like a virgin.'

'I won't tell Hammond. I doubt anybody'll believe Grandzau. Did you do it for money, or revenge?'

'Money . . . But I would have stopped if Hammond had asked me.'

They walked back towards the bridge house. Pickert came out, grinning, his shoulder wrapped in bloodsoaked kitchen rags. Helen started towards him. Chamberlain laid a restraining hand on her arm.

'Helen. Don't make any deals with Pickert.'

She looked at him. 'I don't know what you're talking about.'

'Sure.'

Pickert waved his pipe. 'Thanks for the hand, Chamberlain. Tough sons of bitches. 'Course, when they ran out of ammo we'd a had 'em at a distinct disadvantage.'

'I had a feeling they might have had more ammo than you.'

'We wondered about that. Where's Hammond?'

'Radio room.' He led Pickert up the stairwell. Helen followed, her face a mask. A couple of angry rounds of gunfire echoed through the ship.

'Still holding out,' said Pickert. 'Tough sons of bitches.'

Halfway up the final stairs Chamberlain called through the closed radio room door.

'Miss Isling?'

'Who's there?' Hammond cried hopefully.

'Wrong side. Pete Chamberlain. I want to talk to Miss Isling.'

'*Lady* Isling,' muttered Pickert. 'Can't take you any-where, Chamberlain.'

'Lady Isling,' Chamberlain called. 'I'm the guy who shot out the radio. I did the one on the helicopter and sent it away. You can let Mr Hammond go, now. The Pendragon Auction is over.'

Pickert persuaded an ashen Grandzau to order his men to surrender. They found the ship's crew locked in one of the deck containers and sent a shivering captain and helmsman to the bridge. Plied with hot coffee from the bullet-riddled galley, they determined the freighter's position as less than a hundred miles from Southampton. Five hours later they made VHF radio contact with the Isle of Wight and got patched into the phone lines to London. An evil-looking Royal Navy missile carrier came out to escort them into Portsmouth, where they docked in a thin rain, the only merchant vessel in the fleet of lean, grey fighters.

Inspector Farquhar, lean as their silhouettes, waited at the dockside in the steady rain. At his back was a contingent of Scotland Yard detectives, uniformed police, Royal Navy Marines, and some quietly dressed young men who, Chamberlain assumed, were British Intelligence.

The freighter's captain and crew were led away to make statements. Pickert's men surrendered their weapons to the Royal Marines, who took charge of both them and Grandzau's mercenaries. Farquhar's detectives, many of whom affected his pencil-thin moustache and fitted, single-breasted raincoat, took Chamberlain, the bidders, Karl Graudzau, Lady Janet Isling, Helen Thorp, Charles Hammond, Doug Pickert and the surviving Russian into a nearby hut where Farquhar took statements.

Petrov demanded diplomatic immunity. Farquhar offered a police escort to his embassy in London or Heathrow Airport. The Russian hesitated as if weighing the sort of homecoming in store for him, and with a fatalistic shrug chose the airport.

Farquhar arrested Karl Grandzau for kidnapping, murder, nineteen charges relating to the events at Heathrow Airport, and hijacking the freighter. The German countered with an accusation. He said that Helen Thorp, executive vice president of Comptel, Inc., was his partner.

Charles Hammond, his weary face lined like cracked glass, his ginger hair pasted by the rain to his bare head, had shambled through the proceedings in a stupor. Now he came alert as Helen professed astonishment at the charge. Chamberlain defended her.

Farquhar, openly dubious, sent inquiries to his men who were interrogating Grandzau's mercenaries. None knew a thing about the American business executive. Chamberlain wasn't surprised. Grandzau, obsessed with his secrets to the last, had told no one, not even his prisoner, about his secret partner. Now no one would believe him, no matter whom he accused.

Farquhar seemed relieved. He told Helen and Hammond that they were excused. A limousine was waiting to take them to London. Chamberlain watched bleakly as she took the deal-maker's arm firmly in both hands and led him away without a look or a word for anyone in the room.

Farquhar then excused the other bidders and told them they'd be able to leave England in a day or two. They shuffled out to a waiting bus and when it growled away, Farquhar and two of the quiet intelligence men huddled by the door. Chamberlain, Lady Janet and Doug Pickert waited. They were in a classroom, with rudimentary torpedo diagrams still chalked on the blackboard. They sat side by side in plastic school desks, Chamberlain in the middle.

Chamberlain nudged Pickert. The CIA man had a clean

bandage on his shoulder, and his eyes were glazed with painkillers.

'You owe me one,' Chamberlain said.

'I suppose so.'

'I'll take it now.'

Pickert glanced over at Lady Janet who sat composedly, her hands folded on the desk. 'Bimbo.'

Chamberlain did not bother explaining that from what he had overheard in the radio room she had had more right to be on the ship than any of them. He said, 'Go with me?' and Pickert nodded.

Inspector Farquhar returned, flanked by the intelligence officers, and announced that the national elections in Malagasy had ended without a coup. There was, however, one final matter. Had Lady Janet Isling ever seen Peter Chamberlain before this day?

She answered in a quiet, steady voice. 'I believe I saw him for the first time in Brussels, last week.'

'And then?' asked Farquhar.

'Marseille.'

'Under what circumstances, Lady Janet?'

'I hit him with a pistol.'

Chamberlain thought he saw the merest hint of a smile tug the corner of her mouth, but he wasn't sure because she was looking at Farquhar. Farquhar did not smile.

'And then?'

'Aboard the freighter. Today.'

'Did you not see him at the Savoy the night you shot a Russian KGB agent in Ms Thorp's suite?'

'I haven't been in the Savoy in years.'

'Lady Janet, we have witnesses who saw you in the Savoy the night the Russian was shot. Surely you –'

'The Savoy was Karl Grandzau's favourite hotel,' she interrupted coolly. 'We stayed there often, whenever we had to go to England. It was the only place he ever stayed.' Chamberlain nodded to himself. That's how she'd caught up with the auction. 'But when he died . . . I mean when I *thought* he died . . . I ceased to enter its doors.' She was silent for a moment, then raised her head and spoke very softly. 'I had good memories, there. I didn't want to go there alone.'

'As a matter of fact,' Farquhar said dryly, 'you weren't alone. You were seen with Henri Trefle.'

'As a matter of *fact*, Inspector, I haven't been in England in more than three years, as a simple inspection of my passport will prove. And you will note that my only visits to England since I left home at nineteen were with Grandzau to the Savoy.'

'Immigration is not the only way for an exile to enter England,' snapped Farquhar. 'Just the other day a French boat was found abandoned on the Channel coast. We traced it to Brest, where it had been stolen.'

Lady Janet said nothing.

Farquhar turned to Chamberlain. 'Let's stop messing about, Peter. Is this not the woman you saw in the Savoy? The woman who shot the Russian agent?'

'No.'

'Peter.'

'She's not the same woman, Inspector. What do you want me to say?'

'The truth. Look at her. Stand up, Lady Janet, if you would be so kind. Look at her, Peter. Look! Are you sure?'

Chamberlain looked up at her as she stood and turned to face him, turning gracefully, conveying somehow in the way she moved that she did it by her choice, not Farquhar's. She looked down and met Chamberlain's eyes with a steady gaze he could only call complex. He saw pain, awesome depth, and, incredibly, peace.

'I'm not about to forget a woman who bent a gun barrel over my head,' he said. 'She wasn't in the Savoy.'

Laughter flickered in her eyes for an instant before she sat down.

Farquhar changed tactics. He asked how she happened to be aboard Grandzau's hijacked freighter. Lady Janet sat serenely and said nothing.

Farquhar bored in and the men flanking him moved closer.

'Lady Janet, you've backed yourself into a nasty corner. Either you boarded the freighter as Karl Grandzau's partner, in which case I will charge you with being an accomplice in the kidnapping of Charles Hammond. Or you boarded the helicopter with the other bidders, which means you were in London when the KGB agent was shot.'

Lady Janet said nothing.

'Which is it?'

She sat mute. Chamberlain watched a fine vein pulse to the surface of her white temple. She touched her hair, covering the telltale vein with a wisp of gold.

'*Which?*' shouted Farquhar, suddenly smacking the desk.

'She boarded the ship by herself,' said Chamberlain.

'What?'

'She went aboard alone to rescue Charles Hammond.'

'Shut up, Peter. Which was it, Lady Janet?'

'She's working for the US government.'

Farquhar opened his mouth and looked at him incredulously. 'What?'

'I said Lady Janet was working for the US government.'

'What the devil are you talking about?'

'I don't know the whole story, but one of the agencies hired her because of her connection with Grandzau.'

'What are you saying?'

363

'I'm saying she did a damned good job and she's being kind of loyal not admitting it.'

Farquhar angrily cut him off. 'Do you expect me to believe that nonsense? I'm warning you, Peter, I have enough on you to put you inside for a long time. Starting with the gun you left in your hotel room.'

'I'm just telling you what I heard.'

Doug Pickert raised his pipe. 'Inspector?'

'What do you want?'

'I'm afraid big mouth here is telling the truth. Now I am not empowered to go into this officially and I do not intend to, but since this is a very private meeting and Pete has already blown the lady's cover I can tell you that there's something to what he's saying. This could have been cleared through channels in a few weeks.'

Farquhar stared. At last, he turned back to Lady Janet.

'What do you have to say about all this?'

She smiled serenely.

'She can't come right out and admit it,' argued Chamberlain. 'You wouldn't want her to if she'd worked for you, would you, Inspector?'

Farquhar threw up his hands.

'All right. Mr Pickert, we've an ambulance waiting to take you to hospital. Go with this fellow here. As for you, Peter, see me in London, tomorrow. We'll have lunch, clear up a few details. Go. I'd like to conclude my chat with Lady Janet without your coaching.'

Chamberlain got up slowly. 'She doesn't need any help unless you try to railroad her.'

'I won't. You have my word. I'll see you tomorrow.'

Chamberlain followed Pickert out and said good-bye at the ambulance. A constable offered to drive him to London. He declined and walked out into the rain. He eyed the British navy base with a memory of dozens of such clean, precise places, and walked slowly down a long driveway to the main gate.

The guard saluted. Chamberlain saluted back for the hell of it, then stood alone in the lee of the security hut, protected from the rain by its overhanging roof. A line of wet, black taxis glistened in the street lights, waiting for passengers.

Chamberlain stood a long time, wondering what Helen and Hammond would say to each other in the car to London, and thinking that it might be smart to call Alfred Cowan before she did. Touch base. Not that Helen would do anything to him. She had no reason to, and he had kept her story out of Farquhar's investigation. Besides Helen was not the sort to waste time getting even. She'd rather get ahead. But he ought to find out what kind of bonus Cowan had in mind.

He was thinking how she'd looked running in the Temple Gardens, her black hair flying as it had splayed the night before across her pillow, and as it had blown in the sea wind when she'd pulled the trigger.

Lady Janet came striding through the rain, her hands in her pockets, her head high, a small smile on her face. She saw him outside the gate, and stopped.

'That was awfully decent of you.'

'No problem. I figured we owed you a couple. Not counting Marseille, of course.'

'Would you rather I'd shot you?'

She said it with a smile. He smiled back.

'Thanks for taking the chance.'

'I did the first thing that came into my head . . . You know.'

Chamberlain nodded. 'Sure. When you think it's too late . . . You're fast.'

Shop talk expended, they eyed each other awkwardly over a gulf of mutual loss.

'Did Farquhar give you a hard time?' he asked.

'Nothing that can't be worked out,' said Lady Janet. She glanced at the taxis, as if to motion one over, then changed her mind. 'Was what Karl said true?'

'About what?'

'That your woman was his partner?'

'She wasn't my woman. She was my boss. Yes, she and Grandzau were partners.'

'From the beginning?'

'Since before he faked – disappeared.'

'Were they lovers?'

'No. She was Hammond's. Grandzau found out that Hammond was using her and her company to support his coup plot.' Chamberlain looked up from the wet ground and found her eyes. He wanted to be alone. But first he wanted to tell somebody he could trust. 'We made love one night at the Savoy. After you and Trefle left. I don't think I ever woke up happier the first minute in the morning. But it was a set-up.'

Lady Janet shook her head emphatically. 'It's a rare set-up that's *completely* a set-up.'

Chamberlain shrugged. 'What do you feel? Used? Stupid?'

'Sorry.'

'Good word.'

'And you?'

'Numb. A little mangled.'

The rain fell harder.

Lady Janet nodded at the nearest taxi. It pulled alongside. She got in, lowered the window, and looked at Chamberlain, standing under the overhang.

'Where are you going?' she asked.

'I don't know.'

'Would you like a lift to the station?'

Chamberlain thought about it. 'I think I'm just going to stand here until it stops raining. Thanks.'

Lady Janet regarded him through long, pale eyelashes, studying him carefully.

'When it does, my home is in Gloucestershire. It's called Isling House. Anyone can tell you the way.'